Th

C000214492

The Royal Changeling

JOHN WHITBOURN

EARTHLIGHT

LONDON · SYDNEY · NEW YORK · TOKYO · SINGAPORE · TORONTO

First published in Great Britain by Earthlight 1998
An imprint of Simon & Schuster Ltd
A Viacom Company

Simon & Schuster
West Garden Place
Kendal Street
London W2 2AQ

Simon & Schuster Australia
Sydney

A CIP catalogue record for this book is available
from the British Library.

0-671-01785-3

1 3 5 7 9 10 8 6 4 2

Typeset by SX Composing DTP, Rayleigh, Essex
Printed and bound in Great Britain by
Caledonian International Book Manufacturing, Glasgow.

The World,
according to:
Theophilus
Oglethorpe, gent.
as drawn from sketches
in his commonplace bk.
and from his sundry
comments.

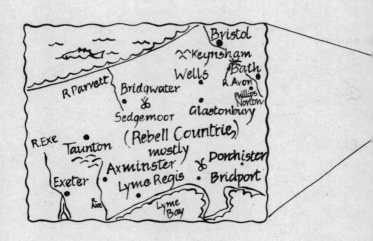

Bristol
Keynsham
Wells   Bath
R.Parrett   Bridgwater   R.Avon
                            Phillips
            Sedgemoor   Glastonbury Norton
         (Rebell Countrie)
R.Exe   Taunton   mostly
                Axminster   Dorchister
Exeter   Lyme Regis   Bridport
         Axe
              Lyme
              Bay

Ye field of Sedgemoor
6 July, in ye year of our
Salvation ; 1685, according
to ye best recollection
and recounting of:
Theophilus Oglethorpe, gent.

ye forces of his Majestic King James II,
commanded by Lt General, LEWIS DURAS-
• Earl of Feversham.

To Bristol

R. PARRETT

① DUMBARTON'S REGIMENT • Scotsmen
② First regiment of King's Guards
③ Second regiment of Kings Guards
   (or Coldstreamers)
④ Queen Dowager's Regiment - Kirke's Lambs, so
   called, commanded by a Godless Rogue
⑤ Queen Consort's Regiment - Trelawney's
⑥ Our gonnes in a useless place, and the
   fighting Bishop of Winchester
⑦ Myself and the Blues

⑧ The Wiltshire Militia, two miles off, where
   they can do no harme
        *   *   *   *   *   *
Ye forces of ye pretended James II but
actually James Walter or Barlow or whatever;
Duke/of Monmouth

Ⓐ Red Regiment, Col. Wade, a estimable rebell,
   though a lawyer
Ⓑ Yellow Regiment, Col, Mathews.
Ⓒ Green Regiment, Col, Abraham Holmes, a savage
   warrior and anabaptist
Ⓓ White Regiment, Col Ffoulkes.
Ⓔ Blue (Taunton) Regiment, Col Bovett or Buffett

Ⓕ 3 small gonnes - splendedly deadly under
   the direction of a stout foreigner.
Ⓖ My Lord Grey of Warke and the rebell
   cavalry

Ⓗ More rebell cavalry probably.

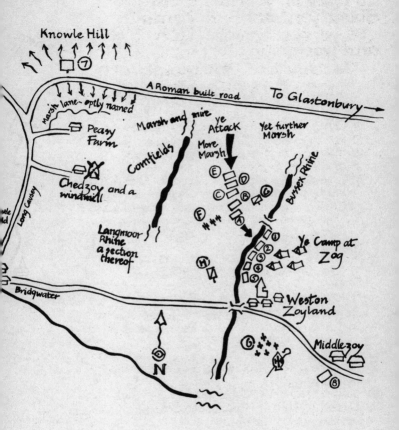

Knowle Hill

A Roman built road

To Glastonbury

Marsh lane - aptly named

Peasy Farm

Marsh and mire

Cornfields

Chedzoy and a windmill

Langmoor Rhine a section thereof

Long Causey

Bridgwater

ye Attack

More Marsh

Yet further Marsh

E

D

C

B

G

F

A

Bussex Rhine

H

1

2

3

5

4

Ye Camp at Zog

Weston Zoyland

Middlezoy

6

7

8

N

DEDICATION

To: Theophilus Oglethorpe, who, in July 1692, wisely said:

> 'Dead men tell no tales . . .'

AND:

D.D. (T'bed lazy ii! and calling prig!) & d; d; & E. N.

AND:

King Charles II, who said:
'He could not believe G*d would damn one of his creatures for taking a little irregular pleasure by the way.'

AND:

in keen anticipation of our own 'Restoration' and deliverance from the hands and laws of po-faced puritans.

History does not tell it this way, but I recount an equally true tale.

Some dates are herein wilfully changed, and events transmogrified: because the records have been known to lie and the victors write them all – and because it suited me so to do.

If in my actions I thus offend, or should my liberties with lives and language upset, may the more accountant-minded find in their hearts to forgive.

'He wanted no other monument than a bare stone with the words "Here Lies King James". He had told his priest to insist on this, but Louis said it was the only thing he could not grant him.

'When everything had been prepared for carrying away his body, the Duke of Berwick, the Earl of Middleton, James's chaplains and other servants set out at seven o'clock in the evening to take it to the church of the English Benedictine monks in Paris. The country people stood silent, and crossed themselves as the cortege passed. When it arrived in Paris, Dr. Ingleton, Almoner to the Queen, delivered the body with an elegant Latin oration to the Prior, to lie in a side chapel "until it pleased God to dispose the people of England to repair in some measure the injuries they did him in his life by the honours they shall think fit to show him after death."

'In the parish church of Saint-Germain, across the square from the great bulk of the chateau, is a splendid memorial to him:

In This Church Lies
JAMES II
King of England
Born in London
in 1633
King in 1685
Dethroned in 1688
Welcomed
in France by Louis XIV
He held his Court in the
Castle of St. Germain en Laye
Where he died on the 16 of September
1701

'His body is not there. Like so many other things it disappeared during the Revolution.'

James II Jock Haswell. 1972.

Herewith, some (small) measure . . .

THE FAIRIES' FAREWELL
Bishop Richard Corbet 1582 – 1635.
(Extract)

Lament, lament, old abbeys;
The fairies lost command.
They did but change priests' babies
But some have changed your land:
And all your children stol'n from thence
Are now grown puritans,
Who live as changelings ever since
for love of your domains.

Witness those rings and roundelays
of theirs, which yet remain
were footed in Queen Mary's days
On many a grassy plain;
But since of late Elizabeth
And later, James, came in
They never danced on any heath
As when the time hath been.

By which we note the fairies
were of the old profession;
Their songs were Ave Marias,
Their dances were procession.
But now, alas! They all are dead
Or gone beyond the seas,
Or farther for religion fled
Or else they take their ease . . .

THE YEAR OF OUR LORD 1685

The army was strung out in a column over a mile long, all the way from the Bridgwater road to right past Peasey Farm. Two abreast, they struggled along in the dark and damp, ignorant of everything bar the back of the man ahead. The Duke had ordered that *'whosoever made a noise should be knocked dead by his neighbour'* and contrary to every expectation, the great silence was kept.

For all that it was July and supposedly summer, a ground mist arose to assist their secret progress and hopes rose with it. The God-given guide seemed to know his way through this maze of brimful ditches, out into the squelching marsh. The house of the government supporter in Bradney Lane was circumvented. No alarm was called, no shot rang out. Soon enough they would be at the Langmoor Stone, which marked the upper plungeon across Bussex Rhine. Then the way would be clear to a surpassing victory. Muskets and pikes and mounted scythe-blades were clutched all the more closely. After all the years of sullen endurance and turning the cheek, they would assuredly be put to good use. In the mighty camp at Zog-by-Zoyland, the Royal forces continued their negligent sleep.

The soldiers of God did not pass entirely unobserved. In purportedly loyal Chedzoy, two men of the village watch stood and quietly observed the long column parade past into Bradney Lane. Strangely enough, it didn't occur to them to discharge a warning blast or hot-foot it to the King's Camp. Instead, *'out of country dullness and slowness'* (in the later, charitable, explanation of their Rector) they just strolled off and made themselves comfortable in a nearby windmill.

1

When dawn came and the mist rose, they'd have a grandstand view of the fight to come.

A young Bridgwater lady, more zealous in his Majesty's cause, had stolen out of the town when the rebels were standing to arms in Castle Field, and hastened to Zog, to warn the Royal Army of impending doom. Unfortunately, the men-in-arms she met had learned their manners in Scotland and Tangiers and were inflamed with Zoyland cider. Brutally dishonoured, she fled in anger and tears, her message undelivered, leaving her ravishers to death in this world and damnation in the next.

Before the rebels marched, their foremost minister, Robert 'the Plotter' Ferguson, had preached to them from *Joshua, 22,* challenging God to turn his face against them that day if their cause was not truly his also. His angry Scottish tones ensured the meaning was largely lost on the West-country audience but the Almighty presumably heard. So far the Presbyterian's rash request had gone unrebuked. On the contrary, his blackmailing of the Infinite was meeting with miraculous success.

On the opposing side, Lieutenant Colonel Theophilus Oglethorpe, attached to the Royal Regiment of Horse, the 'Blues', likewise believed in miracles. It was *implausible*, he granted, that an army of 5000 should promenade at night, undetected – but not *impossible*. Moreover, their 'king' and general, The Duke of Monmouth, wasn't averse to asking favours of Lady Luck – and gaining them by his audacious charm. Thus, for all that it was chill and inhospitable, and the hour of the soul's lowest ebb, Oglethorpe decreed that the intricate dance of the Royal scouts round the rebels must continue. The troopers of the Blues, dreaming of firesides – and other warm spots – in London, were reluctant to comply. Oglethorpe pretended not to notice; once out and about they'd soon rekindle some enthusiasm. Dozing and saucy dreams were better, but there was still a measure of fun to be had in hounding nonconformists.

At his station up on Knowle Hill, that last outcrop of the Poldens, at rest on the old Roman road which crossed it, Theophilus had been tempted to kindly thoughts. Back at

Westbrook House, far away in Surrey, his children would be abed and he wondered what they dreamed of. A curiously clear picture of his home hovered before him, blotting out the weirder landscape below. He saw the River Wey, heading leisurely to the Thames, and the valley-confined streets of industrial Godalming. The Lieutenant Colonel missed those familiar sights more than a man bred to arms sensibly should. The next step would be to consider if he would ever return; an unhelpful meditation for a soldier on the brink of battle. He harshly willed the vision to be gone.

The real view spread before him was less endearing. Out of the moonlit sea of mist rose the steeple of Bawdrip and the Towers of Chedzoy and Westonzoyland Churches. Of the watery world between nothing was visible. Somewhere down there was an insurgent army hell-bent on the overturning of order – and the ending of his own tiny story, given the chance. He had clashed with them once before, at Keynsham, and had the better of it on that occasion. Now it was time to put away soft considerations and bring matters to a final trial of strength. Once, not so long ago, he had fought alongside the Duke, in Scotland and the Low Countries; they had been friends, insofar as men of blood ever are. Now his vaunting ambitions threatened Theophilus with seeing Westbrook no more – not to mention more universal ruin. Their paths, once parallel, had parted and now converged only to collide. It was sad – but the Duke of Monmouth had to go.

Lieutenant Colonel Oglethorpe also had to go: not to the executioner's block and thence to Hell, but down into the white sea below Bawdrip. It was his duty to hazard the Bridgwater 'Long Causey' road and see what went on at the end of it. Feversham and Churchill feared the rebels might flit away by night for another try at Bristol, thereby to prolong the agony. Theophilus was thus minded to rouse them up and pin them down, ensuring a speedier return to Godalming. At his command, the two hundred Blues mounted up and jangled down the hill, along what passed for a road hereabouts, towards Bridgwater.

Ever after, History held Oglethorpe to account for strange inattention. How was it, later scholars not unreasonably asked, that he did not detect the rebels had quit the town? 5000 insurgents were not the sort of thing you easily overlooked. '*Any thing else to report?*' '*Oh, yes, I nearly forgot. There's 5000 maniacs on their way here to slit our throats as we sleep.*' Did it not occur to him, ask the omni-competent commentators, to check that enemy were safely tucked up in their Bridgwater beds? Must not, at one point, the whole rebel army have passed below his position? The night march of the rebels under Oglethorpe's nose was the one great unsolved mystery of Sedgemoor.

The Lieutenant Colonel was never able to defend his good name with the truth. Fortunately he more than made amends later in the day and so didn't have to. It would have been but a poor defence in a court martial to plead prior, pressing, business with a ghost.

The King of *Logres* came floating out of the mist he had created, his rotting boots skimming over, but not touching, the soil of his realm.

'Stand, in the name of the King!' he said. The commanding voice sounded not from the regal body, but from some vast and echoing place far away.

Oglethorpe had gone ahead with four good troopers. Each obeyed directly, despite their advantage in numbers – and their mounts likewise. Men and beasts were frozen, mid-canter; suspended in fluid poses of motion. Theophilus noted their blank, unknowing expressions and saw that the stars had ceased to twinkle. The hooves of the main body following on were heard no more.

Only partly pleased by exemption from the cessation of time, he wheeled his own horse to meet the King. The animal first shied away and then was overcome. It went down on one front knee and made obeisance. Gravity and dignity obliged Oglethorpe to dismount.

The King held out his armoured hand.

'Will you not also do homage?' he hissed, so very reasonably.

4

The Lieutenant Colonel did not approach.

'I know you *can* speak,' he persevered. 'My spell did not include you. Speak words to your King.'

Theophilus did not demean himself by reaching for sword or pistol. He knew that they were vain tools in present circumstances. Integrity was his best remaining weapon.

'I cannot address my King,' he said, quietly. 'He is not here.'

The great figure hovering before him tilted its head, the better to catch the Lieutenant Colonel's speech. It listened, and then the vast helm of iron shook slowly from side to side.

'Such . . . sadness . . .' said the voice from elsewhere.

Courage begat more courage, and therein Theophilus found the strength to burn his bridges.

'My King is James, not Arthur,' he stated calmly. 'I will not betray him as you have me.'

Deep in the shadowy depths of the King's helmet, leathery flesh was drawn back to manufacture a smile.

'Mortal man: he comes . . . and then is gone. His word is like unto his life: mere painting on water.'

Oglethorpe leant on his horse, desperate for contact with any real, truly living, thing. He found that it was trembling. The Lieutenant Colonel was often mocked (behind his back) for soft-heartedness towards the lesser creatures of God. Even friends accused him of compassion to an almost feminine degree. Today however, his weakness stood him in good stead. Pity for the poor beast gave him fresh resolve.

'I have read a different text,' he said stoutly. 'I know that my redeemer liveth.'

Again the royal head rocked, in disappointment and disbelief.

'Hath not childhood ended yet?' he asked. King Arthur's reply was more in sorrow than in anger. 'You have something of mine. I shall ask it of you again – once more: later this very day. By then you will have grounds for a wiser reply.'

Happy not to be just . . . swept away forthwith, Theophilus did not answer. He had done enough to merely stand his ground and save his soul.

The King looked about, taking in the frozen troopers.

'These,' he said, 'might now have tales inconvenient for you. I am kind and slow to anger. They will die today.'

Before Oglethorpe could protest, Arthur swept up his arm and a beam of light detached itself from each soldier. What was sent forth departed reluctantly, torn from its shell of flesh with a scream, before rocketing up into heaven. Theophilus tried to avert his eyes but could not. He saw in every glowing shape the frightened face of its owner. The troopers' souls were not prepared for judgement and they were afraid.

'A new day is dawning,' said King Arthur – and it was. Hours of Oglethorpe's allotted span had been stolen.

The Guardsmen, who'd lost much more but did not know it, looked in puzzlement at their commander. Why was it suddenly light and why did they feel so . . . forlorn?

The King was gone. In his place was a distant sound of cannon and combat.

The Reverend Stephen Toogood had a spring in his step – or at least he would have had but for the quagmire beneath his boots. The Lord constantly led him into the desolate places of the Earth but he did not begrudge it. On the contrary, he hoped for eternal reward for his cheerful treading of *God-forsaken* places. Wading through the freezing waters of the Langmoor Rhine, he had forced himself to thank the Almighty for so putting him to the test.

The Reverend's pious fortitude was strengthened by there being some immediate point to his travails. King Monmouth was, under God, leading them to victory. The fires of the Royal camp at Zog were now less than a mile away. But for the tramp of men and their laboured breathing, all was quiet and their progress remained secret. The Lord had blessed their unbelievable march in the dark, watching over them as he had the soldiers of Gideon. Meanwhile, the warriors of Babylon slept on, spending their last night before the everlasting flames, deep in the arms of Morpheus.

'Dream well,' thought the Reverend, *'enjoy your last sinful con-*

jectures before awakening to death!'

It felt . . . blessed, he had to admit, to have sword and pistol at hand: to at last stand openly in the field against the foes of God. No more covert meetings and mutterings, no more impotent gnashing of teeth at the servants of Beelzebub. Also, Pastor Toogood had his own personal grievances to join to the indictment of the Lord. He'd watched Mayor Timewell of Taunton and his helpers dance, bottles brandished, round a bonfire in the market-place, burning all the pews and pulpits and galleries of the *conventicles* they'd raided. Toogood's little church had been amongst them. In total there were ten cartloads and it took them till three in the morning to finish their revels. They were very merry about it and the Anglican church bells rang all the while in glee. That was five years back but the heat on his face that night, from the fire and from within, was still with him. After that he and his flock took to the hills, like the last generation before the judgement, to skulk in churches under the ground, up in the wilds beyond Axminster. Out there, in the forlorn places of the world, in vast ditches covered by bracken, he held services by night, preaching on texts like *Revelations 12:* 'And the woman fled into the wilderness where she hath a place prepared of God'.

He did no harm but Babylon would not let him be. The Devon militia raided his home and one captain placed his hand up the placket of his wife's gown, saying '*she has a fine bum indeed; good enough for fame in London*'.

The Reverend Toogood forgave but could not forget. Monmouth's call to insurrection fell on fertile ground and the Reverend's flock joined with him, in war as in prayer, marching along as one unit. It was against all hope, and certain proof of Divine favour, that there should arise a true Protestant paladin to lead them on crusade. It would have been a sin indeed not to respond with fervour. Now, this very day they would work the Lord's will and quench their own anger meanwhile.

The password of the hour was '*So-ho!*', the traditional cry of the chase – and, by chance, the site of the Duke's London residence. Toogood had never been a hunting man but tonight he

7

yearned to yell Soho! like any blood-crazed squire. His hand moved to the fine pistol at his side. It had done good work in Cromwell's time, smiting the Amalekites hip and brow, and would do so again.

Out in the darkness, where Lord Grey's rebel cavalry and Wade's Red Regiment were presumed to be, a single shot rang out.

Anton Buyse, 'the Brandenburger', did not have any great hopes of the day. This present commission with the Duke represented something of a dip in career terms. He who had the honour of directing artillery for the Kings of Christendom (and certain mussulman Lords, although that section of his c.v. was less advertised) was now reduced to trundling three childrens' toys through the night. He sought distraction from present discomforts by thinking of what he would really like to have, given free choice, for the coming battle.

This was, of course, only a minor ale-house punch-up by civilised European standards so Buyse moderated his shopping list accordingly. It would be *nice* to have a brace of demi-cannon for a preliminary, long-range duel with the opposing artillery. Pitting one's skill, one to one, guns against guns, against the other Master of the Ordnance, raised mere combat to the art form it ought to be. Sadly, their night-march to surprise the enemy precluded such sophisticated pleasures. Similarly, a restrained number of culverins would have supplied the sheer . . . *punch* essential for the drama of tearing spaces in serried ranks of infantry. Again, 'King' Monmouth's purse did not run to what any petty Rhineland princeling would regard as essentials.

Buyse looked at the reality being hauled in front of him by these enthusiastic but amateur English. So much for fond wishes! A year back, if anyone told him he'd be commanding the grand total of three drakes, (there'd been four but one had a squeaky wheel and was, needs must, left behind tonight), he would have laughed in their face – or maybe killed them. They were mere five-pounders, the sort of thing you gave apprentices to tinker at; something they could do no harm with.

Anton sighed. He was glad his Dad wasn't around to see this come-down. He never thought he'd say such a thing, but it was a good job that fluke-ish Croat saker took his head off when it did. '*Never get involved in a job*', that's what he's always said. '*Ideals are good servants but bad masters*'. The old boy had been right. It wasn't as though he cared about 'Protestantism', whatever that might be. No, he might as well admit it, Monmouth had charmed him and he'd let himself be charmed. So that was that. Anton Buyse had accepted a contract and no Buyse ever bowed out of a job: there was the good name of the family business to consider.

He tightened his grip on his quadrant, a Buyse heirloom handed down to him. Supposedly it had seen service when Constantinople fell and the first Buyse set match to touch-hole. Since then it was like a talisman to them. Father handed it to son when their eyes grew too dim (or practised) to need it.

'*Sorry Dad*,' said the Brandenburger in silent prayer. '*I'll make amends by a really good job. I've brought along some of that hail-shot you designed.*'

He wasn't worried about the day to come. Cannons returned the love his family gave and they never called any member home until his time was done.

Alongside, Anton heard his assistant, John Rose, whispering the artilleryman's litany, touchingly desperate that he should acquit himself well on his first outing. Buyse, who'd learnt the words in his cradle, smiled and joined in:

'*Put back your piece, order your piece to load, search your piece, sponge your piece, fill your ladle, put in your powder, empty your ladle, put home your powder, thrust home your wad, regard your shot, put home your shot gently, thrust home your last wad with three strokes, gauge your piece, discharge your piece . . . put back your piece . . .*'

It warmed Anton's heart to hear those childhood words and observe another introduced to the joys of ordnance. He thought of the son he'd not yet had and the Buyses going ever on and on to better days and bigger guns.

9

'It applies to wenches too,' he softly confided to his pupil.
Somewhere ahead a musket was fired.

Piercy Kirke, late-Governor of the Tangier garrison, now
Colonel of the Queen Dowager's Regiment, slammed his fist
upon the table.

'Well, God damn me, but you're poor entertainment! If
Monmouth's rabble refuse to turn and fight us then I *demand* to
be amused. What d'ye think I woke you up for? Take the poker
out your arse and answer a soldier of the Crown. Come on, it's
a plain enough question!'

The Reverend Thomas Peratt, Vicar of St. Mary's,
Westonzoyland, ignored the table-top earthquake and continued his unwanted supper as best he could. It seemed a
strange and perverse world where the forces of order were as
much to be feared as rebels.

'It is not a subject on which I venture to have an opinion –
nor wish discussed in my house,' he said quietly. 'And whilst
you are billeted here I would ask that you abide by . . .'

'"*No opinion*"?' roared the Colonel. 'Don't give me that.
You're a man made of flesh the same as me. So do tell: what's
your favourite: pure-and-simple or arsey-versey?'

Peratt flushed as pink as the mutton he ate.

'Colonel, kindly consider my wife and daughters who are also
under this roof . . .'

The deeply-tanned soldier was momentarily thrown and set
aside his clay churchwarden pipe. 'God's teeth and bowels,
man!' he exclaimed, puzzlement distorting an already weathered brow. 'Who else d'ye think made me ponder such matters?'

An alternative use for his cutlery occurred to the Reverend,
until he recalled the sixth commandment – and the royal
soldiers posted outside his vicarage. Meanwhile, Colonel Kirke
rampaged on.

'I will have a response of you, God-botherer. Doesn't your big
black book tell you what to say?'

Exasperation gave Peratt the courage to lift his gaze. He
realised that he'd never seen anything as capable of . . . any-

10

thing as this red-coated demon.

'Assuming that you refer to the Holy Bible,' he said, losing the battle of stares, 'I recall that *Romans, 1, 26*, prohibits loathsome acts against nature such as you refer to. Likewise . . .'

Kirke downed an enormous draught of the Vicar's cider and wiped his thin lips on the scarlet and gold of his cuff.

'Cut the cant,' he said angrily. 'I care as little for your text as your company. Chapter two of the equally "Holy" *Koran*, which the Shareef of Fez was gracious enough to show me, says "*women are your fields: go, then, into your fields as you please*". Put that in your pipe and smoke it!'

From outside there was a torrent of inventive invective and the sound of blows. The door opened with a crash and the Bishop of Winchester entered.

'Kirke,' he barked, 'your soldiers are as soft as shit and twice as nasty. "*Don't interrupt our Colonel at his dinner*" indeed! Tell 'em to keep out of my way.'

Both Colonel Piercy and the Vicar stood and bowed to the Right Reverend Dr Peter Mews, who growled at the greeting and crossed over to the dining table. Liberating a mutton chop from the heaped platter, he lowered his bulk on to a convenient stool.

'Couldn't sleep,' he said, in-between savaging the meat and serving himself from the cider flagon. 'Too excited. What were you talking about? The battle to come?'

The Bishop had never really ceased to be a soldier after his lively time in the late Civil War, suffering thirty wounds in the service of Charles, King and Martyr. He carried tokens of his pains in the form of spectacular scars over the left hemisphere of his face. The black silk covering for same in turn bestowed on him his universal nickname: '*Old Patch*'.

For a while, amidst the harrowing of England, he'd been the very epitome of death-on-legs. Then, fortunately for his immortal soul, capture (whilst unconscious, naturally) at Naseby field gave pause for reflection. Upon release, and to general amazement, he entered the Church. The leopard changed its spots – if not its diet . . . Monmouth's invasion had drawn him west, under the pretence of safeguarding nearby Episcopal estates, like a shark to a spray of blood.

With the arrival of such powerful reinforcements, and in Kirke's present abashment, Peratt saw the opportunity for revenge.

'Actually,' he said sweetly, 'the Colonel was expounding on his great attraction to the Koran and the Mussulman religion . . .'

The old Bishop turned his brick-red face on the soldier, the watery eyes therein looking very uncharitable. He'd already had a day of it. At dinner with General Feversham some braggart cavalier – Oggyton . . . Oglethorne or something – had contested his spiritual authority, admitting Winchester's rule over some place called Godalming but claiming ancient exception for *his* manor there, and thus allegiance to the Deans of Salisbury instead. Down here it was uncheckable: possibly true but a bloody cheek nevertheless.

'You don't say?' he rumbled, crunching the chop bone between his teeth. 'I wonder in that case he doesn't *convert*. It's been a while since we've burnt an apostate.'

Colonel Kirke was shameless.

'Tis possible,' he said. 'Religion plays but a small part in my life. However, the King of Morocco had my promise that should I ever change faith, I would embrace Islam. The oath at least saves me from King James's constant promptings to Popery.'

Old Patch's drinking noises turned to bubbling as he misswallowed.

'In fact,' Kirke continued, smooth and sharp as a viper, 'your arrival forestalled a most interesting conversation. Assuming the Vicar, of all people, should know, I'd asked him what this *life* business is about – and do you know, he couldn't *tell* me!'

The Reverend moved to protest but the Bishop waved him to silence.

Old Patch had a special tone of voice, well known to those under the regime of fear at his Farnham Castle seat, which sounded like sweet reason but betokened an eruption to come. He sometimes employed it in sermons and thereby caused many a hardened sinner's knees to knock.

'Well,' he said, smiling and showing off his brown peg teeth, 'pray let *me* enlighten you. The sole purpose of this fleeting life is the worship of its Creator.'

Colonel Kirke looked into the middle distance – about three yards in the context of Westonzoyland Vicarage.

'Worship, you say? Well, I'll give it a whirl. Let me see . . . Almighty God, I worship you; I give you thanks, I adore you, I prostrate myself before your invisible feet, I sing your praises, You are Almighty. . .'

A heavily pregnant – say about nine and a half months – pause hung in the smoky air.

'No,' said the Colonel conclusively. 'Thanks all the same. It doesn't do much for me.'

The Bishop levered himself up, toppling the stool backwards. In youth he'd fought for the blessed Charles, King and Martyr – or anyone else who'd have him – and even now, in autumn years, a relish for combat remained. A be-ringed Episcopal finger was levelled inches from Kirke's smiling face.

Old Patch's Armageddon of abuse was postponed by the sound of musketry from Zog.

Louis Duras, naturalised Frenchman, nephew of the great Marshal Turenne and now Earl of Feversham, Commander of his Majesty's forces in the West, had some black looks for Lieutenant Colonel Oglethorpe when the Blues thundered back into camp at three-thirty. By then light shone in the east and – though far from resolved – battle was well under way. The surprised redcoat line was being luxuriantly bathed in the warm attentions of Monmouth's guns. Being nearest, Dumbarton's regiment of Scotsmen, once the Duke's own, were in particular benefiting from Anton Buyse's expertise and falling in neat swathes. Theophilus was painfully aware that at a quarter to one that morning – shortly before to him but long hours ago to everyone else – he had sent word that all was quiet. The Earl, wig askew and compelled to breakfast on horseback, was not pleased.

13

Seven years back, whilst blasting fire-gaps in Temple Lane, London, to contain yet another major conflagration, his then-commander, the Duke of Monmouth, got over-generous with the powder. A flying beam so stove Feversham's head in that his life was despaired of. However, to the surprise of all and the delight of some, he not only survived the 'remedy' of trepan-ning, but did so with faculties intact. Rising like Lazarus, he was found to be complete – except in one tiny respect. Ever after he was the very devil to rouse from sleep. Awed by the overall miracle, no one had been churlish enough to complain of the defect to date. On this *particular* day though, in the early stages of unexpected battle, it was a trifle . . . inconvenient.

In the end (sic) a bold aide-de-camp applied a plug-bayonet to resolve the matter: that and some refreshing cold water. Accordingly, albeit grumpy and sore and late, the Earl was up and about and, broadly speaking, in control.

Being a gentleman, the Huguenot General did not express his displeasure. He desisted long enough from a chicken drum-stick *a la français* to bid Oglethorpe good morning, and gra-ciously indicated with his ebony baton that some little assistance on the right flank would be appreciated. Theophilus hastened to comply.

Kirke, standing with his Tangier Lambs under the musket storm from across the Bussex Rhine, noted the Lieutenant Colonel's passing and was less restrained. Even had Colonel Piercy led a blameless life up to that point he would still have been damned for the blasphemies he unleashed. Oglethorpe tipped his feathered hat in return, answering: '*and your mother . . .*'

It was not merely that Theophilus wished to atone for his apparent sins of omission, or that he knew the universe was balanced in his gauntleted hand. He also recognised that the fighting madness was coming upon him and for once it was wel-come. Today it would not end in some . . . pointless duel or undignified rage; today it could be harnessed and ridden, and put to good use. Oglethorpe drew the great sword of destiny from an army-issue scabbard and let forth a roar. The following

14

troopers answered in kind.

He was the first across the upper plungeon, heedless of the fire that took away two nearby companions. Fortune – or something – decreed the narrow way was not thereby blocked. These soldiers, foredoomed men from his earlier patrol, fell with a splash into the black waters of the Rhine and sank, bubbling, out of sight. Luckier types came up in support and then they were free on the expanse of Sedgemoor field. The Blues fanned out with Theophilus at their head.

First to be met were some elements of the traitorous Lord Grey's rebel horse. As throughout, they were timorous and unenterprising, and Oglethorpe cleared the way, barely noticing their fleeting presence. In passing Excalibur was blooded for the second time in the campaign.

The enemy horsemen having evaporated, just like the false mist that had concealed their night march, Theophilus sought fresh opponents. He hadn't far to look. Just across the morass there sat, sullen, given pause for thought but still defiant, a bristling clump of pike and shot. This was Monmouth's Green Regiment although Oglethorpe wasn't to know it, for they had scant uniforms to proclaim the fact. The Lieutenant Colonel cared as little for their name as for their welfare. 'For God, for England and St. George – and the old ways!' he cried, whilst crossing himself – and, then charged headlong in.

History judges him rash in so doing. The Green Regiment had been rearwards in the column of march and were still crossing Sedgemoor when the alarm went up. The Taunton weavers and men of London therein had not yet been engaged, their ammunition and fervour were undepleted. Moreover, they were amongst the best of Duke Monmouth's Foot: they had *form*. In the hedgerow to hedgerow, hand to hand stuff at the Philips Norton fight, they'd mauled the King's men into retreat and shot the Duke of Grafton's horse from under him. Their colonel, the old Cromwellian Abraham Holmes, had lost a son there – and an arm besides. He'd amputated the shattered limb himself, field-surgery with a cleaver, and marched on regardless to have his revenge.

Oglethorpe received a torrid welcome.

His mount bucked and reared as it was slashed about, threatening to unseat him. Yelling men attempted to pierce his breast. Deep amongst the forest of pole-arms he saw his deputy, the Irishman, Captain Sarsfield, brought low with a musket-butt and left for dead. It seemed quite likely he also would not emerge from the crazy dance and yet Theophilus was content. There was pleasure in moment-to-moment living and the escape from being . . . himself. Whilst avoiding and delivering death there was no time to ponder which way the world should go.

By contrast, 'King Monmouth' had ample space for that very speculation. Resplendent in scarlet trimmed with gold, armed with a half-pike, he strode up and down the line and thought of little else. For all that his daring plan had stalled he hadn't yet despaired. His every desire and every*thing* – in the truest sense – still hung in the balance. Amid the pre-dawn gloom and powder murk he continued to look for . . . unanswerable reinforcement.

And beneath the tor, at the place the newcomers called Glastonbury, Artorious Rex, *Dux Bellorum*, past and (possibly) future King, began to rise.

'POSTSCRIPT: A MYSTERY OF THE BATTLE'
(Appendix F of Bridgwater Booklet No. 4) by M. Page:
'The Battle of Sedgemoor' (Bridgwater, 1932)

'Although Feversham's story of the battle hangs together fairly well it is a little difficult.

'He tells us that at "a quarter before one" a.m. he rode back from the moor to Westonzoyland. He had waited late for a message from Oglethorpe, who was supposed to be watching on Knowle Hill. As no message came he returned to his quarters in the village.

'But at "a quarter after one" (please note the hour) "came Sir Hugh Mydlleton with one of Collonell Oglethorpe's party" bearing the belated message that he "could not perceive the least motion of the enemy!"

'If we give the trooper half an hour for his ride from Knowle he started about a quarter to one.

'But Lieutenant Dummer, an exact man, says that the rebels reached the fighting line by two o'clock. They must have been swarming, therefore, in the tracks between Knowle Hill and the moor by one o'clock or earlier.

'How, then could the trooper ride right along their path via Langmoor stone without seeing or hearing anything of them?

'It seems almost an impossibility . . .

'All very mysterious. We are almost driven to a suspicion that "Zummerzet Zider" was more potent than they had imagined, which would account for anything.'

THE YEAR OF OUR LORD 1648

'And this, Highness, is Mistress Walter, a fellow expatriate. Goodness, is that the time . . .?'

The Courtier tried to guide the Prince onwards but the way remained barred. He sighed. Factions defeated in war soon got to learn that life could wear a permanent scowl, becoming just one damn thing after another. Even a simple promenade round these dull Dutch streets proved to be studded with misfortune's cowpats.

'Mistress *Lucy* Walter,' simpered the strumpet before them, curtseying deeply and thus directing her face close to the princely crotch. 'At your service, Highness.'

'Well, *hello* . . .' said Charles Stuart, attempting to twirl his adolescent, twelve-a-side, attempt at a moustache in the correct cavalier manner. The young Prince was not quite as experienced as he made out – and certainly less so than this brazen hussy – but he acted the part well enough. Libertines to model himself on were one thing the impoverished court-in-exile didn't lack. Charles recalled, and then rejected, the lines successful with peasant girls whilst cooped up in Jersey. In propositioning the higher classes one didn't need to be so subtle.

'Mistress Lucy, eh?' he smarmed. 'Not *my* mistress as far as I know; not yet anyway.'

The Courtier gaped in admiration and amazement as Walter mustered a halfway convincing blush. If she could so control her capillaries, what other tricks was she capable of?

'Why Sir,' she trilled, half averting her great limpid eyes in a way that said '*yes, yes, YES!*', 'you are too forward . . .'

Prince Charles beamed wolfishly down upon her.

'Well then, missy, if so, there's always *back*wards, is there not?'

They both laughed, intimate conspirators already, two shrewd and unshockable products of their time.

The Courtier was likewise unmoved. His Anglican sensitivities had been deadened in the course of long, loyal service to his King and by the sights civil war had shown him. Prudence, however, remained even if piety was fled. Across the water was England where they soon must go. Parliament's principal fleet had deserted the usurpers and now awaited the Prince's pleasure – for the fickle moment. In a week or so, two at the most, this young Prince must sail with them and cross swords with the arch-fiend Cromwell and his New Model Army. Likewise, even here, eating the bread of exile in the Netherlands, there was no safety or occasion for ease. Parliament's agents and assassins swarmed like blow-flies, ready to save themselves the bother of a battle and thwart God's will with a bullet. This was no time for *soft* considerations. He whispered as much to his Prince.

'Rest easy,' Charles confided back. 'At present I am as hard as could be wished . . .'

The Courtier sighed again. Was it for this he had given up house and home and lost lands held by his family since the Conqueror's time? For the thousandth time since Edgehill and the first effusion of blood, he consulted in memory the motto painted, ages past, above his ancestral hearth: 'Fear God and Honour the King'. Well, that was a stark enough instruction, an incitement to fresh resolve.

'Mistress Walter is a *much-loved* figure in these parts,' he explained to the Prince in a voice heavy with meaning, 'and in other parts as well.'

'My parts agree, so it seems,' said Charles, winking at his breeches.

'And she is currently *very friendly* with loyal Colonel Robert Sidney, great-nephew of the renowned poet and warrior, Sir Philip.'

'I know him well; he's Chamberlain to my sister Mary; a most . . . accommodating fellow.'

20

The Courtier at last despaired of victory in this engagement and drew back a pace to let the two eighteen-year-olds exchange what whispered lewderies they would. Whilst the illicit transaction was arranged, he refreshed mind and eye in dwelling upon the stately buildings and linden-fringed canals of the Hague. It was better, he consoled himself, that what scant influence he mustered be husbanded for some more vital test of strength.

He was never more wrong. Even restraining Charles I from charging to an honourable death when Naseby Field was lost was not such an innocent disservice to the cause he'd given all for. Out of ignorance, everything in the Cosmos he held dear was put at risk. Fortunately though, through God's kindness, the Courtier died soon after, worn out by faithful service and tired of life, still wrapped in that same blessed lack of knowledge.

Meanwhile, Prince Charles eventually returned to his side, pleased and guiltless as a tom-cat with what had been decided.

'Now then,' he purred, 'you were saying about muskets . . .'

Lucy Walter a.k.a. Lucy Barlow, Lucy Sidney – and many other temporary names, departed similarly pleased. Still in the bloom of youth, despite life's rough usage, she'd needed only low level spells to secure the entrapment.

The gentleman-of-the-bedchamber consulted his timepiece by candlelight.

'Fan-my-brow!' he whispered to his colleague. 'It's four o'clock and His Highness is still screaming!'

'Only to be expected. Mistress Walter is Welsh.'

'I did not know that.'

'Indeed so, born and bred.'

'But of what consequence is the information?'

The gentleman was looked on with horror and pity by all the courtiers and bodyguards assembled outside the bedroom doors.

'Do you mean to say,' he was asked, 'that you have never heard of the Welsh erotic arts?'

*

Prince – King-to-be, when his father's head parted from its shoulders – Charles was kept screaming until four o'clock – or even later – throughout his brief stay. Advisors tut-tutted about the dark rings growing beneath his eyes but were powerless to intervene. Bold Lucy Walter had him in her thrall and demanded constant . . . attention. It had to be so. Persistence and repetition were an absolute necessity for what she had in mind. When novelty faded and even her Cymric skills palled, she had recourse to less natural magic to ensure continued jousts. Between proficiency and sorcery she managed to hold on to him for long enough.

Neither were so tedious as to remain faithful for that would have seemed pedestrian and suspicious in the time and place. A superabundance of easy temptation and the climate of a world-turned-upside-down precluded it. Besides, their time together was no idyll. Charles came and went – so to speak – to strive and plot and debate, having the minor matter of a lost throne to deal with. Absence helped ensure that passion's flint continued to spark. And if in the meanwhile either sought alternative comfort, what did that signify? The world had tumbled about their ears long before they met; Englishman killed Englishman and the howling storms of change drowned out quieter counsels. Everyone conformed to the outer chaos in those days.

Lucy was less than quarter-elf but that unhuman portion still made crossbreeding a hit and miss affair. She applied what charms she knew, eschewed all contraception and pampered her ovaries with peppermint in the prescribed way. After that it was a matter of luck and application. There was no question of seeking advice from the elder race, even assuming they would answer. She knew she should not mix her blood with any 'newcomer' king: that was the one forbidden thing. What Lucy proposed would not be approved of – in the most violent manner.

Then, one night in July '48, in the disordered days between their 'chance' meeting and Charles's sailing with the turncoat fleet, the unlikely occurred. Perhaps simple passion made

22

possible what Elf-lore deemed doubtful. Whatever the reason, Lucy's project, for which she'd set aside years, was crowned with prompt success. In a theatre-box at the Hague (disrupting an actor's tragic soliloquy), or a private dining room in Scheveningen, or in a coach en route to Rotterdam – or perhaps another snatched moment of delight – their joint and vigorous efforts were deservedly smiled upon. One Royal sperm, less fastidious than his five hundred million fellow voyagers, took a fancy to an *almost*-human egg. They touched – and embraced. The future Duke of Monmouth began his long, slow, journey towards the light.

Lucy Walter was informed soon after: as chance dictated during a subsequent bout. Better-than-human senses announced it with a roar of joy that emerged on Earth via her coquettish squeak. Prince Charles mistook it for an involuntary round of applause and prided himself on what a jolly dog he was. Lucy noted that superior smirk crossing his dark features and smiled also. Though cruel enough when required – or (Elf-blood coming through) even when not – she didn't disabuse him. On the contrary, made charitable by triumph, she was happy to reward him and bolster his bravado.

'Oh, sire,' she gasped, allowing her at-will Welsh accent to swing wide and free, 'there's . . . *magnificent*, you are.'

Charles had been half-minded to get up and wipe himself on the curtains, but he was willing to linger on for this.

'I've had no complaints,' he mused.

Lucy affected continued breathlessness.

'You *puissant* beast!' she heaved. 'This fortress cannot stand against you!'

'A bit of a conqueror, is that what you think, eh?' He was rather basking in it, for all his dislike and distrust of people.

'Oh . . . yes! A rampaging, victorious Sultan, my oath! If you were to assault these walls again, I should think I might have to surrender . . .'

Charles puffed out his cheeks. 'Actually, best we rest a bit first, there's a limit to what even I . . .'

Lucy sprinkled a little magic on him and he was instantly interested.

'Oh, prime that love-musket again,' she purred, 'and invade the realm of Venus. Ignore my piteous calls for mercy, mercy, mercy . . .'

Her objective was achieved. For once the world was opening wide to *her* command, rather than the usual opposite. She'd had to dance to some peculiar, tiring, music in her time, but now there was every hope, via mothering an exalted child, of more melodic tunes in future. In gate-crashing the Stuart dynasty and injecting the all-knowing older-blood, she even saw hope of composing one or two puppet-shows of her own for the high and mighty to jig to.

Thus, though strictly speaking there was no real point to a further encounter right now, Lucy felt like celebrating. And besides, there was the need to humour Charles. He was as sweet and kind as life allowed him to be – perhaps even a little bit more so – but a dark edge had been grafted on him. It was necessary that he be of a mind to recognise the child when it arrived. Future jousts were also required. She had taken steps to ensure a boy, but even so, another – or a third – would be welcome, just to make sure of things.

'Do you know,' said Charles, 'I'm in a mad mood. A cannon might take me head off next week. You're not like other women. For two shakes of a dog's tail, I'd damn well *marry* you!'

This was unexpected; beyond her wildest dreams. By sheer good fortune, Lucy had tapped into the last remaining vein of warmth in Charles.

'There's no dog to hand,' she said swiftly, lifting up the bed-covers and turning on her belly, 'but a tail I *can* provide. Will its shaking suffice?'

Charles feasted his eyes.

'More than, Madame,' he husked.

'I'll do things for you other girls don't,' she promised. 'Or can't – or won't! And I think we can manage more than just two shakes . . .'

Lucy Walter, for all her faults, was a pleasure to do business

24

with, and the unorthodox marriage contract was soon concluded.

'Well, do you or don't you?' The little Dutch Pastor was so exasperated, he forgot he was in the presence of a Prince and let his anger show.

'Do I what?' slurred Charles as two gentlemen-of-the-bedchamber restored him to upright.

'Take this woman!' repeated the Pastor for the umpteenth time.

Charles screwed up his eyes and tried to make the room stand still. Leaning belligerently close he breathed brandy all over the Dutchman.

'Night and day: all the time,' he bellowed. 'But what's it got to do with you?'

The Pastor was about to throw up his hands but was distracted by someone else, fortunately neither bride nor groom, throwing up for real. Charles turned unsteadily round.

'That's it, Colonel Griff,' he urged the man on, 'better out than in!'

'Speak for yourself!' shrieked Lucy Walter, soon-to-be Stuart, lasciviously eyeing her prospective husband.

The Pastor would have left them but for catching the gaze of one of the bodyguards at the door. This man had been obliged to remain sober and was none too happy about it. A face forged into fury by Marston Moor and Naseby stated that until the job was done, his way was barred.

'Look,' the Pastor pleaded with the Prince, 'just tell me if you take her as your *wife* . . .'

Charles tried to get his fuddled brain round this complicated question. He looked down on the tottering bride. Alcohol converted her into a goddess of desirability, wrapped in liftable liquid silk. However, now he looked, he noticed one of the drunken bridesmaids was quite presentable too – especially sprawled invitingly on the floor like that. Was it the mussulman faith that permitted more than one wife? Which religion was he? He could nearly grasp the name of it – something to do with

25

that Jesus fellow. It was all too difficult to think through: far easier to just agree.

"Course I do. I don't take her for me damned brother, do I?"

The Pastor seized the answer like a drowning man: it would do.

'And what about you?' he asked Lucy, viewing her with mixed amazement and distaste. He was troubled with sinful thoughts of heaving dunes and hills – and just as worried about her heaving all over him.

'Oh, I *do*,' she laughed, giving the little churchman her best 'don't bother thinking about it, you couldn't afford me' look.

'Then, in the *averted*', (he whispered), 'eyes of Almighty God, I pronounce you man and wife – or *something*. Can you sign the certificate?'

'I'll have a go,' said Charles manfully, and lurched out of the grasp of his two bearers towards the table. Moving like a man deep underwater he drew a blotted, erratic, but just recognisable, '*Carolus regis filius*' on the proffered document. Lucy likewise flounced forward and, with immense concentration, tongue gripped between full lips, painstakingly drew a huge 'X'.

'And the witnesses?' said the Pastor, looking longingly out of the window.

Such was the gravity attached to this semi-secret match that no member of Charles's retinue had been willing to put his name to any record of it. The Prince had laughed that off and directed that two innocent Dutch passers-by be seized to do the deed. They now stood shiftily by the door, clutching their gold-sovereign fee, and wondering what the devil this collection of drunken demons were about. It amused the sober guard to encourage them forward with the point of his rapier on their behinds.

'Don't ask,' said the Pastor despairingly, in the local Dutch dialect, 'just sign.'

They did so, taking care to make their signatures indecipherable, and then fled away.

One, a tall man, clad in bourgeois black, lingered enough to humbly bestow a word on the bride. Assuming it to be in the native gobbledegook, no one paid attention – except Lucy. Because of it, the erotic tingle in her limbs, the warm brandy-bath in which she swam, were both instantly stilled and chilled. Sobriety returned like a tidal wave and she was forced to remember what she often forgot: that actions have consequences. Frozen by fright, she could not prevent his departure, nor would it have been wise to try. She had noted the flecks of gold in his oval eyes, observed the unkind smile in the pale face. He was of her race, but a full-breed. It was doubtful these tipsy cavaliers could have detained him.

The tall 'man' had spoken in the old tongue of which Lucy knew few words. 'We' and 'know' were, however, of that number.

It was as well that Lucy had no great expectations of marriage. Though well-born, her childhood was nothing but jagged memories of parental wars, domestic venom and flying cutlery. Even when at last physically separated her mother and father had continued their bloody battle by means of litigation, each seeking custody of the daughter they otherwise ignored. After the law's stately progress at last gave victory to one (she forgot which) Lucy had fled her Welsh homeland and emerged into the world armed only with her wits and nature's generous gifts. All in all she'd done spectacularly well.

Life with Prince (and with effect from the thirtieth of January 1649, King) Charles was pretty much the same as her parents' arrangements, minus the excitement of hatred. He did not follow the contemporary majority in regarding women as an irksome necessity, there was that plus point. Instead, his was the attitude of a keen but neglectful gardener: appreciative of luxuriant blooms – but prone to wander to other parts of the garden. The arrival of a fine baby boy on the ninth of April 1649 also did much to reform him – for a while – since fondness for children was another aspect of his charm.

The English nation was not informed and went unwarned. It mistakenly thought the execution of Charles I, the abolition of the monarchy and John Aubrey's discovery that they possessed a second, greater Stonehenge at Avebury, the most diverting tidings of the year.

Those about Charles, the courtiers and men of ambition, were also forced to fresh considerations by the babe's arrival in the world. Up to then they had whispered harsh and contrary things in his ear about Madame Walter. They said she was a den of entertainment that knew no closing hours, its membership open to all men. The 'marriage' they scoffed at as a jest, a prank taken – *'with respect, Sire, just a little too far'* – and best forgotten. They also had some unsolicited support from several Netherlands Town Councils. The unimpeachably staid black-clad burghers let it be known that only consideration of his Majesty prevented Lucy from being driven forth as an *infamous wench* into drumhead exile. Charles, rather merry that day in a pre-battle mood, had merely smiled at the news, remarking that it was a strange world where he got the pleasure and the whore got the blame. He also dredged into his literary arsenal and fired off a quote from the Bard of Avon, to wit:

> *'Thou rascal beadle, hold thy bloody hand!*
> *Why dost thou lash that whore? Strip thine own back;*
> *Thou hotly lust'st to use her in that kind*
> *For which thou whipp'st her.'*

They'd had no answer for that.

Lucy had two powerful weapons against these (admittedly truthful) calumnies. Firstly, a viable son and heir could not be disregarded in a time of heart-tearing infant mortality. Secondly she had the wedding certificate: big, bold and brazen – like herself – in (slightly shaky) black and white. Despite having abandoned her first wild hopes of queenship, all requests from the Royal party to *'inspect'* said document, to *'put it in safe keeping'*, met with sturdy refusal. If insurance had been invented just then, Lucy would have called it her insurance policy against single-parenthood and a cast-off old age. She informed them that it was secured very nicely, thank you, safe and sound in a robust black box . . . somewhere. Much money was thrown about in seeking it, and much enamel was ground from cavalier teeth in thought of it, but the 'box' remained unfound.

Charles's son first saw the light of the world in Rotterdam, at the end of a crushing twelve hour labour – for the unnatural never arrive naturally or without pain. All admired his lusty cries and pale skin – and then he was sent away with an English nursemaid to nearby Schiedam to see if he would survive. Their lodgings, in the home of a Dutch merchant, plainly agreed with him and he grew strong. Then, this hurdle over, when he seemed like to live, his mother and father allowed themselves to grow fond – after their own casual fashion. King Charles saw him as often as he could – which was not often, and Lucy seriously inconvenienced several love-affairs to periodically inspect the child. Most importantly, funds were always found from the meagre royal purse to see that he lacked for nothing material. They called him James; James Barlow – a surname plucked from the list of Lucy's past companions. It was as good a one as any: Lucy recalled the man's face and that Knight was content, at Royal request, to make the loan. Lucy borrowed 'Barlow' also; happy to bear a gentle name as well as gentlemen at last.

Thus, everyone was satisfied with events and arrangements – for they did not enquire too closely. They were not there to see the baby's feeding, when the nursemaid looked down on him and allowed the gold in her eyes to show. The infant, likewise blessed, lay strangely still and quiet – and smiled knowingly back.

'Have the coachman halt.'

Lucy Barlow's gentleman-retainer conveyed the instruction upwards and outwards. Madame was too grand and well-provided for nowadays to bellow her own orders. The sumptuous conveyance juddered to a halt, pitching its occupants forward in an undignified heap. Lucy, no stranger to exotic positions, was the first to right herself and resume her seat. She peered intently out of the mud splattered window.

'What is my lady's pleasure?' asked her gentleman-in-waiting, speaking passably courtly English and bowing as best as a sitting position permits. Since they had novelty value, his mistress was still very partial to a bit of bowing and scraping. The servant was happy to oblige, being one of the very few men willing to please her for nothing in return.

'I think I recognise this place,' she replied, still quizzing the landscape as though one bit of these flatlands stolen from the sea was distinguishable from any other, 'but the recollection is dim . . .'

Her gentleman had made it his business to have an encyclopaedic recall of his mistress's extensive acquaintance.

'It is quite possible, Madame,' he answered, 'though you were a trifle . . . over-refreshed on your last visit. We are not far from the residence of your good friend, the Compte de Verteillac, cruelly and falsely banished from his native lands for alleged crimes of . . .'

Some memory cells flared in Lucy's languid brain.

'Tall dashing chap,' she prompted, 'abundant codpiece and, hmmmm . . . all those Moorish servants?'

'The very same, my Lady.'

'Hmmmm . . . it's a damned long way from Antwerp to Schiedam . . .'

'Nigh fifty miles in all,' agreed the gentleman. 'We are but halfway.'

'And my bum's as sore as a whore on Monday with being jolted all these hours . . .'

'I'm sure the Compte would be glad to soothe it, Madame . . .' he silenced a lady's maid's guffaw with a savage glance, 'by his hospitality, I mean.'

Lucy took no offence. *To thine own self be true* was her motto – along with *Why not?*

'Just so. It seems a shame to come all this way and not pay one's respects to the old boy. The child will still be there in Schiedam when we attend it in due course.'

'But of course, Madame,' said the gentleman, favouring her with an unusually complete and white display of teeth. 'A babe of just one year is not like to be roistering about town . . .'

They chortled at the jest and the lady's maids joined in. One thing you could say about service with Lucy Barlow in her new Antwerp establishment: the wages might be late and the life irregular, but you could have a giggle.

'No, you're right; young James is not going anywhere. So that's settled then. Tell the coachman our new destination.'

'Willingly, my lady – but may I be excused this outing? It chances that I too have a friend hereabouts who merits a hello. Besides, I recall that the Compte's largest Moor had conceived a powerful fancy to me: I might have to fend him off at sword-point . . .'

Lucy couldn't see the need for such coyness, but it was in her nature to be obliging to people – and men in particular.

'As you please, my fine fellow. Attend us back at these cross-roads in . . . oh, five hours should be ample.'

The gentleman dismounted and stood to watch the carriage clatter away into the distance and its appointment with Venus. He shuddered. Association with the newcomers was like cont-amination. They were . . . warm, with animal heat; they swarmed over each other in bed and in towns, like lizards in a pit. Worst of all, they had *emotions*.

He studied the blue, cloudless sky, arching over the unend-ing plain, and wondered whether their God really did look down upon them and 'love' them. Incredible.

A soundless signal was sent to the nearest horse and, soon enough, trembling, unwilling but helpless, a suitable beast answered the call. Its breast was bloodied where it had burst its fence or stable. The gentleman found and fingered the stiletto concealed in his sleeve.

Yes, five hours should be *ample*. Then he would be free.

Sated and relaxed and cosy, Lucy was content to wait a little while when her gentleman-retainer did not show. An hour passed, then another, and still the carriage waited at the cross-roads. It came on to rain and the horses stamped and steamed as dusk drew on. Suddenly, independent of any prior train of thought, alarm flared like a beacon in Lucy's heart. Her eyes narrowed and that which was non-human within her was allowed free rein. Those senses she could not put a name to, let alone describe, reached out into the dark and found that all was not as it should be.

The sodden, miserable coachman was awoken from his doze by the carriage door being flung aside and his mistress's scream from below. Crazed, heedless of the rain, she appeared beside him and ordered, in words not to be queried or denied, that they make Schiedam by nightfall.

It almost killed the horses but it was rather that than thwart the possessed woman who urged the driver on. The lady's maids were ditched, drenched and protesting, on the roadside, to lessen the burden and the carriage fairly flew along the pitted roads, balanced on two wheels as they took corners, in a way it was not designed to do. The driver dared not slacken the pace for fear of the harpy alongside him. One yard per hour slower she warned him, and she'd reduce the weight still further, run him through with her hairpiece-bodkin and take the reins herself. The servant could tell the difference between threat and promise when he heard it.

Somehow they made it to town without crashing into gore and matchwood. The carriage availed itself of the Dutch merchant's house-wall to come to a final halt. Lucy leapt down, regardless of modesty, her skirts billowing outwards, and hit the ground running, armed with bodkin and the coachman's pistol. A room-to-room search took all of two minutes, the longest of Lucy's eventful life.

The place was like it had never been lived in. Merchant, nursemaid and baby were gone.

Before astounded Dutch citizens, Lucy rent her clothes and tore at her hair, bewailing in an unknown tongue the greatness of the injury done her. Another mad night ride to Maaslandsluys, the nearest port, had already done little to improve her appearance. The Town Mayor and his bodyguard, preparing to embark for the Hague, shrank back from such a terrifying apparition.

Lucy saw that her passion was counterproductive and was instantly calm, collected and focused; as worthy of attention as an oncoming sabre. She explained, in quiet, rational, words her dilemma and stoked high the fires of sympathy. She blamed Charles, she blamed Cromwell, she blamed herself for the tragedy. A purse full of gold was thrust at the frightened Mayor as token of worldly worth and merit, and genuine intent. If she'd thought it might help, she'd have thrust her mound at the old man, crowd or no crowd. Eventually, by one means or another, he – and all the other Hollanders – were convinced.

A search of every ship at every quay was ordered by his Worship. His musketeers welcomed the chance to have a nose in other people's business. Many things of interest fell out in shaking up the town – but nothing of relevance to Lucy. A stop order was then placed on the other ports and people's lawful transactions were much disrupted in the days that followed. Somehow, across the nation, Dutch sympathies were enlisted on the side of this poor woman and against the machinations of baby-snatching foreigners. Charles and the Royalists were obliged to display their innocence and confirm it by assisting the search-cum-crusade. For a while, everyone enjoyed the interlude of hysteria as a relief from day-to-day life.

Then, just when interest was flagging and more important matters – such as tulip bulbs – reasserted themselves, the baby was found, healthy and safe and sound, in the little town of Loosduinen. Somebody had left young James Barlow, well wrapped and snug in a basket, in the porch of the Church there. His name and proper address were helpfully attached to the container.

Lucy was straightaway fetched and, a good mother after her fashion, finding him clean and cared for, sang sweet thanks to the sky. It was only later, for the first time ever preparing him for bath and bed herself, that she found the band of parchment around his tiny wrist. The swirling, spidery script thereon would have been meaningless to most – but it had significance for Lucy. Decipherment took a whole evening and unaccustomed mental exertion but, by the dawn succeeding the day of her deliverance, she had it.

'*We cannot harm him,*' said the message. '*He will be King but he will break your heart.*'

As her baby slept alongside her, Lucy considered the proposition – but only for a second.

'*Fair enough,*' she thought.

There were other, more earthly, attempts on the child as he grew straight and strong and a better dynastic proposition. King Charles's advisors could not accept the boy's continued connection with such a 'flighty trollop' – as they termed her – for all she might be his mother. A head that one day might wear the crown of England should not have its character formed in a den of iniquity. Charles waspishly answered that he didn't see why not: it would fit that head for the company it would later keep. However, he took their point. By that stage it was all over between him and Lucy. Her magic had faded and he was puzzled – and shamed – by the fierceness of the first attraction. He did not mean to be cruel; that was never his pleasure or his way. It was just that the stern idol, Duty, required another sacrifice at its altar. He had put valued portions of his own life to the knife there, and now it was Lucy's turn.

Mrs Barlow didn't see it that way. Lucy had never accepted that mere concepts like 'honour' and 'duty' should abort even a moment of human happiness: heaven knew that there was little enough of it around. Instead, she rented a large and secure house at Boxtel, near Breda, and kept James ever close by her. There was a second miracle by now, a baby girl called Mary, by the Dutch Lord Taafe (maybe), though Lucy had withheld her exotic side on that occasion and the girl was purely human. She loved them both equally, like a scatty tiger.

The Royalists were angered by her stubbornness, but not deterred. First, whilst Charles was downing great draughts of humiliation in Scotland, his lackey, Lord Craven, laid crafty hands on James. Lucy went to Dutch Law, pawning her jewels to a Jew and her body to a judge. Between the two she got her verdict and her boy back.

Then, one cold Brussels night, when James was eight, Lucy let her snarling guard slip. Deceived by the monstrous rectitude of Sir Arthur Slingsby, the great and good Cavalier, she accepted accommodation with him arranged by Charles. Indeed, her greater fear was for the Knight's reputation. She would, she said, offer him a signed document to the effect that ,though they passed a night under the same roof, she had made no assault on his honour. He had gravely thanked her for her consideration.

In fact, the crusade he had given his life to had just made its greatest demand on him. He had been asked to act in a squalid manner – for the very best of reasons, of course – and fealty was (mis)used to bludgeon him into surrender.

It was all done simply enough, for he could not be bothered with cunning in such a cause. The Officers of the Court Guard were ordered to arrest Madame Barlow in respect of an unpaid loan. Strictly speaking, though the spirit of hospitality was thereby ravished, he was entitled to do so. Lucy owed money to most of the kinder-hearted members of the Cavalier community, since her preferred lifestyle, even subsidised by an ever-changing cast of lovers, didn't come cheaply. Moreover, though she never forgot an ill-turn, her recall of favours was more shaky. However, Slingsby's sudden zeal for repayment seemed suspect. Certainly, that was Lucy's assessment. With her locked up, however briefly, James would be theirs; perhaps for ever.

Her octave ranging and ear-threatening screams were remembered in the vicinity for generations to come. Whole blocks around were awakened. When the soldiers fell back, scratch-marked, from their first attempt, she grasped the child to her ample bosom and would not let go. The fight continued through the house, wrecking the fixtures and spilling out into the street. There the deeply embarrassed Sir Arthur found an audience of night-attired Netherlanders come to see the show.

Lucy screeched a highly biased resume of the play so far and the mood of the mob swung against him. Then the Town Watch arrived, muskets, lanterns and all, to add their pompous two-penneth, till Slingsby wasn't sure if he was at a pantomime or the start of a lynching. For a moment, tormented by the Babel of noise, he was minded to shoot his way out and get some sense and peace that way. Fortunately however, discretion, and the sentiments of religion, prevailed and he backed down. His charges were withdrawn and slowly, very slowly, the mob dispersed. Lucy and James went with them, dishevelled but victorious.

Sir Arthur withdrew indoors for a stiff ministration of brandy. He would, he reflected, sooner face Cromwell's Ironsides, any day, than tangle with that banshee and her unnaturally calm child again. He'd caught young James's eye as they parted and it had unnerved him. That knowing half-smile wasn't normal or nice. Let 'em go; into hiding and damnation: the House of Stuart was better off without them.

Later that night, someone threw cobblestones through all his windows.

The bare office was as unwelcoming as the conversation.

'So let me see if I've got this correct: you're the widow of a Dutch sea-captain . . .'

'That's right,' said Lucy, dabbing at her eye with a lace kerchief, all the while sizing up her military interrogator. 'A poor widow cast adrift . . .'

'Though you speak no Dutch . . .'

'There was no time to learn. We were given such a short time together.' She repressed a very convincing sob.

The red-coat smiled wearily and laid down his quill.

'So, Madame, am I to presume it was a match of just loving looks and silent communion?'

'You may presume what you wish, sirrah,' flared Lucy. 'Do not mock the best thing that ever happened to me!'

'How then did he propose to you?'

'By the loving eloquence of his visage. Cupid has no need of language.'

'What was his name?'

'Um . . . Hendrik . . . um, van der . . .'

36

'Pray do not exert yourself, Madame,' said the soldier. 'The name of your spouse temporarily escapes you. Tis a common phenomenon – though usually found in longer married couples . . .'

'Thank you for being so under . . .'

'*Enough*!' He slammed his massive fist on the table and made Lucy jump. 'If I wish for comedy – which I don't – I'll attend a theatre. Which I can't, because the Lord Protector has closed 'em. Why are you in England? It's coming up to dinnertime and I want the truth out of you.'

Lucy shied at the word: in her experience truth was, at best, inconvenient and more often painful. She poked gingerly at her memories in search of this 'truth' business. Then inspiration occurred.

'*What is truth?*' she asked, quoting the words of Pontius Pilate. Her father had shown her a Bible once, and she'd just recalled that the Cromwellians were keen on that sort of thing.

The Colonel was both amused and bemused by his prisoner's citing of scripture: an experience akin to coming home and finding his hound reflecting on Holy Writ.

'Look into my eyes,' he said softly. 'What do you see?'

Movement onto the physical plane was very welcome, even though Lucy could detect nothing amorous in the order. She complied. The soldier was broad and flaxen-haired, a west-countryman by his burring accent, with a face made up of curves that should have been friendly but was not. His eyes were light blue and very still.

'I see war,' she answered, speaking by instinct. He nodded agreement.

'And harsh deeds through necessity,' he expanded. 'And charity worn down by experience. In your instance, you may also see an unhappy future: prison and separation and weeping. My sole business latterly is in death sentences and life-long incarcerations. Such is the condition of England. That being so, your future is yours to shape – for a moment or two longer . . .'

'I will tell you what I know' she said swiftly.

'That's good. I'd rather my upcoming beef and beer isn't

37

soured by recent severity. So, we find you, a notorious exile, lodging with a curious menagerie, above a barber's shop in the Strand. What's it all about then?'

Lucy didn't like to hear her family and current lover, Colonel Thomas Howard, compared to a zoo of exotica. The slur emboldened her to further deception.

'Well, maybe Charles Stuart did sire a child off me – but it died. I've not seen the King these two years back, oh no. The children with me were by other men – I'm not sure who: it was dark. We're here to collect my legacy from my dear departed mother's will. There's a thousand pounds, no, more than that, waiting for me. When we have it, we'll be away from here and trouble you no more, oh yes . . .'

The soldier flattened his lips in mockery of a smile and, taking from the desk a page of vellum from which dangled a legal seal, held it up before her. Lucy quizzed it innocently: sometimes there were advantages to illiteracy.

'Call me inattentive if you like,' he said, gazing sadly out the window across the rooftops of the capital, thinking of all the plotters sheltered beneath, 'but I've read this a dozen times. My distinct impression was your mother loved you so much you're not mentioned in her will. Perhaps you can show me the particular clause . . .'

'Um . . .'

'And, before you think of it, your Dad's will is likewise.'

'I'm not surprised; the black-hearted old . . .'

'*And*, when you have secrets to hide, it doesn't do to fall out with your servants. Your maid, Anne Hill, informs us of a more . . . interesting begetter for your boy than you admit.'

'That witch wouldn't know the truth if it got in bed and swived her. If she had children I wouldn't want one of the kittens. She borrowed my marble utensils of love and . . .'

The soldier held up his plate of a hand to stem the tide of invective.

'Attend me, Madame,' he said, lumbering up and beckoning her to join him at the window. 'Do you know what that is?'

Lucy followed the pointing finger.

'The sky?' she hazarded. He looked reprovingly at her, as though expecting better of such a spirit.

'The Tower of London,' Lucy admitted.

'Well,' he said, imitating her Welsh tones, 'there's handy.'

Actually, the Tower wasn't as bad as centuries of careful Crown indoctrination had led people to believe. There were greens for the children to play on, pleasing promenades for her and Howard to walk, and interesting sights for them all to see. The accommodation provided was quite civilised. When fear engendered piety Lucy attended divine service at the Tower Church of St Peter *ad Vincula*. Between these and other distractions, whole hours could pass without contemplating the proximity of Traitor's Gate, the headman's block and a state-of-the-art torture chamber.

Lucy had fled Charles and Holland and the kidnap attempts thinking to find shelter under the wing of an even worse demon. Her enemies feared Lord Protector Cromwell more than they did God – although that wasn't saying much. They cursed him nightly in their prayers, but blanched as they did so. He was an object of dread. In 1644, the day before the crucial battle of Marston Moor, Prince Rupert had just one question for the first roundhead prisoner taken. It wasn't about numbers or plans but simply: 'Is Cromwell there?' And, if that was true so early on, it was correct to a higher power now that 'Old Noll' ruled the four nations. His authority was so absolute, his daring so infinite, that he had even squared up to the legal establishment and punched them on the nose (and in their pockets!) Not even Good Queen Bess dreamed of getting the law out of *their* claws. Such superhuman confidence didn't just command respect, it hoicked you up by your collar and dared you to withhold it.

Lucy preferred instinct to reason, but reasoned, insofar as lack of practice allowed, that they would not be pursued into the maw of such an ogre. She forgot that the ogre might have an appetite of his own.

There were further interviews with the Lieutenant of the

Tower, a gentlemanly old soul concealing a mind like a knife. That Officer had seen just about everything in his time and was accordingly not too upset about oncoming death – or threatening others with it – in a gentlemanly way, of course. He had the full story out of them inside an hour of their meeting, without recourse to hot irons, the eye-spoon or Scottish-boot – or even harsh words. Lucy endured it reasonably well but Colonel Howard was reduced to jelly – and lasting impotence – by the experience. Whilst they were in the Tower their relationship did not prosper.

Then, for a while, Lucy and her party were left pretty much at peace as higher minds decided what to do with the information extracted. Young James and his younger half-sister played football with the children of the gaolers. A kindly executioner showed them the axe used to deal with his late Majesty, Charles I, and James gravely hefted the blade that had killed the grandfather he never knew. In the pleasant weather of that summer the days drifted easily away.

Finally, one bright morning – but far earlier than was her custom or preference – Lucy and young James were roused up by soldiers they'd not encountered before. These were hard-faced, taciturn men, marked with old wounds, and both grim and efficient in a manner unlike the usual guardians of the Tower. When Lucy protested the bed was tipped over, spilling her on to the cold floor. Then, to add insult to injury, they took no more notice of her glorious naked form than the task in hand required. James, bold beyond his years and fearing the worse, snatched up a clasp-knife and sought to protect himself (but not, it seemed, his mother . . .). A gauntleted hand casually squeezed the boy's upper arm until the blade was dropped. Lucy was thrown a fur coat to protect her modesty and, when she ventured her 'screaming, hysterical scene' stratagem, a boot helped her on her way. From cosy sleep to venturing forth, the bedroom was cleared of life in mere seconds.

They issued out, blinking, into the sun and were closely escorted across the green. Lucy's howls were silenced by one soldier raising a finger to his lips and smiling a smile that was no smile. The Lieutenant of the Tower joined them en route but he had no *good morning* for them today. His easy courtesy appeared switched off.

In the base of one minor bastion, there was a little door that Lucy had paid no heed to till now. Now it stood ajar and was guarded by two of the monster-soldiers. Lucy and James and the Lieutenant were ushered in and the door slammed behind them. Before them, at a desk and in all his glory, sat the Regicide.

Actually, there was not much of the glorious about him. Cromwell was dressed in simple black, the sort of thing you'd see on the back of a grocer. He sat easy in the plain wooden chair, old, worn boots sprawled before him, toying with the Great Seal of England. His face was etched with care, his eyes somewhat weary – perhaps with the hour, perhaps more generally. One callused hand gestured them to be seated.

Stricken silent by awe they hurriedly obeyed. Then the church-like reverence was spoilt by the Lieutenant of the Tower's 'aargh' of pain. He leapt into the air as he had not done for many decades, clutching his backside. A tin tack protruded from the fleshy parts thereof.

Cromwell was possessed with laughter and thumped the table in glee.

'Never fails!' he gasped. 'Never fails. They never look at the seat, only at me!'

The Lieutenant extracted the article from his behind and constructed a half-convincing smile.

'Your Highness is most . . . jocular,' he said, having chosen the term carefully from an extensive menu of possibilities.

'Say what you like about my regime,' Cromwell said, still chuckling and addressing Lucy and her son in the most amiable manner imaginable, 'but we *do* have a laugh!'

'Do you?' said Lucy in her surprise. She'd always heard otherwise.

'Certainly we do,' answered the Lord Protector. 'Admiral Blake got me with a squishy-tomato-on-the-seat at the last but one High Council meeting. I thought I'd die laughing!'

41

'Heaven forfend,' said the Lieutenant – quite genuinely. He was all too aware that the retention of his own head on his shoulders was connected with Cromwell's longevity.

Mention of the metaphysical rendered the Lord Protector serious again. He did not jest about such matters.

'I'll go when the Lord summons me,' he said stoutly. 'According to His own sweet will. Meanwhile, Madame, what are we to do with you?'

'Let us go?' suggested Lucy, not sounding too hopeful.

Cromwell gave her a friendly 'oh come on' look.

'I think not, alas. If you were just Charles's current . . . in deference to the boy's presence, *close friend*, I'd not stand in your way. That's a thing between the Lord and your conscience. No, it's because you've brought the heir to the throne with you that . . .'

Lucy opened her mouth to protest, but the words coughed and expired on her lips. She didn't feel like insulting this homely fiend with her unconvincing alibis.

Cromwell read her inmost thoughts.

'Yes,' he agreed, 'let's skip the stuff about dead Dutch sea-captains and alternative paternities. We know whose he is; he even looks like Charles. No, we shall have to keep . . .'

In remarking James's resemblance to his father, Cromwell had glanced at the boy. His words stumbled on a while longer but his mind was clearly elsewhere. The Lord Protector fell silent and looked again, conducting a full scrutiny. The room became very still.

James stood up to the baleful gaze most manfully but Lucy was host to a new army of fears. The Lieutenant of the Tower looked at her in puzzlement, hopeful of some explanation of what was going on, but she would not provide it. Lucy was on her mettle as never before and inscrutable as a stone. Desperate thoughts scampered through her mind. Should she show some leg and flash her cleavage? Was there any hope in confession? She pondered furiously but each avenue of escape ended only in despair. Did he *know*?

He did. Before he was Lord Protector, before all the wars and titles, Cromwell was called 'Lord of the Fens' – because he came from there and made his reputation with the poor commoners therein. He had heard things in that strange place – and seen things. He was aware of what flitted about on the edges of life – and sometimes even closer in.

'Well, well, well,' he said to Lucy, at long, very long last. 'Who'd have thought it?'

The Lieutenant was lost and let it be known. Cromwell waved him quiet. He was thinking something through; something, it seemed, of supreme import. All the easy-going warmth and kindliness was fled away. His stare held no charity for Madame Walter.

'So it shall be,' he finally decreed, speaking the words like a sentence in court. 'It is the Lord's will and the world must suffer it patiently. I will do no harm to infants – of whatever type . . .'

Lucy sobbed in relief – to the Lieutenant's further baffled consternation.

'. . . But you'll not set foot in England again – not in my time. Expel them both,' he ordered the Lieutenant, 'today. Let Charles have his viper. Set them down on the shores of Flanders. Then burn the ship they travel in.'

Lucy's party were left on the beach, abandoned like some contagion, but Miss Walter picked up her skirts and marched inland and to the years beyond like a conquering amazon. She deluded herself that she had won. She should have thought deeper.

Enraged by his only heir being offered to the mercies of Cromwell, Charles and his partisans redoubled their efforts. Sir Arthur Slingsby would try no more but there were the attempts of Edward Progers in '57, and that of a Manx mercenary soon after. Each came closer to success and the Dutch were tired of protecting one stubborn mother, however fair and noisy. Lucy was worn down and offered a truce: Charles could have and raise the boy so long as she had free access. They would share a house together and it would be like the old days. The King pretended to be interested. That was in January '58. By April they had James to themselves. He would not see his mother again.

On the fourth day of that month, Thomas Ross, a Scot and minor poet, sat and wrote to Charles's Private Secretary concerning a certain commission. *'Pray tell his Majesty,'* he said, *'his little son is out of the hands he was in and bestowed in another place, both out of his mother's knowledge or anyone else's . . .'* He was rewarded with the promise that Charles would almost *certainly* read his latest book of verse.

Lucy never recovered. She also never gave up, travelling the continent in poverty, from rebuff to rebuff, in search of her son. Mercy came in the form of death, whilst she was hot on the trail in Paris in '59. The cause was never ascertained, for no one much enquired; not Charles, not James, not anyone. At the age of twenty-eight Lucy had served her purpose to everyone's satisfaction – except her own.

THE YEAR OF OUR LORD 1663

A pot-pourri of cold-eyed conversation.

'The theatre's coming back, one hears.' 'Killigrew's "King's Players" has got a licence. He's to have the Drury Lane place.' 'The Theatre Royal. Only I heard D'Avenant's "Duke's Players" secured it.' 'He claims to be Shakespeare's natural son you know. His parents had the Crown Inn at Oxford where the Bard often stayed.' 'And the Bard had his mother, one supposes.' 'There'll be actresses, I hear.' 'An innovation by royal warrant, no less. Can't imagine what prompted his Majesty there . . .'

'Did you hear about Buckingham?' 'Yes . . . quite skewered the poor Earl of Shrewsbury, apparently.' 'Well, he's sunk his pork-sword in the man's wife long enough.' 'Hence the duel.' 'The Countess cheered on the contest, there disguised as a page.' 'The minx!' 'And was bedded straight after by the victor to celebrate, all soaked in her husband's gore. You have to laugh . . .' 'It's the devil to get out of silk, blood. That's why I tend to red apparel. Scarlet deeds and women: best cover 'em in matching hues.'

'I see that Sir Charles Sedley got done.' 'Bound over in the sum of £500, friend of Charles or no.' 'Shitting off the Cock Tavern balcony into Covent Garden, that's one thing . . .' 'We've all been a bit tipsy from time to time . . .' 'Oxford Kate'll be pleased – she could lose her licence.' 'It was the blasphemous sermon to the crowd that followed . . .' 'Whilst naked.' 'One should know when to stop. That'll clip his wings.' 'And keep his breeches on.' 'Don't bet the farm on it.'

'I'd recommend you try it, Madame.' ' "Tea" you say, Mister Pepys?' 'Just so. It is as reviving as it is, alas, expensive. The duty

45

levied is quintuple the initial cost. A small quantity first came ten years back, captured off a Netherlands ship.' 'And what was the other thing?' 'My proposal to pleasure your portals at the earliest oppor . . .' 'You rapscallion!' 'Any port in a storm, Madame!' 'No, I meant before that.' 'Ah, the "fountain pen", a real boon to those with regular writing obligations.' 'You are likewise a fountain of innovations, Master Samuel. I hope you can maintain that level of satisfaction . . .'

Dispute as you may the wisdom of restoring the monarchy to England but it was a great step forward for party people. This particular royal rave at Windsor had really taken off. Two fortunes had been lost at cards, three duels commissioned and a score of assignations arranged (not counting two already consummated behind the curtains) and it was still only seven o'clock.

'You dance well, sir. You are to be c-c-complimented on your facility and g-g-grace.'

Lord Monmouth, James Walter-Croft-Barlow and maybe Stuart, bowed thanks for the Duke of York's fulsome, albeit stuttered, compliment.

Lord Rochester, slumped drunk in a nearby chair, agreed with the Duke of York.

'He gets it from his mother. She used to do a lot of dancing.'

'Just so,' snapped the Duke primly.

'The mattress minuet, for the most part.'

'We're *obliged* for the intelligence, sir,' insisted the King's brother, turning his long face on Rochester. When he wished it could look as merciful as marble. 'We'd likewise t-t-thank you to mind the proximity of the boy.'

The courtier, soldier, poet and libertine was not intimidated. He knew he was a blazing comet, designed for a bright but brief career.

'His *proximity* is much on my mind, Highness: such fair skin, such well-formed limbs. He prompts recollection of a recent – alas unpublished, verse of mine:

> *'and if ever busy love entrenches,*
> *then thou, soft sweet page of mine,*
> *doth the trick worth forty wenches . . .'*

James Stuart, Duke of York and heir apparent, a moralist by the undemanding standards of the Court and already well on his way to Catholicism, permitted his nostrils to flare. Rochester merely took it as a tribute to the muse and toasted his audience from one of the bottles he held.

The Duke swivelled on his high-heeled boots and guided Monmouth away across the ballroom. The Great Hall of Windsor Castle provided ample room for escape from areas overheated by the flames of Hell.

'You will find no shortage of v-v-vicious company in your new life,' James advised the youngster, casting a protective arm around his slim shoulders. 'People will seek to profit from the favours showered upon you. Acquire the w-w-wisdom to spurn them. In this and all other respects, I will always be here to assist you.'

It was a valuable offer: James was a man of his word: in fact notorious for it. Despite the *Restoration* and return of Stuart fortunes, he'd even honoured his marriage pledge of exile days to the . . . buxom (and papist!) Anne Hyde, a mere politician's daughter. Mighty efforts had been made to dissuade him, his mother even finding a courtier who'd *'eased the pain of love with Miss Hyde in a water-closet'*, but the Duke stuck to his guns and girl. True, she'd do the decent thing by dying early but he wasn't to know that at the time.

Monmouth directed disturbing sloe-eyes onto his would-be protector.

'Surely not *"always"*, sire,' he said. 'You are much older than I.'

James halted in his tracks. The mob of dancing couples respectfully afforded them space – whilst tuning in to every word.

'Well no,' conceded the Duke, striving to retain the convivial tone, 'no m-m-man is immortal, but . . .'

'Do not think me ungrateful: whilst you are still with us I shall learn from you all I can.'

No one likes reminders of mortality; least of all Princes of the Blood mindful of the Crown. James Stuart bridled at . . . well, not the words; they were blameless enough, but rather the tone.

'And learn to what end, may I ask?' he said icily, outrage overpowering his speech impediment.

'Why, for my betterment,' answered Monmouth, with an innocent smile. 'And the benefit of England.'

'I'm g-g-glad to hear it, *young* sir.'

'Though you need not worry overmuch for me. Rochester's banter did not offend. Likewise, one has heard that you are not always so averse to bawdy. We are already well acquainted with mama's reputation – and the Earl's . . . catholic tastes.'

That last word was carefully chosen, a silken shoe directed at the groin. The Duke's sympathies for the Old Faith were open knowledge. York now drew himself up to his full imposing height, looking over the youth; the aggression-display greatly assisted by the scarlet and ermine of Knight-of-the-Garter robes.

'I understand,' he said, still struggling to be patient, 'that you have already had *one* s-s-sojourn in the Tower . . .'

Monmouth was merely amused, as though it were a sheep growling at him, instead of the second man of the Realm.

'Indeed,' he answered glibly. 'And there, though young in years, I met the arch-monster Cromwell – and outfaced him. I don't believe you can say the same . . .'

Onlookers thought that James's eyeballs would venture forth to dangle on his cheeks. A famous, history-changing, dynasty-disrupting, 'Stuart Explosion' seemed in the offing. No one had ever thought to impugn the Duke's bravery; not even the blackest republican. After the unhappy, neglected, childhood that had tied a knot in his tongue, he'd spent his life fighting. From the age of nine all dolled-up in a padded buff-coat at Edgehill, through sterling service for the French Sun-King, to killing Englishmen if need be, he'd been in the thick of everything going. Though he'd felt fear he'd never shown it – and that was

48

true heroism. It was hardly his fault if fate deprived him of a tussle with Old Noll himself.

Charles II set down his spoon. From the vantage point of a temporary throne at the Hall's end, he saw the disaster-in-the-making. Exile and a decade of conspiracy had given him a sixth sense in such matters: the one and only benefit from that heart-tearing period. Whenever the atmosphere became toxic beyond a certain expected level, Charles knew of it, whichever way his eyes were facing, whatever he might be about. The (suppressed) memoirs of Nell Gwyn recount even an interrupted romp when the King surmised, she knew not how, that the infamous Lord Shaftesbury had entered the Palace. 'A *plotter has come – and so I must not*' she records him as saying. A falling-out in the Royal Family was of even greater import than an ambitious politician and Charles left his pease-pudding to cool.

The king was half a foot taller than the average guest present, taller even than the chosen guardsmen at the doors. Thus his upper portions and periwig were easily visible above the heads of the dancing throng, ploughing through them like a shark amidst sardines. On arrival at the epicentre of ill-will a pretend-friendly Regal embrace soon separated the antagonists.

'Well, isn't this nice?' he asked, in a *you-might-be-family-but-watch-it* . . . tone of voice he retained for special occasions. 'Chatter, chatter, chatter, best o'pals, eh?'

James, Duke of York, told his brother all he wanted to with a look. Monmouth's oval face was a blank palate. A long silence ensued.

The King had an ironic expression at the best of times. He intensified it.

'Asked a question . . . not speaking Abyssinian . . . Waiting . . .'

'Quite so,' obliged the Duke. 'I'm finding our c-c-conversation most instructive . . .'

'Me too,' replied Monmouth.

'Well, knock me down and call me Nelly, I'm pleased to hear it. Can't have any *discord* in the regime, can we? We don't want

49

to go on our travels again, do we? No indeed not.'

He bore down on Monmouth. 'So then, how's married life? Plenty of the old *cuckoo-in-the-nest*, chase-you-to-the-cornfield, business, eh!'

Monmouth shrugged.

'The Bride's mother – may she grow a tail – feels it is best we wait awhile. She says delay consummation till we are both fifteen: something to so with childbearing hips or the like.'

Charles made a noise of derision.

'Modern nonsense! Don't hold with it myself. There's a poem Rochester wrote:

> '*When roses are red, they're ready for plucking.*
> *When girls are fourteen, they're ready for . . .*'

'Good-*day* to you b-b-both,' snorted the Duke, interrupting the recitation and stalking off.

King Charles watched his brother go, not showing the sadness he felt in order to deprive the onlookers of their pleasure.

'Don't flatter yourself with my favour,' he whispered to Monmouth, never ceasing to gauge reaction all around. 'I only spoke saucy to soak the gunpowder. Though a garter-grasper of the first order – save for redheads apparently,' the King paused and puzzled for a second, 'the Duke does not like such talk. I knew he would leave.'

'I'm obliged to you, father,' answered the boy, with smooth confidence.

Charles looked down upon him from a great height.

'Oh it's that you are,' he said firmly. 'Let me tell you about it.'

He bore Monmouth off to a refreshments table at the side of the hall.

'Here,' he said, thrusting a slice of duck at Monmouth, 'stop your mouth with this and pretend you're listening to chit-chat.' The boy daintily obliged, shredding the dark meat with perfect teeth.

'Disputes weaken families,' said Charles. 'And the family is everything. Out of the little kindness in his thin heart the

Duke would be good to you. I will not have him thwarted in that.'

Monmouth signalled full comprehension and agreement.

'You've come very far; from the wrong side of the blanket to dizzy exaltation. The view from high up is wonderful: enjoy it and have a happy life. From where I've put you there's a long way to fall.'

Monmouth conceded the point with an economic nod and freed his mouth to reply.

'But that won't happen,' he said, smiling.

The King could not help but frown.

'Why not?'

'Because you love me.' It was a bald statement of fact.

Charles started to reply but found the words would not come. He was considerate of the few fondnesses he felt and lacked the strength to abort any of them.

'Look,' he said finally, a caricature exasperated, fond father, 'I'm not Methuselah; I'll be off elsewhere one day. There's more poison than sunshine in this world, especially at our rank. You need to have other friends.'

'But I *do*,' answered the boy, looking along the table for fresh diversion. 'Don't worry.'

The King closed his eyes for a second, wondering why everything good was just that *little* more effort than it was worth. Opening them again, he beheld necessary reinforcement for his argument.

'You boy, yes you, over here if you please.'

The Page, much the same age as Monmouth but stockier and less blessed with looks and grace, hastened to them.

'Now,' said Charles, 'here's just the lad. You're an Oglethorpe, aren't you?'

'Yes, Majesty, Theophilus, son of Sutton Oglethorpe.'

'Couldn't be better. What do you think of family loyalty?'

Theophilus wasn't expecting that, anticipating instead a request for food or for a message to be run. Even so, his reply was sure.

'Well, Majesty, it's everything, isn't it?'

51

The King beamed on him. If only all his subjects were so plain and simple and obliging.

'*Exactly*: my very words. Now mark this, Monmouth, this boy's family gave all for my father's cause; they fought and suffered, they lost loved ones and endured harsh penalties, penury and exile for us. Not one of them broke ranks and brought shame on their name. They did not count the cost and now they have come into their reward. Have I stinted in my gratitude, young Oglethorpe?'

The page-of-honour shook his head vehemently.

'No, sire. My dad never ceases to praise providence. Our fortunes are restored, my brothers hold position in the law, the army and at court. You and the Lord have been good to us – in the long run.' He seemed troubled by the slight qualification – but obliged in honesty to make it. Charles appeared not to notice.

'And this despite my exchequers calling me mad to repay all my debts of honour. So then, Master Theophilus, if you are grateful for what you and yours have received, what would you say if someone were to marry you off to an heiress – say the Countess of Buccleuch – with long white legs (so I'm told)? What then if your patron festooned you with titles: Duke of Buccleuch, Earl of Dalkeith, Lord Scott, Baron Tynedale, Earl of Doncaster, Duke of Monmouth and – this very day – Knight of the Garter? And that's not to mention M.A.s at Oxford and Cambridge, new houses in Whitehall and Chiswick, a pension of £6000 per year from the excise rights for Yorkshire and £8000 on the export of Welsh white draperies. God smack me but I've even turned over the receipts from wrecks and salvage! Now, would you be mildly pleased or what?'

Theophilus looked at Monmouth, knowing full well that it was he they were talking of. The page could hardly fail to be aware; that flood of fortune was on every educated tongue and this very ball was in honour of Monmouth's en-gartering. Lavish festivities, bonfires and fireworks had not abated since his marriage three days earlier. The lucky recipient returned the gaze without malice, indicating he might speak his mind.

'Um,' answered Oglethorpe – and, seeing from the Royal visage this was not the reply required, added, 'well, truth to tell, I'd say my cup runneth over.'

'And you'd say right,' confirmed the King. 'Forget your present duties. Here's one of these new-fangled gold guineas to stir your zeal. Stay with Monmouth and repeat your last statement at five minute intervals. Pray do me the service of *convincing* him, for I weary of the task.'

In fact, Charles had noted an unfamiliar cleavage, insecurely constrained in scarlet silk. The engines of passion lumbered into life, forcing him to move on. Monmouth and Oglethorpe were left alone.

The young Duke, Earl, etc., etc., subjected Theophilus to the closest scrutiny, as though on a tour of inspection of his soul. Monmouth's face would not release the page's more homely counterpart. Oglethorpe, a very literal boy, submitted to the search whilst counting down the minutes to the first of his repetitions.

Monmouth at least released him, having read what he wished.

'You need not heed the letter of his Majesty's instruction,' he said, friendly as you like. 'I accept the sentiments already.'

Theophilus was glad to hear it. Keeping track of each five minute interval would stilt conversation.

'Do you know what I think?' asked Monmouth, passing a dainty parcel of chicken-cornflour wrapped in pastry. Oglethorpe waited for the second part of the question but it did not arrive. He had to assume it to be a genuine enquiry.

'No,' he said, truthfully. Monmouth was unreadable when he so chose.

'I think our meeting was no accident. I detect that we shall not part. Are you content for our fates to entwine?'

Theophilus bit into the confection, at ease now that frankness was the order of the day.

'I can think of worse predictions,' he admitted. Monmouth looked approvingly at him.

'That is because you lack imagination – at present. However,

53

your acceptance is good: for it is futile to fight destiny.'

'If you say so, Lord . . .'

'I do, though I cannot yet see the end of the matter between us. Its conclusion is presently shrouded by contingencies. What I do say is . . .'

His attention was suddenly severed. He looked about, scenting the air like a wild animal.

'I suspect,' he said, as though to himself and just the smallest part alarmed, 'that someone seeks me.'

So it proved. Within moments a note was passed to Monmouth requesting his presence in the antechamber. Theophilus had to read it to him, for Lucy Walter had not laboured overmuch on his education. He was surprised at the Duke's acceptance and willingness to comply. Every exalted gathering attracted its swarm of petitioners and importuners and generally they were greeted with as much joy as wasps at a picnic. For one so presumptuous as to interrupt a ball only stern rebukes seemed appropriate. Instead Monmouth was keen to meet this 'Mr Pelling'.

Indicating Theophilus should follow, the Duke swept from the room, glorious in his cut-down garter-robes, and a Yeoman-of-the-Guard opened the door into the adjoining waiting area. The echoing buzz of conversation from the patient hordes ceased at the sight. Hope flared briefly in the eyes of those seeking appeal from some outrageous legal verdict or finance for a pet project. The bearers of new popish plots and informers on priests hurriedly rehearsed their lines. Monmouth conceded them a smile but nothing else. He appeared to know with whom his business lay. A tall man at the far end of the vast hall answered the Duke's summons.

Theophilus studied him with just as much interest as the guards. He moved with grace, equal in easy balance and economy of effort to that shown by Monmouth on the dance-floor. The confidence he displayed did not seem entirely fitting to his status: a plain 'Mr', in simple clothes, begging from his betters. Such boldness, and the honour shown him, awoke hatred in the assembled cadgers and caution in the sentinels. Yet as he passed each, the hostility simply fled away and he was looked upon with favour. Even Theophilus, a no-nonsense youth, found himself smiling at his approach.

Close up he was of still greater interest. Oglethorpe could not decide whether Pelling was of advanced years but well-preserved, or prematurely aged. Fifty years before he would have been the height of fashion – amongst the mercantile classes; but now appeared a strange visitation. He did not boast a wig but retained his natural hair, worn long and flowing. His low bow was exquisitely executed.

Only Monmouth appeared immune from the charm offensive. He too wore a smile, but it was more challenging, less charitable.

'Why, sir, Mr . . . Pelling,' he said, 'at long last, eh?'

Pelling's voice was clear and musical but curiously short-ranged. Though Theophilus heard well enough, he felt sure it did not carry far. The mendicants strained to eavesdrop but puzzled faces betokened failure.

'Long postponed,' agreed Mr Pelling, 'to some perspectives perhaps. We do not think our timing is amiss. At least, such is our hope.'

'Hope,' answered Monmouth, 'is usually a vain thing.'

This caused the visitor's eyes to widen. Theophilus sought for the pupils therein but could find none.

'We are in complete earnest,' he went on, 'I assure you. Moreover, we evidence our sincerity with a gift.'

A tiny scroll, banded with golden ribbon was proffered. Monmouth didn't hesitate to accept.

'I like presents. What might this be?'

'A prophecy, my Lord,' said Pelling. 'A whisper clawed down from the ether by our more venturesome explorers. It definitely concerns you and your earthly path, though doubtless its meaning is presently obscure.'

The Duke elegantly flicked off the bow and spread the scroll with two long fingers.

'"Between the darkness and the shine
Duke Monmouth, Duke Monmouth
Beware of the Rhine!"'

'A warning, eh?'

'Indisputably. Even in your doggerel translation the sense is clear. Note also the underlying significance, Lord: we never forewarn those not high in our favour.'

'Or fears,' added Monmouth, brusquely.

Mr Pelling conceded that by silence.

The message was allowed to flutter to the ground, where, though not the most enquiring of scholars, Theophilus noted the text of curious circles and whorls. He'd shed tears over Greek (to no avail) in recent years but not even that struck his eye as so utterly alien.

'I am grateful for this valuable offering, Emissary,' Monmouth advised. 'Though gratitude is a short-lived sentiment, as you'll appreciate. I'm likewise impressed – and informed – by your foolishness in making it.'

'We had intended,' Pelling said slowly, looking all around, 'to make you a most . . . attractive offer.'

Monmouth gave him a dismissive 'oh, *did you now*' glance and caused another petitioner to venture forward. This new-comer was less abundantly blessed by nature but equally self-assured.

'Mr . . . Pelling,' introduced Monmouth, 'I give you Master Nicholas Boson of Newlyn in the County of Cornwall.'

'The *Country* of Cornwall, with your kind indulgence, Highness,' said Boson, daring to correct the Duke. Monmouth didn't seem to mind in the slightest.

'Just so,' he confirmed. 'Or *Kernow* as it is properly known.'

Theophilus had at length found the features he looked for in Pelling's oval eyes, though a puzzling trick of the light made those pupils seem golden. He then turned his attention to the comic provincial wilting under their gaze.

Boson was shaped by and for scholarship. Theophilus took leave to doubt he'd ever played tennis or poked a sword in anger. His clothing and demeanour were those of the small-town pedant; starved of female admiration and therefore despairing-careless. The man's accent was as impermissible as his linen. He could not stand against the visitor's adverse judgement. Pelling, by contrast, appeared sprung from some superior breed.

'Your Highness . . .' Boson quavered, appealing for help.

'This gentleman,' said Monmouth, supplying it, 'is the foremost scholar and revivalist of Cornubic-British . . .'

'A dying tongue,' snapped Pelling; his tone impertinent in present company. Somehow the spark that should have lit the guards' ire failed to ignite.

'The dying may be revived,' countered Monmouth, just as convinced. 'Even the dead themselves may rise – so Scripture advises us.'

Pelling shook his pale face in disbelief.

'I reject my breeding,' crowed the Duke, 'and turn my coat. I have been offered better terms.'

'No,' protested Pelling. 'Listen: Arthur deceives . . .'

Monmouth was unappeased.

'We tire of you – begone. The final struggle is underway. Boson: show him the future.'

The Cornishman nigh tore the buttons off his coat in his zeal to draw some object from within. It proved to be a rough-hewn cross of lead, hand-sized and irregular. Held helpfully before his eyes, Pelling could study the angular script covering its surface. Something he saw or read quite mortified him.

'*Resurgam*,' confirmed the Duke unpleasantly.

Pelling, his mission miscarried, fled Windsor Castle in defeat.

THE YEAR OF OUR LORD 1674

'So talk us through it,' said King Charles, from amidst his swarm of giggling mistresses. 'And give us no false modesty, sirrah.'

Monmouth was now additionally honoured with the titles of Privy Councillor, Lord Great Chamberlain of Scotland, Governor of the Arsenals in the North at Kingston-upon-Hull and Lord Lieutenant of East Yorkshire – and a fashionable type of cocked-hat was named after him. Most recently he had been Lieutenant Colonel of the Royal English Regiment, His Majesty's contribution to Louis XIV's war against the Dutch. They were well regarded in continental circles. Their practice, inherited from Cromwell's New Model Army days, of advancing in silence – save to cheer on first sight of the enemy – intimidated as much now as when initially noted by the Great Marshall Turrenne himself.

Armed with such an instrument Monmouth had covered himself in martial glory in the service of the French and returned to England, bathed in the favour of both the *Roi Soleil* and his own royal Father. Even James, Duke of York, being an honest man and temporarily sweetened by a lively new wife, was forced to admit he'd done well. Success had even improved Monmouth, rather than ruined him, and the wild boy of years gone by was replaced by a more mature, more thoughtful man. No one could report him bragging of his deeds. He'd even learned to read and write.

'I have little to tell,' he said, turning his unfairly handsome face on the gaggle of courtiers. 'We came, we saw, we conquered. My gallant Englishers did all the work. There was *such* a lot of smoke: I just waved my sword around and suddenly the city was ours . . .'

Theophilus Oglethorpe, standing alongside his friend and commander, had different recollections. To him the taking of Maastricht was a military miracle – as was his survival of it. In the final charge the ground rang with shot like hailstones.

Captain John Churchill likewise disagreed – and strongly enough to contradict the third man in the Realm.

'Over there,' he said, pointing across Windsor Great-Park to where the replica city-wall had been erected, 'by the half-moon of paving beyond the counterscarp: that is where the Duke saved my life.' Monmouth demurred most attractively but Churchill shook his wig. 'No, Highness, I *will* have it said.'

'Indeed you will,' echoed the King. 'We shall attend the spot.'

The courtiers rustled across the lawn to the convincing array of bastions, bulwarks, ramparts and walkways erected for the wargame that evening. A thousand favoured guests would be attending to see Monmouth (and, to appease him, the Duke of York) recreate the siege and a full programme of approaches, sallies, trenching, mine-springing, parleys and assaults was arranged. Two little armies of English and imitation-Dutch camped nearby under a bitterly resented teetotal regime.

It was a delightful late August day, warm but not oppressive: by evening it would be perfect for the event. Afterwards, they could have fireworks and party the night away. For once, there seemed to be no fly-in-the-ointment; no half-a-maggot in the apple. King Charles's over-tested heart was cheered by something going right. He looked paternally on the advancing Monmouth and, noting that, the Court took their tone from him. After the ups and downs of previous times, he could do no wrong.

They reached the paved expanse meant to represent Maastricht's Brussels Gate. Monmouth seemed very thoughtful.

'If my son is so maidenly-modest,' laughed the King, 'then some other must speak for him. Take it away, Churchill: give us some of that madcap, martial mayhem!'

The Captain was delighted to repay his debt and further his career at one and the same time.

'Majesty,' he said theatrically, bowing like a huckster, 'Lords, Ladies, Gentlemen, members of the Quality – and Nell Gwyn.' The mob shrieked joyfully at specific mention of the erotically-talented, but socially-challenged, one-time orange-girl attending the King. She and her lover laughed not one jot less, for, alone of all vices, hypocrisy found no welcome in Charles's Court.

'Pray attend,' Churchill continued, once he could be heard, 'to the glorious feat of arms I shall unfold. We marched to Charleroi, to add our two thousand Englishmen to the hundred thousand Frenchies slung together by Lewis, the fourteenth of that name. The army's fighting prowess was doubled – at least – thereby. Don't titter so immodestly, Madame, you'll wet yourself. Where was I? Oh yes, we stomped through the flatlands taking more boring towns than I care to recall and put the Dutch burghers – no, lady, I said *burghers* – to flight. They, unable to face English steel – assisted by a few frog-molesters, resolved to ruin the country instead: not a titanic task, I admit. The dykes were opened and the sea came to claim what is rightfully its own. We halted on the shores of an expanded ocean. I went fishing from a Dutch church steeple.'

'Did you catch anything?' yelled the Duchess of Portsmouth, a frighteningly forward mopsy.

'Only a cold and the clap, Madame,' replied the Captain. 'But that's another story.'

'Cancel our assignation!' she roared back.

'*Anyway*,' said Churchill, feigning massive disappointment, 'come June, a month as wet as a Scottish holiday, we entrenched before Maastricht. We had already acquired honour enough and shown the French how fighting is done. His Majesty, Lewis, presented our Colonel with a diamond-crusted ring and sword in token of his gap-mouthed amazement. My Lord Monmouth honours *him* by condescending to wear them.'

The Duke obligingly showed off the dazzling items. The audience duly '*oooooo*'ed its approval.

'Now, the continentals conduct a siege with the patience of a corpse. Inch a trench forward here, erect some *gabbions* there, have a parley and start again. That is not the English way and certainly not Colonel Monmouth's! One foul evening our volunteers got before the city walls and set to silent work under the squat Dutch noses. Come morning, we'd got three new batteries and twenty-six guns at "*hello, how are you?*" range. Did we then *give* them some or what?'

'We did,' conceded Monmouth, with a wry smile.

'Soon we could venture an assault and, leaving the French behind, Monmouth cleared the way! Over the outer line we went, beyond the counterscarp, putting the defenders to the sword, establishing a bridgehead on this half-moon here. The last thing I recall is attacking a flatlander's musket-butt with my brow. I was spark-out and fit to be skewered, but the Duke here stood over me with pistol and blade, laying all-comers low until help arrived. I am here today,' said Churchill, suddenly solemn, 'because he was there then.'

The Duke acknowledged the heartfelt tribute with a brisk nod of his fair head.

'We held our position,' continued the Captain, 'till relieved at dusk, and retired, we thought, to earned repose beneath the stars. It was not to be. A single well-placed mine slew sixty-two of the new garrison. Then, the Dutch, revived by this luck, sallied out to drive the blackened survivors from our gains. We saw all, out on the plain, and the sight wearied our limbs even more. We had striven so valiantly, it seemed, to no end. It was the Duke that then rallied us and no other! He dashed back with but a sword, and we were shamed into following. There was me, and Oglethorpe here, and Kirke, despite his hangover, and some few waifs-and-strays plus a few foreigners, including Lewis's famous musketeer, D'Artagnan: twelve men in all and precious few for the task.'

Churchill looked about and saw by the rapt faces he still had his audience. Drawing his sword he darted about the ersatz Brussels Gate, engaging invisible enemies.

'We met our fleeing comrades not twenty paces from the

oncoming foe. The Duke repaired these broken men with nothing but his example. The tide was turned and we swept back against a sea of opposition. The gallant D'Artagnan fell, most of us fell; my top-coat had more holes in it than a beggar's britches. Then,' he paused for dramatic effect, halfway through dispatching some unseen Dutchman, 'there was a lull, a quiet. We looked about. Only two types remained in the breach: Englishmen and dead-men. The Hollanders were all gone to a better place – which is anywhere but their own nation. We had won.'

The courtiers broke into wild spontaneous applause. Nell Gwyn punched the air and shouted 'Eng-er-land!'

'Maastricht surrendered soon after,' concluded Churchill quietly, with excellent bathos.

The murderous mêlée was re-enacted but this time in more friendly fashion. Monmouth was mobbed, not by Dutch grenadiers but by courtiers; streamlined human weather-vanes adept in tacking to the prevailing winds. He suffered more ill-usage from back-slapping and fervent kisses than he ever did at the real siege of Maastricht.

For a moment King Charles was left behind, no longer the sole fountain of worldly blessings. Only the stolid Oglethorpe remained by him, unwilling, or perhaps unable, to join in the easy expressions of joy. Charles noted that too, pleased to find at least one real human at his court.

He was likewise . . . glad that things had ended well. There'd been times when even paternal love – which is almost limitless if real – had sighted its furthermost shores and faltered over the boy Monmouth. For every peak of pleasure or pride, there had been accompanying sloughs: messy patches to wade through. Sometimes the King recalled his son aboard the *Royal Charles* at Solebay, blasting the Dutch flagship *Eendracht* apart – and Admiral Opdam with it. Elsewhen though, he saw the widow and little children of the harmless Beadle his son had murdered. What was the name, Vernell? Viddle? Charles ought to know for he signed their generous pension every year. A drunken celebration at Lincoln's Inn, some worthless noble cronies, a 'lark' – and a watchman died to round off the evening. Charles recalled the puzzled faces of the beheaded family each time Monmouth's charm tempted him to affection. The righteous uproar from that night's work had been deafening. He'd been minded to abandon his son to justice and not sign a pardon.

That was the trouble with the boy; every good thing was balanced by a bad, woven into a seamless garment. There was no encouraging the one at the expense of the other, without rending him in two. Whereas virtue warred with evil in the hearts of most men, in Monmouth a truce seemed declared and the two lived alongside each other in accord. It showed in his actions. For every day of good company and service: days of wagers and racing at Newmarket, or deeds of daring in the Great Fire of London, there were overbalancing months of pain and worry. Charles felt sure other parents didn't have to put up with that.

For instance, when Monmouth slit the nose of Sir John Coventry, MP – or hired bullies to do so, that wasn't for the man's maligning of his Father's name; oh no. Charles was sure of it for he'd closely enquired. The true motive was his son's prickly honour, and enjoyment of the deed – and its tumultuous aftermath. Parliament had been fit to send the Stuarts on their travels again for that infringement of their liberties. Charles had dined on piled helpings of humble pie for months – and for what? If some three-a-farthing tribune from the Shires implied the King was keen on the company of actresses, what of it? It was nothing less than the plain truth anyway – and no cause for fanning the embers of civil war.

The same applied to his feud with the Duke of York: whence did that come and to what purpose? Charles's brother, stiff-necked though he was, would be friends with the boy if only he was met half-way. James didn't – altogether – deserve the 'Dismal Jimmy' nickname Nell Gwyn had coined for him. He had a good heart when he cared to turn it on. The two men had no true *grounds* to fall out: it was just discord for its own sake. And the bounteous harvest raised of that bitter crop was no sur-prise given the company Monmouth kept. Villains like

Shaftesbury and Oates and all the green-ribbon 'no-popery!' crowd were strange friends to choose. Sparks from the disloyal conspiracies Monmouth circled round leapt back to burn Charles when he heard of them.

So, the boy had been sent to the wars: the traditional making or breaking of wayward youths from time immemorial. It seemed to have worked. In battle things were simple: black and white, and character was put to the test. The boy came back a man, his mettle proved, and so much . . . quieter.

And thus Charles smiled on his son and the blessing was returned in kind. The King rested content: for once self-deceiving. Love blinded him. He would not see that Monmouth's smile was mixed with hunger.

THE YEAR OF OUR LORD 1679

'He's a liar and a sodomite, a murderer of innocents. Every time I see his lantern chin I want to stamp on it.'

Brigadier Oglethorpe turned in the saddle, looking at General Monmouth in amazement born of hearing these words. Amidst the dour Scottish landscape his commander's scarlet and lace array made him seem all the more vibrant.

'Why then,' Theophilus asked, almost angry when sufficiently recovered from shock, 'are you and Titus Oates such warm associates?'

Monmouth was merely amused. He always seemed to value his friend's naivety rather than mock it.

'The man serves a purpose,' came the blunt reply, sugared by courteous tones. No further explanation was deemed necessary.

Theophilus disagreed. His outrage made him no respecter of persons, causing him to press the point.

'He spouts the wildest fantasies,' he growled, 'careless of consistency or truth, and stirs the unwashed to fresh atrocities. His Majesty is forced to sign the death warrants of guiltless men: harmless old priests and loyal patriots. I . . .' anger caused him to splutter and stumble, 'I'd like to . . .'

Monmouth rode on at the head of the column, unaffected, unoffended.

'To gut him slowly,' he agreed calmly, 'yes. I've told you that I wish likewise. Perhaps that day will come and I'll defer the pleasure of the deed to you. In the meanwhile, Titus Oates and his Popish Plot suit me very well. If I'm to be Prince of Wales and succeed the throne, then the Catholic Duke of York must be discomfited: disinherited even. The fever of the nation must be stoked until James is as welcome as plague in a play-ground – though 'tis sad that men must perish to see that day. Mark me, Oglethorpe, I speak plain to you because of our bond. I can rely on your discretion if not your approval. However, I'd advise less volume in your virtuous views: many of our men lap up each unfolding instalment of the plot as Oates dreams it up.'

Rather than heed that advice or embrace such cynicism, Oglethorpe stared balefully back at the long line of soldiers behind them. Those foremost avoided his eye.

'I'll speak as I see fit and expose the spine of any trooper who gainsays me. If it should chance to be an officer I'll call him out and . . .'

Monmouth shook his head ruefully. 'Your temper, Theo, old friend – and all these duels. You'll come unstuck sooner or later.'

'Offended honour does not weigh the odds, my Lord.'

'Speak for yourself. Still, I'm pleased to find you in your usual martial spirit; it will come in useful. I heard about Crookham-by-Flodden.'

Mention of the skirmish roused Oglethorpe from the melancholy into which he had spiralled. Between them, the madness gripping England and the sights of Scotland had quite depressed his spirit. Edinburgh in particular made him feel he languished on the edge of the world, far from Christendom. The huts, the weather, the lack of trees, the accents and pastimes were all . . . unacceptable. It was even said that there were still *wolves* hereabouts, though if so they were discreet; too few and wise to disturb the night with howls.

'My oath, yes!' he beamed, cheered by the recollection of battle. 'That was good. Your average Covenanter horseman, well, he makes a good show, beating his breast in prayer, but get up close, stick a pistol in his visage and he's off!'

Monmouth signalled his agreement. 'The dragoons performed well, I understand.'

'Passably. They all followed me and got stuck in. I don't recall having to hang anyone afterwards for laggardness. All in all it was a signal honour to disperse His Majesty's enemies on such a hallowed site.'

'Hallowed?' asked Monmouth, his pallid face en route to a sneer. 'How so?'

'Look to your History, my Lord,' chided Oglethorpe. It was one of very few school lessons to have set grappling hooks in *his* mind. 'Flodden Field was the occasion of our nation's most glorious victory over the barbarians amongst whom we campaign. In 1513 the Earl of Surrey slew their invading King James IV – and twelve Earls – and nineteen Barons – and three hundred assorted Knights and lairds; not to mention the Archbishop of St. Andrews, two Bishops, two Abbots and the Provost of Edinburgh and . . .'

'Not to mention, that is right,' advised Monmouth fervently. 'Best not to mention.'

Oglethorpe looked about, again surprised. He could see no reason for restraint. Their Scottish auxiliaries were well back in the line of march, and if one should hear, well, so what?

'I cultivate a certain . . . delicacy in such matters,' explained the Duke. 'It is not my wish to excite the sensitivities of our partners in these Isles in any way. As with the loathsome Oates, I have my uses for them.'

Theophilus accepted that Monmouth moved in circles which imposed restrictions on free expression, but didn't see why he should be similarly afflicted. If it had come from anyone else another duel might have been in the offing.

'I only spoke the facts, my Lord. We have our history and they have theirs.'

Monmouth was keen that his point be made. He reined in his horse and leant close to his friend. The army lumbered to a halt behind them.

'Exactly,' he hissed. 'And *history* is the record of the contest of life – but one with no court of appeal. The losers mislike to hear past decisions. Humour me in this Theophilus, or we shall walk together no more!'

Monmouth's propensity to consort with scholars of the Celtic persuasion and entertain paladins of their dying tongues

69

was well known. In London there had been many a time when Theophilus needed to fight his way through a swarm of Druidic types to get to see his patron. Though strange and inconvenient he'd always thought it to be a harmless interest. Far better that than the less innocent enthusiasms of the Duke's youth. Now Theophilus was less sure. For it to threaten a rupture between them, the Duke was clearly more engaged than was thought.

'I defer,' said Oglethorpe, still puzzled, but constrained to obey this shadow of the Crown.

'As I knew you would,' said Monmouth, most warmly and graciously, resuming their progress. 'For you are . . . faithful. I never doubted you, Theophilus; not ever. You shall have your reward in due season. Meanwhile, for the moment, oblige me in this. Whilst we are here to kill Scotsmen, let us do so without upsetting them.'

In 1513, as Theophilus said, an Archbishop of St. Andrews (who just chanced to be the Scottish King's teenage, illegitimate son) was killed by the English. Times moved on and in 1679 the Scots felt up to doing the job themselves. On the third of May of that year, a band of Covenanters hauled His Grace, James Sharp (a Caledonian who'd dared to negotiate with Cromwell himself), from his coach and hacked him into bits. There was no plainer way of showing their opinion of Charles's Episcopal policy in his family's ancestral nation. In case some lingering doubt remained, eighty well-armed cavalry rode into Rutherglen, not far from Glasgow, and nailed a proclamation to the church door. Among other things it declared King Charles an usurper and 'King Jesus' as their only rightful Lord. United for once, Scotland awaited the King's reply.

'Sorry' might have been the appropriate response, for Charles's Northern Kingdom had been sorely provoked just recently. First there was Montrose and his Irish troops, making the Covenanters look silly all through the Civil War years. Then came Cromwell and 'the Lord delivering them into his hands', making 'Preston' and 'Dunbar' and 'Ironsides' unwise words to bandy at a Scottish social gathering. James, Duke of

York, Charles's regent in the North, was the proverbial sick-in-the-bedspread following all that. Taking full advantage of the Scottish legal loophole which allowed torture (unlike boring England), he made sure everyone knew he was not happy being exiled. Scots were prodded at pike-point to hear the wonderful phrasing of the Book of Common Prayer each Sabbath and pastors' feet were made to fit that leaden instrument of torment, the Scottish boot. After such a long scourging mere self-respect dictated Scotland should revolt once James was allowed home.

Sadly for them, the age of sympathy for injustice had not yet arrived. The Duke of Monmouth was appointed 'General of all the Forces in Scotland' and headed that way with two thousand men. Theophilus Oglethorpe, his friend and newly-promoted Major of the King's Own Regiment of Dragoons, preceded him, anxious to promote repentance and a gnashing of teeth. Meanwhile, Lord Ross's loyal lowland militia barricaded Glasgow against the Covenanters and were only driven forth after a bloody battle. They retreated in good order towards the oncoming English, pestered by fanatics with pistol-fire and preaching. For good measure, the frenzied assassins of Archbishop Sharp emerged from their Highland bolt-holes to reinforce the Covenanter general staff and supply bloodthirsty advice.

Those most foremost and eager in the support of 'King Jesus' had hurried ahead to martyrdom and/or glory, meeting Oglethorpe over the border. He was able to convince them that piety and justification were no guarantors of victory. One charge of his less-than-holy but hard-bitten Cockneys and Home-counties men cleared the way. The pursuit was only curtailed by nightfall and local peasantry found bodies in odd corners for years to come. The Oglethorpe family could add 'Flodden II' to their personal battle standard.

Hamilton, Balfour and Baxter, the Covenanter chiefs, were undeterred. The concept of predestination, given a peculiarly Scottish twist, made them strangers to doubt. From newly-won Glasgow they marched to Stirling and considered the whole western portion of the nation theirs. The army of liberation-cum-salvation swelled to eight thousand strong, many of whom knew the psalms by heart.

Monmouth, with one-quarter that number of less scripturally aware men, was strangely but equally sanguine. He earned the respect of his men by his nonchalance, and the love of the populace by not burning his way north. Whatever his army took, be it food, drink, shelter or sexual favours, he ensured was paid for in full. That was not the usual way of his time and, for the expenditure of a few thousand of his own pounds, he acquired vast reserves of affection. The time was fast coming, he knew, when he might need to draw on it, perhaps unto overdraft.

His whole perception was that if blood must be spilt, best spill it soon and lance the infection before it turned gangrenous. Monmouth hastened from London to Edinburgh with unprecedented speed, preferring an expedite expedition rather than a large one. Spurning the delights of that gritty city, he marched his troops by night, ardent for the rebels' embrace. That they might foretaste just what a swine life can be, the fiery Brigadier Oglethorpe was again sent on ahead.

The two forces, idealism and order, collided nine miles south of Glasgow, at Bothwell Bridge (or 'Brig') by the River Clyde. The rebels were amateurs, better at slicing Archbishops than mixing it with armed men. They'd set no pickets and posted no night sentinels. The first they knew of Theophilus's approach was the famous English 'single cheer' and the fireworm glow of his dragoons' matchlocks in the dusk.

Oglethorpe confirmed the worst with a jovial hello from out of the night:

'Hey, savages . . . we're coming to ge-e-ttt you . . .!'

'Wherefore, as regents-designate and anointed appointees over the sinful subjects of the Realm of King Jesus, first and last; we order those holding office, title or power under any dispensation of any previous existing realm, authority or sovereign state, to surrender themselves to the new government – as defined in clauses two to eighteen inclusive of the proclamation hitherto read – and to place themselves and their servants, heirs, spouses and possessions at the disposal of King Jesus – and those wielding his authority in his name. Any wretch failing to do so without demur shall be whipped with cords of scorpions in the life everlasting to come and in this world be subject to such punishments as have never been . . .'

'Can *you* understand a word of it?' asked Monmouth, out of the corner of his mouth.

Theophilus Oglethorpe shook his head. 'About one in ten,' he answered. 'The accent's luxurious. You'd have thought he'd become clearer after a quarter hour . . .'

'Twenty minutes now,' Monmouth corrected him, consulting his timepiece.

Theophilus tutted quietly. 'If it's any help, I'm sure he keeps saying "*Jesus*".'

Monmouth frowned.

'Yes . . . I thought that. Should we nod our respect at each mention, do you think?'

'Unwise. We only *reckon* that's what he's saying: best just smile if there's any doubt.'

Monmouth pondered and then agreed. It was a strange kind of parley: being harangued incomprehensibly by a shaggy man atop a barricade. Odder still, though armed to the teeth, he appeared to be wearing some kind of clerical collar. This was not, they presumed, an Anglican divine – although he canted like one. How on earth could he fit so much blather on to one scroll of paper? Still, it was what the enemy requested, just as soon as dawn broke and Oglethorpe's regiment advanced to pistol range. Retaining vestigial hopes of resolving all without gore, the Duke was happy to oblige. He and Theophilus approached the ramshackle barrier of stone, wood and farmcarts across the bridge to listen to what the Covenant proposed. It proved to be more of a monologue.

'I've heard *of* the statement called the Covenant,' whispered Monmouth, 'but I never thought to *hear* it.'

'Nor me,' replied Oglethorpe, similarly discreet. 'And I don't find the experience agreeable. One feels the desire to shoot him.'

73

'You brought a gun – to a parley?'

Theophilus shrugged. 'We are beyond civilisation, my Lord. Things are more . . . flexible here.'

Monmouth sagely conceded there was wisdom in these words.

'Even so,' he said, 'restrain your emotions. Let us hear him out before we blast him out.'

Happily, the Covenanter's oration was meanwhile drawing to a close. Spittle flying freely he wound fury and conviction into a searing blaze of words, passionate enough to reform Satan himself. How amazed then he was, when eyes and arms ceased spinning, to discover the devil's lesser lieutenants unimpressed.

Monmouth and Oglethorpe looked up, surprised by the sudden silence, finding that something was clearly expected of them. They consulted in looks and finally agreed on a polite round of applause.

What bloodless creatures these southrons were, thought the Covenanter. Here he was, Pastor Cameron, the foremost preacher in the land, a converter of sinners and the inspiration of this present venture: yet even he could not reach these people: they were beyond salvation. Had he not just explained it was *they*, not he, who were rebels, risen in arms against THE LORD JEHOVAH? It was no use talking to them: the English had ice in their veins.

Cameron disappeared behind the barricade, with a dismissal as opaque as the rest, save that it contained the word '*sassenach*'. Shortly after, the weaver of words was replaced by even less amiable types. They openly bore weapons – and minimal good will towards the soldiers below. It seemed the time for talk was over.

'Back you go, there's a good fellow.'

To emphasise his point, Monmouth cocked his pistol and held it to the fleeing gunner's brow.

The pressed-man from Leith garrison was distraught. His arms gestured wildly even as his head stayed rock-still under the gentle pressure of the flintlock.

'Hell, man,' he shrilled – rather rudely Theophilus thought – 'will you send us to our death?'

'If necessary,' said the Duke in tones of sweetness. 'Of course.'

To be fair, the army's four guns were being liberally hosed by Covenanter shot – and they *were* placed nearer to the enemy than strict wisdom required. There again, Brigadier Oglethorpe had seen worse stations to man – although not many.

In silent consultation the artillerymen weighed certain death against likely death – and returned, like children heading schoolwards, to the guns.

Monmouth accompanied them, ignoring the dragonfly-passing sounds of hostile fire. Theophilus would have joined him but was waved back.

'Be with your dragoons,' the General told him. 'Charge when the way is cleared.'

Some of the gunners fell and writhed about a while, but the survivors served their pieces, finding welcome distraction in the routine. Two rounds each of partridge shot made a satisfyingly loud response to their afflictions and, at such close range, blew the barricade to splinters. A few blackened Covenanters stood, shocked and passive, where the blockage had been.

Monmouth looked back at the waiting cavalry.

'In your own time, gentlemen,' he called.

Just as he was about to set spur to horseflesh, Theophilus observed a lone rider issue from the main Covenanter army drawn up on the hill beyond the bridge. He cursed to note the man flapped a white cloth. He also knew just what to expect.

'Merde!' he shouted and his soldiers laughed. Their Brigadier's passion for conflict in all its rich and stormy tones, was painfully familiar to them.

Already Monmouth was signalling him to hold, ever ready to hear yet another parley. Oglethorpe couldn't understand his friend's ceaseless moderation. Surely, if things were set out, stark as you like, there was nothing more to say and that was the way the Lord wished it. The art of Politics was as clear as mud to Theophilus.

And yes, sure enough, Duke Monmouth showed he was will-

75

ing to listen to further prevarication. The horseman was allowed forward to shouting range when the guns could have easily sent him back to God in component parts. Oglethorpe was again summoned to hear the nonsense.

This time they'd wisely selected a more anglicised speaker. Less advisedly he was just as much a ranter as the last. Whipping out an identical parchment, the man began to read.

Monmouth could now comprehend every incendiary word and when they reached the part about just who were the rebels and who were not, he called a halt.

'I've heard all this – I think,' he said, almost angrily. 'Have you nothing new or more conciliatory to say?'

The Covenanter was all offended innocence. 'We were told,' he growled, 'that the Duke was a merciful man, with no delight in the blood of God's children . . .'

'My mercy,' came the good-natured reply, 'is attested by my patience in hearing sedition told twice. Sadly we are at an impasse. Negotiations must be handed to gentlemen skilled in the removal of such obstacles. Master Oglethorpe . . .'

Theophilus was by his side in an instant. 'My Lord?'

'Edge matters forward a little, will you?'

The dragoons were at the charge within moments, their Major to the fore and giving voice to his enjoyment. The artillerymen had to shift rapidly to avoid being trampled.

Theophilus was the first one on the bridge, cutting to left and right, a parade-ground exercise unspoilt by his blade often biting home. Long ago, a deceptively sleepy-looking old monster of a sergeant, all adorned with white scar-tissue, had told him it was never necessary to kill. *'Just cut and shock'*, he'd advised. *'The hooves of those following will finish the job.'* It was good counsel, speeding you up, making you less of a target. Likewise, the wisdom of an officer joining in the fun. All the high-ranking casualties he'd known were prone to standing aloof, observing the scrum but not *of* it. It was in the middle of the mob, paradoxically enough, where one was safest and most useful.

After the great good fortune of re-meeting – and slicing – the second, intelligible, parleyer, Theophilus suddenly burst

76

beyond the bridge. On the slope above, the Covenanter main body jostled and heaved out of line, clearly irresolute and torn between two options. It was often the way, he reflected, as he dealt with a stray Scot, of such fanatics. Whilst never doubting the Lord's long-term favour, there came a point when they wondered if he was with them *today*. Only Cromwell's Ironsides had convinced themselves of permanent oversight but Theophilus preferred not to think of that particular exception to the rule . . .

Checking that he had some company (he wasn't entirely careless) Oglethorpe headed up the hill. Though he was dangerous company to keep, his men admired him for his leading-from-the-front valour and a respectable number caught up to make a line. Gaps made by Covenanter musketry were mostly filled.

Observing benignly from below, General Monmouth pondered whether it was stupidity or lust for death that made his friend act so. It was by no means the first occasion he'd had cause to wonder; nor had he ever come to a conclusion. Certainly it was a very useful quality, but such a lack of . . . respect for the Grim Reaper worried him. Theophilus Oglethorpe had many good things to live for, and if he stayed by Monmouth he might have many more. Yet he acted as though he had some surer hope beyond the grave, or as if he *believed* all that bravery and honour stuff. Most strange. The Duke could not resolve the quandary and there was no time to consider further. Oglethorpe needed rescuing again.

Unfortunately for him, using impeccably democratic means, the Covenanter General Hamilton had organised a counter-attack. Its prospects were auspicious. Every military text advised against detachments pressing too far forward, regardless of initial success. They were equally pessimistic about the fate of horsemen facing a downhill charge. Theophilus had read most of them, but, typically bull-headed, didn't take anything they said as gospel.

He and his men disputed the issue all the way but they were slowly shoved and stabbed back down the hill, right the way to the bridge. If Hamilton hadn't spent time consulting opinion and persuading comrades of his wisdom, the dragoons would have been back over the Clyde, and the English, chastened, back to square one. Happily for them, Monmouth didn't have to first discuss what he should do.

Sufficient elements of the Royalist's main force squeezed over the brig in time. The oncoming Scots hit them at the gallop – but not in entire good heart. The outnumbered Dragoons were fun enough but these rock-steady regular troops spoilt the game. Here and there resolution failed and they bounced back, as though meeting a wall. In the narrow play-area superior numbers couldn't be brought to bear. Individuals began to arrive at informed, individualistic, opinions about the likely final score. Pretty soon the Covenanters didn't have superior numbers any more. Their ranks grew ragged as the sensible started to flee.

Monmouth fought his way to the front and found that Oglethorpe was still alive and enjoying himself. He made no criticism of him for he knew it would do no good. Best leave the innocent in innocence of wrong-doing.

'You may pursue,' he informed him – and then curtailed the expression of glee produced, 'in moderation only. Be back within the hour.'

Traditionally, '*the pursuit*' was when victors reaped the benefit of all their hard work and sacrifice. The harvest metaphor was quite apposite because that was also when they reaped the unresisting defeated as they sought safety. The habitual wild discrepancy in casualty figures between winners and losers could always be accounted for by the pursuit. For it to be artificially curtailed, as General Monmouth instructed, was an act of madness, the throwing away of four aces in a high stakes game.

Oglethorpe was enraged – although silently so – and strived all the harder to make the most of his time.

Fortunately, some of the stubborner Scots met him halfway and tried to make a stand. Hamilton rallied a handful on the aptly named Hamilton Heath and obligingly waited long enough for the guns to be brought up. Then, though hosed down with 'case' and easy target practice for the Dragoons, they were also good enough to linger on so Oglethorpe could smash them with a charge. There was adequate action for him to be content with the foreshortened banquet.

As a *gratis* 'disgestif' on the following day, he had the pleasure of a skirmish on Cumlock Moor. One hundred and forty Covenanters sinfully put their God to the test by presenting themselves for combat. In such circumstances Monmouth could hardly deny Brigadier Oglethorpe the honour of trampling them into the turf. Theophilus thus re-met the enigmatic Preacher Cameron, and, in cleaving his head, ended both him and the rebellion.

'Master Oglethorpe, I am glad to see you safely home,' said the girl. 'My thoughts were often with you.'

The soldier looked down on her, somewhat puzzled.

'Are you? Were they? Do I know you?'

Some nearby courtiers sniggered. Though generally neglectful of scripture they were aware of the Biblical sense of the verb 'to know'. Theophilus shut them up with a look.

'Eleanor Wall attends His Majesty's . . . close friend the Duchess of Portsmouth as her Maid of Honour,' Monmouth informed him. 'Access to that powerful lady lies through this Hiberian lass. Her star rides accordingly high.'

'Though not in the same manner as my Mistress,' added the girl, smiling. 'Let there be no misunderstanding.'

'No indeed,' Monmouth graciously conceded. 'All your rides are purely equestrian and pure to boot. Even *my* proposals have been daintily rebuffed and yet friendship remains. I'm surprised you've not noted her, Theophilus; she's absolutely your sort.'

'Not a tang of scandal attaches to me,' explained Eleanor to the embarrassed soldier. 'And there's precious few at Court that could be said of.' She amiably studied Oglethorpe from head toe. 'In fact, I suspect you are the only other such.'

Theophilus didn't care for slips of girls to be so in charge of converse with grown men except – maybe – in this case.

Though capable of putting regiments of hardened troopers in mortal fear, and fighting duels at the drop of a careless word, self-contained seventeen-year-old lady's maids rendered him tongue-tied.

'Perhaps we should make better acquaintance?' he said – and meant it. He hadn't thought to find unsullied goods at Court.

'We shall, sir,' she replied, matter-of-factly. 'I'm to have a position in the Palace . . .'

'The word is as "Head Laundress and Seamstress",' Monmouth obligingly interrupted. 'It's a plum: £2000 per annum and the slaves do all the work.'

Lely and Purcell drifted by in conversation. Blinded by linear time and the shell of flesh round genius, no one paid much heed.

'I shall have a Whitehall apartment besides,' she continued matter-of-factly. 'Possibly beside your own . . .'

'Though you must move swift,' the Duke cheerfully advised her. 'The new year sees Colonel Oglethorpe bound for *Afrique* and command of the Tangier garrison. It is a prodigious promotion and I just can't conceive what might make him give it up.'

'I'm not wedded to it,' blurted Theophilus. 'Would you like to stroll in St. James' with me one day?'

He was drawing on greater courage than ever required at Bothwell Brig. Leaps through transient windows of opportunity intimidated him far more than staring down death. One had to live on with the upshot of the former, whereas the latter was merely the end.

Monmouth doubled up and laughed. He thought it so *nice* that a little naivety should survive in the world: a museum curio for future ages.

Oglethorpe had no chance to protest nor Eleanor to reply. The Chamberlain emerged from the inner room and said the King would see them now.

Mistress Wall watched them go and thus saw Oglethorpe's fleeting backward glance. She smiled at him. Some essence of each travelled along the line of sight and met – and meshed –

beyond all hope of untanglement. The door closed but did not sever the link. Henceforth material barriers could not bar keen awareness of each other's spark of life.

For all her youth Eleanor knew better than to wrestle overlong with fate. Her family had dipped in short order from comfort to ruin through war and Cromwellian 'transplanting' to the wilds of Connaught. Throughout they'd kept the faith and ate what was put before them: sometimes with relish, sometimes not, but never complaining. Revived good fortune was no cause to change their ways. One chapter closed, another began and one should just accept it.

'Well, well, well,' she thought, 'who'd have dreamt it? A kind man in London! Kiss Tangiers goodbye, Theophilus. You'll do.'

' . . . the final tally being eight hundred traitors slain in battle, a further four hundred in subsequent pursuit and twelve hundred taken captive who await your pleasure.'

Monmouth bowed to the King at the end of his account.

Charles raised his eyes over the edge of the report in which he had been following the tale.

'And what "pleasure",' the King asked, less ecstatic than he might be, 'shall I have of twelve hundred canting Pharisees? Do I make them scullions here at Windsor, to scowl and mutter as I and my mistresses pass? Is there any shortage of hypocrites here in London that we require reinforcement? One was not aware of it.'

Monmouth didn't appear upset. The explosions of welcome which had greeted him in Edinburgh and down into England advised him of the true value of his achievement. Even Charles's faint praise was mostly feigned. His son had only to do anything half-right for the Royal heart to swell with pride.

'Besides, four hundred isn't much for a pursuit. Lagging back were you, Oglethorpe, eh?'

Theophilus, ever easy to reel in, would have given his eyebrows to be able to reply and defend himself. To his credit he didn't even look to Monmouth for vindication. To Monmouth's credit he didn't need to.

'Oglethorpe excelled himself, as always,' said the Duke, well aware of the winding up. 'It was I who reined him in.'

The King nodded, signalling with a look that Theophilus's stock remained high.

'So one hears. The same informants state you had your own surgeon minister to the wounded on *both* sides. Can this be true?'

'It is,' answered Monmouth, boldly.

Charles favoured him with one of his long, investigative looks.

'*Most* Christian,' he said dryly, in long postponed due course. '*Most* commendable.'

The Duke chose, on the basis of negligible evidence, to take the compliment at face value.

'Thank you, father. I perceived that they were all your subjects and charges under God, however misguided.'

Charles made a '*hmmmmm*' sound, which could have been agreement – or something else. The King had his own opinion of the Northern Kingdom, born of the humiliations it had inflicted on him whilst in exile there. As the price of military aid, the Covenanters had made him confess his iniquity on a daily basis and expound, in writing, on his father's 'wickedness'. Then, for all that, Cromwell had scattered them like chaff at Worcester. Despite their bloodthirsty boasts, Charles well recalled leading the crucial charge and looking back to find only English courtiers following. Prisoners and surgeons was it . . .

'My brother and *heir*, the Duke of York and Prince of Wales, thinks that you acted kindly out of self-interest, in the hope of reconciliation and gratitude; in expectation of a Caledonian Monmouth faction . . .'

'Psalm 140, verse 3,' quoted Monmouth, '"*They have sharpened their tongues like a serpent: adders' poison is under their lips.*"'

'Then perhaps your little court of Celts influenced you to mercy . . .'

'The Scots are not Celts, father, as you should know. Likewise, the scholars whose company I keep are incapable of deflecting me from my proper duty, as you also know – or your spies have told you. If it were not so you would have long since dispersed 'em.'

'If *I* had been there,' grumbled Charles, running out of good arguments, 'I would not have had the trouble of prisoners.'

This last feeble shot glanced off Monmouth's self-assurance like all the others.

'In your service, Father,' he said graciously, 'nothing is too much trouble. Also take note: I cannot kill men in cold blood. That's work only for butchers.'

At last the King had him. He leaned back in his chair and smiled sadly.

'Then downgrade your ambitions, dear son. To be and remain a King one must learn the jolly butcher's trade. This last month alone, I've signed the warrants for eight old priests hounded out of hiding, who are innocent of anything I know of – and I assure you I'm on nodding terms with most sins. Because of the conspiracies excreted from Oates's brain they must hang and be cut down before dead, to have their guts extracted and burnt before them. That is just part of the price I pay for Parliament to accede to its dissolution. They must have their blood sacrifice or civil war.'

'Or else sit on,' interrupted Monmouth, unimpressed, 'and pass an exclusion bill denying your papist brother the throne. On such a day, *I'd* be Prince of Wales. For such a prize eight old pimps of Babylon are a bargain price I'd say.'

For the first time Charles looked at his son the same way he did all other humans – which was a very bad sign.

'Maybe I erred,' he said, as though tired of every last thing – and released of a burden thereby. 'Maybe you are Kingly material. I wish I didn't love you.'

THE YEAR OF OUR LORD 1683

'And where do you think *you're* going, matey?'

Lieutenant Colonel Oglethorpe halted comically in mid tread on his way to the door. He'd thought his wife occupied elsewhere with her embroidery or intrigues.

'Just a tour of the estate, my dear: nothing untoward.'

Eleanor, 'Ellen', Oglethorpe, nee Wall, descended the stairs like an oncoming regiment of Turks. Two years of marriage and a child to bless each one had not lessened her frightening charms.

'Why,' she said archly, 'and to think I judged, from your purposeful tread, you were about something more sinister . . .'

She had never let him forget his slipping away to fight a duel at St. Martins-in-the-Fields. At the time he didn't see it was any business of a wife to be informed of such appointments but the ensuing marital tempest convinced him otherwise. The pain of all the might-have-beens lent her strength. Theophilus's military career and fighting hand-to-hand with the best of France, Holland and Scotland, proved no preparation for a mêlée with the fiery, crockery wielding girl from Tipperary. After that, the legal consequences of placing a blade in the navel of John Richardson esq. were easily endured. When the man died the next day in Covent Garden, Theophilus was acquitted of murder but convicted of manslaughter. Before the wheels of justice could grind on, he'd claimed 'benefit of clergy', asking for a Bible and proving he could read from it. Sentence was accordingly passed under more moderate statutes and he'd stoically endured branding on the face – with a stone-cold branding iron. He was fortunate to have the sympathy of the Court with him. Onlookers mistakenly thought Mr Richardson had acquitted himself well in combat — for Theophilus was visibly marked with wounds inflicted by Ellen.

Ever after, the loving wife kept a beady eye on her husband's wanderings, particularly on early mornings after a night in company, putting pay to his duelling-fancy as she had the Tangiers appointment. She appreciated that death would come to part them soon enough, without Theophilus chasing after the Grim Reaper and tugging his gown. Ellen was prepared to take infinite trouble to hang on to something of infinite worth.

'Well then,' she said sweetly, brushing his lace ruff and simultaneously relieving him of his sword, 'you won't be needing this then, will you?'

Theophilus didn't dare resist: for she was now armed and he wasn't. Futile protests were however permitted.

'Madame,' he said, raising his hands in supplication. 'I cannot wander abroad with an empty scabbard. Wits will ask if I'm searching for Excalibur . . .'

Ellen was unmoved, tucking the foil under one silken sleeve. 'Then take it off,' she riposted. 'Or appease your temper by giving them a boot. You do not need a sword hereabouts, Theophilus, and that is the end of it. What is it you fear? Is the Surrey puma prowling? Do you anticipate a mussulman invasion of Godalming this morning? If so hadn't you better rouse the militia rather than deal with it yourself?'

For all her confidence, Ellen knew better than to stir the sleeping beast. She could calculate the boundaries of safe sarcasm to perfection.

'Go disarmed,' she asked him nicely. 'For me. So can I rest easy.'

Put like that he could hardly refuse. Kissing her hand like the secret romantic he was, Theophilus swept his feathered hat over his periwig and ventured out into the world.

There were caches of spare swords all over the house and grounds for just such eventualities. He collected them like he did stray or injured cats and dogs, the prisoner of ingrained compulsions. One swift detour to the hollow oak by the summer house and he was re-equipped and free to march down the short avenue from Westbrook Manor, out of sight of its plentiful windows. It was not that there was anything nefarious about his outing: merely the fact that a lack of arms felt unnatural. Without the reassuring tug of a blade by his side, Theophilus was always conscious of the lack – something akin to an amputated limb, or so he was told.

He gave up trying to remember what Richardson had done to offend and turned his thoughts to more friendly matters. Dear Ellen was right about the absurdity of martial readiness in such circumstances. Looking back on his stately property, he could detect no cause for alarm. He was glad to have lashed out and bought the place. For two generations the Oglethorpes had been a mobile-column, pitching temporary camp where events threw them. The hurricane years of Civil War, the crippling fines and exiles, had allowed little option. Now however, coming into their just reward and with the benevolent face of the King shining upon them, they dared to sink some roots. Buying Westbrook had nigh cleared him out of cash, and that had called for nerve in a man happiest when ready to ship out, bag and baggage, the minute fate turned ugly. In the end it was marriage and the arrival of children that had provided the anchoring force – that and confidence of ongoing favour. So long as he faithfully served the Lord above and his Royal representative below, surely the good times would continue.

Westbrook was square and solid; a two-storey red-brick place, only thirty years old: not terribly defensible, granted, but comfortable. Its position was good, on a hillside behind Godalming town, with a commanding view of the Portsmouth–London road and Wey valley. If perchance God should frown and the world turn upside down again it could soon present a more . . . robust face to enemies. In idle moments, Theophilus had already sketched plans for a perimeter wall studded with fortlets. A modicum of effort might convert Westbrook into a useful citadel for legitimacy and right.

Leaving behind its concealing groves of oaks and beeches,

Theophilus addressed his boots in the direction of the town. It was an agreeable March morning; the sun giving notice of approaching spring but discreet enough to leave a pleasant chill in the air. Lieutenant Colonel Oglethorpe didn't hold with excessive warmth: it made one lazy and frumpish. If he had his way each household, be it never so grand, would have one fire-place apiece. Sadly, Ellen didn't concur – and within the home her views prevailed.

Theophilus studied the trees and hedges along the way, and gravely bade the birds good morning. They replied in song and his spirits, never very low at the worst of times, rose to their moderate maximum. This was settled country and Theophilus approved. Uncounted, uncelebrated, generations had striven here, engaged in improving toil; raising replacements to carry on the work before laying down to well-earned rest. By tiny increments Mother Nature had been cured of her wild excesses and made fruitful and friendly to man. If this wasn't what the state and order existed to protect, then he didn't know what they *were* for. Theophilus's dim recollections of the ancestral lands in Yorkshire provided the necessary contrast. There was little virtue, to his mind, in a life hid up in stone towers and ploughing one handed, the other resting on a gun. Things were . . . better here and the natives not minded to believe in *bogles*, *bodach* and other beasties of the night.

The tower of Godalming Church was never out of sight in this little valley and mere minutes of steady tread brought him to the ancient structure beneath. If he had not been otherwise engaged Theophilus might have entered in for a swift conver-sation with the Almighty, but since exercise was the order of the day he chose not to dawdle. Unlike most of his contempo-raries, Oglethorpe thought the body merited attention just as much as the soul, in order to preserve its mettle. Besides, he was sure the Lord would understand and if chance presented he would call in on his return. It was a subject of regret to him that he could not share the fervent (albeit papistical) faith of his wife, but regular Sunday communion, topped up with periodic christenings and weddings gave him quiet grounds for metaphysical confidence. It seemed plausible that the Almighty was a kind father, rather like himself, not given to undue chastisement of his children.

The narrow High Street was almost empty, for this was a working day and most people had been at the stocking-weaving looms and paper mills since the work bell struck at eight. Only a few of the more economically blessed had the freedom to be out and about in mid-morning, peering in the shops or just taking the air like Theophilus. He nodded to them all and was gracious enough to briskly pass the time of day with the local notary and surgeon. Then, ignoring the temptations of the *Angel* and *King's Arms* coaching inns, and turning a blind eye to the affront of the Quaker conventicle, he was soon out of Town. Blithely assuming permission to use the privately owned bridge over the Wey, he turned aside from the ford used by lesser mortals and crossed the tributary of the Thames dryshod.

Beyond, in the wide expanse of the common or *Lammas*, lands, the sights and sounds of industrial Godalming could be set aside. There was precious little here that wasn't natural creation, innocent of man's busybody hand. Theophilus could commend its tranquillity and the wide prospect of green but he was not reconciled to it. If the Wey would only refrain from its winter floods, if some Dutch drainage-engineers were set loose on the tussocky waste, then someone might wrench prosperity from it. That might be sad for the birds and conies but there was always somewhere else for them to go. Lieutenant Colonel Oglethorpe had seen too much of 'light land' in one lifetime for him to tolerate it in his homeland.

After a few necessary meanders round particularly boggy spots, the coach-road ran pretty straight out towards Loseley and Guildford. To either side what Theophilus called 'proper countryside' closed in again. It was a landscape of fields and hamlets, paths and woods, where you could lose yourself if wished – but also earn a living. Since both Godalming and Guildford were tucked out of sight from here, the entire panorama was unblighted by a town.

A mere mile or so north, along a branching track, was the

Manor of Binscombe, which had come to him as part of the Westbrook package. He might well have turned his feet in that direction for a tour of inspection but decided against. The hamlet of that name was easy-on-the-eye for sure, and the ancient wood on the ridge above an ideal place to relish silence, but the inbred, surly natives – Quaker-nonconformists all – had yet to take him to their hearts. Theophilus could do without their joyless sidelong glances today, thank you very much.

Instead, in accord with his inner nature, he pressed on, making good time along the metalled road until encountering a recalcitrant herd of cattle out by Farncombe. The way forward was well and truly blocked. The thought occurred to enforce his will with flat of sword on both beast and drover but he declined to do so. Again differing from so many of his time he found it distasteful to bully the lower orders of whatever sort. He thought they had a sufficiently rough deal from creation as it was, without him rubbing salt in the wound. The herdsman had a job to do and the heifers had a dark appointment to keep; whereas he was wandering free. As a gentleman and proven soldier it was no dishonour for him to ignore the challenge and stand meekly aside.

Happily, 'aside' included at this point the *Leathern Bottle*, the *Skinner's Arms* and the *Tanner's Arms*: three rustic inns catering to the humbler parts of the passing Portsmouth–London trade. They also turned a penny grazing out the relays of coach horses and refreshing the yokels of Farncombe, Binscombe and Catteshall. Not wishing to show favour, Theophilus's humane forbearance was rewarded by ale and no-nonsense company in each. Exercise could go hang.

By and by, all thought of beating his personal record for the walk from Westbrook to Shalford and back was similarly abandoned without rancour. He'd shown willing and for once it wouldn't hurt to grant himself a holiday. The initial rush of John Barleycorn in his veins made him mellow and forgiving – even to himself. Therefore, a gentle turn round Broadwater Lake would serve to cap the outing and appease the spirit of employment.

There were actually two watery expanses under that title, Old Pond and New Pond, the former incongruously half the size of the latter, linked by the Northbourne, a minuscule streamlet en-route to the Wey. No local memory touched on a time when they weren't there and so the mystery of the naming was now lost. Collectively they served as an incontestable dividing line between the rival civic ambitions of Godalming and Guildford; an obvious border thoughtfully sited by providence to prevent argument. First seeing the light of day to the right or left of the yard's-breadth Northbourne determined one's loyalties for life.

Theophilus was a 'furriner' and thus exempt from local classification as sheep or goat. As yet, the local geography was, for him, an open book in which he might browse at will. Knowledge of the invisible lines beneath his feet and the hallowed legends lingering in the fields was still some generations away for his family. Yet it would come, he sensed that, and these walks were the foundation trenches of the edifice of affection later Oglethorpes might feel.

Today though, Broadwater was just a view, a pleasant stroll and the promise of good fishing. Old Pond was only fit for ducks and child's-play but New Pond was more imposing: depth enough to drown in, tree-shrouded and mysterious in parts, and with a population of swans and pike and bream. Early on, whilst seeking somewhere to begin married life, he'd even considered commissioning a brand new house to stand beside it. Sadly, although the King had been generous with forfeited Scottish estates (Theophilus even owned a coal-mine up there), that idea was beyond his purse. Westbrook had been as grand as he'd dared go. To compensate, Oglethorpe conjured up that spectral mansion in his mind's eye as he wandered round the Lake edge. What quirk of personality was it, he wondered, that made him imagine gun emplacements amidst the formal gardens?

A suspiciously circular island, wooded and obscure, presumably man-made, the work of forgotten hands, lay offshore and off-centre in the Lake. Local gentry used it for picnics and alfresco illicit liaisons. More legitimately and in-betweenwhiles, a host of avian life found refuge from humankind there, to rest and raise fresh generations. Theophilus recalled planning a stone tower or citadel to be placed on it; the site for a desperate last stand against . . . well, someone or other.

Due to lack of maintenance, there were parts of the bank where water merged into land with no clear division. Away from positions favoured and revetted by anglers the ground often turned to marsh and Theophilus had to watch his step. He'd already nigh on lost one boot in a quagmire by the Portsmouth Road and now trod with caution. Therefore the arm might have been visible for some time before he chanced to see it.

Sighting the shapely protruding limb from the corner of his eye, he paused, looked again – and almost went headlong into a clump of reeds. He could not, in the truest sense, believe it, and swivelled round, hoping for another human to confirm or deny the hallucination. There was no one about. Theophilus was on the Farncombe side of the Lake and the people of that little hamlet had business to keep them indoors on a weekday morning. He turned again and the problem was still there – a white, slender arm in a wide sleeve of silk, emerging from the middle of the Lake and brandishing a sword.

His first rational thought was that this was a joke: and a very good one at that – which would have sad consequences for the prankster when he caught them. He'd see if they still thought it so funny with a foil up their fundament. Then closer observation brought doubt with it and his anger ebbed away. The arm was absolutely still, whereas a submerged yokel would thrash about and disturb the still face of the water. Nor would they be able to remain under for so long without being claimed by death. And besides, the arm was that of a fine lady, unspoilt by the kiss of the sun or muscle-enhancing labour. This was no farm-girl put up to a jape by a mischievous Lord Rochester type and Theophilus could hardly conceive any lady of quality would play such a game. In his experience, most of them found getting out of bed exertion enough.

Also, there was the matter of the sword. Even from a distance he saw that it was a kingly blade, broad and well-crafted, pommeled in gold. It was not a type he'd ever seen in any modern military context, though he'd observed the kind before. Its poorer relations hung in ancient Castle halls and in the Tower's Royal armoury.

The arm held its position, thrust from the water like an offer or accusation, pointing the sword to the sky. A chill, quite independent of earthly weather, now promenaded Theophilus's spine.

A less intrepid man might have walked on, relying on fallible memory and the myriad cares of life to one day erase the sight. Theophilus could not be so dishonest. Centuries of duty and honour grooved into the family genes obliged him to investigate and see off this assault on normality, one way or another. Never lifting his gaze from the vision, even at the risk of falling headlong, he made his way closer.

At one end of the Lake there was a small boathouse, where gentlemen kept rowboats for summer's-day jaunts or for the purpose of keeping aloof from more hoi polloi fishermen. Though it was fastened shut during the winter months, Theophilus's cavalry boot secured him gate-crashing entry to the select little club. Likewise, the boats themselves were moored up with cunning and intricate knots, proof against ordinary would-be borrowers – but not against Oglethorpe's more direct approach and sword. Similar means soon procured him two sprays of broom, good enough oar-substitutes for an inelegant row. Minutes later he was upon the water.

He'd hoped (one-quarter) or feared (three-quarters) that the racket would scare the strangeness away, but it had not. The arm and blade were still there, unmoved and unchanged. Theophilus dared to look around, still anxious for some onlooker to share the scene, but there was no one. If this *was* oncoming madness, there was at least benefit in it being unwitnessed. On the other hand, it would have been nice to have someone to applaud his daring or report his end.

The arm was right in the middle of the Lake and with such inefficient propellers Theophilus's course to it was slow and erratic. There was ample opportunity for him to think again and head for home, but he could no more do that than walk away from his children. Even with no mortal observers present, the shades of all the Oglethorpes back to Eden were around the Lake shore, urging him on. They were a tribunal he could not outface.

Eventually, with painful effort, he was there. The arm and hand stretched out of the water three yards to starboard. Shipping 'oars' he awaited developments. Curiously, there were none.

Close up, the lustrous skin of the sword-bearer was too white to be human – although it might have had that status once. The fingers gripping the pommel were long and elegant and tipped with gleaming black nails. They looked dainty and refined enough but Theophilus got the impression of crushing strength within. He noticed also that the cream-silk sleeve was not dampened by immersion.

A minute passed without event. Ever one to bring matters to a conclusion, Oglethorpe kneed fear aside and paddled closer. Rising unsteadily to his feet, he peered gingerly over the edge.

There ought to have been comfort in the discovery it was no disembodied arm. The limb continued down to join with a shoulder and head just beneath the surface. However, that discovery was spoilt by study of their owner.

The woman looked at Oglethorpe, as he did at her, and with equal fascination. Her eyes were black and fathomless. Theophilus had never beheld anyone so beautiful – or so cruel.

She proved less impressed. 'You,' she "said", 'are *not* the one.' There was no movement of the ebony lips, stark in contrast to the parchment pale skin around. The speech just . . . arrived in Oglethorpe's head, sounding like the Queen of spiders.

'I beg your pardon?' he replied politely, unable to think of anything less lame.

'*Not* the one,' she repeated, in similar manner. Her golden, floating, tresses shook in agitation. A second arm reached out of the water towards him.

No matter what Ellen said, Oglethorpe never went anywhere

without a concealed firearm. One practised motion drew the little lady-pistol from its pocket. A steady thumb cocked the flintlock.

'I am for *you!*' he retorted, and shot her through the head, just before the claw could reach him.

The Lady of the Lake lowered her wonderful face, now alas spoilt, and sank slowly down. Theophilus watched her progress without regret; for even chivalry made allowances for self defence. Within seconds she was lost to sight in the lower depths. Oglethorpe was left alone on the Lake as the shot echoed round the fringing trees and birds rose cawing from them in protest.

The suspension of nature continued a little longer. From his seat in the boat, where he'd retired to reload, he noticed the sword remained, resting on the water in a way that it strictly should not. When armed again, he ventured to reach out and grab it. Half-expecting the witch to intercept him and aiming into the water, he was not prepared for the weight of the thing, almost losing his balance. Wobbling on the edge, he was minded to release the sword rather than share the Lake with the Lady, dead or not, but stubbornness prevailed. Then, stowing the great object in the bottom of the boat, he made haste for land.

To his relief, she did not surge from the water to board him, either for revenge or to recover her charge. There was no sign of her at all, though in Theophilus's experience, Neptune invariably offered up its victims in due course. Once assured of survival he began to wonder how he should recount what had passed. This was not Argyll or Connaught where floating dead females were nothing to get excited about. Presumably he'd need to make some kind of confession and clear his name of murder. However, second thoughts soon arrived as to just what that confession might be, and how it would sound in the cold light of Law. They gave him pause. He waited awhile, recharged pistol to hand, waiting for her to show. Five long minutes passed but the still surface of the Lake remained unbroken. To break the monotony he replaced the boat and re-hung the door of its shelter. A gold guinea piece left on the row-board would pay for repairs and assuage his conscience – in that minor matter at least.

Once again at the Lake's edge and at a loose end, he detected no change. The criminal damage to the boathouse, two murdered sprays of broom, the expenditure of a shot and a little powder, these were the only evidence of the bizarre event – those and a certain sword.

In the excess of other worries Theophilus had given no thought to his trophy. He'd used it to force one edge of the sundered door back into approximate place and then, suddenly fearful of contamination, planted it in the ground. For want of anything more constructive to do he now went to retrieve the Lady's 'gift'.

It was not there. No one could have visited the spot in the few intervening moments without Theophilus's knowledge, and so he was forced to more radical conclusions. In its place, in the exact place where he had thrust it, now sat a more prosaic blade. Oglethorpe had seen hundreds, if not thousands, of the type in every cavalry barracks he'd ever frequented. The standard cavalry sabre was much the same right across Christendom and hadn't changed since the Roman *spatha* went out of style. He supposed a spontaneous change in shape was not out of the question, given the greater strangeness of its delivery, but even so . . . Just when he had one dark miracle to cope with, fresh wonders were as welcome as plague boils.

The unhappy notions continued to disembark. Theophilus rehearsed interesting conversations with ascending levels of Justice: none of which concluded in a meeting of minds. The more he pondered the less promising the options seemed. Revealed for promiscuous delectation this morning's work might well land him at the loon-house or Tyburn: places where pleas for 'benefit of clergy' went unheard.

Theophilus looked again at the unruffled Lake, and then at the transmogrified sword. It was clear *something* had occurred but his wits were not up to naming it. He'd had enough for the moment. Both the question and the weapon were stowed away out of sight; the first in an innocent expression, the second in the enveloping folds of his great-coat.

Theophilus had always found that the next best thing to an adequate explanation for misdeeds was swift removal elsewhere. After one last check of Broadwater for incriminating carrion, he composed himself into an 'I'm just out for a walk' manner and headed home.

As described, when he needed company there had been none. Now when its absence would be pleasing, there arrived a surfeit. Half a musket-shot along the circumnavigating path Godalming-wards, he was intercepted.

Ordinarily, Theophilus could place, class and classify strangers to a tee. Clothing, deportment and confidence of approach rarely failed to slot people into their appropriate social niche. However, the oncoming gaggle were a puzzle. Ill-fits to any classification, a mysterious sight in the Home Counties, Oglethorpe questioned whether their fine, court-style, clothing actually belonged to them. They shambled too close together for his liking, more like a conspiracy than half a dozen normal men about their business. Likewise, there was something about them that rankled, a bobbing, one-pace-side-ways-two-steps-on sort of gait betokening both purpose and hesitation – like a snot-rag of schoolboys egging each other on to some mischief.

Theophilus relocated his pistol but did not yet draw it. An hour back he'd have smiled upon such potential-rich diversion but one chat with the Dark Angel per day was quite sufficient for him. Right now, the newcomers were only gravel in the timepiece of life. Besides, there were six of them – even if, man for man, they weren't up to much. It was a lot of people to lay low at the best of times. Undaunted, he walked on towards the nuisances.

Beholding him they halted and conferred, one or two be-wigged faces occasionally emerging from the huddle for a fresh look. Much as he would have liked to, Theophilus could not pass for they collectively blocked the way. To one side lay a quagmire, on the other the Lake. The group now officially constituted a problem and he called to mind the sword strokes required to unbung the stoppage.

'Good day,' he said, affably enough and drawing close. 'Be so good as to free my route, gentlemen, *if* you please.'

They didn't please. Instead, the request was discussed amongst themselves, a low babble emerging from the inward facing group. They were not to know that Theophilus's temper could leap from moderation to mayhem in one lithe move, but even so, the discourtesy was inadvisable. The inner Oglethorpian beast stirred and growled.

They heard that well enough and turned to face. Their attention was then more than fully engaged by sight of the (plain and simple) sword he'd drawn.

'Mister Blade,' he advised them, 'often motivates when manners do not.' Theophilus advanced to *en garde*.

Though King Fear held court in their eyes, some even greater power overruled him. Oglethorpe had been prepared for almost any response from them bar a burning scrutiny of the foil he held. He was temporarily thrown. It was no special sword, a plain gentleman's companion little different from the scores secreted at Westbrook. In those circumstances, for all they'd ignored him, it seemed unsporting to use the weapon to wound its admirers.

'I'd be obliged for an answer,' he barked. 'Or prepare to make even closer inspection.'

Happily, at that moment they seemed to conclude their study and drew back as one, showing the respect due a naked weapon.

'Meea navidna cowza sawsneck,' snarled one of them, a chippy little black-haired man – who then contradicted himself by translating: 'I won't speak any Saxon!' The challenge was undermined by his shrinking even further back, till only his brow and burning eyes remained visible peeping round a colleague's shoulder.

Another of the group, the eldest and most stately, looked pained by this opening, and ventured marginally forward himself.

98

'No. It is apologies we offer,' he said, as genteel as Oglethorpe could wish. 'Understand, if you will, we have little facility with the English tongue.'

So that was it. Theophilus had been around and knew that not everyone in the world was fortunate enough to speak French or English. In Scotland he'd met (and killed) monoglots of the lingering Gaelic language. Somewhere or other he'd read that the same applied to the less blessed portions of Wales and Cornwall. To understand all was to forgive all.

'If I was deficient in lucidity,' he said, 'then I withdraw. My apologies.' The foil was smoothly re-sheathed even though unblooded. To a true gentleman, ignorance or innocence offered full restitution for offended honour.

'Gracious you are,' replied the spokesman – and then frowned, shaking his snowy locks. 'No, I mean you are gracious. It is we who should sorry say.'

His comrades bobbed and weaved even more, miming agreement.

This was all very nice but the way was still congested. Theophilus attempted to stamp out the inner embers of irritation, before they reached the abundant combustibles nearby.

'So,' he said, through grim lips, 'a visit from Wales, is it?'

'In part,' answered the old man, looking at some of the scrum around him. 'And Kernow – or Cornwall as you doubtless term it. And Alba and Mannin – or Scotland and Mann on the same principle.'

'I see.' Theophilus couldn't help but glance Lake-wards, half expecting an inopportune returnee. 'Well, welcome to England and good day to you, gentlemen.'

A firm step forward caused them to flinch – but not part. Theophilus halted abruptly and spoke likewise.

'Is there some additional way I can be of service?' he asked. If Ellen had been present she'd have recognised that the fuse was nearing the barrel.

'Yes, indeed,' said another of the gang, a combatant Cymric voice emerging from unpromising, runtish, material. 'Has anything happened lately?'

Oglethorpe *looked* at him and the man seemed to recede further into his luxuriant beard.

'See this?' rumbled Theophilus, indicating his sword hilt.

'Yes, we have,' answered the man, still defiant though paler. 'And it's not what we're looking for.'

The first spokesman glared balefully upon his companion, shaming him to silence.

'What my friend *meant*,' he explained, 'is things untoward; which interested in we are. Scholars of the paradoxical we are; see?'

'No,' replied Theophilus, bluntly, and made as to march forward again.

'Please, patience, look you,' the old man asked, so sweetly as to oblige compliance. 'We intend no offence. Only it's an *appointment* we have: here and just lately. *Delayed* we were, on the road, see.'

'*Wickedly* post-poned and de-layed, we were,' echoed another, younger, man clad in Erin-green plaid.

'By the blocking herd of cattle, moo-beasts, along the road,' concluded the spokesman, 'together with their hindering herdsman – may his eyes rot.'

'Oh, them. Yes, I met them,' said Theophilus, glad of at least one fragment of affinity with the Celtic mob.

'Our carriage could not pass. And it's missed our meeting we fear we have.'

Theophilus shrugged his false sympathy. 'Well, if it's any comfort, I've been here half an hour and not seen anyone: not a soul.' This was near enough the truth to satisfy conscience. He rather doubted the deceased Lady was the type to boast a soul. 'Who is it you hope to meet?'

The straightforward question floored them. They looked at one another like some invisible member of the party alone knew the answer.

'A lady,' said the spokesman, at long last and made hasty as the delay in reply grew dangerous. 'She had something for us.'

'Possible it is she's here,' said the hirsute, cocky one. 'Not certain. She may wait some other place.'

'The time is right though, as to really,' chimed in another, hitherto silent, a pop-eyed wildman, improbably clad as a dandy.

Theophilus's mind was by no means his nimblest faculty but it generally got where it should in the end. Some metaphorical cogs and wheels finally meshed and turned to produce enlightenment.

'*Just* one moment, sirrahs,' he asked. 'Are you in Duke Monmouth's employ?'

Their panicky denials were all the confirmation needed. He should have guessed earlier. Who else clothed and fed a menagerie of learned Celts this side of their twilight homelands?

'It's he who put the unsuited finery on your backs isn't it?' Theophilus stated, as bold as you like – for he had their measure now. 'Did he send you here? Did he mention me?'

They shrank back in earnest now, like a vicar meeting his bastard.

'Who you talk about,' gabbled the spokesman, 'we don't know. Nonsense you talk it is. Come on boys, maybe we're not too late if we don't dawdle. The conjunction might still persist.'

And then Theophilus's most immediate problem was solved by the group flooding past him, a busy river flowing round a granite island. His person was shunned even as they pretended he did not exist; the muttering scholars cringing away from proximity and contamination. Before he could protest (even had he a mind to) they were past and reformed into the same strange dancing group, heedlessly spoiling their silks in the bankside mire.

Theophilus could have puzzled deeply about the encounter but decided not to. It was just too . . . tiring an accumulation of thoughts for one day. And anyway, he could always ask the Duke what he thought he was up to, letting his house-trained madmen roam the countryside. They were bound to meet at Court pretty shortly.

The brief mutually troubling encounter over, the participants parted without sorrow. Neither looked back. Thus, in their great haste to be away from the fury-faced *Sutangli*, the Celts failed to notice something that might have interested them. Lieutenant Colonel Oglethorpe was not his normal agile self. His brisk stride was hindered by something concealed beneath his coat.

Theophilus re-met the heifer herd, making slow progress back along the Portsmouth road. This time he was less inconvenienced. The herdsman exercised rare powers of control to clear a path for him and the beasts most wonderfully obeyed.

'*You see*,' thought Theophilus once through, '*every human, however humble, can aspire to excellence in something.*'

He was right of course, for the most part, in principle if not in fact. The herdsman was not human.

The pretence was maintained for a little while and the purpose-built roadblock ambled on. Then, their purpose fulfilled, the animals' minds were released. They fled in all directions lowing in fear, back perhaps to the fields from which they'd been unnaturally gathered. By then, Theophilus was too far away – and committed – to see or hear or change what would be.

The 'herdsman' studied the retreating soldier, the gold in his eyes being permitted to show. Thus unfettered he saw more, the distant Oglethorpe blurring into multiple images; the man seen in past, present and future conditions. He studied the last in particular, and smiled – in the perverse, misusing, fashion of his race. It was done.

'He's here!'

Theophilus hardly needed telling. The gaudy coach and arrogant outriders parked at Westbrook said all. The latter had already caused swaggering offence, he could tell, judging by the set or flushed expressions – male and female respectively – of his servants. They were rushing back and forth trying to gather in their Master's menagerie of strays, for fear these cavaliers would while away their wait in tormenting the dumb animals. That anxiety was well-founded but could now be set aside and the hounds left to bark at the hostile humans. Even Monmouth's hired blades would be on best behaviour under the eye of Oglethorpe.

That same eye noted that their sleeves bore tokens of the Green Ribbon Club, a Protestant street-trouble society operating out of sundry City taverns like the vast King's Head in Chancery Lane. Likewise they brandished the 'Protestant Flail': deadly iron-enhanced coshes and a feature of that brethren. It was a new and revealing development.

'Where is he, Ellen?'

'In your library, Theo. I've arranged wine and wafers. A cold collation is being prepared.'

Theophilus nodded approval. Ellen Oglethorpe was rock-solid, a dependable fixed point in the maelstrom of life.

He'd taken care to dispose of one sword, the more ordinary one, before entering the house and Ellen-range. The second, intriguing and newly acquired, blade was more carefully hidden, wrapped in his coat in an obscure closet for later consideration. Just now, the third-down-from-top-dog in England commanded greater priority.

Monmouth was lolling in a horsehair armchair, idly flicking through one of Theophilus's dusty books. His friend's arrival was doubly welcome therefore, providing an excuse to ditch dull learning.

'Oglethorpe, how goes it?' Plutarch's *Parallel Lives* was tossed aside.

'Passably well, my Lord. And you seem hale enough . . .'

Monmouth stood and stretched. His aversion to repose was widely known.

'Never better. And drop that "lord" business: we're alone. Out of starchy company I shall always be plain James to you.'

'And I'm honoured by it. By the bye, *James*, I think I bumped into some of your druids today!'

For some reason the Duke wasn't best pleased to hear it. This wasn't the start he obviously wanted.

'Well, yes, perhaps. My little hobby, eh? Yes, I think I recall scattering a few of them in these parts. There's some research that needs doing. They . . . reckon they're on the track of some-thing. Who knows with such people?'

Theophilus laughed: a manly sort of bark. 'Least of all them it seems. I thought I'd have to cut my way through 'em like a bunch of Covenanters. I tell you, James, their coats are better than their manners.'

On this point Monmouth could share in the joke.

'Well, it saves on wages, Theophilus. I can hardly wear the same ensembles twice, and they'd sooner have my colourful cast-offs than good English guineas. It makes for a comical sight en masse, I grant you. Anyway, never mind them: it's good to see you, you old swine!'

They shook hands warmly and Theophilus doled out the decanter of Cadiz sack.

'To James, then,' he toasted, 'Duke of Monmouth and apple of His Majesty's eye!'

'And Prince of Wales.' It was added glibly enough, but derailed conversation like a pike to the face.

Oglethorpe lowered his glass, doubt writ large across his honest red face.

'I . . . had not heard that news,' he said, choosing his words most carefully. 'I thought another James, Duke of York, was heir to the Throne.'

'At the moment,' admitted Monmouth, quite unabashed. 'For a while and in theory. Facts and his papistical professions suggest otherwise. He may have implausibly survived our three successive Exclusion Bills in Parliament – but we'll have him yet. The title is rightfully mine. I am the *Protestant* heir.'

Theophilus's notions of a cheerful chat had gone sourer than a witch's milk. The law – and honour – drew small distinction between hearing or speaking treason. For both his own house and his friend's sake, he would have to tread warily.

'Hence, I presume,' said Theophilus, now spelling out the implications slowly and clearly, 'your retainers' tokens . . .'

Monmouth grinned and nodded, seeking to engage his old comrade's gaze.

'My membership of the Green Ribbon Club is no secret,

104

Theo. It is now time for partisans of the reformed faith to stand forward. Vital issues are at last in the open. I thought you were all for that sort of straightforwardness.'

He peered sympathetically at Oglethorpe, widening his elegant eyes. They met no encouraging response. As he rather feared he might, he'd run aground on his friend's tiresome core of steel-clad ethics. There'd been hopes that honeyed words and an appeal to loyalty might tack round it. How weary-making . . .

'The title of heir,' recited Theophilus, looking at his boots, though in no way ashamed, 'is the gift of the King. It isn't voted by the multitude or seized. James, my friend . . . my good friend, if we've not learnt the principle of legitimacy yet, then what was the Civil War for?'

'What indeed?' answered Monmouth, brightly, in contrast to Oglethorpe's anguished tone. 'Perhaps it isn't over yet.'

That jabbed at the scab-less wound in most British hearts. If there was something to unite all factions and confessions it was the desire to never see those days again.

'You jest!' exclaimed Theophilus.

Monmouth subsided back into the chair, the opposite of relaxed. He steepled long tapered fingers under his chin.

'For once, no,' he replied. 'The Restoration settlement has proved to be no final solution. If "legitimacy" prods forward a papist successor, then patriots must look for a re-definition.'

Theophilus shook his head. A reviving swig of sack failed to warm his veins.

'I pray that is not so. I most earnestly pray not.'

Monmouth shrugged dismissively. 'Well, pray on by all means, if you think it some help. Should you still believe in a deity who's in the least concerned with us, then I won't stand in your way. Now, Theophilus, the question is, will you stand in *mine*?'

The last drop of comradeship drained from his voice. The query was a challenge. In terms of his audience it was also a mistake. Considering he thought himself so subtle, Monmouth should have known better.

'If need be,' Oglethorpe answered him. 'You, and all men, know full well where I stand.'

Monmouth could hardly deny it and conceded the point with a (strained) smile. It was Theophilus's old-fashioned notions and consequent stupidity that were the foundation stones of his usefulness to men of power. There was no point in dashing yourself against those foundations, or prising them out, thus undermining the very fortress he sought to employ. It was time to regroup prior to a more considered attack.

'Let's start again,' he said, unleashing every reserve of charm. 'Be unborn my words.'

Theophilus remained suspicious and grudging. He'd seen this 'sweet reasonableness' before, employed to tip the most virtuous of wives on their backs or to avert the King's anger. It seemed contrary to the spirit of friendship for those seductive skills to be unleashed.

He withdrew to the matching partner of Monmouth's place of rest and looked unhappily round. Why, he wondered, did he have three copies of Burton's 'Anatomy of Melancholy'? Why had he got one copy?

'If you must,' he replied, sadly. 'If this isn't the social call I'd hoped for.'

Monmouth was all false reassurance; every expression and gesture and look – and for the first time Theophilus perceived its insubstantial nature, seeing right through it and out the other side. It was a revelation, and he was unused to those.

'This is,' protested the Duke. 'A social call, I mean. Nothing more sinister than a call on an old and valued comrade, I promise you. I've not come as some unholy recruiting sergeant. There's no need for that. You and I took the King's shilling together long ago.'

'The King's shilling,' Theophilus reminded him. 'Note that.'

'Who else's?' Monmouth feigned puzzlement. 'To what other possible end? Yet surely you don't maintain there is but one way to serve His Majesty?'

Theophilus thought about it.

'Well, yes I do actually,' he answered, frowning. 'You serve him loyally.'

At that unhappy moment, Eleanor Oglethorpe chose to enter, leading a train of flunkies bearing vittals. Her curt dismissal, via identical-twin, imperious, waves of the hand by Husband and Guest, so stunned her that she even complied. From behind the re-closed Library door came the sounds of servants being barged backwards and the crash of falling trays. Ellen's lively curses then joined the rough music. Oglethorpe and Monmouth took no notice.

'But not *blind* loyalty,' the Duke countered. 'There is such a thing as higher duty.'

'Is there?' Theophilus sounded interested.

'Most certainly. Consider the matter, Oglethorpe. A King occupies his position for a purpose. He is placed there – by God, if you like – to play a role. He must fulfil it, even at the cost of his life if required.'

'Like Charles the Martyr, you mean?' hazarded Theophilus, willing to be helpful but still uncertain. Monmouth leapt upon the cooperation.

'*Exactly*. You understand all. Well, the same applies to his son, my father. Now tell me, have you ever heard of Rye House?'

Nowadays, every glorified merchant's shack dignified itself as such-and-such 'house'. Theophilus troubled his memory for the name.

'Can't say I have. Were we billeted there once?'

Monmouth smirked at some private joke.

'Not to date – though we might be soon. You may come to know the place well – just before it assumes a glorious place in our history.'

Theophilus hadn't thought to go on any travels. His Majesty, and through him, the Army, were allowing him a little time to enjoy his new rootedness.

'How so?'

Monmouth leant forward; the very epitome of easy-going frankness.

107

'Said abode occupies a most advantageous position, fortified, moated and discreet; yet beside the London–Newmarket toll-road. I have inspected it most closely accompanied by the present owner, Master Richard Rumbold, and can conceive nowhere better in all Hertfordshire for my purpose.'

Monmouth was plainly waiting for the next obvious query but Theophilus failed to oblige. As a professional cavalryman he was wary of charging into prepared positions. At the same time, there was something about that precision of siting which jangled certain nerves.

'I don't think I've had the honour . . .'

The Duke sat back, disappointed.

'No, you haven't. I thought it best to keep you apart. Unprepared, you might not see eye to eye . . .'

Theophilus was horrified. 'One of them?'

'One of them,' Monmouth confirmed. 'One of the blackest of "them" in your book I expect: an Ironside right from the start and a volunteer guard at the blessed Charles's execution in '49. So there, you see, he already understands all about the self-sacrificing nature of Kingship . . .'

'Has it come to this? Cromwellians and regicides? Murderers of your own Grandfather? The sort of people who separate hens and cocks on the Sabbath for fear they might have fun?'

Monmouth shrugged. 'If you like. Also the sort of person who put it across us at Marston Moor, Naseby, Preston, Dunbar, Worcester, the Battle of the Dunes . . . and sundry other places too saddening to mention. The track record suggests we could do with their help. And speaking of tracks . . .'

Theophilus understood now, and had to accept that the best might also be most false.

'The races at Newmarket . . .' he said slowly, spilling out the extent of his distress in those few words. Strangely, Monmouth did not pick up on it. Wild ambition had swept away his finer judgements.

'To which his Majesty is most partial: precisely. Riding meat, eating meat and putting meat into meat – the three great pleasures of life as my Father explained to me: actually, a proverb plagiarised from the Arabs I believe. Accordingly we can depend both on his presence at the Newmarket Spring Races and his haste to get back to his doxies at Court. There's been the very closest study made. Father always dashes ahead of his retinue. By the time Rye House is passed there's rarely more than a half dozen outriders plus his coachman. A haywain toppled in the road will draw forth the guards to clear it – and marksmen in the ditch beside will clear them. Then our horsemen concealed in the courtyard can sally forth to finish the deed.'

Theophilus looked solemnly at his ex-friend.

'So one King dies,' he said, 'and another is proclaimed.'

'Oh no, not so,' Monmouth lied stoutly, unaware that his batteries of deceit now fired blanks. 'We shall just deprive the King of his misleading advisors. Then, under our protection, he will perceive the justice of my cause.'

'How could he fail to?' asked Theophilus, looking out of the window, into a world now drained of comfort and colour. Monmouth was falsely encouraged.

'The Duke of York must die though,' he added candidly. 'We know he'll be with the King. It ties up loose ends. You shall see to that. Rumbold is fiery enough but past his best. I need a dependable warrior who likes to charge home. You'll enjoy it: the Gentlemen Pensioners will put up a good fight I expect.'

He looked up in expectation of gratitude for the great favour offered. The handsome face soured upon not finding it.

'What's this, Oglethorpe? Not enthused? I've outlined your patriotic and religious duty. What do you say?'

Theophilus expelled a held breath through gritted teeth, and numerous illusions fled with it.

'What I say,' he replied softly, 'is *en garde*, traitor. Kindly wait here while I fetch me sword.'

No one could accuse Monmouth of flat-footedness. His moment of terror was commendably brief.

'Ahh . . .' he said sorrowfully, driven to fresh calculations. 'So you really do believe in all that *honour* business. How quaint.'

Theophilus paused on his way to the bookcase where, hidden

behind vast volumes of something or other, he'd months before cached two foils.

'It wounds, I confess,' he answered, 'to realise you ever doubted it.'

The Duke spread his hands in a 'oh well, never mind, that's life I suppose' sort of gesture. Unplacated, Oglethorpe continued with his errand of deadly intent. Trusting even where no trust was due, his back remained offered up to a treacherous shot or strike as he hefted the concealing tomes aside.

The Duke of course considered it, but settled for simpler ways out of present difficulties. There was ample time for him to search his pockets for subtler weapons.

'Replace the swords,' he said shortly. 'Come back. Sit down. Forgive me and forget all that's been said.'

In due course Oglethorpe did exactly as he was told.

The coach leaving Westbrook contained an unhappy Duke. Yapping mongrels pursued it down the drive. Even the sight of the cloud of green-ribboned outriders, harbinger-vision of glories to come, failed to cheer him. He'd invested a great deal in Lieutenant Colonel Oglethorpe, only to receive pitiful dividends. So now he had to rush matters; a deplorable necessity, contrary to the rules of conspiracy. Where else would he find that rare Oglethorpian combination of savagery and sophistication? The present day contained violent madmen enough, for sure, but precious few so suited to present needs. The mere killing of Kings was not enough; it had to be done with *honour*, by men the succeeding regime could laud – and then, with great regret, visit justice upon. Theophilus had been a part of their elegant plans so long that they'd forgotten he had any independent existence.

Monmouth was now reminded of that fact by the fierce heat pulsing out from the little box beside him. Despite a lining of lead and dense heartwood construction, the casket couldn't contain all the warmth of Oglethorpe's emotions. The sorcerous *leech-stone* within must be fairly throbbing with its burden of stolen anger, too hot to be long held in hand or pocket. Fear of scorching to his parts had obliged the Duke to thrust it aside as soon as he was out of sight. By the time the coach was on the London road the box had become a tongs-job, blackening the expensive upholstery. It was quite some man they'd lost.

Nor was that all. Monmouth had hoped to husband the limited supply of 'leechers', reserving them for more important minds. His Cymric wizards courted perilous company to gain them, sacrificing years of earthly life and risking the one beyond. That was nothing to the Duke, of course, but their quest carried problematic side-effects. One mage had just . . . disappeared, along with his London lodgings, leaving only a sulphurous smell and difficult questions to answer. Besides, he needed their knowledge of the 'unseelie realms' – for the moment.

Theophilus had frowned at the leech-stone at first viewing, and then queried Monmouth's triggering phrase. Soon enough though the harsh face had softened and all his fury flowed away, along with certain . . . inconvenient memories. With those safely stored in the stone, the Duke could draw a happier picture on the resultant blank canvas. Theophilus would recall a jolly chat, a verbal refight of Maastricht – and perhaps a bit too much sack at midday, an explanation for the headache he'd have. Nothing was lost – but on the other hand, nothing was gained either. Dealings with humans – under the present dispensation – was like that. What a nuisance.

Monmouth realised he was hungry. The fiasco at Westbrook meant they'd gone without sustenance – and Madame Oglethorpe questioned that when he'd left. 'Getting too grand for plain rations, are we?' she'd asked, in a tone less respectful than appropriate; as though they were still friends like in days gone by. Things had moved on since then. He'd mumbled some excuse about poor appetites but saw she wasn't deceived. Mouthy cow – though mettlesome perhaps: likely good fun to shake the sheets with. He'd bear that in mind when his time came. In the meanwhile, people should accept he was not the rough-edged lucky bastard King Charles first brought over. He was on his way up – and to places the unenlightened didn't

111

even suspect existed. There'd arrive an occasion of reckoning for these over-familiar types, and it wouldn't be long delayed. That Irish *colleen* Theophilus had bred with would be just one of many to sing a different song under the new regime.

It then occurred to him he could buy some bread on the way to Soho and toast it over Theophilus's anger.

'So what *did* you talk about then?'

Theophilus, in the grip of powerful emotions, swept the wig off his head and hurled it to the ground.

'For the ten-thousandth time, woman,' he roared, 'I've already told you. I've had nothing else this week. What d'you want? Blood? An affidavit from Almighty God?'

'I'll-tell-you-what-I-want,' replied Ellen Oglethorpe, punctuating each word with a jab at her husband's chest and driving him back. 'I want the *truth*!'

Theophilus reached the wall and could retreat no further. He looked to the heavens (or the hallway ceiling in present context) for assistance.

'I've told you the truth.' His hands cupped involuntarily en-route to Ellen's throat but were reined in just in time. 'We talked. We joked. I went on about the siege of Maastricht and he told a *risqué* story about Nell Gwyn's tongue. That's it. C'*est tout*. Is this song the only one you sing?'

'It is – and you'll jig to the tune before I'm finished with you; you see if you don't. I know James Croft Duke of Monmouth and that was no chit-chat face he had on him. His eyes didn't even take my clothes off like normal. He was *embroiling* you and don't you dare deny it!'

She could have bit her lip on saying so. What possessed her to pick on the one wrong word in the Oglethorpian universe.

'*Dare?*' Theophilus shrugged himself free from the wall. '*Dare* is it! Don't you dare me, Madame. You attend to your duties and, by God, I'll discharge mine! Be so good as to *clear the way*.'

Ellen had lost the skirmish but not the war. She stood by, hands on hips, whilst the Theophilian forces quit the field, in passable order but under token verbal pursuit. The Lieutenant

Colonel scooped up his abandoned wig (now a little dusty and dishevelled), and having replaced it, swept from the house. Mrs Oglethorpe followed as far as the door.

'And don't go bothering with the hollow tree,' she yelled after him. 'I found those swords.'

Theophilus's shoulders stiffened but he made no other response. A column of gardeners passed him along the drive, politely oblivious to the domestic fray amongst their employers. They were used to it.

'Morning, Master,' said their foreman, Mr Grimes. 'Don't fret, I gets far worse from my wench.'

'And don't be *embroiled*!' Mrs Oglethorpe's parting shot bowled down the drive before she withdrew indoors. Theophilus snarled at either or both bits of advice and turned aside into the grounds.

Mutually invisible, he could not observe Ellen's anguished closing of her eyes and biting upon her knuckles. She never saw him pausing for thought. Anger born of affection has a short but lusty life.

In no fit state, sartorially or otherwise, for company, Theophilus abandoned notions of a trip to Town and distraction of the fire-water type. Instead, he took his confusion to a yew-shaded wrought-iron bench thoughtfully set on the edge of the estate. It was there that in years to come his fanatic-Jacobite daughters would construct sturdy fortlets commanding the narrow valley, in anticipation of Bonnie Prince Charlie's arrival. However, in 1683, that was generations of low-politics and betrayal away and the site was still innocent of any martial presence – save Theophilus's own swirling-purple thoughts. It should have been a citadel of calm and orderly sensations – and yet it was not. Somehow its flint wouldn't spark; its powder was wet and the civil stronghold was betrayed to malign forces.

He sat and studied the prospect of the Wey and Godalming-town seeking respite from the undefined unease he felt, but comfort proved elusive. For Ellen to be right, and he wrong, was bad enough in itself. Yet, worse still, was this girlie malaise. He'd always thought himself proof against the scourge of *melan-*

113

cholia, only to find he was on the same rack as any poet. All through the last week, Theophilus could not rid himself of a vast feeling of . . . disappointment.

'It is hardly surprising,' said the tall man suddenly alongside him on the bench. 'Feeling lost in the universal expanse your kind put such value on *attachments*.'

To his credit, Theophilus remained seated, the master of his feelings. The impulse to rise or attack lived out a mere mayfly span. He didn't even challenge the stranger's trespassing presence. He could guess.

The newcomer approved and was willing to assist. Prosaic queries were aborted by the most expressive, if silent, reproof. '*No, of course this isn't* normal,' said the message in his golden eyes, '*but don't demean yourself with dull questions.*'

'I see . . .' said Theophilus, in due course. 'Well, good morning to you then.'

The visitor smiled and leaned back, stretching out his long legs and making himself at ease on the bench. He appeared to find some imperceptible fault in the green and gold splendour of his sleeve.

'That's right,' he explained, eventually. 'I am.'

Theophilus studied the uninvited guest, recognising the aristocratic spirit when he saw it.

'You're what?' he asked, lost in contemplation of the too-fine features and dead-white skin.

'I just am. It seems only polite to permit you at least a "*who?*" or "*why?*" – just to get preliminaries out of the way. We are only what you've long suspected; that which you've half-glimpsed in the landscape – and then rejected as fancy.'

'I never *dis*believed in elves,' said Theophilus, 'only kept it quiet.'

The visitor was suddenly weary. He expelled his breath and its glancing blow was like the most seductive of perfumes.

'That name again. We do so tire of it . . .'

Even alongside the numinous-made-flesh Theophilus's temper was still in working order. 'Is that so?' he snapped. 'Well, then perhaps you'd oblige with an alternative.'

114

The stranger left off examination of his cuff and the arm thus released settled gently to his side like falling gossamer.

'Therein lies a problem,' he replied. 'I have no name all to myself as you do. We are less . . . separated. I could perhaps, for present purposes, adopt the name of my homeland . . .'

'If it's all you have,' agreed Theophilus, helpfully.

'Suth-Rege it is then. How do you do.'

'Well enough up to now. And where might *Suth-Rege* be?'

The newly christened stranger turned to look at Oglethorpe whilst sweeping wide one hand.

'Why, here, of course,' he said simply. 'This land that was taken from us.'

'Ah . . .' answered Theophilus. He was used to such expressions of grievance, having heard it *ad nauseam* from Monmouth's Celtic 'court'. 'Sorry. Nothing personal.'

'I quite understand,' Suth-Rege reassured him. 'And in fact our overthrow long predates the arrival of the English. It lies more invasions back than are presently known of. One's thirst for revenge is not thereby diminished, of course . . .'

'Naturally.'

'. . . but patience is meanwhile acquired. We hope that long patience will soon be rewarded. Do you still have the sword you found?'

Theophilus's *'What sword might that be?'* faltered and expired on his lips. Attempts at deception seemed merely shabby in present company.

'So you know about that then?'

Suth-Rege mock-apologised for his omniscience. 'Our little role in its giving earned us some knowledge. Your forgiveness, please. Our scrutiny of you has, I promise, been kept to a decent minimum.'

Theophilus was untroubled by the news for he fashioned his life into pretty much an open book. It was simpler that way – less things to remember. Besides, his Father had always told him: *'Never do anything – in daylight – you'd not be happy for your Mother to see'*. To date, abiding to that had stood him in good stead – aided by the fact that mother had been a half-wild northerner (and an Anglican Archbishop's granddaughter!) anyway.

'Yes, I've still got it. It's safe. Can you tell me about it?'

'No.' The blunt refusal was said so charmingly that it was hard to take offence – but Theophilus managed it. 'Not yet,' added Suth-Rege, as swiftly as good grace would allow. 'The timing is not quite proper.' His tone was so regretful, so understanding of hurt feelings, that even Oglethorpe was (almost) appeased.

'When will it be *proper* then?' he asked, only marginally more florid than usual.

'When we see the King. That is what you must arrange.' The answer was unhesitating – and Theophilus was silenced. Suth-Rege spoke as though he sought admission to the Mayor of Godalming; something of no great shakes – to be fixed up when he'd a free moment. 'And bring the blade with you.'

Oglethorpe re-orientated himself by studying the sky. It remained clear and untroubled – unlike his thoughts. Birds traversed it in a way they'd always done. It was not the world that had gone awry; merely his little portion of it.

'And what, pray, shall I say to him?' he asked, when words at length returned. 'That the elves crave audience?'

'Yes,' agreed Suth-Rege, unexpectedly. 'Then tell him this, so he will believe.'

Before it could be prevented, the Elf's left hand lightly brushed Oglethorpe's brow. The charge in those slim fingers singed the skin and caused Theophilus's wig to stir, but these sensations were neglected nothings compared to the tidal rush of liberated memory and gifted sights.

Oglethorpe's gratitude for the flood of remembrance was matched by relief for being lifted from despond's slough. Once its conjuring-up was recalled, the demon melancholy could be booted back to hell. Not only that, but he was now free to do his duty.

Theophilus recollected his true conversation with Monmouth; he saw the conspirators meet to plot and then mass for attack at Rye House. He was shocked to recognise so many. The

116

armed mob then faded and the scene changed. In his mind's eye he witnessed a tall and shadowy figure, not unlike his present companion, raising sorcerous fire in Newmarket. The Spring Race meeting went the way of all the incinerated stables and horses, and Charles came home early. The would-be regicides barricaded the toll-road in vain and gnashed their teeth at the non-arrival. Surveying the scene from angelic heights Oglethorpe observed them dispersing on horse or by foot, but all in confusion, back to Court or Scotland or Holland, and fresh calculations.

Theophilus looked to heaven. 'Only give me the chance,' he vowed, through pursed lips, 'and they will plot no more!'

Suth-Rege fastidiously avoided following that particular line of sight. 'Quite so,' he agreed, coughing politely. 'Meanwhile, we have plotting of our own to do. Times are such that humans and forerunners must work together. You will tell and your King will be grateful. Then Charles must hear the awful news.'

'About Rye House, you mean?' queried Theophilus, looking for some, or any, sign in those aquiline features. 'About his son's treason?'

'What?' the voice was puzzled though the face remained corpse-like. 'Oh, I see: no, nothing so simple. Much worse. Arthur has awoken.'

Watching from an upstairs window, Eleanor Oglethorpe saw all – or almost all. Sometimes she could see her husband's companion; at others he was just shifting grey shadow. The black-haired youth slipped in and out of mortal view according to shifts in an unseen sea.

And yet, for all that was uncanny, she was less afraid than for some days past. A message of cheer might be read in Theophilus's renewed vigour and the set of his jaw. This was not the stoic front of last week but a return of purpose. His boundless courage was back. In Ellen's book, love was trust and trust ought not to be crippled by reason. If Theophilus decreed the spectral visitation was for the good, then, for the moment, that was sufficient for her.

Even so, as she drew cautiously back from the pane, Ellen had to admit to a little surprise – and a degree of patriotic pique. For all the talk of the 'Grey Neighbours' back home in Tipperary, she'd never so much as glimpsed them. How perverse then, that they should wait for a move to Surrey to bless her with a garden party.

The change in room temperature was so swift and profound that the Duke of Monmouth could not continue. A sudden onslaught of cold deprived him of both the means and will to go on. In front, the Duchess's derrière grew goose-pimples and was much less fun to board. Husband and wife disengaged with a 'brrrr' and adjusted their dress.

When decent and able, the Duke crossed to the box which had hitherto heated the room. He gingerly tapped it – but to no avail. Its snug-creating properties were gone.

Now, that meant one of two things: either Oglethorpe was dead or else his memories were free. There was little difference between them. Should the second prove to be the case, then the first must soon follow.

He snatched up the little casket and shook it, frowning. The expended stone rattled, inert, within.

'Friends!' he said dismissively; perhaps to the ravished, weeping Duchess, perhaps to himself. 'You can't trust anyone nowadays.'

King Charles II listened, and then raged, and then wept as his heart broke. Even before the news he'd made clear his desire to be elsewhere. A man called Newton was propounding a new theory about the tides to the Royal Society that evening and the King, a keen amateur scientist, had hoped to be present. That was now out of the question and Charles would miss the exposition on 'gravity'. A similarly powerful, but more metaphysical, force dragged his spirit down.

From outside came the sound and fury of Piercy Kirke and Samuel Pepys, lost in their episodic, air-singeing argument about the Colonel's late rule in Tangiers, its 'bestial depravity' and whether it mattered, and if 'canting quill-duellists' should visit outposts of empire 'peddling meddling'. Normally it amused the King: now he sent someone out to shut them up.

He could not conceive what he'd done to deserve this knife twisted into his autumn days. As Kings went, as much as the world permitted, he was a kindly soul. He'd had his carpenter fit a false leg on an injured crane in St James's Park. And this was the thanks he got.

The Duke of York stood beside his brother as Theophilus's tale unfolded, offering what consolation his own battered charity would allow.

'Is this God's punishment?' wailed the King. 'I've not been *that* bad. All this because I tupped a few doxies?'

'Be cautious, Majesty,' warned the Archbishop of Canterbury. 'Our Lord can only act justly. We must endure his stripes patiently.'

Neither Charles nor James had any high opinion of the Anglican Church but they reined back the ripostes that naturally sprang to mind. For all that his timing and chosen church might be uncertain, the aged Archbishop Sancroft's integrity was not in doubt. Charles appointed him and kept him at Court for that very reason: a quaint relic of former days and ways.

'Mebbe so,' growled the King. 'But I question whether he need lay on with such a will – or if there ain't backs more ripe for whipping.'

The Archbishop thought that a fair point and so remained silent.

'Still,' Charles went on, now rallying a fraction, 'it remains to *check* these grave allegations. No offence, Oglethorpe, but you'll concede they emanate from strange sources . . .'

The Duke of York was having none of this prevarication. 'Done, checked, t-true,' he crisply advised his brother, causing Charles's shoulders to slump again. 'You were warned in general terms before but would not believe. Lieutenant Colonel Oglethorpe has but c-coloured in the picture. Accept.'

The select gathering in the throne-room saw him do so,

observing the grim notions proceed from brain to eye to body. A few seconds on, Charles seemed a smaller, older, man.

'Very well,' he said in a voice from far away, 'let it be done. Remind me of these vipers, this "Council of Six".'

'Lord William Russell,' recited Theophilus.

'High Treason,' answered the King, and a secretary noted it down. 'The Tower. The axe. Though *he* insisted on proper execution of drawing and quartering for my father's innocent servant, Stafford, I am more merciful. He also has great estates I recall: his widow and orphans may retain them.'

'Sir Algernon Sidley.'

'A republican,' said Charles, his lip curling. 'He approved my father's death. Let him feast from the same table.'

'The Earl of Essex.'

'Likewise – though he may look for reprieve. Since his father died for mine, I owe him a life.'

'John Hampden.'

'We had enough trouble with his father of the same name. The blood of that tribe scalds when spilt. Let him live, but break him with fines.'

'Lord Howard of Esrick.'

'He's invertebrate. Allow him to turn King's evidence and convict the rest before a Grand Jury. Then let me see him no more. Use the lesser fry in similar manner but ensure only a brace or two get as far as Tyburn. Just a little gore serves to drown treason; excess only makes it grow.'

He sighed and sat back, tired of all this worldly wisdom. 'And thus there's an end to it.'

James Stuart disagreed. 'Not so,' he said, coldly, 'unless my numeracy's at fault. We are dealing with a "Council of S-six".'

'So?' The King's voice contained a warning but the Duke of York ignored it.

'I,' he answered, 'have only heard *five* names.'

'That is true,' said Theophilus, speaking out of turn and out of duty. 'The sixth and chief conspirator is James Croft, Duke of Monmouth.'

Charles visited Oglethorpe with the most glacial of gazes.

120

'We are *obliged* to you, sir,' he said. 'May you one day have someone so . . . remindful of a child's ingratitude. Yes, my Lord Monmouth, son and snake: he too must have his reward as he has rewarded me. A bill of High Treason and £500 for the man that hunts him down.'

The Duke of York was unwise enough to rejoice in at last seeing justice done. His brother saw and noted it.

'As to the other thing, Oglethorpe,' Charles commanded, 'you may proceed. We have seen much in a long life, perhaps too much, but one is still attended by surprises. Tell them the English Realm is honoured by Elfland's diplomatic recognition.'

'It is the ripest half a thousand pounds we are ever like to see,' said Lord Rochester to Oglethorpe. 'But who would dare collect it?'

Tipsiness led the perfumed courtier-poet to misconstrue Theophilus's status, mistaking him for a mere guardsman and possible pick-up.

The room was still decorated festival-style for Princess Anne's hilarious marriage to Prince George of Denmark. Charles in particular found it hard to credit a man as boring as George might still remain observable to the natural world. The thought of his conjoining with lumpen, lesbian, Anne had kept the King amused for months and culminated in embarrassing outbreaks of laughter during the ceremony. '*I've tried him drunk and I've tried him sober*', he confided to the prospective father-in-law, James, '*and there's nothing in him.*' Nevertheless, the politic, Protestant match went ahead and something of the associated unkind lightness of mood lingered in the palace.

'I suppose, my dear,' the Earl inadvisedly surged on, 'it depends on just what you'd do for money. I mean, the whole world knows that Monmouth lurks at Toddington in Bedfordshire, enjoying the company – and so much else, I don't doubt – of Lady Henrietta Wentworth. You might say, ho, ho,' and here he went so far as to nudge the Oglethorpian ribs with his elbow, 'he's hiding in "*Beds*"; get it?'

'Yes, I do,' answered Theophilus, calmly. 'And you get this.'

Thereafter the Earl took little interest in proceedings. Falling-down drunks were hardly unknown at King Charles's Court and soon enough some flunkies dragged him away to sleep whatever it was off.

Theophilus had little patience for *mollyfrocks* at the best of times and right now was hardly that. Rochester had no business being around at this, by Royal command, most private of audiences. Goodness only knew how he'd managed to blag his way into Windsor. It being Oglethorpe's assigned duty to keep the ante-chamber clear, even a 'Southwark Hello' (or head-butt) for an Earl was regally permitted. Rochester wouldn't mind, even assuming he remembered.

The incident was in keeping with the times. Just lately, joke-weddings aside, the Royal Court was not a pleasant place to be. Aside from increased security, the steady drip-drip-drip of blood from the Rye House business cast a dampening pall. Lords Howard and Russell had gone well, with the fortitude of true Christians. My Lord Essex had pre-empted his King's forgiveness and, in emulation of the ancient stoics he so admired, slit his throat in the Tower. By unhappy coincidence, Charles was inspecting the fortress at the time, giving rise to all kinds of insinuations. Lord Howard played his expected part and betrayed all, whilst John Hampden thought himself lucky just to be £40,000 poorer – and thus very, very poor. Monmouth meanwhile, awaited developments.

Left to himself, Theophilus would have gone and fetched the Duke, regardless of past affections. If asked to he'd have even visited sentence upon him. In the end though, his lust for justice was restrained by the King's example. That silly, doting, father pretended ignorance of his son's whereabouts and wanted nothing but the merest expression of regret to make all things well. Lieutenant Colonel Oglethorpe might not approve but it ill-behoved him to take more offence than the worst wounded party.

The door leading to the great Hall of Approach was tapped upon with the agreed signal. Theophilus hissed at the last remaining servitor-elements to begone and they slipped away through obscure exits back to the flunky labyrinth which honeycombed the Castle. Only then, and assured that he was alone, could he cross the chamber and crack the double-doors ajar.

A shrouded visitor awaited beyond, muffled and coated and nondescript. Amidst the aspirant peacocks of the Windsor Castle community he could hardly have stood out more. Theophilus was mortified.

'You misunderstood,' he said, in distress. 'I told you *inconspicuous*.'

'And so I am,' maintained the stranger. The glorious, cultured, liquidity of his voice negated his counting-house appearance. Whatever he might at first seem, this was no book-keeper.

'For a Quaker orgy mayhap,' Theophilus answered, with heat and speed. 'But this is the *Court*, man!' The stranger's eyes widened to be thus addressed and Oglethorpe glimpsed their golden core. Even his Etna-style temper was accordingly cooled.

'I am not a "man",' came the icy reply and Theophilus drew back before its frigid breath. The doors parted for the arrival to pass through and then closed with great violence behind him, all without assistance. 'And it would be well for you to recall it. We might well . . . speak to you, but do not expect concern for your feelings or a study of your ways, newcomer. Lengthy consideration of humanity we find . . . distasteful.'

He seemed minded to develop the theme, a passionless sort of fury building slowly in tone and stance. Fortunately fresh considerations intruded. 'However,' he added, and more temperately, 'I recollect I am an ambassador and should dissemble and oblige. Here, is this more likely to suit?'

The dowdy mercantile coverings were gracefully swept aside to reveal a glory of scarlet and thread of gold. He was like the visitor to Westbrook but not, Theophilus suspected, the 'man' himself. In their unpleasant beauty and poise, the breed tended to similarity. This one's inky locks were shaved, the better to reveal the sharp long lines of his skull, but otherwise he was much like the previous specimen. The whole was less than the sum of promising parts; nominally appealing ingredients adding up to excess. *'Nature'*, Theophilus thought, *'has over-blessed them. The first-born child is often spoilt.'*

Whether the gold was showing or not, they were also unable to keep the . . . neutrality from their eyes. That was both unwise and impolite. Theophilus had observed men look at midges that way.

'Far more fitting,' he lied. 'If, that is, one overlooks the mud and rips.'

The Elf was undismayed. 'We reside in forests,' he said proudly, 'because you drove us there. We do not fear them out of guilty conscience or wish them ill as you do. We live therein and love and use them. Why then should we not bear signs of their embrace?'

Theophilus was not sure he could answer that. Far better for him to take refuge behind pressing time. 'They await you,' he hinted.

His opponent operated to his own unhurried schedule and would not be rushed. 'You were asked to bring the sword . . .' The tone was reproving.

'And so I have.'

The Elf looked again at the apparently standard-issue sabre attached to Oglethorpe's belt. For all that plain sight denied it, he seemed to have no difficulty in accepting Theophilus's word.

'Good. Are you not joining us?'

'I'm alternatively charged: to ensure you are not disturbed. Be advised; in this engagement I am just a common soldier.'

The Elf thought he knew better. 'How can that be so,' he asked, smirkingly amused, 'when you carry a general's weapon?'

Such talk sounded . . . inopportune; particularly so given the rewards doled out to ambition and treason just lately. And whilst on that subject, Theophilus called to mind the exalted company gathered just the other side of the antechamber's second door. It was undesirable, not to mention unwise, that the King, Prince of Wales, Archbishop of Canterbury and (undercover) senior British Jesuit should have their hopes and curiosities tantalised any further.

Theophilus knocked to gain entry and heard the Regal assent. 'Your Majesty, my Lord, Your Grace, Your Eminence,' he said, in quiet but otherwise normal tones, 'His Excellency, the Elfland Ambassador.'

Oglethorpe was too honourable to eavesdrop through the door but there were parts of the conversation he could hardly fail to hear. It was a thing unknown for the kindly Archbishop Sancroft to raise his voice in anger but Theophilus could make no other attribution. There seemed to be some theological sticking-point which roused him to frenzy; a dervish-style mood made worse by the Ambassador's calm replies. On several occasions it sounded as if only the Jesuit Cardinal's bodily interposition prevented an Anglican assault on the Elf.

Charles and the Duke of York, being seated further back on the throne dais, were less clearly audible. If mere intonation was any guide, they started off the souls of amiable welcome – and then became increasingly troubled. Having less (if any) of a confessional position, the King (supreme head of the Church of England) could be more reasonable than his Archbishop. Likewise, the Catholic Duke and Jesuit-Cardinal, occupying a house built on firmer ground, might listen carefully and provide mutual support. Yet even so, one and all, they seemed less than enthused about the Ambassador's unfolding tale. The Elf was unfailingly polite but implacable. Theophilus heard him being very persistent about something called '*childhood's end*'.

Theophilus held himself – and his gifted sword – in readiness for intervention. The persons of accredited diplomats were meant to be inviolate, but that didn't give them free licence. He felt responsible in some degree for the behaviour of this invitee of his. Somehow or other, he was caught up in a maelstrom of events greatly detrimental to the peace of anyone it gusted upon.

'That is correct, Oglethorpe,' came the Ambassador's voice, clear as a pagan bell, from beyond the door. 'You are.'

Before Theophilus could query his proxy-inclusion in the debate, that door opened and the King popped his head through. He seemed . . . saddened or diminished, and quite oblivious to the scandal of him playing pageboy.

'He wants to see you,' he told Oglethorpe. 'Otherwise he won't go on.'

Theophilus's confusion was only heightened by obedience to the call. The Throne Room looked like the aftermath of some bloodless battle. Elements of the defeated were scattered round the edges whilst the Ambassador, unruffled and demure, stood centre-stage in triumph. He acknowledged Oglethorpe's arrival with a fluid bow.

'We need you,' he said, 'rather than these others.'

The 'others' looked glad to hear it. Archbishop Sancroft was slumped in a chair, and refreshing himself from a brandy flask in shockingly plebeian manner. From time to time he shook his snowy head and muttered under his breath, but otherwise declared himself 'out of it.' The Cardinal was more composed but deep in thought, staring chin in hand into a private middle-distance. Only Charles and James, soldiers in their time and thus armoured against shock, were still mobile, but even they were both as pale as paper.

'I cannot bear to repeat,' the Ambassador went on. 'Usurper company fatigues me. Besides, I am not sent just to bandy words. You must come and see and believe.'

'It seems we Stuarts are faced with ruin and displacement, Oglethorpe,' said the King, setting off to prise the brandy from the Archbishop. 'And not just us either. We've all rather had an excess of straight-talk right now but I commend your attention to the quandary. Run along and sort it out will you, there's a loyal chap. Good luck.'

'You shall come too,' added the Elf, confounding him. 'And the Welsh Prince.'

'P-Prince *of* Wales,' James corrected him, courageously resigned and master once again of his own features.

'Whatever. You three have been allocated parts. You must play them.'

'Must,' growled Charles, glad to have some affront to bite on, 'is not a word to speak to Kings.'

126

'I agree,' replied the Ambassador, as cool as you like. 'But equals may so converse. Amongst my own people I am accounted a King.'

'Of where?' asked Charles, genuinely curious, despite all the distractions. Having once lost a crown made him particular in accounting others'.

'You wouldn't know the name,' answered the Ambassador, minus his usual verve and suddenly all sad staccato. 'Don't like to speak of it – painful memories. But it was a good place: before you vermin came. Sorry: realise not diplomatic terms: no offence.'

He was on his way to one side of the room, and for the merest second no longer moved as though feather-light and panther-strong. Burdensome thoughts broke his graceful stride and turned his boots to lead. If you blinked you might have missed it, but Oglethorpe did not. There were, it seemed, keys to their hearts after all. He noted that.

'Well, *where* is it then?' persisted Charles.

The Ambassador, his poise restored, was distracted by a close search of the wall. He played his elongated fingers upon its surface, and peered intently at the papered surface.

'I beg your pardon? Where? Ah, yes, that is easier answered. It is here.'

'*Where?*' repeated Charles.

'Here,' replied the Ambassador – and opened the door he had discovered.

Life might have dealt them some interesting hands before now but Charles and James could not but look on gap-mouthed. There'd never been a door there; certainly not a massive old oak-and-iron-nail job like that. And even if there had been, it would have revealed the cardroom they knew full well lay the other side of the wall. Nothing in the natural order of things could have permitted the view of the great torch-lit, descending corridor revealed by the Ambassador.

'It is here,' he said, as though asserting his right. 'And everywhere.' A sweep of the hand regally invited them through. 'My land is connected with all parts of your "*England*": should anyone

127

wish it to be. Most homes have such an entrance. Step forward.'

This was all very well, if opaque, but they no longer knew where 'here' was. Moreover, it was contrary to state policy for both monarch and heir to venture together into unknown seas.

'If I wished you ill,' said the Ambassador, privy, it appeared, to their innermost thoughts, 'it would be done by now.'

As bald statements of fact go, it was plausible – if insufficiently respectful. Charles and James silently conferred, using the code constructed by a shared and troubled childhood. Agreement was swift and the Stuarts stepped forward as one.

The Ambassador had already gone on and they followed him. Theophilus brought up the rear, the one member of the group not blessed with royal blood and thus landed with mundane matters like security.

'Your blessings please,' he asked the Archbishop and Cardinal. 'And hold the fort till we return.'

Sancroft wasn't up to complying but the Jesuit had rallied sufficiently to oblige.

'May the eternal Eye shine love upon you,' he said, with great sincerity, 'even though you forget him.'

Theophilus closed the door in the clergyman's face and left the world behind.

They hadn't waited for him and he had to run to catch up. There was no opportunity to inspect the wonders of this shadowy labyrinth which joined Windsor to . . . somewhere else. It was enough that the floor was paved and flat, and the flares sufficiently bright to see your footing. He rushed on until in hailing distance of the Royal party.

At least he *assumed* it was they. His greeting met with more surprise and less welcome than should have been the case. The trio who turned to respond were pasty-faced, curly-headed men in white – and strangers: though the rough crosses about each neck prodded some elusive recollection.

As a soldier he should have known how fatal assumptions can be, especially in foreign climes. It had never occurred to him that these corridors might not be for his use and instruction only. Even with the evidence of normality's suspension beneath his boots, he'd discounted the chance of opposition somehow interposing betwixt himself and his companions. In his refusal to accept life's tricky tendencies, Theophilus would always be the proverbial bull-in-a-china-shop.

Still, that simplicity also could stand him in good stead, or extricate him from the snares he blundered into. Whilst lesser or more reasonable men might have queried the black looks he was receiving, or sought to turn aside the hostile reception, Theophilus was content to eat the meal laid before him. He drew his sword and advanced.

They weren't expecting that. The distance between them was too short and the corridor too confined for safe retreat. Turning their backs on the stranger would only expose them to a steely thrust and oblivion from behind. Neither, it seemed, were they armed. Their options limited, the three men settled for moderating their malice and speaking to the stranger. Theophilus slowed, and listened, and didn't understand. He told them so.

That short speech converted shock into full-blown horror. They gaped – and gestured – and looked at each other in disbelief.

'Saesneg!' said one, expelling the word like vomit.

Whatever it meant, it had the effect of impelling them to action. Two moved forward to block the way, whilst the third fell to his knees and implored the heavens (or roof) with a flood of words and frenzied shaking of hands.

Theophilus was puzzled. Who were these apparitions in gowns and why did they dislike him so? He tried to think it all through but, being realistic, recognised that wasn't a promising approach. All he could conclude was that prayers were being offered, to some or other deity; and not for his continued health and happiness either. Unfortunately for them, Theophilus believed in the power of prayer.

'Stop that wailing,' he advised the man, and leaning forward, nicked his ear with the sword.

It did the trick. They all of them looked at the blade and their horror – even the blooded man's – blossomed wonderfully

129

into something else. Theophilus got the impression they weren't beholding the plain state-issue sabre that he was. If true, what they saw served to inspire them. They forgot their fear and positively fell on Oglethorpe like furies. He was obliged to take a whole step back and kill them one by one.

'*Odd people,*' he thought, as the last went down – and then trod over the bodies to press on.

Actually, the King and Duke and Ambassador weren't that far away. Hearing sounds of conflict, and with every faith in Oglethorpe's direct way with such things, they'd paused for him to deal with it and then catch up.

'But how did they miss you?' he asked, having briefly explained the hold-up. 'You must have come through them.'

'The very word,' agreed the Elf, loftily. 'We penetrated them unseen, unheard, like wraiths. My sorcery permits that. If you'd be so good as to keep up, you'll be included in it.'

'But the corpses . . .' protested Oglethorpe, practical and prosaic even at this inappropriate moment. 'An alarm will be raised.'

'It is raised already,' said the Ambassador, matter of factly.

King Charles cocked his head to one side and listened.

'I don't hear it,' he whispered.

'It is raised nevertheless,' the Elf answered. 'If you were as evolved as I you would feel it. Do not fear, they will not see us.'

Nor did they. Time and again they passed through clouds of scurrying acolytes, much the same as Theophilus had disposed of, all bearing the asymmetric cross but in various stages of panic or armed preparation. They emerged from branching corridors, massed in the wider spaces or disappeared down forks in the path to pastures new, taking their drill from the flock-of-sheep school of military thought. If there was some coordinating intelligence to their actions, it seemed to be a jittery one – and prone to frequent changes of mind. The Ambassador's little group went on, unhindered, ever downwards.

'There's enough of 'em!' said Theophilus, curiosity leading him to speak out of turn.

'They attempt great things,' replied the Ambassador.

'History cannot be conquered by one man and a dog.'

There wasn't the material for a sensible argument in that. James, Duke of York recognised the technique. Politicians often employed enigma to kill a promising line of enquiry stone-dead. He wouldn't have it.

'Then, s-sirrah,' he asked impatiently, 'what are they about? Likewise impart where we are. Also kindly c-confide the nature of this place. Do we wander in a subterranean cathedral?'

'Or an underground university?' added Charles, who, as usual, had been saying little and learning much. 'God knows it's as musty as Oxford.'

There were grounds for both identifications. They'd traversed places which in other contexts would be counted chapels or halls of learning.

The Ambassador considered as they marched.

'As to where,' he said, at long last, 'this was mine once and I do not care to speak its name. As to what: well, a slice of both suggestions. Prayers are offered here and there are courses of instruction. One might justly term it a church and an academy – each devoted to your demise.'

This last morsel was delivered with a smile.

'But for the most part,' the Elf added, forestalling their protests, 'it is a tomb. Look.'

They did so and saw he spoke the truth.

As royal residences go, it was none too impressive.

'Well, well, well,' said Charles, as though hearing news of a very distant relative.

The Ambassador seemed to want more.

'Is that your full reaction?' he asked. 'I expected something less insipid.'

'Don't hold your breath,' growled the King. 'It's all you're getting.'

Actually, all three humans, King, Duke and Lieutenant Colonel, were as shocked as could be wished, though brought up not to show it. But for that they would have been gap-mouthed – through both amazement and necessity. The overpowering charnel-house smell made nasal respiration painful.

They knew they were intruders, the sense of detection was acute. Each had the feeling of hostile intent, invisible but there all the same, standing just behind them.

'We are not welcome here,' said James.

'No,' agreed the Ambassador, little to their comfort. 'Far from it.'

The long low hall was dimly lit but from no perceptible source. The torches in brackets stopped at its start, precisely where the change in atmosphere began. The endless corridors had been bad enough but there was a division between there and here. This place was alive and aware and full of malevolence.

Theophilus experimented by retreating a pace over the threshold. Instantly the ill-will ceased like stepping out of a too-hot bath. For a second he relished the relief – and then rejoined his King.

Charles's title was not in doubt and the Ambassador's bearing bore out his regal claims, but both were mere impostors compared to the Master of that hall. He lay in state at its far end, in a starburst of light from nowhere. It ebbed and flowed with the beat of his heart. They could see the red pulse within his ruined chest, through black chainmail and exposed ribs, pumping sometimes with ease, at others in spasm, but without cease. The great King's body was composed in an attitude of prayer but one decayed gauntlet gripped an empty scabbard. For all that he was just dry sinew and bone there was an expression of energy to him, a force so very *nearly* able to lift him from his grave. They were thankful the crowned head was turned away from them, not wishing to behold those empty eyes.

'Approach,' the Ambassador asked them, in a whisper.

Charles looked at the ground, not from fear, but unsure of his path. He noted that the floor was thick with undisturbed dust.

'We are the first,' he said quietly, warning the Elf, 'for many a long year. Is this wise?'

'Yes, we are first,' came the reply. 'The stolen babes that top up the life force are merely flung in. You will observe their little unformed bones all about. And no, it's not wise. Others are forbidden entry and we only come here at great cost. You must look and learn.'

The term *cost* was always a goad to Charles, who'd spent a lifetime considering expense and the hold it gave Parliament over him. He stepped boldly forward, leaving a line of prints in the virgin grime. The others followed.

Their way lay down an avenue of altars, placed regularly to either side. On each reposed a warrior. They had been put to rest embracing a sword, with a war-horse set beside them. Time had tarnished their glory, visiting flesh with decay and metal with corrosion, and though all were recognisable for what they had been, some had tumbled into final disarray.

'The magic failed them,' the Ambassador informed his companions, noting their gaze, 'or they it. The centuries were a test and trial. Only the most implacable can cross the gulf of years. But note the others.'

They did so and observed a scarlet beat in all the better preserved chests, of man and beast alike.

'Most linger on,' said the Elf, almost sadly, 'unaware but biding still. We cannot touch them.'

'Then how are we h-here at all?' asked James, Duke of York, permitting his flabberghastment just a minor sortie.

'The spell is almost impenetrable,' answered the Ambassador, still walking and with a smile, 'but not quite. Though not to be overthrown, vast sacrifice prises the door ajar to permit a glimpse. Our coming here will be the death of me but it is worth it.'

The humans stopped in their tracks and the Elf, surprised, paused with them.

'Literally?' asked Charles.

'Of course,' said the Elf, puzzled by their puzzlement. 'My race rarely joke. The price of this outing is my remaining millennia. A score of my brothers and sisters are likewise surrendered to dark forces to bring you here safely.'

They thought about it and, alas, it was Oglethorpe's more forward, less discriminating, mind that framed words first.

'Thanks very much,' he said, briskly. Both King and Duke grimaced at him.

'It was nothing,' replied the Ambassador, courteously taking the hobnailed gratitude at face value. 'If I thought you could hear it and live on I'd speak of the tally paid to set *this* place up.'

They followed the line of his hand and perceived for the first time that the altars were thickly coated in something dark. It was not so even-textured as paint and in a few, very few, places the white stone beneath peeped through. Patterns of flow could be observed, minor rivers and streams, ending in long dried pools of purply-black. The very walls and ceiling of the hall-cum-sepulchre, both suspiciously ruddy, now took on a sinister aspect. The men were glad to pursue him when the Ambassador moved on.

At last, hundreds of paces along, they came to the King-in-glory, set high up on a titanic cube of marble. Even lying prone, they saw he had been a giant and proportionally built. A simple, undecorated, iron crown bit into his skull, increasing his stature to rival Goliath's.

The humans didn't dare to speak but they could still point.

'The bones?' queried their guide, the sound of his voice causing them to flinch. 'I mentioned those. Sacrifices. Children mostly.'

They hadn't meant the shattered skulls piled at the base of the stone. 'There's words,' hissed Charles, indicating the marble itself.

They were arranged in that curious, cruciform style seen before and sight of them finally twisted the key of memory in Theophilus's mind. Recollection surfaced like a whale. That shape, that message – in scaled-down guise – had adorned the neck of Master Boson from Kernow, the night, two decades ago, when Monmouth repelled Pelling, the emissary of the Elves. He didn't doubt, now enlightenment dawned, that enquiry would have revealed the same about the persons of the Celtic rabble beside Broadwater Lake. This was the fountainhead and founding statement of a widespread fraternity.

'That's right,' said the Ambassador, either to Charles or to

Oglethorpe's thoughts – and at alarmingly normal volume, 'words of power: that's why they glow. "ANOETH BID BET Y ARTHUR" The language is lost but it could be rendered: "CONCEALED TILL THE FINAL DAY, THE RESTING PLACE OF ARTHUR".' He let this sink in awhile before applying the coup de grace.

'So, gentlemen,' the Elf said, waving them forward like an impresario presenting a turn, 'as was once said in another context: "behold the man"!'

To their horror, he then snatched up a long-bone and rapped it upon the blood-dappled bier. 'A-hem,' he coughed.

King Arthur slowly turned his head. The flesh fragments joining it to his body creaked and protested but complied. They then saw that though his eyes were long gone a light still burned in their sockets.

'Your Majesty,' said the Ambassador, at his most courtly, to Charles. 'May I present to you: His Majesty.'

The two Kings looked at one another, neither happy with the sight. It lasted only a second. Thereafter, Arthur only had eyes for Oglethorpe – or at least something he carried.

'Mine,' he said, a voice from a million miles away and yet hurrying to be amongst them. One withered claw sought to reach out towards the sword. 'Mine!'

Theophilus backed away.

'No point,' observed the Ambassador, politely chiding him – and gloating at the same time. 'He knows now. There's no way back!'

A sound like the lament of souls in purgatory came from behind, a caterwauling powered by long-brewed anger and frustration. The undead warriors were turned towards them, and feebly attempting to rise. Their bony limbs flailed at the still air, grating against armour and rending rotten fabrics, stretching impotently forth to beseech and threaten.

'They are stirring,' said the Elf-King, rather redundantly. 'Agreed?'

Charles, James and Theophilus were in no position to refute his opinions. Yet he awaited their reply, calm and more alien than ever amidst the hellish chorus. They hastily affirmed.

'Are you *sure*?'

They certainly were.

'Good.' The Ambassador nodded grave approval as Arthur loomed, huge and horrible over his left shoulder. Only then would he relent to save them – and contradict himself – and show a way back.

'I know where *this* is,' said King Charles, wildly grateful just to be free. 'I've been here.'

'L-likewise,' confirmed the Duke of York. 'It's Glastonbury. There's the ruined Abbey.'

'*Ynys-witrin*, the "Isle of Glass" as your first ancestors termed it,' agreed the Ambassador. 'And were perceptive in so doing. It was once a means of glimpsing somewhere else. We've arrived on Wearyall Hill,' he added, making himself elegantly at ease on the springy turf, 'where once grew St. Joseph's Thorn. Over there is the Tor from whence we came.'

That killed conversation as they looked at that conical eminence, surmounted by St. Michael's Tower. They'd left not a moment too soon. The Elf had relinquished the power permitting their trespass, and the scene had suddenly changed. They'd thought to find themselves back at Windsor but this sunny hilltop was just as welcome. Compared to beneath the Tor, a dunghill in Dundee would have been paradise itself.

The Ambassador failed to share in their unease. He was cat-like in his focus on the present moment alone; content now to play at tourist-guide.

'Do not look for the Thorn,' he informed them. 'Your *Puritans* took exception to the pleasure it gave, and chopped it down in the Civil War times; thereby severing roots they could not suspect. It was once a fine sight: *Crataegus oxyacantha praecox*: a Syrian breed – rather like your religion that claimed it. We who were here before called it a *Yggdrasil* Tree and knew it bound Earth to the realms above. Still,' he conceded reasonably, 'it was good of your Jesus and his Uncle to bless it when they came here. They were charming people.'

136

Then he faltered, forcing them to pay fresh attention to him. The Ambassador now looked drawn, insofar as it was possible for his kind to descend from perfection. His companions realised that it was not just languor that drew him to the ground.

'That is right,' he answered their unspoken queries. 'My time is short and strength diminished. I regret you must make your own way to London; I cannot reach there. It also seemed . . . apt to finish at "Weary-all".'

'You appear unconcerned,' said the Duke, frowning down at him. 'Are you so c-certain of s-salvation?'

'Sure of its irrelevance,' replied the Elf, shocking James. 'We are barred from Heaven – and the other place. My story just ends. What more solace is needed?'

The Duke had an answer to that but was Christian enough to see this wasn't the time or place.

'There are a few other things,' the Ambassador went on, lying back, his hands crossed behind his head, 'before I go. Mere odds and ends. It's tedious but I must be thorough. Listen: Arthur may lie in Avalon but he fell at Camlann. He left his sword there and this man . . . found it.'

The King and the Duke looked at Oglethorpe but met a blank wall of wilful innocence.

'That was our doing and choice – besides being amusing. It is more than a blade to Arthur and he will seek it. Don't oblige him. And what else is there . . .? Oh yes, we once had a pet called . . . *Nostradim*, I think that was its name – or something similar. He scribbled down things he overheard. Book 6, number 22 might amuse you. Also you'll have to track down the *Armes Prydain*. Raid Monmouth's house in Soho; there's bound to be a copy there.'

Again he stumbled and had to pause to revive.

'That will do,' he said, perhaps to himself. 'I have done what I can.' The Ambassador looked up, to check they were attending. 'You are equipped to attend the High-Moot,' he told them, as though presenting a prize.

It was not like Charles to be pedestrian but he failed to restrain himself in this instance.

'What is the "*High M . . .*"?'

'No,' commanded the Elf, lost now in a study of the sky. 'My business is concluded. Enough.'

And so they were silent, honouring his occasion. They sat cross-legged beside him, three respectful Englishmen, providing quiet company for the departure of a King.

A strong wind blew up, streaming back their hair and causing the grass to dance. Black clouds raced to intrude on the sunshine. The Ambassador sighed.

'It is time for my last song,' he mused, 'so what can I say? I've learnt that both sky and time are infinite – and that is very beautiful. It would be good to see more but I have lived, and touched the universe, and that also suffices. I thus declare that nothing is true and everything is permissible!'

The Duke of York tutted disapproval.

Exquisitely courteous, even at the end of things, the Elf-King regretted giving offence. He raised himself, in evident pain, on one elbow.

'I'm sorry,' he said, the effort making him wince. 'I realise that is not to your tastes. I shall think of something else. Forgive me.'

James happily did so, though aware absolution could not avail the soulless.

The Elf settled back and smiled once more. He looked wickedly at the surrounding humans.

'How about,' he said, ' "*It is done*".'

That was his second scriptural borrowing of the day. The oval eyes then closed for the last time and he faded into the turf.

It was akin to the melting of ice, although his substance flowed more like molten gold. For a second the ground around was gilded and shone more glorious than a treasury, and then he was gone, streaming down into the earth from which he came. There were no remains or memorial to say he'd ever been, save that the grass where he'd lain now grew more verdant and lush. His last words echoed awhile and ascended the sky, but weakened and died as he had, falling far short of Heaven.

138

THE YEAR OF OUR LORD 1684

. . . *The warriors will scatter the foreigners as far as Caer weir [Durham]*
They will rejoice after the devastation,
And there will be concord between the Cymry and the men of Dublin,
The Gaels of Ireland and Anglesey and Pictland, the men of Cornwall and
of Strathclyde will be made welcome among us,
The Britons will rise again . . .

They will ask the Saxons what they wanted,
What right they have to the land they hold,
Where are the lands from which they set out,
Where are the kinsfolk, from what country, are they come?
Let them begone as exiles
Ere the Welsh are stripped of their land . . .

There will be widows and riderless horses,
There will be woeful wailing before the rush of the warriors,
And many a wounded hand before the scattering of armies
The messengers of death will gather
When corpses stand one by another . . .

For the English there will be no returning.
The Gaels will return to their comrades.
The Welsh will arise in a mighty fellowship,
Armies around the ale, and a throng of warriors,
And chosen Kings who kept their faith . . .

The English race will be called warriors no more,
But bondsmen of Cadwaladr and his hucksters . . .
From the *Armes Prydein Vawr: The Great Prophecy of Britain.*

Written circa 930 AD, probably by a southern-Cymric monk, on the occasion of the High King, Athelstan of Wessex, *Rex Angul-Sexna and Northhymbra Imperator Paganorum Gubernator Brittanorumque Propugnator*, extorting tribute from Wales, after harrying Scotland, by land and sea, as far north as Caithness.

'In the land of the great heavenly temple
a nephew at London is murdered through a false peace'

Nostradamus. *The Centuries*, Book VI, number 22.

'I'm waiting . . .' Ellen moved the fizzing taper closer to the fuse. 'My patience is wearing thin . . .'

By contrast, those she addressed – whoever they might be – appeared possessed of boundless restraint. Her threats provoked no response.

At the time it had seemed a promising idea, the lusty bastard child of desperation. When the Elf creature visited Westbrook that day, Ellen had covertly observed his respectful bow to the ancient yew before joining Theophilus on the bench. It was evidence of some attachment between the two and thus something she might work upon.

'*Mebbe* thousands *of years*', Grimes the gardener had told her. '*Man's like a mayfly compared to father yew. Why jew arsk?*'

He'd got an answer to that in being told to bury a brandy-barrel of black-powder around the tree's base. There was a near mutiny amongst the outdoor staff at such wantonness but Ellen was equal to quelling it. Spartacus himself would have risen in vain against Madame Oglethorpe's regime. Grimes in particular had gone purple and supplied his considered opinion in thankfully opaque Surrey-Saxon terms. In return she'd been indulgent and dismissed no one, merely boxing a few ears. Their insolence sprang from the purest of sources and the resultant torrent could thus be forgiven. Besides, there ought to be no need to actually carry out the deed.

'Last chance. Tell me all or else!'

There was also the matter of the ruin. Several times she and Theophilus had wondered how so age-old a tree might have

143

what looked like a wall incorporated within its very trunk. Previously they'd doubted any structure could have predated the yew and put it down to a freak of nature. Now Ellen was less sure. Whilst tumbled and moss-rotted the blocks of stone had been most delicately, precisely, laid, though cyclopean enough to defend a city. The few surviving yards above ground also suggested far longer spans in the silence below. In short, there were all the signs. If it was some relic of theirs they might be eager to preserve it.

Ellen had anticipated trouble in procuring such a quantity of gunpowder, especially in these troubled times, but was pleasantly surprised. In the event, no one, from Godalming supplier to Chilworth producer, expressed suspicions or thought it strange.

'A gift for your husband I take it, Madame,' was the only comment – and she found it instructive.

'Right, I'll count to five and then . . .'

All Ellen wanted to know was the same story told to Theophilus. Surely that was only a courtesy and not too much to ask. If *he* would not impart it then someone else must, even at the cost of some prompting.

There was no reply, no sudden granting of enlightenment.

'It'll be your loss. I'm not demanding the moon.'

Apparently she was. Ellen continued to address only empty air. Her hand hovered over the powder trail.

'1 . . . 2 . . . 3 . . . 4 . . . I'm serious . . . 5!'

She couldn't do it. Perhaps she was just haranguing a silence, threatening nemesis to a blameless tree and appearing ridiculous. A sigh of relief rose from the watching gardening staff gathered out of earshot to witness the cruel execution.

Ellen spat on the taper and swung away, leaving savage footprints on the turf. She didn't like being faced down.

Come to that, she didn't like being face down either. However, that's where Mrs Oglethorpe found herself after the explosion. A humid giant's breath flung her to the ground, acquainting her face with the springy, scented grass. In passing, the powder-gale also shredded Ellen's skirts and blew the rib-

144

boned remnants round her waist, granting the gardeners a compensatory eye-full. It was a pleasing side – amongst other places – of the mistress not seen before and, lost in contemplation of these hills and valleys of delight, they forgot to bemoan the murdered yew.

Stone and soil and splinters rained down on Ellen and a lancing pain in one nether-cheek convinced her she'd been struck. However, this proved not to be the tree's revenge – or not directly so – for the cause of the white-hot discomfort buzzed round to her face to admit liability.

Ellen had been stung by wasps before but never by one with an Elven visage. It flitted before her nose and smiled at her.

'We are not put to the test,' it chittered. 'Nor swayed by fondness of mere earthly things.'

'But . . .' wailed Ellen. 'Who . . .?'

'Our Yggdrasil tree and last remnant of our capital is gone. We are saddened: but only a little, only for a while. We do not allow the material to bind us.'

'I just wanted . . .' said Ellen, scrambling to her knees and strewing off a layer of dirt and bark and leaves. It was hard to express oneself properly whilst grovelling and clutching an agonised backside.

'As always in your life,' the insect-elf interrupted, still smiling, 'what you want you shall have. The knowledge is yours. It is injected along with my sting, for they share the same properties. Likewise they both leave a permanent mark.'

Then the wasp-toxin hit Ellen's bloodstream – with understanding riding pillion. In an instant she knew all that Theophilus knew – but was not made glad. She was afflicted with two types of poison.

'Thank you *so* much,' she told the wasp.

It flipped and spiralled in celebration of insectoid mobility.

'There are more tears over answered prayers . . .' quipped the altered Elven voice.

Ellen tried to swat it but the creature laughingly evaded her and streaked away into the wide blue sky.

*

145

'Tally Ho!'

'I beg your pardon?' asked Charles, frowning in disbelief.

'T-tally Ho,' repeated his brother James, reining in his mount. 'It is the correct usage when about to give chase.'

'I don't follow this at all,' said the King in exasperation. 'If the hounds have scented the fox-vermin then let them go after it. Why must we get involved?'

Patience was not the Duke of York's strong point, but in addition to being a brother, Charles was also his divinely anointed sovereign. He forced himself to go over the ground again.

'The chase is the p-purpose of the exercise,' he explained, eager for others to share in the pleasure of his latest hobby. 'The dogs utilise their snouty faculties and we pursue, over field and b-brake, displaying the utmost of our equestrian skills, to keep up with them. Therein's the nub of this new sport.'

Charles looked round at the cloud of courtiers who were all waiting to take their tone from him.

'And I'm expected, am I,' he queried, 'to gallop around, at the risk of m' neck, with no view but dog's arses, so as to be present at the kill?'

This wasn't developing as James would wish, but, deficient in humour and the detection of sarcasm, he gamely persevered.

'Just so. You have grasped the knack of it.'

'Though we can't consume what we slay, even assuming we get it off the hounds in recognisable shape, and don't call to mind what dogs oftimes do with their tongues.'

'Well n-no,' conceded the Duke. 'But there is some utility even so. Brother Reynard is a plague to farmers and keepers of hens.'

Charles was both puzzled and disgruntled. 'Well, let *them* kill the fox then. They have guns and dogs, don't they? Lazy bastards. At least that way their fields don't get trampled in the process. Now, if it was a deer you could put on a plate I might see the point . . .'

In his earlier days as a soldier, James was renowned for his reluctance to quit the field of battle, however badly things were going.

146

'It is all the rage on the c-c-continent,' he said, playing his last and trump card. 'All the most sophisticated courts, including France, have taken it up with relish.'

That did it. Charles resented the craven reflex deference to all things foreign that possessed his upper classes. He was happy to speak French as the language of diplomacy and international polite-society, but that didn't make Gallic culture synonymous with civilisation – whatever the French might say. If people thought it all so screamingly wonderful why didn't they go and bloody live there?

'Ah, well then,' he answered, 'that may rule out us coarse-as-coalbunkers, mere beef-and-beer English folk. We're too plain and simple and slow on the uptake. Still, if King Louis and the Prince of Orange discern merit in something, then that suffices. Say no more. Send this lot off into battle with the fox and we shall watch and be instructed.'

Both brothers, in the course of long lives richly visited by misfortune, had learnt the trick of disengaging their faces from their emotions. Only Charles could tell that the Duke was saddened by his failure to enthuse.

'*Poor old James,*' he reflected, adding a drop or two to his own ocean of sadness. '*So hard on himself and so easily hurt. When would he learn to sever connections with people? They only ever lead to sorrow.*'

'Stay with me,' he told him, beckoning him close. 'Further words from you may yet endear me to this new sport. And you too, Oglethorpe.'

The Duke inwardly brightened and hastened to comply. Theophilus was likewise glad. He disliked wanton destruction of God's dumb creation (though happy enough to deal with human vermin) and had not been looking forward to this outing. Had he known of it, he'd have sooner been with Ellen, blowing up their garden at Westbrook at that precise moment, rather than sip from this particular cup. The King, who could read men like books, knew it.

'I thought I'd save you,' he confided, 'knowing your tender love for furry beasts.'

147

Theophilus coloured up. Such weird, unfashionable views were a terrible embarrassment.

The waiting nobles had their smirks wiped away by Charles's baleful glance.

'Off you trot,' he ordered. 'A terrible foe waits you in the woods. How's it go? Tally ho-ho!'

They thundered off to the blare of horns and woofing. The King watched them with disdain.

'It'll never catch on,' he muttered. No reply seemed expected. The remaining trio ambled along slowly in the hunt's noisy, mud-strewn wake.

After the Great Frost of the previous winter, the coldest in memory, it still felt good just to be out and about, however weak the excuse. Charles had enjoyed the month-long Frost Fayre on the solid Thames, a wild carnival of commerce and fun, sword-swallowers, bear-baiting, dancing and plays, all egged on into a frenzy by the suspension of nature. He'd also marvelled to observe the sea frozen two miles offshore, not expecting to behold the like again. In time though it all rather palled and his true favourite pastimes were grossly inhibited by the chill and imprisonment indoors. He was glad to feel the embrace of the Sun (amongst others) again.

Charles drew forth a hip-flask and sipped daintily from it. The rustic view seemed to hold all of his attention.

'It's all *go*, innit?' he commented meaninglessly, when sufficiently refreshed.

Neither companion answered. For all they might love and serve him, both knew Charles Stuart never said anything in innocence. They also saw a dark spirit had arrived to perch on his shoulders.

'Any news from Holland?' he eventually asked Oglethorpe. It sounded a simple enquiry but was not.

'Monmouth and I are estranged,' stated Theophilus. 'He knows not to seek kind words from me.'

The Duke of York nodded wholehearted approval.

'That was *not*,' snapped the King, 'what one asked.'

'No news, your Majesty; no word, nor hope or wish of any. I

148

was as much betrayed as you were.'

It was an unhappy assertion, although Charles made due allowance for a less than sprightly mind.

'I don't think so,' he said. 'Not by a long chalk – but let that pass. There's no word from the boy then?'

Theophilus shook his wig. 'Not to me. I only know what the "Observator" reports: that he skulks in Netherlands exile, tupping his mistress and frequenting with rebels. Your agents can surely tell you more than me.'

They surely could. Charles had turned more blind eyes than a statue and broken all his own rules, desperate to keep his son by his side. Whilst others lost their heads and innards over the Rye House business, Monmouth remained inviolate. Trusted envoys raced back and forth between them to no great reward. Then, when with trouble worse than childbirth, a written confession and expression of regret was at last pulled from him, (and published in the *Gazette*!) he plain denied it days later. First there was shock and next the stockpiled anger of decades. Face to face, Charles told his son he might '*go to Hell!*' – and then downgraded that to Holland (which was much the same thing). The order of banishment was signed and the Crown's few true friends sighed in relief. A King cannot afford to look foolish or appear the prisoner of sentiment if he wishes to cleave to his title.

Nevertheless, a soft heart, even one so selective as Charles's, is not converted to sense by miles or betrayal. Spies assumed his parental mantle and told him everything. Monmouth had found a new home and love besides, at the Netherlandish Court. His aunt, Queen Mary, and the Prince of Orange made him as welcome as they knew how, and distraction from intrigue was found in the arms and other welcoming places of Lady Henrietta Wentworth. His affection for her was accounted genuine – an eyebrow-raising revelation in that day and age. He had even begun to dance again, using up excess energy and entrancing the anti-vivacious Flemings, with his grace and skill in that innocent art. Charles's rage-born-of-injury would have been soothed but for stories of the other company he kept. In time though, the regal eyes tended to glaze over when reading those less happy titbits.

'He's b-biding his time,' expostulated James. 'The serpent merely seems asleep. M-m-mark my words.'

'He's not the only one,' growled the King in reply. 'There's no shortage of people keeping us waiting at present. When are we going to hear from your damn Elves again, Oglethorpe?'

'*Mine*, Majesty?' protested Theophilus.

'Well, you appear higher in their confidence than us mere monarchs and princes. It's nigh six months since our jaunt to Glastonbury. We were led to expect a more sprightly course of events and frequent chats with the fantastic. God's ankles, man, if a Duchess led me on like that I'd have lost interest by now. You shouldn't flash the furry hoop and then refuse to play: I detest prick-teasers. If you don't want to sell, don't open shop, that's what I say. Can't you give 'em a nudge?'

Theophilus flicked at his horse's ears in exasperation. Life, marriage, the Army: it was all one impossible demand after the other.

'How do you suggest, Majesty? Shall I dig into Glastonbury Tor and await developments?'

Charles liked sturdy responses – in moderation. He smiled on Oglethorpe.

'If you like. And wave your magic sword whilst about it. That should get a response.'

'I should imagine it would,' commented Theophilus dryly. His hand dropped instinctively to Excalibur-in-disguise which now rarely left his side. 'Though whether you'd hear any more of me is another matter.'

'It's a t-thought,' mused James, embracing the 'plan' with apparent relish. He had all of Oglethorpe's thirst for battle – and none of his sense.

Charles sadly shook his head. Sometimes he couldn't credit they had the same mother.

'A thought – but not a good one, brother. The Lieutenant Colonel is a faithful servant and, not being overburdened with such, we'd be sad to lose him. Moreover he's our link with the worries in question. Now that he has been good enough to *confide* in us . . .'

'I didn't see how to explain about the sword,' protested Theophilus. 'No one would have believed. Besides, I shot the Lady . . .'

Charles stopped his horse abruptly, taking them by surprise.

'It's in our power,' he said, 'to pardon such trifles. Deception's another matter. Are you sure there's no other . . . difficult items to disclose?'

'On my oath not,' answered Oglethorpe.

'Good enough for me,' snapped the King and moved on. 'Then there's nothing to do but wait their good pleasure. Perhaps no slight's intended. We shall calm our thwarted thirst for prodigies. Maybe such weird issues have a pace all their own. We've made what preparation we can.'

'And the balance is up to G-God,' added James.

'Or someone,' commented the King, tweaking the Duke's tail. 'We've dutifully acquired the 'Army Friday' and that Nostril chap's book . . .' Charles knew very well it was the *'Armes Prydain'* and *'Nostradamus'* but he wasn't going to accord them the honour of twisting his tongue on their behalf. 'We've even gone so far as to peruse the balderdash within . . .'

'I've memorised both!' boasted James.

Charles grimaced. He defined a gentleman as someone who could recite poetry but didn't. Fortunately, the Duke desisted from proving his achievement.

'The first,' said the King, before James could, 'speaks plain enough of its intentions – damned cheek! The second is a black cat in a dark alley and about as useful.'

'The Druidic construction at Stone-henge-by-Salisbury might be termed a temple,' suggested the Duke of York, revealing unsuspected private researches. 'Its alignment may well relate to the heavens.'

'As does St Paul's,' retorted Charles, 'and m' chapel at Windsor and Glastonbury-cursed-Tor for all we know. Does this propel us the slightest bit forward, brother?'

151

'And Monmouth *is* my nephew,' added James, out of painful honesty.

'And mine also, for regal bastards are often so described. Are either of us to murder him?'

'No.' The Duke's straight answer could be readily accepted.

'Nor I. And as for *"a false peace"*, well . . . We stumble and guess like drunks at a barndance. So, whilst comprehension eludes us, let us forget King Arthur and Celts and Elves, and other such rings on the bath-tub of history. Maybe they will moot this "Moot", maybe not. We shall not hold our breath. Meanwhile let us enjoy life as though the bad dream is over.'

A dream of another sort cantered back to join them. Though too pale and streamlined for some contemporary tastes, Lady Arabella Godfrey, *nee* Churchill, had boyish charms rated highly by those in a position to know. James might be counted an expert on the subject, having fathered four children upon her.

'Sorry to spoil the men-talk,' she trilled, blasting them with volleys of charm, 'but the buggers have gorn and left me behind.'

'M-madam,' answered the Duke, a pushover as always, 'you are never less than welcome.'

Charles grinned, effortlessly giving his cares the heave-ho. He liked anyone (though particularly women, of course) who were eager to please, who met you halfway. Arabella was practised and polished but not so much so as to be brassy. This was the world he felt more at home in.

'My dear Lady,' he husked, joining in the fun, 'your behind should never be so neglected.'

Madame Godfrey shrieked in amusement.

'Wicked boy!' she said, wagging her finger. 'What I meant was they went so fast I couldn't keep m' seat!'

'How so?' exclaimed the King, poking the disapproving Duke with his riding crop. 'My brother here used to say you had a very fine seat!'

'And so she did,' said James, firmly and not in the least amused. 'The Lady was one of my f-f-finest equestrian pupils.'

152

That only prompted his tormentors to fresh hilarity. Even Theophilus's straight face was sorely tested. The whole world knew that James's liaison with her had begun under the cover of riding lessons.

The King wiped a tear from his eye. It was an abiding joy to him that his brother couldn't just *admit* to worship of the female form in addition to his Catholicism. He wasn't so troubled. Though no theologian, it struck Charles as disrespectful to God to think Him so concerned about *little* sins.

'Come on Oglethorpe, we'd best be off. To work, brother! Arabella stands in need of further instruction. Who better than you to re-teach her control of a powerful beast between her legs?'

The King spurred his horse away, with Oglethorpe close behind, before James could sufficiently master his stutter to reply. Arabella put an end to those sputterings by leaning across to peck his brow. Time, separate ways and marriage had not dimmed her affection for him.

'He's a tease,' she said, her voice less strident, less theatrical, now she wasn't acting for the King. 'Don't rise to it.'

'Good j-job he can't hear you,' answered James glumly. '"*Rise to it*" – d'you see? Can't say anything r-round him if there's a lady present.'

Arabella snorted dismissively.

'Well, Jimmy, you should know I'm no lady. Come on, let's ride side by side and depart from their sight.'

She led on, away from Windsor, away from the distant sounds of the hunt, out into the silence of the green fields. James jogged amiably along, resuming the companionable ease that had dignified their years together. He meanwhile noted there was nothing at all amiss with her horsemanship – the minx!

At length they chanced on a woodland arbour and, without a word passing between them, both consented to stop. Private, dry and well provided with springy turf, it might have been designed by Venus herself. Thus mugged by fate, James hardly felt guilty at all about the thoughts that surged into his loins.

Arabella surveyed the scene with knowing eyes.

'It reminds me of somewhere,' she smirked.

'Likewise.'

'Do you remember that first time?'

The Duke's snort dismissed any doubts of it.

'We were hunting just like now,' she went on, reminiscing dead days as much for her benefit as his.

'Greyhound coursing,' James corrected her. 'We got t-thirty hares.'

'You didn't.'

'Ah, no . . . not me personally.'

'You played the hero, charging to the rescue of some young gel whose horse had bolted and thrown her.'

'I was concerned for your safety.'

'And relieved to find me prostrate but alive, in a swoon but unhurt. Alas, cruel chance decreed the disarranging of my dress. M'gown was round m'neck, no less. Quite inadvertently, I was displaying the grotto of delight for your delectation.'

'A slave to the s-sight, I dismounted my s-steed.'

'And mounted me instead.'

'And you woke up and asked for a j-job for your brother.'

Arabella laughed, unabashed.

'I was only seventeen, a mere Maid of Honour to your wife, starting out in life and in a hurry. Us Churchills have a way to make. Do you regret taking John as your page?'

James shook his head.

'I regret nothing I took that day,' he said firmly.

'I'm glad to hear it. Johnny-boy has proved a fine soldier and servant of the Crown: he'll be a great general one day, for he's even more ambitious than I. You see, greater good can sometimes come of minor naughtiness . . .'

James frowned. If only he could accept that, life would be so much easier . . . Lady Godfrey noted the slump in his shoulders – and wasn't having it.

'Do you know,' she said, raising one white hand to her brow, 'all this . . . recollection is so exhausting. I declare I feel quite woozy . . .'

With one suspiciously liquid and elegant motion, she slid slowly from horseback to the ground.

James couldn't help but smile. Looking over the neck of his mount, he found a recreation of that delicious scene from years ago. Mere seconds later he was beside her.

'This time,' she said, miraculously restored to full awareness, 'there's no price tag.'

The Duke was wrestling with his hunting jacket, and finally taught it a lesson by just bursting the buttons.

'More f-fool you. I'd have paid it.'

'But . . . there's something I should say . . .'

James didn't like the sound of that and ceased to molest his breeches.

'Would it change things,' she said, mock frightened, 'if I admitted to a teeny-*weeny* bit of Elf blood – from way back and long ago?'

The Duke considered, comically half de-bagged. 'No, not really,' he said eventually. 'Knowing your clan I should have guessed.'

'We don't keep in touch – hardly spoken for centuries: not till last week anyway.'

'Oh yes . . . ?' said James, warily.

'They left a message – about the High Moot: about when and where.'

'And?'

'Don't stop, wicked-jimmy,' she moaned lasciviously. 'I always mix business with pleasure.'

Ever-ready, even when thinking of *business*, James complied and trod out of his drawers.

'And?' he repeated.

She drew him down upon her, long-lashed dark eyes widening with pleasure.

'What a waste to memorise the place,' Arabella giggled, 'when I've got *you* to remind me, big-boy. They said it's a week from now – and – oh! – at *The Long Man*.'

'Though I have now travelled the Sussex Downs upwards of thirty

155

years, yet I still investigate that chain of majestic mountains with fresh admiration year by year, and I think I see new beauties each time I traverse it . . . For my own part, I think there is something peculiarly sweet and amusing in the shapely-figured aspect of chalk hills, in preference to those of stone, which are rugged, broken, abrupt and shapeless. Perhaps I may be singular in my opinion, but I never contemplate these mountains without thinking I perceive somewhat analogous to growth in their gentle swellings and smooth fungus-like protuberances, their fluted sides and regular hollows and slopes, that carry at once the air of vegetative dilation and expansion: or was there ever a time when the calcareous masses were thrown into fermentation . . . by some plastic power, and so made to swell and heave their broad backs into the sky, so much above the less animated clay of the wild below?'

'The Natural History of Selbourne'
Gilbert White. 1789.

'It is amongst these modestly proportioned yet majestic hills that the great, silent figure of the Giant patiently awaits the solution of the mystery of his origin. Known variously as the Wilmington Giant or the Long Man of Wilmington, he stands on a hillside four miles north-west of Eastbourne, some two hundred and forty feet tall in his original state. If – strange fancy – he were able to tear himself from his turf prison, rise up from the hills and stride to Canterbury, he would by several feet overtop Bell Harry, the central tower of the Cathedral . . . the Statue of Liberty, which is only two-thirds as tall as the Giant . . .

'The Wilmington Giant'
Rodney Castelden. 1983.

'. . . He must be the tallest human figure in Europe, for he is two hundred and twenty-six feet high and the staves he holds in his hands two hundred and thirty and two hundred and thirty-five feet: the outlines are now preserved by a filling of white bricks, having become very faint a century ago . . . He is first mentioned in the eighteenth *century Burrell MSS. where he is shown holding scythe and rake, but he is clearly older. Sir Flinders Petrie ascribed him to the Bronze Age, others to the Druids: some have seen him as Balder opening the gates of dawn. The theory that he was set up by the monks of the neighbouring monastery . . . is merely perverse . . . It may or may not be significant that he was set up just below the concentration of earthworks on Windover Hill. Within the last century the outline of another giant could be seen on Hindover Hill south of Alfriston, but he has now vanished.'*

'Along the South Downs'
David Harrison. 1958.

'Eyeless, noseless, mouthless, he is like a face waiting to be born or a revelation that is imminent. He is the familiar spirit of the Weald, the phantom essence of those chalky epochs, the lingering spirit of Downland Man etched upon the green.'

'Gods and Graven Images – The Chalk Hill-figures of Britain.'
Paul Newman. 1987.

'*What* a palaver,' said King Charles, alighting, less than impressed, into what passed for the hamlet's main street. 'Why the devil couldn't they just post an invitation like normal people?'

The Duke of York joined him in surveying the rustic scene.

'Your query contains its own answer. You thirst in v-vain for "*normality*". It's simply not their way I suppose.'

Force of habit made the King raise his pomaded handkerchief only to realise there was no need. This wasn't BabyLondon. The air of the South Downs was sweeter than any artificial concoction.

'You should know,' he quipped, only momentarily appeased. 'It transpires *our* intercourse with Elves is less long-standing than yours – if you see what I mean.'

The gibe struck home. 'Only in innocence,' James protested. 'And all unknowing.'

Charles flashed his famous dry smile. 'Well, *unknowing* maybe. I misdoubt the innocence of up-ending Elf-maids. Perhaps your confessor can advise you.'

Leaving his brother to think that one through, he moved on, beckoning Oglethorpe to attend him.

'Master Theophilus,' he asked, studying without condescension the few humble cottages, 'kindly remind me of our location.'

'The village of Folkington, in Pevensey-*Rape*, in the county of Sussex, Majesty. Or so 'tis spelt. The aborigines remind us, to the point of impudence, it's spoken as Fowington.'

'Then we shall respect their South-Saxon sensibilities. Fowington it is. Incidentally, where are our loyal local subjects that one may thus oblige them?'

'Evacuated, Majesty: for the duration – at sword point.'

Charles sighed heavily. 'Your temper, Oglethorpe, sometimes exasperates. I suppose one yokel corrected your pronouncing . . .'

'More than one, Majesty.'

'Two or three?' said the King, with heavy sarcasm. 'Gracious, these people must be stopped . . .'

Anything less subtle than a sabre-cut was wasted on Theophilus.

'Don't worry, Sire, I put 'em straight!'

'I bet you did. See they each get a florin afterwards. I'll pay you back – probably.'

His meditation complete, James hurried to catch them.

'I cannot conceive,' he blustered, 'that any blame attaches to me. I mean, the Churchills? Who would have t-thought it?'

'Me for one,' answered Charles, bluntly. 'That family-cum-conspiracy makes the Borgias look casual. And don't talk to me about failing to *conceive*. Was it four or five bubbies you had by her?'

'Only four,' replied the Duke, sounding hurt.

'More vipers in our bosom. Didn't you *suspect*? Tell me that's why you threw Arabella over for that Sedley woman . . . .'

The Duke, alas, was a prisoner of the truth.

'Well n-no,' he admitted. 'That was an accident. Coming upon Lady Catherine bent over and packing some linen, I mistook her for a serving maid, and not my wife's lady-of-the-bedchamber. S-she was so gracious about . . . the ensuing confusion that my heart w-warmed to her.'

Charles clapped his hand to his brow. 'I am almost reconciled to the ordeal to come. Lead on, Oglethorpe, before he tells me more.'

Theophilus know that his King had a lively curiosity about the obscurer corners of his Realm, and so had forearmed himself with dreary knowledge. He divested himself of it as they walked.

'To our left is a Church dedicated to St. Peter, the priest of which – who sadly cannot be with us – told me, under duress, that it is of flint-faced stone, built in the thirteenth century of our deliverance. The wretched settlement under its shelter is best known for the cultivation of the teazle plant for dressing broadcloth and as the one-time residence of the herbalist and astrologer, Culpeper. Observe the . . .'

'Is that where we must go?' interrupted Charles, raising his eyes to the cloud-topped protuberances of the Downs above them. For once he was not so interested in the by-ways of the land entrusted to him. He had the gut-feeling that his claims over it would today be disputed.

'Windover Hill,' confirmed Theophilus. 'That is the appointed place.'

'I cannot see this *Long Man*.'

'He is only seen from head-on, Majesty, set back in his own fold of the hills. That view is from Wilmington village, which I've likewise cleared and secured with soldiery, over a spur of the Downs from here. Fowington, if you please, nestles under Windover and is close beset by trees. It seemed happiest to arrive by the less obvious route.'

Charles's history provided ample example of the wisdom of such caution. His subtle mind judged it wasted effort amidst the present suspension of nature, but he could approve the general policy.

'You have done well, Oglethorpe. Our safety seems well pro-vided for.'

It certainly was. Theophilus had commissioned the first ever detailed map of the area and, employing same, arranged it to be sealed off from the world. All human life had been 'persuaded' out of the way. Small detachments of the Duke of York's Horse, of which he now had the honour to be Lieutenant Colonel, stood over the approaches to ensure a degree of privacy. A larger group were held in reserve for darker duties. Should Theophilus not countermand the order and confirm the King's welfare by nightfall, they were to sweep the Downs clear of life – of whatever sort they might find.

Theophilus reconsidered his plans for the thousandth time and 'saw that they were good'. He was then punished for his misuse of Holy writ by the King's attention to detail.

'No wonder I'm always broke,' said Charles, good-naturedly, as they started to ascend the hill-path out of Folkington, 'when my troops sport uniforms as gaudy as that.' He pointed to the ring of armed sentinels they now glimpsed through the trees. 'What regiment are they?'

Theophilus looked and then ground his teeth.

'I couldn't say, your Majesty,' he replied, sadly. 'It's not our army.'

The sun came out to accompany their climb along the narrow chalky track. Charles took the lead, striding ahead with his long legs, although the oldest of the group. James, Duke of York, and Theophilus puffed along after him as best they could.

'Nice day for it,' the King shouted back at them. 'Is that this Long Man?'

Indeed it was, glimpsed obliquely on what antiquarians sus-pected was the artificially levelled side of Windover. He looked blankly out over the Weald, patiently awaiting his own purpose and putting mere transient 'Kings' and 'Dukes' into proper per-spective. As the path wove up the hill-spur, a few yards to left or right removed him from view.

'Marvellous panorama,' said Charles, coming to a sudden

160

stop. 'Can see for miles. What's that booby-shaped thing?'

Theophilus almost cannoned into the regal back. He followed the pointing arm.

'Mount Caburn, sire. An outpost of the Downs. There's an ancient citadel atop it and legends of a Roman buried in a gold coffin. I've stationed lookouts there.'

The King stared. 'That's thoughtful,' he said, after a long pause. 'Though perhaps wasted effort. They'd be better employed hunting that gold. It seems our person is already well guarded.'

Theophilus took the reproof in silence. He had no explanation for the other sentinels who'd walked through his cordon.

'Sulk not, Theo, at least we're alone now. Our friends have left us behind.'

That was true. The Elf-soldiers had suffered them to pass and they now had the hill to themselves.

'Never mind,' laughed Charles. 'Onwards and upwards, lads. Let us ascend, like Christ, into the clouds.'

This was also true. The cloud-cover had dipped even as they walked, hiding the top of Windover in ethereal white.

It was hard going and the slope in places sheer. Their riding boots slipped and rolled on the crumbly chalk. In other circumstances it would have been a relief to gain the summit but as it was they were in no hurry to leave the world behind. In the end, however, neither inclination, nor gravity or terrain could forever postpone their arrival at the High Moot of the Old Ways.

A sound of disapproval, like a distant threatening storm greeted them. They could not see all of the groups gathered on the hilltop, or any of them at all distinctly. In the ebb and flow of cloud groups of figures presented themselves for inspection and then were gone. Hostility enhanced the chill.

The congregation was gathered in a circle, bunched into discreet little knots right round the top of Windover, crowning it with strange life. By luck or design, the humans emerged at the one point on the circumference where they might enter safely. They were met and escorted in.

161

'And so it begins,' said the Elf-King, portentously, to his train of lieutenants. They scattered at his command, each to their separate clans on the outer reaches of the hill.

He was much like his predecessor, blandly beautiful and glorious in mud-besmirched cloth-of-gold. His cool neutrality was tantamount to friendship in the present context and they were glad to see him.

'If you please . . .' he said to Theophilus, gesturing him forward.

'If I please what?' he asked, not used to being spoken to first in Charles's presence.

'The sword: display it.'

'You do it.' He wasn't keen on stepping out into the field of fire.

'We cannot touch Excalibur,' explained the King, as patient as could be wished. 'It is abomination to us.'

Theophilus looked to Charles and received the Royal assent in a shrug.

'To the centre,' commanded the Elf, 'but no further. There are some here you best not approach.'

'But the c-cloud,' quibbled James. 'They won't see.'

'They will see,' replied the King, with quiet confidence.

So there was nothing else for it but to put best foot forward, as bravely as possible for the honour of his race. All unknowing, Theophilus trod over the bumps and dips that were the barrow-graves of long lost dynasties, till he stood clear and alone. The counterfeit sabre was then whisked free of its sheath and brandished aloft as though to signal a charge.

It met with an octave-transcending acclamation from all round. Hisses and howls and lamentations soared briefly as if he'd opened the door of Limbo.

'He is rising!' announced the Elf-King, in a clear, unraised, voice that somehow covered the hill. 'I spoke the truth!'

Amidst the maelstrom of noise Theophilus glimpsed some of the more outlandish participants – and wished he had not. He had not been aware that man shared the Earth with such a variety of life. Without waiting for permission, though with

162

creditable calm, he returned to his own kind.

The Elf-King heard more than just sorrow in the cacophony.

'We need them,' he told the Moot, matter-of-factly. 'We must treat with them.'

The angry babble was heard again. Though it inspired them to draw closer together, the three humans could make no sense of it. The Elf-King, however, found cause for exasperation therein.

'Old grievances must be set aside,' he replied over the roar. 'Dream no more! We are weak! We can influence and meddle and appear strong, but that is not enough. Only these fast-breeders, these swarming soul-bearers, can grasp the world and swing it round. This day is the usurpers'. It is their time: ours is gone or not-yet!'

He seemed to gain a measure of agreement to that: Reluctant, grudging acquiescence perhaps, but good enough for his purpose.

'Do they mean *us*?' asked James, out the corner of his mouth. 'Should we b-be offended?'

'If you like,' replied Charles, sardonically. 'Oglethorpe here's a duellist. Mebbe he should call the fellow out.'

The Duke couldn't spot humour at five paces. 'Later, perhaps,' he gravely advised Theophilus. 'Now's n-not the occasion.'

Oglethorpe wasn't going to argue. Unlike his companions, he had seen the more monstrous delegates close up. Some of the larger entities would require cannon-fire to finish off.

The Elf-King pointed back at Charles. Monarch though he might be, the King of England, Scotland and Ireland shrank back under the scrutiny of a thousand non-human eyes.

'This one's faction must now be our own,' announced the Elf. 'Our interests for once coincide. Who here thinks to survive the coming storm without allies? No, we must ignore our disgust and confess our needs . . .'

He left the audience to stew on that awhile. The circling growl of disapproval diminished as they thought on. Then, picking his moment perfectly, the Elf-King stepped forward to harvest the crop of doubt.

163

'And lest you think otherwise,' he said, theatrically sad, 'my own people must also confess. We are not given to the pain of "guilt": that is a newcomer notion. Yet I say to you this day we have wronged you; you survivors of better times, and we shall therefore bear the brunt of what is to come. We have dabbled among the usurpers, for mischief and for sport. We have put our changelings amongst them, for our amusement and their tears. Yet not until now, never in all the ages since the last High Moot, not since the ice last retreated from this flank of Mother Earth, has there been a *renegade*-elf. Only now are all our secret thoughts betrayed to the enemy. He rises and exults, and that is our fault. I confess it.'

Strangely, the revelation didn't provoke the spontaneous rage that earlier rose to greet the human delegation. A new realisation of peril instead gave rise to silence. Like a cuckolded spouse, the gathering seemed crushed by disappointment.

'Monmouth is with him,' the Elf-King admitted. 'And we suffer for it. But with the newcomers' help, we will repay in full. The traitor will sorrow even as we made his forsworn mother, our disobedient half-breed and this King's wife, sip the cup of wormwood.'

Even amidst such wonders, there was a lot in those few words for the humans to reel in. A number of skeletons surged from the cupboard of the past to cavort before them. Each had had their suspicions about Monmouth but the blow of confirmation wasn't thereby softened. Still worse was the 'wife' thing. Five years back Charles had published a solemn declaration that '*on the word of a King and Faith of a Christian*' he and Lucy Walter had never tied the knot. Doubt was thus cast on his right to either title. His brother looked at him and saw a stranger.

'But you s-s-swore . . .' he gasped.

For once in his eel-like progress through life Charles Stuart was caught red-handed and he knew it. His loveable rogue image could not avail him.

'Not now!' he commanded. Happily, the Elf-King came to his rescue.

'These creatures are half-blind,' he told the assembly,

thereby distracting James. 'They live amidst reality but do not perceive it. If we are to cleave to them, they must know what we know and see as we see. You all must agree to such an obscenity. Shall it be done?'

Perhaps his audience had pondered the question before or were not fettered to a mortal pace of thought. Whatever the reason, they did not dispute the fleeting space allowed for consultation.

'All the known tribes have come from hiding,' said the King. 'An unprecedented array. This present age has not seen its like. I speak for the Southrons and I say yes. What say Albion?'

A tuneful assent came from one part of the circle.

'And Black Crow?' They cawed likewise.

'Shining-Path and Dalriada?' The two clans affirmed as one.

And so the solemn litany went on, through *'Tenement-Elves'*, *'Morisco's'* and *'Goddodin-Riders'*, *'Citadel-stock from the man-free Tyrol'*, *'Feather-cloaks of Paris'* and *'Old-City Zion orthodox Elves'*. The question was demanded of the *'Camague lancers'*, the *'Low-Country barge-Elves'*, the *'Burgundian stradiots'*, *'Constantinople Blues and Greens'* and the *'Englisc Companions'* – and numerous others the humans didn't catch. Universal, melodic, consent was obtained.

'There is one more thing that is needful,' said the King, when the secret register seemed called. 'Nothing can proceed without the Keeper of the Gate.'

For a moment there was quiet and Charles was about to voice his need for brandy. That was soon forgotten though, when the Hill beneath them spoke.

The answer came, not like thunder or a giant's roar, but as a quiet, private, voice beside each and every ear, perhaps even to the nearby resting Neolithic barley-Lords in their barrows.

'The Long Man hears,' it whispered softly, the sound of a young man far away, emanating from the earth itself. *'The door is open. You are not dead but you may enter.'*

King Charles reckoned he could sound confident when he wanted to, but this was something else. A true ruler had spoken.

Then, if that wasn't amazement enough, they saw the Elf-King prostrate himself in homage.

When his fearful respects were paid, he summoned them over.

'"Jacob called his sons to bless them",' he said, mocking them with scripture. 'And he said "gather together and I will tell you what will happen to you in the end of days . . ."'

He pointed and they looked. Windover's summit was no longer so bald and bare and windswept as before. A grove of slender trees now improbably graced its crown, high above their natural habitat and set a-dance by the gusting breeze. Then they looked closer and saw that wasn't so. The sylvan ring was independent of worldly weather and subject to its own laws. The movement of the boughs proved to be an illusion; the outward sign of shifting shapes. A legion of trees, each similar but slightly different, came and went in swift succession, mimicking obedience to the Sussex blow. A gentle light came from within, transmuting the air around to gold.

'The Grove of Possibilities,' the Elf-King told them. 'It is raised for you. Proceed within.'

It is no reflection on them to recount that the three men looked about, seeking excuses not to comply. It was thus they noticed the dying begin.

'What's happening?' asked Theophilus, aghast.

The Elf-King humoured them and turned to see. He noted that individuals in most groups round the hill had started to fall. Some tribes were only mildly afflicted, but others had gaps torn in their ranks.

'Magic is costly,' he informed them, blandly; not able to share their concern. 'Even with the Gate-Keeper's assistance, some things are not cheaply gained. Each of the First-born retains only a little magic within. We must yield up many to pay the price.'

He would have left it at that but saw that his guests were unappeased. That puzzled him, for how was this any worse than one of their 'plagues' or 'battles'? Surely it was better to rationally decide on a day to die? The King found it hard to keep in

166

mind that newcomers were of a higher order than dumb beasts. You could see why some tribes used them as meat animals.

In what might have been an act of kindness, he turned back to add more.

'Don't worry,' he said. 'We think it's worth it.'

Charles studied the trees as they approached, intent on retaining a fingergrip on reality, but couldn't readily identify the type. Bare and leafless at this stage in their own seasonal round, they might have been any one of a dozen British species. The inner light which bathed them did not assist recognition. Realising the task would be difficult, he abandoned it and surrendered to the flow.

The second they stepped within, the landscape changed, the strange light flickered. From inside the grove they looked out into a world transformed.

A soldier still, Theophilus's first thought was his unprotected back. Finding that safeguarded by a high brick wall he scouted their immediate confines. The grove had become ordinary, just half a dozen trees, a plain and simple copse in the corner of a field.

As befitted a King, Charles was more interested in the prospect before them. Keeping his feelings from his face, he regally surveyed the scene.

'And where might this be?' he asked, affecting unconcern.

'*This* is what might be,' answered the other King present. 'If you believe such theories, the world has travelled round the sun over three hundred times since your day.'

They separately decided to let that news be. Whatever they might say, no human can truly credit a future not favoured by their living presence.

'But w-where are we?' said James, gesturing to the rows of brick houses beyond the field. 'What is this city?'

'It is not a city,' the Elf informed him. 'The current age thinks it only a village. We are in . . .' he seemed to commune with some data borne on the air, ' . . . the Valley of the Ferns.'

Oglethorpe forced his brain to work. 'Farncombe, do you mean?'

The Elf-King nodded his long head. 'That is the current designation,' he confirmed.

'I live near here!' Theophilus exclaimed, happy to find one point of reference.

'Lived,' said the King, with casual brutality. 'Yes, your God-al-ming is over there, a few miles away. Even your house still survives, after a fashion.'

'And my descendants?' asked Theophilus, unable to deny the desire for proxy immortality.

Again the Elf-King consulted his invisible informant.

'I do not see any there. Others have inherited.'

'Oh . . .'

'I can offer some comfort. A nearby "museum" boasts an "Oglethorpe Room". A society bearing your name fosters friendship with the Americas. Your memory still stalks this place.'

'And what about the Stuarts?' asked Charles, keen to get in on the prophecy dispensing. 'Do we manage to . . .'

The Elf cut him short.

'We are not here for petty thoughts,' he reproved them. 'You will ask me the result of horse races next. Besides, this is only what *may* be.'

'I'm g-glad to hear it,' said James. Believing that the days to come were a matter for God alone, he'd had no questions anyway. 'Look at the way the buildings pile one on another. Our Southwark stews are more spacious.'

The Elf-King smiled.

'Times change. This is accounted countryside now. There are patches of open left but they are ruled and regulated: not wild. You have bred and spread.'

Charles didn't care for the relish displayed for present misfortune.

'Must be hard for you people then,' he said. 'I thought you didn't care for our company or crowds.'

The King had no difficulty in agreeing.

'We survive,' he said, without sorrow or self-pity. 'Unseen and disregarded, lingering in odd corners, in the places you do not want or cannot have. This age does not believe in us, you see, and that is our salvation. We can await better days. Meanwhile, since we are here, let us assess this slice of happenstance.'

The grove flared again and then flew, carrying them with it like gossamer on the wind. The prosaic little copse it had hidden in was left far below.

The Elf-King appeared at perfect ease with both the place and means of transport. Ever-watchful, Charles noted that and lay aside kingly dignity (and fright and nausea) to query the knack.

'You *know* this place, don't you?' he asked the Elf, determined, by hook or by crook to get a handle on him like he had on everyone else.

'I will be here,' the King confirmed. 'Or I am here, if you prefer. The two I's share the same matter and we communicate. I tread in a time I will one day walk. It therefore has a certain . . . familiarity.'

Being of an experimental, press-things-to-the-limit-and-see-what-happens sort of temperament, Charles wanted to enquire the consequences of the two 'I's' meeting. Perhaps fortunately he didn't get the chance. The grove rematerialised to show a new scene.

They were on a high hill crowned with houses. A grander sort of dwelling graced one side of the street, whilst plank fencing shut off the drop on the other.

Gaudy wheeled boxes lining the road were the initial focus of curiosity until the Elf-King dismissed them in tones of hatred. '*Cars*,' he spat. The humans' attention was re-directed over the fence.

'See,' he commanded. 'This is all that remains.'

Charles, at six foot and two inches could look over with ease, but James and Theophilus had to crane. None of them knew whether to be consoled or cast down.

The horizon was green. There were fields and woods and farms as far as the eye could see. This 'village' came to end and then the country began. That was the cheering part. It was only a second, closer, inspection that revealed the canker in the bud.

Distant and silent, they observed the path of a mighty highway and the ceaseless progress of 'cars'. The verdant panorama was delineated with cut-off lines of concrete-grey.

'They call such reservations a "green belt",' the Elf-King told them. 'Beyond that London is waiting.'

'For what?' asked Charles, resignedly.

The King ignored him, lost in his own thoughts.

'There are parts the car-bound ones do not visit for decades on end,' he mused. 'We can survive there: there and similar places – for a while. We sicken and sadden – but we survive.'

The man-King shook his head decisively. 'I see now – and believe. There's weightier matters at stake here than my dynasty – and Lord knows that's dear enough to this old heart. It would be hard to be fully human amidst such pandemonium, such a wound upon the world. This shall – *must* – not be. We have brought hell to live on Earth.'

The Elf turned on Charles, alarmed.

'Have you understood nothing?' he asked, as animated as they'd ever seen his kind. 'This is the *best* that can be hoped. You have not yet seen Hell!'

He then opened a door in the fence and took them there.

'Speak freely,' the Elf-King advised them. 'He cannot hear you.'

They studied the slim black-clad young man busying himself round his tiny abode. Though pale and wan, he seemed possessed of all his faculties.

Somehow crammed into this poky space, the grove likewise went unnoticed. Its shifting branches scratched the walls and ceiling. Anyone with eyes to see should have seen.

'Deaf, is he?' asked Charles. 'The constant noise I suppose.'

It was a good guess. Traffic noise and uproar permeated even up to this dwelling in the sky.

'No,' said the Elf, quashing the neat theory. 'I have removed us one or two degrees. We can be neither seen nor heard.'

With that comforting news they felt at liberty to inspect this cubby-hole the fence-door had opened onto. The task didn't long delay them. A few hundred square feet were all the man had to call his own. Likewise, seventeenth-century taste led them not to dwell on the scanty fittings. Their eyes flitted over a utilitarian wilderness of metal and black cloth, of geometry and abstraction, failing to find refreshment.

'The window tells all,' said the Elf-King. 'You look. I will not.'

'Are you here also?' enquired Charles, remembering the King's previous easy orientation.

'No,' he replied, looking blankly ahead. 'I am alone here. My people are gone.'

The three men crossed to the one small pane of glass alleviating the half-gloom. The grey City started many, many floors below and went on without end.

'The year is the same as before,' the Elf-King told them, whilst averting his eyes from the scene. 'But here you have made different decisions regarding the questions put you. Observe and be wise.'

In fact there was little to observe. One part of the metropolis was the same as any other. In the distance there were hills, but they too were coated with towers. In-between them all the 'cars' flowed like blood.

'Where are we then?' asked Theophilus, a country-boy by birth and thus marginally more chilled than the others. 'London?'

'As was,' nodded the Elf. 'It is *Solent-City* now.'

They turned to look again, vainly hoping perhaps to glimpse the sea and thus a limit to the horror. Then the tinny chiming of a bell distracted them.

They had forgotten their busy companion. Ignorant of uninvited guests he was attending to his devotions.

That rather surprised them. Metaphysics in such a world seemed out of place. The Elf-King wryly noted their disbelief.

'Do not revise your opinions,' he said. 'It is not what it seems.'

Having sounded a tiny bell, the man now knelt before the small, matt-black altar on which it stood. Three times he slowly touched his forehead to the floor in homage.

'Oh, Market,' he said with both love and fear hand-in-hand in his voice, 'you are ace, you are ace, you are ace. Don't make me a mug, give me the edge. Tell me your secrets. Let me know you more closely and love you more dearly and give me the edge . . .'

There was more but the Elf-King tuned him out. The fervent mouthings and carpet-bashing continued in silence.

'He buys and sells things,' the humans were told. 'Invisible, intangible things; things not yet made or never to be made or that might be made. He speaks down invisible channels to trade, shaving profit from speed and wafer-margins. Thus, though the age professes to believe in nothing, a strange faith has crept in along its fault lines. They so often seek the mind of "the market" that men now credit it with life. Decades of terming it each day "nervous" or "confident" have brought it to incarnation. This man would not confess his creed to his cold colleagues but many secretly share it.'

'Blasphemy!' exclaimed James, regarding the worshipper with horror. 'A f-false god!'

The Elf-King was less moved. 'But one that might answer prayers,' he observed caustically. 'Unlike some.'

The Duke's further protest was aborted by a languid raising of a palm. 'It is an arid creed, I grant you. There is no room within for the likes of you or I. My folk are gone, and so is anything you might conceive as fully human. A deity called Account-ancy has prevailed and it demands cruel sacrifices.'

'For what reward?' asked Theophilus. 'I can't see the appeal.'

'Look about,' answered the Elf. Its bounty is spread before you.'

'What?' spluttered Charles disbelieving, and angrily indicating the view. 'That?'

The Elf-King confirmed it with a nod. 'Man can learn to abide anything,' he said. 'That is both your species' strength and curse. In time even bitter fruits become bearable. Ash acquires a taste; nerves deaden and the pain goes away.'

'And does all this likewise depart, pray God?' persisted Charles.

'Nothing lasts for ever, King-of-England. I will spin the wheel of time and show you.'

They looked out again to see the sun streak across the copper-coloured, polluted sky. A day passed in a wink. Then the solar round became a golden arc and finally so swift as to be invisible. The leviathan-city changed.

First there was decay, then ruins, then revival leading to more ruins. For a short while there were mosques but they too fell. They saw movement in the wreckage and signs of human toil – but less and less and finally none.

'At last,' said the Elf-King. 'The Earth lies at peace – without you.'

'Same again?' asked King Charles, reviving already, and helping himself from the barrels behind the bar.

James, Duke of York, was less able to put facts behind him and his tankard remained untouched. Beer was of no help in matters appertaining to the soul.

'When *was* that?' he asked the Elf, his brow still furrowed.

The second King present stretched his long legs out on the pub bench.

'Sooner than you think – to use a later literary phrase. A few brief centuries, a few decisions – and Arthur – lay between you and . . . that.'

There'd been little conversation since leaving the hellish end-time. They'd escaped it to emerge, shocked and silenced, in the hollowed trunk of a vast and ancient yew-tree in Wilmington Churchyard.

'*Another portal,*' the Elf-King had explained as they freed themselves from its embrace. '*They are thick on the ground hereabouts.*'

They could well believe it. The great tree looked like one of Adam's early plantings, split by long-ago lightning and reliant on huge chains wrapped round its upper trunk to hold it intact. Since Theophilus had noted it before – albeit from the outside – the testimony of location was as welcome as a mother's cuddle. Further reassurance arrived in the form of the soldier

173

sentinels left behind – firmly fixing their temporal position. Less convenient were their officers' natural enquiries – about how their Sovereign came to be in a tree and so on – but these were brushed aside. Left alone at last, the foursome had staggered into the village and looked back on Windover.

The Long Man returned their gaze. Above him the cloud was lifting and down the sides of the hill streamed the remnants of the Moot, away to . . . wherever it was they went when people weren't watching.

'*In the words of my predecessor – and someone else*,' said the Elf-King, '*it is done.*'

So, as it happened, were the humans. A tremendous weariness assailed them, a draining of obscure reserves being the least consequence of sailing the time-waves. Charles had turned his back on the sights and thus spotted Wilmington's one inn, *The Giant's Rest*. Though humble, it was open and deserted, as alluring as another man's neglected wife. The King's policy in both cases was pre-programmed. He entered in.

Now, a few drinks later, they felt better – or leastways, less involved. The Elf did not indulge, regarding them without expression and stirring his ale with a stiletto. If they'd been inclined to return that scrutiny, the men would have seen that he too was tired. Most un-Elflike, signs of age could now be seen about his golden eyes. At length the graph-lines of their revival crossed his declining strength.

'Soon you will ask questions,' he said, 'and I cannot bear that. There is no time. Listen and I will speak plain.'

Something – though not his fading tones – told the men they should pay heed. Even Charles set down his pot.

'Arthur deems his time has come. He is probably right – he usually was. It is now or never for him. He will take the Celtic peoples with him as his soldiery. There was such an alliance long ago and it can be forged again. His legend has been trivialised but they remember him. He will pose, as before, as the enemy of the English and that will suffice. We do not wish him to prevail and nor should you – you have seen where that leads. Arthur knows us for what we really are and the Celts believe in

174

us more than you. They have cause to, for it was they who dis-possessed the first-born races with blades of iron. Their guilt makes them burn inside, and bad conscience turns people sour. Arthur can convince them to finish that holocaust. Your folk, however, came later. You have only second-hand record of us, and a disbelief which suits very well. There is no blood-quarrel between us and we can coexist in mutual disdain. I have shown that you will leave us a niche to live in. Purported to be tiny tinsel-winged creatures we survive under your dispensation. Arthur would be more . . . realistic.'

Despite the previous admonition, James could not quell the inner Babel of enquiry.

'But what is A-Arthur? Mortal man has a certain s-span and then . . .'

'Would that he was a man,' said the Elf-King, regretfully. 'Then there would an end to him. No, Arthur is a force; he both *is*, and serves, the Null.'

'And who might they be?' asked Charles. 'I thought I knew all my enemies.'

The Elf smiled at such presumption. 'You have not the slightest idea,' he said, 'of the powers that prowl on the edge of this sleepy garden world. There . . .' he seemed to draw back from some revelation, though desirous to deliver it. 'No, I will not deprive you of all illusions. But understand this: you con-ceive of two opposed poles, "good" and "evil" – which is all very . . . nice for you. Consider though – just for a moment – an alter-native. There is also a choice between a life of the senses or the imagination. For the former stand the Null – and you have seen their aim. They have their emissaries in every dimension. In some I have seen them personified, twice as tall as men, jade-black and blind, with the strength of giants. There they destroy all, the more swiftly to forever enjoy hibernating peace, slum-bering in intermingled heaps. Here they do more subtly. They wield reason, and dullness and *civilisation*.'

'I always presumed,' interrupted Charles, dryly, 'to be serving that last notion myself . . .'

The Elf-King shook his head. 'Your race does not understand

the term. You are comparatively new on the scene. Centuries of suffering are still required before that boast may be made. On his last outing Arthur lay claim to the great heritage of Rome and the Celts, the *Cymry*, believed him. Your rough forebears were almost swept back into the sea. Future antiquarians will discern in the ground that slaughter and the sudden end of all your forward settlements.'

'So how are we here then?' asked Theophilus. 'By what means did we endure?'

'You had help then, as now,' answered the Elf-King. 'But it was a close-run thing. We have weakened since, whilst *he* has rested. His dupes will rally to him again and who can condemn them? What have you to set against all that was Rome and the Empire?'

A few things like beer, cricket, Shakespeare, irony and 'The Book of Common Prayer' sprang to mind, but there was no short answer to his point.

'This is an auspicious time for him,' the King continued, unopposed. 'This land is war-tired and wracked and ripe for cantonisation. Your Cromwell-King,' (and here Charles's lip curled), 'who knew us well, feared that and said as much. Likewise "religion" is factious and discredited by chop and change. Recovery from your *Reformation* is a millennium away.'

'Ha!' crowed James. 'T-told you so.'

'And thus you hear why,' said the Elf, indicating the Duke of York to Charles, 'we would have this man rule after you. The Elves like Catholic kings. Their confident creed can accommodate us, made easy by believing itself possessor of the truth. An indulgent eye is usually turned. Whilst puritans and Protestants condemn and exterminate, *they* leave us to our own devices. When one considers the alternative . . .'

For the first time anyone present could recall, Charles looked guilty.

'Ah . . .' he said, tentatively. 'You mean my son, Monmouth . . .'

'Your *legitimate* son,' added James, glowering reprovingly at him.

176

'The same,' agreed the Elf-King. 'It is he who tips the balance and decides Arthur's timing. We have never had a renegade in all the many years, but fear of it still led us to forbid dalliance with the kings of Men. We never seek to come to undue prominence: all our safety has ever lain in discretion. It is one thing to mate with lesser species, though we find the deed chancy, to make eighth or quarter or even halfbreeds for our amusement. But to permit a full effusion of our pattern, to overwhelm the human type and make an Elf in mortal form, that we deplore. Complete knowledge is granted them but unlike us they are free in their use of it. Lucy Walter knew our law but wilfully disobeyed. She wished to shake the world as the world made her shake beds.'

Again James cast a rueful eye at his brother – which was unfair for he was just as promiscuous as Charles, though, it transpired, more lucky. The perils of promiscuity proved to be not just spiritual or venereal.

'Well, that's easily solved,' said Charles, keen to regain ground. 'I'll disinherit the boy.'

'What would that achieve?' asked the Elf, dismissively. 'When you are gone what weight will your word have?'

He was short on detail but supported by history. The humans reluctantly recognised his point.

'Then dispose of him,' suggested Theophilus, to Charles's and – to his credit – James's distress. 'He's one of yours.'

'Which is why,' answered the King, succinctly, 'we cannot. We are not like you. Elves kill their own kind in battle or in jest, but sordid acts are as poison to us. Assassination is a newcomer trait.'

'Oh . . .' Previous notions of superiority – in moral terms at least – evaporated away.

The King was rather pleased about that. It was a nice way to take his leave.

'So now you know all,' he said. 'As tennis-playing men you will understand when I say that the ball is in your court. Strike it as best you may.'

Charles, who got up at six each day for an hour on the courts,

177

regardless of the night before, could see the analogy but wished it were that simple. As he understood it, this particular game was supposed to be doubles, humans and elves versus Arthur and Monmouth. Now his partner appeared to be about to leave the match.

'But what about you?' he asked, finding it hateful to be so reliant.

The King was already on his feet. 'I am tired,' he replied, 'and have an appointment.'

It seemed pointless to protest and so they left together, forgetting to pay the bill. They parted without farewell, within sight of the Long Man, and the humans went off to the Brighton road, to find their carriage, and return to London and the struggle to come. The Elf meanwhile, took the opposite direction.

He knew of a second tally to pay that would not await settlement. The wonders of the High Moot were by no means free and its price, exacted by merciless creditors, already caused his feet to stumble. It had amused them to demand his line should end before he did. Stripped of joy as well as centuries, he might see the futures displayed today, but he would not be glad of it.

It was thus a slow and painful progress for him to re-ascend Windover, in order to see his family die.

'Hell's boundaries, you gave me a shock! What are you doing here?'

Ellen Oglethorpe looked over Theophilus's shoulders at the empty Whitehall corridor beyond.

'Why so horrified?' she asked, feigning offence. 'What's more natural than a wife should come to see her husband? Up to something are we? I don't *see* a giggle of ladies-in-waiting with you. Rochester tells me dressing them as page-boys is the latest lark: was that your plan for the evening 'fore I spoilt it? It's an intriguing tickle-me-fancy – and might explain the frigid welcome . . .'

Theophilus always had difficulty spotting a joke unless it came up close and introduced itself plainly.

'You're mad, woman!' he spluttered. 'If you listen to Rochester you'd believe all courtiers mate with squirrels and Manxmen. I've got better things to do. It's just . . . I thought you were at Westbrook.'

'I was. Now I'm here. There's a reason.'

Theophilus didn't hear her. He was justifying his neglect of his family to himself.

'The King demands my permanent presence. He'll confirm that. There's news expected from . . . somewhere,' he ended limply.

'The Elves, Theo, yes, I know.'

'That's right, and when it comes he wants me by his side to . . . what did you say?'

'I *know*.'

Theophilus eyed her cautiously. He was well aware that in verbal duels he wore lead boots against her spring-heeled shoes.

'Do you? Know what?'

'Everything that you do: about that.' She lightly brushed the 'sabre' Excalibur attached to his belt and smiled flirtatiously. 'About Arthur and Monmouth and all those other trifles.'

In his mind's eye, if not in actual fact, Theophilus's jaw was upon his cravat. He should not have bothered trying to restrain it, for words would have escaped him more easily thereby.

'How?' he snapped, not sure whether to rejoice or rage.

'The knowledge came rearward,' she explained, 'and by dint of radical gardening.'

At that point he could have stumbled down a treacherous slope of pedestrian questions and arrived breathless at the bottom, much later but little wiser. Instead, trusting to instincts and first notions, he resisted the temptation to clerkish linear-thought. Taking the easier path of wisdom, he chose just to admire the view and admit that his wife was a remarkable woman.

'I'm glad,' he said. 'Now it's shared.'

They were silent for a moment and Ellen looked about, recalling pre-motherhood days, now distant and unreal as the stars, when the King's ripped shirts and Lady Portsmouth's politicking had seemed important.

'Our quarters were near here, remember?' she asked.

'Opposite each other, I recall. That was handy – being at the back of the Palace, I mean, near the steps down to the Thames barges.'

'That's right.' Ellen smiled again. 'Charles was very clever in allocating those particular rooms. It meant you could slip in and out very easily.'

The upright military man just managed to stifle an unrequested smirk.

'There were,' he admitted, 'some instances, when your proximity was convenient. One may have crept across the landing once or twice . . .'

'As loud as an elephant on heat; always finding that ill-fitting floorboard. Everyone heard and knew – and laughed to see us at last conform.'

'It wasn't quite the standard game,' Theophilus protested. 'We married.'

'Eventually, and only just in time. Baby Lewis was well on the way.'

Oglethorpe wouldn't have it that they were just as bad as the rest.

'We made the effort,' he maintained. 'There's a difference.'

Ellen laughingly agreed.

'Oh yes, there was that. Don't think you got through that door on a whim. I chose carefully – and well, as it turns out. Lewis misses you – as do I. When will you be home again?'

Theophilus shook his wig sadly. It seemed a time for truth rather than well-intended lies.

'No idea. We totter on the precipice of other parties' own good time. They dole out the courses of this gruesome meal at a leisurely pace. Charles won't release me until the next bowel-churning plate arrives. It could be any period, measured in days or months or . . .' Theophilus grimaced, rejecting the next increment of time. 'Besides, Monmouth has fled the realm and an entirely more earthly invasion is expected from that quarter. My services are likewise required for that prosaic eventuality.

180

However, Madame, in the meanwhile you are infinitely welcome . . .'

His attention had wandered to the panorama of dusk over Whitehall visible through the nearby window. It was seized back by a rustle of silk and cotton from Ellen's direction.

'As you are, kind sir . . .' she lisped.

Theophilus looked and gaped.

'Madame! Cover yourself! This is a public corridor . . .'

'We spoke of our old accommodation, Theo. Do you recall *these* quarters?'

Acting independently of orders his hands formed claws and advanced – only to be leashed back at the last moment.

'Most nights,' he husked, answering truthfully. 'And mornings and afternoons.'

'Is that your room nearby?'

'It is.'

'Then ignore my piteous whispers of *no, no, oh!*'

Oglethorpe had swept her up and over his shoulder, like a sultan taking his choice of captured Constantinople. Then, halfway over the threshold and engaged in intimate study of her nearest portions, he noticed something.

'You've been stung,' he said.

Ellen proved she was just as capable of encouraging, flattering feminine ploys as the more practised Arabella Churchill.

'"Twas only a little prick,' she teased. 'I hardly felt a thing. Whereas *now* . . .'

'Naughty boy, you shall stay as long as you wish. We love your presence in our country.'

From Mary Stuart such words could be accepted at face value. Monmouth knew not to make that mistake about Dutch William's agreement.

'Just so,' said the pale *Stadtholder*, aware that myriad courtiers were listening in. 'Our welcome to you no bounds knows.'

The only other time Monmouth had seen a face so consistently devoid of expression was on a hanged man brought to the dissection table. If William of Orange ever had any human

181

emotions in him they'd died long ago for lack of sunshine, through never being allowed out to play.

'You are too kind,' answered the exiled Duke, bowing his thanks and going along with the charade. 'But I hesitate to impose. Perhaps I could find employ with the Holy Roman Emperor – though that might involve campaigning near the Rhine which, for private reasons, I am loathe to do. Still, there are bound to be outlets for my talents *somewhere*. One would rather take service with the Turk than cause you embarrassment or harm.'

Mary's warm nature was happily missing all the sub-texts in the conversation.

'Stop your jabberment,' she said, smiling down on him from her tulip-festooned throne. 'If Uncle Charles and you have had another falling out, that need not concern us. You will stay here and brighten our court until he comes to his senses.'

'Yesss,' "agreed" William, nodding his wigless, avian head. 'Our tulip – I mean guest you will be absolutely – if nothing more.'

Monmouth took that to be a reference to the incident during his previous visit. William had pinched his bottom and then, not meeting the desired response, passed it off as a joke. For sure, the Duke was keen to cement powerful alliances – but not at any price. The Stadtholder had sulked for a day but then accepted he'd drawn a blank. After that he was as icy to Monmouth as he was to everyone else. It was as near to forgiveness as he came.

King Charles of England however, had never been pardoned. His tipsy jests before, during and right through William and Mary's wedding day six years before, remained fresh in the Stadtholder's memory. That merry monarch had accompanied them right to the nuptial bed with jests about '*putting his past* behind *him*' and '*forsaking the* Netherlands *tonight*'. Even the innocent Archbishop of Canterbury eventually got the point. Drawing the four-poster curtains on them, Charles had ringingly recommended '*Now nephew, to your work! St. George for England! A change is as good as a rest!*' William had smiled like

182

he was sucking razorblades but vowed to have revenge. That long-awaited moment had now arrived. This viper in England's bosom would find nurture here.

Mary only saw a handsome young rascal-relative who'd gotten into hot water. In the same way she rescued cat-savaged birds or depressed-looking dogs, it seemed only right to offer sanctuary. She didn't understand there might be deeper implications. In fact she was blessed in not understanding much at all. Raised in the all female and fervidly lesbian atmosphere of Richmond Palace, along with Ann her sister and half a dozen other aristocratic *gels*, her education had solely concerned the depravity of papists. That, once drummed in, was deemed sufficient, and if she cared to 'marry' an older girl, Lady Apsley, as Ann did with Sarah Churchill, no one paid much heed. In consequence, the ways of the world brushed only lightly against her – to the great benefit of her happiness. On being told, at the age of fifteen, she must marry – for real and to a *man*, Prince William – she'd cried the whole afternoon and following day, but ultimately her innocence was her salvation. She did not see her husband's strangeness or ponder on their lack of children or how good-looking all the male servants happened to be. Then, because it was what one ought to do, she made herself fond of William. In the end it had all worked out rather well.

'You dance so well and converse so sweetly,' she told Monmouth, 'we shall have you. Our stolid court is thus enlivened. England's loss will be our gain until Charles comes round.'

William nodded and rose. 'May that day be soon,' he said, 'but not too soon. Meanwhile let us make arrangements for your diversion.' He stepped forward to join the Duke, raising his skinny arm to link his shoulders – and then thought better of it: the latest grenadier was insanely jealous. He and Monmouth forged into the crowd, ostensibly convivial host and guest.

'So when do you make your move,' he whispered, his sliver-thin lips returning to their normal twenty-past-eight.

'Not yet,' answered the Duke, seeing this was a time to be candid. 'I will charm my way back to Charles's favour. My hour will come when God calls him home.'

183

'Word is you tried to remove him.'

'My own father? Never!' The words denied it but the tone meant *'well, yes'*.

William was sympathetic. Happily, *his* father had been seen off by smallpox nine days before his son entered the world. It greatly simplified things. He didn't approve of sentiment in politics.

'I agree. To wait the best policy is. Bide till the succession. James is papist and thus repugnant to a Protestant nation.'

'And thus to yourself also,' Monmouth reminded. William shrugged.

'The tags serve to distinguish friend and foe,' he replied, 'but it is all one to me. They may call themselves black and white for all I care. I take it you do not *believe* any of the nonsense.'

'Oh, no,' the Duke reassured him.

'That is good. Otherwise your judgement trust I cannot. Very well, I shall help. The English Ambassador asks me to arrest you but it will not be. Fobbed off he will be. When the day comes, guns and ships you will have.'

'And men?'

The Stadtholder halted, as though a sensitive spot had been touched.

'Understand,' he wheezed, momentarily afflicted by his asthma, 'this great gamble yours alone is. I cannot be too forward – England a great navy has! Many English conspirators this land harbours. Recruit you must amongst them.'

'I've already started. The dregs of the Rye House business ended up here, to join the Cromwellian colony. There's a mad, murderous preacher called Ferguson who daily implores me to invade.'

'These are the sort of men,' William agreed, recovering from his panic attack. 'Best to receive the crown in London when Charles goes to judgement – but if love you cannot make him, then sail with fanatics of that ilk. Have you plans to tell?'

Monmouth could not repress a secret smile. This stolen-sealand kingling could little guess what allies he had to call upon.

'The aboriginal Celts will rise for me,' he confided. 'That is arranged. Even so, I have many options. It might suit me to join them via a remote landing, to first weaken the English by inciting civil war.'

William regarded him with new respect.

'This is good and I like,' he said. 'But best it is to triumph with words and charm. You have much of the last. Employ that which you waste to tip Dutch court-ladies on their back to win your Father's love.'

'It's as good as done,' answered the Duke, tormenting William with a dazzling smile. 'What can stop me?'

Extracts deciphered from the diary of the Duke of Monmouth:

1685. January 5. I received a letter from Lord Halifax marked by the King in the margin . . . that in February I should certainly have leave to return . . . that the Duke of York had no suspicion, notwithstanding my reception here.

1685. February 3. A letter from Halifax, that my business was almost as well as done, but must be so sudden as not to leave room for the Duke of York's party to counterplot . . .

1685. February 16. The sad news of his death . . . O, cruel fate!

When Charles II went to bed, very late, on Sunday, the first of February, 1685, an untoward thing occurred. At the door of his bedchamber a sigh from nowhere blew the only candle out. The King and his companions, old Earl Ailesbury and Harry Killigrew, stood for a moment in the Whitehall gallery's inky dark and puzzled at the absence of any gust to account for it. Then they laughed at the happenstance. Up to then, Charles had been light-hearted, having just emerged from the Countess of Portsmouth's chambers (and the Countess). Once light was restored, the Gentlemen-of-the-Bedchamber, believing the world was all there was, thought no more of it. The King, however, was secretly less sanguine.

He concealed his feelings as he had all his life, and bantered to his old friends about the new residence taking shape in

Winchester. By next week, he said, he hoped the roof might be leaded and the place fit for regal habitation. Away from London's prying eye, it would be ideal for his scientific investigations into the properties of mercury and lady's maids' netherlips and suchlike intriguing topics.

His friends laughed again and Ailesbury asked for a commission in the Guards for a cousin of his. The King was in his nightgown by then and making water in a po. He seemed cheerful enough and told the Earl he'd be happy to bestow such a trifle.

The following night was restless. A huge fire of scotch coal made the room hot and airless and the King's hounds stirred and prowled without cease. Ailesbury and Killigrew were plagued by the room's numerous clocks, gifts over the years from the monarchs of Christendom, which seemed to have slipped out of sync. The striking of every quarter, separately defined by each, chopped their repose into jagged bits. Charles slept through it all but tossed and turned, ill at ease. Several times he mumbled in distress and sought to wrestle free from his blankets.

A new day came at last and Charles woke between four and five, as was his custom. Though he pretended otherwise, the kindest witness could see he was not well. His face was puffed and as pale as paper. Most mornings he would play tennis or stroll in his Physic Garden where he grew herbs for his laboratory, or else trot through St. James Park and feed the maimed crane he'd repaired with a jointed wooden leg. Even the offer of a blow-job from the expert Duchess of Portsmouth did not intrigue as usual. No longer tempted by the *'mouthful of fresh air'* (or anything else) and *'a little ingenious raillery'* he once so loved, he declined each in slurred speech.

The weak illusion of normality lasted till his barber arrived. Consideration of a shave seemed too much to endure, and Charles shrieked in pain, falling back in a fit. He foamed at the mouth and thrashed about on the floor, eyes screwing horribly up till just white showed. Only the lancing of a vein and generous bleeding (so they thought) saved him from death there and then.

186

James was fetched, arriving breathless with a boot on one foot and a slipper on the other, and his heart was torn – because he straightaway knew. Whilst the emetics and purgatives, the blisters and pans of hot coal, were applied, the Duke bid swift farewell to his brother, and forced himself to think of mere worldly matters. The nation's ports were ordered closed, lest Monmouth be advised, and the Guards were posted about town against an insurrection. It pained him to think that so many malignants awaited this day, to rejoice and make their move.

About midday, Charles rallied, despite all the doctors had done. In a voice already halfway from some other place, he asked for his wife – and Theophilus Oglethorpe.

'Though there be but t-t-two doors to his room, the people we can trust do not outnumber them. What a s-sad comment on this life.'

'No one shall enter through either,' Theophilus told James. 'Ellen and I will guard them well.'

The Duke already had proof of that. Mistress Oglethorpe had routed an imposing delegation of Anglican clergy that very morning, threatening them with a chamber-pot and hatpin when they imperiously sought audience with the dying Head of their Church.

'We shall not forget,' said James, gratefully, calling that noisy incident to mind. Neither would 'Old Patch', Bishop of Winchester, who'd been anointed with the one implement and prodded with the other. There'd ensued an ugly tussle as Archbishop strived with Bishop to get the retaliatory sabre back in its scabbard.

'In particular, beware the Church of England,' James advised, 'for they've not given up yet.'

They ought to have done, for they'd received little encouragement to date. In the two days he'd been slipping away Charles had refused their offer of the sacrament, either saying it was too soon or, when the pain bit, denying they were *real* bishops. His secret disdain for their Church was long suspected but still a shock to hear announced out loud. Even little Bishop

Ken of Bath and Wells, a man of known saintliness, could not persuade him. The King had nothing but respect for the man, even though – or perhaps because – he'd refused to share lodgings with Nell Gwyn when Charles came visiting; but for his office there seemed none. One and all, with greater or less charm, they were rebuffed.

The strange spectacle was enough to stir the slumbering piety of Ellen's ex-employer, the Duchess of Portsmouth. A Catholic herself, she contacted the French Ambassador who in turn alerted the distracted James to his plain duty. Like a veil falling from his eyes, he realised there were more important issues than placing his behind securely on the still-warm throne. The Duke had many faults but once shown a moral obligation he was at it like a fox with a hen. The Oglethorpes' fiery talents were directly put to use in securing some Royal privacy.

Theophilus didn't catch the question James put to the King as he made to leave the room, but Charles' reply was loud and clear: 'Yes, yes, with all my heart!'

In the England of the Popish Plot and riotous Guy Fawkes nights, it was no easy matter to lay hands on a Catholic priest. For them to be both alive and in the Kingdom was a capital crime. The Queen was attended by monks from her native Portugal but none of them spoke English. Fetching a chaplain from one of the Embassies would attract undue attention. They were in a quandary till Ellen Oglethorpe recalled Father John Huddleston, a Benedictine who resided at Whitehall. Her lodgings as Royal seamstress had been near his. Long ago he'd saved Charles's life in the mad flight from Worcester, and, his loyalty proven beyond reproach, he was always excepted by name from every step of anti-papist legislation. Fortune smiled and he was soon found and brought, more than willing to risk his life a second time.

Excalibur to hand, Theophilus stood guard outside while the dying King revisited his little sins and then came home to the faith of his fathers.

'He will n-not be long now.'

For a second Theophilus thought it was James. He was wrong. Arthur had mimicked his voice. Oglethorpe whirled round to face the spectre sitting, vast and vile, on one of the broad sunlit windowsills overlooking the Thames. Though tired by his night-long vigil a sword was soon between him and this other King.

Arthur either felt or feigned no fear of it. On the contrary, his empty eye-sockets regarded Excalibur with love.

'Yes, please,' he said, in his own withered voice, extending a mail-shod claw.

Theophilus realised his mistake and stepped back, sheathing the blade.

'It is mine,' whispered Arthur, appealing to the human sense of property.

'*Was*, perhaps,' counted Theophilus, not taken in by wrong's misuse of right.

'And shall be again,' the King persisted. 'But it must be given; willingly given. The presiding Power demands the owner's permission; be they false holders or not. As you humans say: "*possession is nine-tenths of the Law*" – and there are Lawmakers even I must obey. You will give me the sword.'

Theophilus was about to say '*don't hold your breath*', but saw in time it was hardly appropriate. Arthur no longer had need of air.

'Tell me something,' he ventured, seeing the King was minded to conversation rather than violence. 'What if I should call the guards? What if we should hose you down with musket shot? Would that be an end to our troubles?'

Arthur was absolutely still, as fixed as a statue, and Theophilus liked that least of all. There was no gauging his reactions.

'Unlikely,' came the hissed reply. 'Some bones might be broken, my scanty chest further sundered, but the force that binds all would go on. Should I be at any risk I would answer in kind and my power, I think, would be the stronger. Besides, it cannot be, for I have seized this room. Time is excluded and there will be no interruptions. Life goes on around but not here.'

'I might be needed . . .' said Theophilus, concerned.

'And a facsimile you would answer the call,' Arthur reassured him. 'I have placed us slightly sideways and no one will notice. We must have time to talk.'

Oglethorpe would have asked *what about* but he was damned if he'd play by the kidnapper's rules. The King seemed unconcerned by the ensuing silence.

'There is a false dawn,' he mused eventually. 'Charles fools them again by making a last stand. He was never one to husband his spark.'

Theophilus had no choice but to believe him. When there is only one source of news people will make do with it.

'How is he?' he asked.

Arthur seemed almost sad. 'Fading,' he replied. 'But with customary charm. He has just apologised to the waiting horde *"for being so long a-dying"*. Now he implores James to *"let not poor Nelly starve"*. Having embraced the false fantasy of religion he goes easily, without fear of the everlasting dark.'

'To beyond your reach, at least,' said Theophilus, combatively.

'What makes you so sure, human? What is your knowledge of such things?'

The *'human'* wouldn't be drawn. He looked round the now confined seeming anteroom, wondering whether to attempt escape. He suspected it might prove undignified.

'It would,' confirmed Arthur. 'Listen to my words and then we will soon be done. Be reasonable – and patriotic: you can save your beloved country from endless harm.'

Theophilus objected to attempts to play him like a harpsichord.

'I've learnt,' he answered back, 'that my kind can expect little from you.'

The King appeared interested by the response. Perhaps he sensed an opening.

'Ah, now there you are wrong,' he said. 'What allies I have is of no interest to me, so long as I have some. Last time the Celts served well enough, and it's simplest for them to do so again –

they are prepared ground and the prophecies are the seed in it. But there's no other reason. I could just as well lead you and do great things for your nation. Besides, one was obliged to ride the Celts hard, as you'll note from their earliest legends of me. The "good and fair" King is a much later fiction. Doubtless a certain resentment abides. It might suit to dispense with them and rally other foot-soldiers. Had you thought of that?'

'No,' said Theophilus, bluntly; refusing to think of it.

'Even Monmouth is a means to an end. One by one I have bargained his secrets from him, till his presence is almost super-fluous. Once I'm recovered enough to unleash my Knights it will hardly matter when or where he invades. Any rising might serve as cover, an English one as good as a Celtic. I require only two things. One is a diversion, which Monmouth will provide. The second is in that scabbard attached to your belt. I *need* it.'

Theophilus's straightforward mind chewed on that, vaguely sensing some leverage.

'If you can do all this,' he asked, waving to indicate the iso-lated room, Arthur's presence there, his survival into the modern age – and all the other wonders he'd seen and suffered from of late, 'why do you await a simple blade?'

'That is easy,' replied the King, his bony arm extended once again. 'Even you can comprehend. I cannot trust my essence to mere flesh and blood. It lasts, as you see,' he demonstrated by plucking at the dried sinews working his raised hand, 'but not for an indefinite span. I thought – and still do think – it safer to place most of that which is me into more durable form. The bulk of what I am, or could be, is in that sword, whereas the "I" you see is but a husk, a portion of the whole: a rearguard, to put it in terms you would approve.'

'So how did you come to be divided?'

'Treachery, deceit, betrayal: normally weapons I wield myself but lethal nonetheless against me. I thought that virtue was just a chain around my foes but at Camlann I learnt its absence sometimes costs. I died for a while and my attention was stunned. Excalibur was taken and concealed. When at last I reawoke, we called one to the other and like magnets started

191

the road to reunion. That process is now almost complete. To you falls the honour of the final yard. Pass it to me.'

'I shall not.' Theophilus sounded stout enough but in reality he pondered what there was to do. A being of Arthur's size demanded a double-charged musket at least. Fortunately, the King showed not the slightest sign of hostile intent. On the contrary, he grew more and more reasonable.

'To what purpose is this negativity?' he asked. 'What end do you seek?'

'Yours.' Oglethorpe's reply was succinct but heartfelt.

Arthur lowered his head in apparent despair. 'Do you believe the *Elves?*' he spat in exasperation. 'Stealers of babies and haters of men? Do you take all you know of me from *them?*'

'Well . . .' Doomed by upbringing to be obliging, Theophilus had to admit there was the ghost of the genesis of an embryo of a good point in that.

'Well,' said Arthur, 'it is time to look and learn another story.' He waved at the high window behind him and the scene changed.

Whitehall, Westminster, the Thames were gone, replaced by an equally recognisable landscape. It wasn't a view of Glastonbury he'd seen before, not being a bird or having access to aircraft, but there was no mistaking it. Arthur creakingly turned his head to study the panorama along with Theophilus.

'You see a possibility so strong,' he said, 'it is up and running, parallel to this time. The merest push to the fabric of reality brings it into being.'

'The town is bigger,' observed Oglethorpe, intrigued, despite all his misgivings. 'But neat though . . .' This looked better than anything the Elf-King had shown.

'Humanity thrives and prospers under my rule,' Arthur agreed. 'Consider all the surrounding green and tranquil countryside. Ponder the modest and quiet roads. Yet this is the new capital of England, a mighty realm and seat of happiness. Note the fortifications and tokens of war.'

Theophilus peered closer. 'I don't see any.'

'Exactly. There are none. There is no need. In this time they are but bad memories.'

'What, no war?' Oglethorpe knew his religion decreed he ought to be pleased, but no one swallows the bitter pill of redundancy with pleasure.

'This is a future time,' the King comforted him. 'But not far future. In reaching it there were struggles with men of ill will. You would still find employment – and fun.'

'It's not that I enjoy . . .' Theophilus protested, for form's sake. 'Only . . .'

'Peace is not made by milksops,' Arthur agreed. 'You do not have to explain.'

He moved aside to let Oglethorpe come closer. The window showed a wider scene than human eyes would normally permit. He felt he could see all over England – and beyond – and though he looked hard, he discerned nothing to distress.

'And in a few short years . . .' said the King. The view changed, though very little. This capital of England was still a small market town, although grown in prosperity. If anything, the amount of green had increased. Then Theophilus noticed golden veins in the ground, tracking across the landscape and glowing – dimly at first and then in full glory. The network emanated from the Tor and spread all over the Land. He could see they were not roads or pathways, but the evidence of some marvellous energy.

'Mother Earth at last recovers,' explained Arthur. 'Man joins in partnership with her, forgetting black dreams of dominance and rape. She smiles in return. The ley-lines awake, the old powers revive. Humankind and Nature join hand in marriage and . . .'

The process reached critical mass, and Glastonbury and England and the World burst into life, bathed and suffused in wonderful light. The Earth was made anew.

'Behold the new Jerusalem,' said Arthur.

Theophilus forgot all the sorrows he had ever had, and all the strains built into being human slipped away. Even seen remotely this age reached out to him and healed. He undid the scabbard from his belt.

193

'I . . .'

Arthur graciously understood. He held out his hand. 'There is no need to say sorry. Your King forgives.'

If all his vices were subdued, Oglethorpe's virtues were enhanced by the vision. Ever-present loyalty and honour recalled oaths of allegiance to another King who had been good to him. Charles, not Arthur, was still his sovereign.

'I must just check,' he murmured, apologetic but resolved.

Arthur realised the peril, but too late. His roar of '*No!*' could not prevent Theophilus touching Excalibur to the window.

The new scene mortified as much as the other pleased. Arthur's false vision drained into the soil of the true picture. In fact there was precious little soil for it to occupy for in most places this Glastonbury was down to bedrock. Oglethorpe didn't know what pylons and power-stations and 'freeways' were, but he could deplore their mastery of the landscape.

'Lies!' he spat, reversing the sword point-wards to the King. Arthur now found grounds for terror in a beloved thing and retreated before it. He said nothing, knowing there were no words to endear the blackened desolation just shown to an uncorrupted human. A foul breeze, the merest token of the storms which raged within, emerged from this future to make the room acrid.

'Your own magic betrays you,' said Theophilus, calm and deadly and powered by fury, 'as you sought to betray me.' Excalibur was now drawn, its sharp tip aimed at Arthur's empty eyes.

'We shall yet be friends,' said the King evenly. 'And that is the worst of it for you. The old Oglethorpe will be so lost and remade that you will lust after the future you now despise.'

Theophilus advanced crab-like warily into striking range. 'Never!'

The blade turned sleepily in his hand, somehow sensing a mission not to its tastes. Arthur observed that.

'It knows me, human. It *is* me. I need fear no harm.' The tone convinced but caution in his stance belied his words.

Theophilus tightened his grip.

'I can overman it,' he spat, wrenching the weapon round to obey his will. 'And you!'

The stroke was a treat to see, abducting the extra effort required for countermanding Excalibur to add speed and force to the blow. Even so, the mutinous spirit within decreed a crucial turning aside, a mere one or two degrees. It permitted Arthur to save his head.

'Soon,' that King repeated. His cracked voice was free of doubt. 'Soon we shall be friends. But first you shall acquire *discipline*. I tire of persuasion. Henceforth, each time we fruitlessly meet, I may deprive you of something you love.'

He again raised his huge right arm, this time as though lifting an unseen weight on his palm.

'Or perhaps some*one* you love.' The iron gauntlet slowly squeezed shut.

From King Charles's bedchamber there came the sound of women's wailing and the torn howls of men.

King Arthur's future vanished when he did. Theophilus could once again observe the contemporary Thames. A second later the door to the bedchamber slammed open. James, Duke of York, came out, unaware and unseeing, wrapped in a world of his own. He had no eyes or feelings save for his own pain. The lingering taint of the cancerous Glastonbury did not touch him.

'My beloved brother,' he said softly, not knowing who he was talking to, 'is gone.'

Theophilus Oglethorpe knelt and wept also, now sure beyond any further temptings as to where his loyalties lay.

'Your Majesty,' he said. 'Long live the King!'

Ellen Oglethorpe re-affixed her spectacles and had another go at it.

'*Dearest Wyfe*', the letter read (probably) – a warm and promising start. '*I rite in haste.*' That was nothing but the baldest truth. Theophilus's missives were always pushed by time or lack of words. '*He sails & so we ride – to the West – tho that is secrete so do not rede that part or else forgit it.*'

195

It was a tall order but Ellen dutifully pretended to comply.

'*Yu no how our* ~~separ seper sepper~~ *parting pains me and i never-the-least respectfully ask yu recall me kind-ly amidst this grim bisyness. Sell the orchard crop to Perrior the Mayor for he is a honest fellawe – not to Master Janaway for he is a tippler and a rogge – or else put it to scrumpy you-self.*

'Ever roughly considerate,' she thought. 'I'd been wondering about that.'

'*Meanwhile be arseurred that cum civil-warre, dis-comfort or the reaper, my first and last thort shall or should be of yu.*

I remain, madame, your devoted husbind'

Theophilus Oglethorpe. Gent.

It once again occurred to Ellen to ponder what precisely Theophilus had done during all his expensive years of education. She was equally inspired to clasp the childlike communication to her heart.

'May God be between you and harm in all the empty places you tread,' she prayed.

'Amen,' echoed Lewis, who had read alongside her.

There was also a second, more polished, billet-doux. The Duke of Monmouth had written from the Hague.

'*Madame,*' it said, in some other man's impeccable copperplate, '*my breast is fair riven when I contemplate the impression you may have gained from our last, soured, meeting, or the wicked tales that mayhap have since been imparted to you. If only Heaven would relent that I might correct and reverse any poison attributed to my name during this wicked season. And if, dearest lady, in forgiving any fault of mine, you might recall sweet friendship past and dampen the anger raging in your headstrong husband's soul, then I would be so . . .*'

Ellen put the remaining pages down unread.

'Assist your mama, Lewis,' she asked her son, handing him the Duke's bulky letter, 'and convey this to its proper place.'

The child obediently trotted off, and then paused to consider

196

just where that might be.

'Mama?'

'Fold and quarter each sheaf,' Ellen advised him. 'And then hang the divided sheets in the servant's privy.'

There at least, she felt sure, it would find a receptive audience.

'He never misses his Thursday bowls,' said Mrs Tye. 'Not ever.'

Mr Gregory Alford, Mayor of Lyme Regis and fellow pillar of the Town's Bowls Club, knew that to be true but was unwilling to accept the implications.

'Maybe the Frenchies' hospitality is good,' he replied unconvincingly. 'Mr Tye likes a cup of wine . . .'

Mrs Tye snorted her disbelief, and the little group on the Cobb stared once again at the three ships anchored off Lyme Harbour. Their silent anonymity made them seem sinister. Long hours had passed since Tye, Customs 'Surveyor' for the Port of Lyme, rowed out to enquire their business.

'If they're French – or Dutch,' (this being the other clutched-straw suggestion) 'then I'm a mussulman,' said the tigerish Deputy 'Searcher of the Customs', Samuel Dassell. 'Which I'm not. If they're furriners or up to any good, why don't they show a flag?'

There was no answer to that, though the Mayor tried to construct one. He'd been seeking an innocent explanation for the visitors since they were first spotted at daybreak. The strong off-shore wind made their plying inwards slow and laborious, giving him ample time to cast around for a likely happy ending to this June day. Sadly, the frigate and its companions, a *pink* and a *dogger*, had not cooperated. It wasn't so long ago that Barbary Corsairs had plied these waters, in competition with the sea-scum of all Europe, on the sniff for easy pickings. The English Navy had put pay to them, more or less, making it safe to live on the Isle of Wight or venture forth to fish, but right now Mayor Alford would have almost welcomed such an uncompli-cated explanation. In the darker cupboards of his mind a more monstrous proposition was knocking to come out.

'Their gun ports are closed,' he offered hopefully, knowing full well how weak-kneed he sounded. 'There is that . . .'

'Well then,' barked Dassell, apparently coming to his own decision, 'let's test their Christian passivity! Break out the gunpowder and bark a hello.'

Mayor Alford shook his head firmly. 'You can't.'

'I'm taking charge here,' replied the Customsman, drawing himself to his full five feet and adjusting his periwig. 'So what's to stop me? The Town cannon works, don't it?'

Alford had no way of knowing but plumped for a positive response.

'I expect so.'

'So where's the powder then?'

The Mayor smiled in what he thought a placatory fashion.

'There ain't none. That's what I meant.'

'What?

'It went bad: a long time ago – under a previous mayor. Have you any idea just how expensive the stuff is to buy? Besides, it's dangerous . . .'

Dassell wrenched his wig from his head and danced a swift jig on it. The spectators quietly observed, recollecting the scene for future generations.

'Well, call me a catamite,' he said, when he'd done, 'but I thought that was the idea of the stuff. Do you mean to say . . .'

'There might be some on the *Saucy Sue*,' interrupted the Mayor hurriedly, before the reproach got too memorable. 'It's just in from Barbados and they carry a brace of cannon. I'm sure the Captain . . .'

'And call out the militia!' ordered Dassell, already on his way to the *Sue*.

Alford was glad of the man's abruptness. Leisure might have permitted realisation that muskets need powder just as much as their larger brethren.

The Mail coach from London generally rolled into Lyme around five-ish on Thursday. This week it brought official warning that the Duke of Monmouth had set sail from Holland

198

with a posse of rebels borne in three ships. Their presumed destination was a south coast port.

The revelation supplied the key that let Mr Alford's darkest suspicions free and out to play. It unhappily coincided with the customs-house boat's return, along with three others, crammed to sinking point with strangers bearing arms. The Mayor took that as permission to get on his horse and ride.

The armed forces of Lyme Regis had all heard the call but most declined to answer. They sensibly saw little use in pointing empty, rusting, firearms at a cause many could only commend. When the invaders landed only one militia red-coat, John Holloway, tobacconist of Lyme, barred the way. Monmouth's army of eighty fanatics decently paused to allow the lone defender time for fresh considerations. A few seconds later the Duke had his first mainland recruit.

As decisions go, it was reasonable enough at the time, but ultimately fatal. Like the simple Charmouth fisherman who'd earlier came aboard the frigate *Helderenberg* to sell herring, Mr Holloway had started a walk that would end on the gallows.

England's defences thus swept away, and it being plain there'd be no undignified scuffle, Monmouth came ashore. He was dressed in purple, livened only by the splendid star of the Garter on his breast. A tall slender figure, he looked every inch the saviour of Faith and Nation. Behind him, confirming the point for the slow of understanding, was carried a great banner of green and gold, bearing the motto 'Fear Nothing but God'. It amused the Duke to delude the yokels with a flag in the Elven colours, openly proclaiming a hidden truth. If they knew but a fraction of what he did about the Null, that great 'Nothing', they would indeed fear it.

A quarter-century back, King Charles, his father, had landed at Dover on the way to reclaim his throne and Land. The Duke had consulted eye-witness accounts of the scene and rehearsed its imitation during the ten days at sea. Falling to his knees on the beach to pray, he implored in ringing tones, the Almighty's blessing on this sacred undertaking. Then, peeking through his fingertips, he saw the Lymians were lapping it up.

His devotions were heard out in silence but when he rose and drew his sword, the greeting crowd could contain themselves no more. Planted agents supplied the actual chorus but it was taken up with glee.

'A Monmouth! A Monmouth! The Protestant Religion!'

A cloud of well-wishers accompanied him into the Town, the more forward rushing up to kiss his elegant hands. By the time they got to the Cobb many had joined the cause. Customsman Dassell, who'd been occupied rolling powder barrels from out of the *Saucy Sue*, noted that and decided he could make better use of his time. By then Mayor Alford was well on the way to Honiton and the Militia forces gathered there.

The Duke's in-joke standard was set up by Church Cliff. Men jostled around it to enlist. Monmouth laughed and reproved them, urging the mob to patience.

'Restrain your elbows, lads,' he advised. 'Be you twenty or thirty thousand men, I've got arms enough for all!'

In fact, that was the one scorpion-in-the-privy. He only wished it were true. The Null, or its current King Arthur manifestation, had rather let him down. Their promised funding, in the form of ancient buried gold and bullion, had failed to arrive. It had taken the pawning of all he owned, and Lady Henrietta Wentworth's jewellery as well, to get this far. Just hiring the *Helderenberg*, a mere thirty-two gunner, had cost £5000. Putting fifteen hundred muskets, pikes and breastplates, plus four small cannon and an expert to work them, in the two smaller ships had cleared him out of everything. Suggestions that Lady Henrietta went to work on her back to raise further sums hadn't met with much welcome. She'd countered that he should come to a similar arrangement with William of Orange – and the subject was allowed to drop. It was a shame though. She was so . . . mettlesome and inventive that, given enough warning, they could have darkened the sea with their fleet and arrived here with an armada clad in gold. Still, it was not to be.

The way things were going they might not notice the lack of cash. All of the Town ventured out to hear the Duke's proclamation but even before that his army had doubled in size. The

'Independent Lyme Regiment', eighty strong and growing, was born without so much as being asked.

Robert 'The Plotter' Ferguson, preacher and wildman, had written the ringing declaration, but couldn't be trusted to deliver it. Whilst a master of the rabble-rousing phrase, the Scot was prone to pistol-waving and profanity to emphasise his argument. His volcanic delivery would terrify rather than convince. A calmer, more comely, youth was deputised and stood up in the marketplace to read the Duke's claim.

'Hear ye, hear ye,' he called. 'Attend the declaration of James, Duke of Monmouth, and the Noblemen, Gentlemen, and others now in arms for the defence and vindication of the Protestant Religion, and the Laws, Rights, and Privileges of England, from the invasion made upon them; and for delivering the Kingdom from the usurpation and tyranny of James Duke of York . . .'

It was extraordinarily effective, Old Testament cadences meeting and mating with ruffian slang, to provide something incendiary for everyone. Those who thought themselves 'of the better sort' heard and approved of the call for constitutional democracy: free elections, annual parliaments and *Habeas Corpus*. The more normal relished the charges against 'King James': that he poisoned his brother, started the Great Fire of London and was on at least 'how do you do?' terms with Satan.

Even the Papists themselves, had there been any dense enough to stick around, were nodded at. Amidst the obligatory references to 'Romish idolatries' the wisely absent Catholics were assured of survival, providing they 'withdrew from the tents of our enemies'. It was very reasonable, considering.

No less reasonable were Monmouth's personal claims. Though confident of his legitimacy and right to the throne, he left the matter to the decision of an unsuborned Parliament. For the moment he was content to be just 'Captain-General of the Protestant Forces of this Kingdom.' Resolving the paradox of there being two would-be James IIs was thus happily postponed.

Ferguson well knew that speeches were like sex: the aftermath of both contained illogical guilt at getting so worked up.

It was always an idea therefore to end by fastening one's teeth in the listener's ideals, providing a whimper not a bang. Pitched in general enough terms the targets were thus left exalted instead of furtive.

'People of England,' the youth concluded, 'all we ask is that never more may it be in the power of any person on the throne to deprive their subjects of their rights, or subvert the fundamental laws of Government designed for their preservation. Now let us play the man for our people and may the Lord do that which seemeth good unto him! Will you join us?'

By nightfall of the second day, there were fifteen hundred rebels under arms and blood had been shed.

Samuel Dassell had been on the edge of the marketplace crowd and, a conspicuous abstainer from the general enthusiasm, had come close to arrest. One of the invaders asked why he was so po-faced? For a while therefore he was obliged to affect ecstasy with all the rest, damning his rightful King with the best invective at his command, whilst an eagle eye was kept on him. It was not until early evening that opportunity arose for escape. Setting out as though on a summer stroll, hatless and in shirt-sleeves, he just kept on walking. All the way out of Town his shoulders were hunched as he visualised a musket taking aim to fell him. Poor Mr Dassell felt the focus of every eye and stepped strangely, imagining each pace his last. In the event no shot came, the invaders having other pressing business to attend to.

Beyond the Town boundaries he let out a mighty sigh and hijacked a passing carriage-and-two. By claiming Crown business, waving his (empty) pistol, and giving every appearance of being a desperate man, he made it to Crewkerne. There were militia there and though their first inclination was to hang him as a highwayman, reason eventually prevailed. The Customs-man was authorised to use post-horses and thus sped to London, raising the alarm (and alarm) as he went.

As it happened London wasn't very interested, since everyone was asleep when he arrived. A blunderbuss was shoved in his face when he hammered the door of Winston Churchill, the

MP for Lyme, at two in the morning, and he grew weary in repeating his story before it was accepted (and the firearm lowered). Finally convinced, Mr Churchill then rushed to the Royal Chambers, together with his rising-star soldier son, John, and dared to wake his Majesty at that unearthly hour.

Dassell retold his now embellished tale by the Royal bedside, as he would soon after to the Privy Council and at the bar of the House of Commons. James listened carefully, propped up on pillows and glad that the blankets were thick enough to conceal the giggling strumpet beneath. Pretending not to hear those tokens, his visitors were impressed by James's lack of concern. This was indeed a King, they severally concluded, who could surface from sleep to look cruel fate in the eye, and still keep a straight face. Dassell was rewarded with £20 and certain promotion before being sent to well-earned rest. The Churchills were told to withdraw but return shortly with their martial proposals.

Thus no one saw King James fairly leap from bed, not even the young actress under the sheets. She was likewise soon uncovered, thanked and sent on her way. Most unlike a seventeenth-century man in his mid-fifties, there was a spring in James's step to match the lightness of his heart. Akin to Bunyan's Christian, he felt like a smothering burden had just slipped from his back.

For most of his life, forces and factions had contended against him, his loved-ones and ideals, but always keeping to the shadows: remote-striking by malice and intrigue, preferring the alley-assassin's blow to the fairness of battle. The puritans had been threatening rebellion this last quarter-century but never got round to it. Their allies the deists and atheists issued their sneery little pamphlets without actually *doing* anything. Monmouth, meanwhile, the friend of all opposition, conducted the cacophonous tune and whipped it to a frenzy. Now all that was ended. Everything James hated had edged out into the light and was standing forth in arms. Previously the spirit of the age was like a fog, all pervading but elusive. Today, *Deo gratias*, it saw fit to take shape: it had a nose one could bop. A plain and simple military man, disgusted by the cack and distorting-mirrors of politics, James knew that this was the time he was born for.

By a quarter-past-four, on the morning of Saturday, the thirteenth of June, 1685, thirty hours after Monmouth set foot in Lyme, King James was at his desk writing orders.

'That's the way to do it!' smirked Monmouth to himself, and allowed his cautious soul to give way to exultation. Two days after King James's early awakening the Duke was high up on Trinity Hill above Axminster. The position gave a fine view of the Axe Valley and, just at that moment, also of the utter rout of the Royal militia.

The Duke was not only pleased but relieved. After a disappointing skirmish at Bridport he'd begun to have doubts about his recruits. They continued to stream in bravely enough, enabling him to form four regiments of foot, the Red, the White, the Yellow and Green. When they issued in column out of Lyme he had three thousand under command; a riotous expansion of his initial tiny force and an imposing sight with their regimental tokens and hat-badges of green sprigs. Though more accustomed to the drilled-to-idiocy machine-armies of continental Europe, Monmouth recognised the equal value of fervour. If one glanced over the plough-horse cavalry that was all he could get, and the embarrassing mere two-brace of guns, he remembered seeing moderate grounds for optimism. Then the niggling misfortunes began.

Firstly, he'd lost both his Commander of Horse, Andrew Fletcher, a volcanic Scottish laird but able professional soldier, and likewise his Paymaster, Thomas Dare, a useful local Man-of-Influence with fingers-in-many-pies. One had argued with the other over possession of a horse and the matter was settled with a bullet to the brain. The Duke was thus obliged to put Fletcher back on board ship and Dare in the ground. Not the least disagreeable outcome of that business was that Lord Grey now succeeded to the cavalry command. For creating cuckolds and drinking ordinary mortals dead, one could hope for no better chap, but Monmouth doubted his other manly qualities. Sure enough, his Lordship's invertebrate tendencies were soon amply displayed. During the try-out probe at Bridport, Grey had fled like a girly at the first shot, snatching a mere draw from a promising situation. There was a nasty fire-fight at the *Bull Inn* and Colonel Venner of the Reds had killed several gentlemen within before being grievously shot in the guts. Stout Wade, his second-in-command, had saved the day (and secured his promotion) by pulling the foot back in good order. The Militia's nose was well-blooded and though three times the stronger they did not press the issue. Insults were exchanged beyond musket-shot and honour was shared. Even so, it was not the good start one could have wished for. The retiring force met the Duke at Charmouth and the lawyer Wade gave a far from rave review of Grey's role. Inexplicably the veteran rake and conspirator was neither replaced or disgraced.

That was because of one of the other problems: Grey was the only aristocrat they had. For all that the body bearing it was useless they needed his *name*. It worried Monmouth that no other quality had come in to them. The lower orders were vital, to be sure, and for wielding weapons and dying in the cause, there were no substitutes. Nevertheless, social mountaineers were also required to supply guidance to the top. They alone were able to smooth the slippery paths up the pyramid of the social structure. The sincerity of weavers and farmboys could not, of itself, propel one to the highest altitudes.

And so, to continue his chosen metaphor, Monmouth decided that he must come to the mountain if it would not heed his call. A push at the present edifice might convince the gimlet-eyed ambitious classes which way things were heading and get their juices flowing. The army's training in Lyme was curtailed and they issued forth.

It could hardly have gone better. Against them was Lord Albemarle, commander of all the mobilised militias and thirsting for an opportunity to shine forever in his Monarch's favour. He'd once read that armies were at their most vulnerable on the march, a principle presumably richly multiplied when applied to a rag-tag, new-raised force. My Lord did not agonise over-long. The assembled loyal might of Somerset and Devon converged in a dash on Axminster. Somerset got there first but it turned out not to matter. Monmouth's men swept in and swept them out.

The Reverend Stephen Toogood of Axminster beheld the sight and was inspired, along with all the male members of his little congregation, to join this patently God-blessed crusade. '*The Lord*', he later wrote, '*eminently appeared . . . sending an hornett of fear amongst those who came to oppose . . . so that a dreadfull consternation of spirit ceized on them . . . some ran away in amazement, some were so strikken with terror that they were even bereft of their reason, and like distracted persons. Others threw away their weapons of war, and would take them up no more: and many watched opportunities to leave their colours and old officers, and came and joyned with this new company . . .*'

Monmouth couldn't quite believe it and came to check. He posted Wade and the Red Regiment at the further approaches to the Town, dissuading him from pursuit, and placed Buyse and his guns in support. When the men of Devonshire belatedly arrived, they chose to mistake these few poor pieces, together with some logs protruding from the hedgerows, for a mighty array of ordnance. Thus finding cause to join the great impromptu 'fun-run', they fled away, screaming like stuck pigs and shedding their red-coats and muskets. Added to the yellow-jackets of their Somerset brethren, a pretty effect was unintentionally made upon the green fields.

The Duke had no eye for it, being given to even stranger considerations. He could come to no harm amongst these headless chickens and so rode out amongst them, the better to ponder. Looking back he saw that Wade's position was good but no grounds, even so, for such an excess of terror. He frowned, not knowing whether to be pleased or annoyed, but was not given further time for doubt. The conclusion he was sadly edging towards came to meet him.

Arthur killed men as he came, striking left and right with an empty scabbard. Those struck fell silently, torn from life by something more shocking than the gentle taps they took. The King's leather face contorted into his own version of glee but he was gracious enough to withhold the great terror from the Duke and his army. It seemed that only Monmouth could see him.

Traversing the intervening fields like a slow arrow, unhurried but purposeful, he made straight towards the Duke. In the places where his war-boots skimmed the turf it died. An interposing hedge shrank away from him, dividing like the scriptural Red Sea. Arthur passed through the gap but his broad shoulders still brushed against the branches insufficiently drawn back. They shrivelled and warped and perished.

'You see how good I am to you,' he said upon arrival. 'Your enterprise thereby . . . inches on.' His voice was like the whisper of an advancing glacier.

Monmouth's mount only stood its ground because it was frozen, bulging-eyed and froth-mouthed, into the last extremities of fear. Dumb beast and yokel militiamen knew the truth though they neither saw nor heard. The Duke was less wise and stayed to converse.

'It was not needed. We could have prevailed alone.'

Arthur smiled again, mockingly this time. He directed his empty eyes beyond the Duke to the ranks of his army.

'Do you think so?' he asked, making his own opinion clear.

The Duke allowed himself to rage. He had been promised a more . . . spectacular advance to London and the Throne. Valiant though his West-Country men might be he wished for regiments of regulars and trains of cannon, gloriously attired and backed by every evidence of supernatural support. His daydreams envisaged the highest and the best of England swearing allegiance under the eyes of an unanswerable army, and sweating in awe of his weirder allies.

'If I am just the King of Lyme Regis,' he spat bitterly, 'with an army to match, whose fault is that? Where are your much vaunted Celts? Where the columns of your undead Knights?'

The giant spectre was unmoved, though it was relief to see his false amusement go.

'The former are for the most part sunk in sleep,' he replied, 'forgetful of their history. When I rise again at last then they will remember me and serve. Meanwhile it suits that you land among the English and divide their strength in civil war. Likewise, my knights, my first and best myrmidons, are harboured and reserved. I cannot commit them yet. You must make your own way to London.'

For all that he used betrayal, Monmouth powerfully misliked being betrayed.

'A bargain was struck!' he shouted angrily. 'It's me that keeps the Elves from your back. Recall that nothing we attempt can prosper without the wardings I supply!'

'Supplied,' Arthur brutally corrected him. 'You have delivered was what contracted. I will pay the agreed price . . . probably . . . in my own good time.'

The Duke knew it was undignified to fume and bluster but couldn't help himself. Arthur was merciless.

'You have divulged the secrets necessary to divert the antipathy of your race,' he went on. 'I do not think you have held anything back. Your shop is empty of stock. Therefore, do not *ever* again try to wield the whip over me. I will impose my will in my own time and you must abide with that. Do you understand?'

Monmouth forced himself, with maximum effort and minimum grace, to signal wordlessly that he did – all too well. His fingertips left pinch marks in the tough leather of the reins he held.

'Besides,' the King continued, more conciliatory than before, 'there are reasons for my lack of faith. I am weakened and unable to exert my best on your behalf. This is all you shall see of me before the final battle.'

The Duke was interested. More than ever now he needed to know about faults in his patron's armour. 'How so?' he asked politely. 'I thought you grew in power towards your coming day . . .'

Arthur seemed willing to be candid about his problems.

'I am stretched,' he said, 'forced to turn my face to many fronts. The trip to London to kill Charles the King fatigued. Likewise, our enemies held a summit against us, beside the old chalk-god in the South-country. Though I strived mightily against it I could not disrupt or overhear their deliberations. These things have depleted me.'

Monmouth nodded sympathetically, taking the revelation about his father commendably in his stride.

'You should know,' added Arthur, 'that much of me is backed up in Excalibur and I am still deprived access to it. Exposition of my full glory, my liberation and resolution of all our troubles awaits its recovery. Your friend, Oglethorpe, will not relinquish possession. What do you suggest?'

'Former friend,' the Duke advised him, just to be on the safe side. 'He and I have a one-sided score to settle. Does the blade really have to be freely given?'

'Sadly so, Elf. It is monogamous and faithful, albeit in this case with reluctance and regret, to each happenstance owner. That is the primary law of its forging. The weapon, for all that it is, must obey. Fortunately, the Oglethorpe human is slow and does not think to draw upon its full services.'

The Duke was glad to hear it, mindful of Theophilus's ridiculous devotion to joke virtues like loyalty and duty. Then he almost cheered up as that led him on to consider how apt it would be if those same weaknesses were to be made his ruin . . .

'Come to think of it,' he mused, 'one idea does occur to me . . .'

By the fifteenth of June the Royal flying column of four hundred troopers, all King James could muster at short notice, were just beyond Salisbury. If any had cared to look back the Cathedral spire was still in sight. Five companies of the Queens Regiment of Foot, Colonel Piercy Kirke's 'Lambs', fresh from educational times in Tangiers, trudged on more sedately a day's march in their wake. It was a beautiful day and, being headed for his native West Country, their joint commander, John Churchill, might be expected to entertain cheerful thoughts. If so, he gave no sign of it.

'So you feel no conflict of loyalty? How interesting.'

Coming from someone as paint-smooth (and slippery) as

Churchill, the query could be taken in any way one liked: a simple enquiry, an accusation, a reproach, a metaphysical musing . . .

Theophilus Oglethorpe settled for one of the downside interpretations and reined in his horse – but not his feelings.

'None whatever – *since* you ask,' he replied hotly. 'No more than the Royal Dragoons we ride with. They were once Monmouth's own, and with him in France and at Bothwell Brig, the same as I. Another now commands and we – being *loyal* – obey. Are you doubting me?'

Churchill looked back at the jangling column of cavalry behind. The four troops of the Royal Regiment of Horse or Blues, were to the fore and thrown into confusion by their colonel's sudden halt. The two troops of Dragoons beyond them cantered obliviously on to add to the anarchy. They were not expecting any unscheduled stops in the dash West ordered by the King.

'Monmouth was but their commander,' countered Churchill, 'albeit well-loved. You were his friend.'

Again it was difficult to take offence, since the remark was so innocently phrased – but Theophilus managed it.

'As you were!' he sallied, ever believing one should attack to defend. 'I well recall your constant attachment to Monmouth's side after Maastricht fight and . . .'

Churchill both conceded the point and silenced him with a gracious nod. He indicated they should ride on.

'All true, quite true,' he said, as the march resumed. 'I don't deny it. But that was twelve years back. Times change. Take Titus Oates, for instance; latterly the hero of the hour and saviour of his nation from papist conspiracies. Last month I watched the hangman whip him half dead through the streets of London. The treatment's to be repeated annually during his life imprisonment. One day fortune kisses and the next she spits. There's no constancy in this world, Oglethorpe. Likewise with our . . . acquaintance, Monmouth. Once the apple of every eye but now there's a £5000 "dead-or-alive" reward on his head. Parliament's passed an act of attainder against him and voted

£400000 to his destruction. In these altered circumstances I find my memories of past fondness suddenly grow hazy.'

Oglethorpe was slightly unfair to single Churchill out for inconsistency. Not a few others were experiencing similar difficulties in recollection. Arrests of the Duke's associates were occurring daily, whilst Monmouth's written summons to his cause to various exalted ones were getting dusty replies. Churchill could well have left it there and claimed vindication, but he seemed anxious that the full sad truth be known.

'Understand, Theophilus,' he said, not unkindly. 'I've since set my feet on a path where friendship is but a burden. What "friends" I may – or may not – have had are long since left behind.'

As he always did when shocked, Oglethorpe frowned – at both Churchill and the World.

'You speak very plain, my Lord . . .' he said slowly. Churchill smiled upon him.

'I can afford to, Theo. Your obvious fondness for the warmer qualities of life debar you from the heights I aspire to. Consequently you will neither ally or rival be. I can thus be honest with you – and friendly even. How are your charming wife and family?'

The Lieutenant Colonel of the 'Blues' was still at sea, hauling in his superior's frank litany.

'Very well, thank you,' he answered, abstracted. 'As far as I know.'

'And who might you be?' asked Eleanor Oglethorpe.

'Your salvation,' replied the Elf, 'did you but know it.'

Ellen wasn't having that from anyone, no matter how exotic.

'My only saviour is in Heaven till he comes again,' she countered firmly, pointing the bread-knife she'd seized at the intruder's slim chest. She was more peeved than frightened, having plans to chop a lot of logs that morning (Grimes the gardener having not 'got round' to it). 'So I'll ask you once more: who might you be?'

The disturbingly beautiful youth raised one long hand to his

211

chin, mimicking depth of thought. 'I'd question the theology of what you state. Surely your Christ person is not detained in Paradise but . . .' The blade traversed the space his heart had occupied one beat before. Ellen followed through with all her strength and crashed against the kitchen wall. The Elf's graceful evasion took him as far away as the room would permit.

'I am merely that which you have always hoped might be,' he informed her, not noticeably put out by the attempt on his life. 'Proof that the world is not yet entirely mankind's and mundane. We told your husband much the same. You and he are alike.'

Ellen was now content just to talk. If the Elf intended harm he could have struck as she blundered, mad-dog style, past him.

'Neither of us like uninvited guests, I'll admit that much. How did you get into Westbrook?'

The Elf ignored the workaday query. Instead he looked round the low-ceilinged kitchen as though in a palace of marvels. Ellen could not detect if he was impressed or dismayed.

'You *know* who I am and we are,' he said suddenly. 'You have met with others of my kind. Your Theophilus, at length, accepted our existence with good grace, and even pleasure. Will you not follow your husband?'

'Such is my custom,' she agreed warily, 'if he's going in the right direction . . .'

'Our late King saw you spying at the window that day. We conversed with you regarding our Yggdrasil Tree. In years past, others of our race observed your childish play in Tipperary. We know of you and that you will not deny us.'

Ellen was intrigued despite herself. 'You're in league with the Elves of Ireland?'

Her guest smiled, a chilling sight, and agreed.

'We do not recognise your names or frontiers but yes, there is marriage and war between us – sometimes both in the same day.'

'And what have you come here to do?' Mrs Oglethorpe enquired, slipping more confidently back into her role as Empress of Westbrook.

212

'I have said, mistress newcomer: to save you – and thereby much else. I am your last welcome visitor for some time. No doubt your pup could kill me, but my advice, dispassionately offered, is that he shouldn't.'

Ellen did not see how the Elf might know that. As best she could judge, her eldest son had entered the room as softly as only a five-year-old can. Well brought up by his father, Lewis now trained one of Theophilus's pistols on the stranger's back, holding it firmly in two hands, awaiting his mother's word.

'My humble suggestion might be,' the Elf calmly continued, 'that he save the shot for those.'

Ellen looked, as directed, out of the kitchen window to see that a modest army of half-formed monsters were hurtling house-wards across Westbrook's lawns.

'I agree,' she said, unable to tear her gaze from the oncoming soldiery. 'Do as the nice man says, Lewis.'

The sturdy boy obediently changed his aim and shot the first one through the open door. As it screeched and thrashed about and died others trampled in to take its bestial place. They looked like eel/man hybrids; humble aquatic life much promoted, though little pleased by the honour. Each owned an unseemly amount of teeth and tusks.

From beneath his cloak the Elf drew a complex little cross-bow and baroquely formed blade.

'So begins,' he told them, with every appearance of sunny cheerfulness, 'the siege of Godalming.'

Churchill and Oglethorpe raced ahead with only a light escort. They got to Axminster on the eighteenth of June, just three days after the great rout of the County Militias. Monmouth's army was long gone by then, permitting shamefaced Albermarle to reoccupy the Town and hang a few malcontents.

By 'mighty strivings', he said, attempting some salvage of his reputation, he had rallied a few battalions and they might suffice for minding road-blocks and prisoners – though he advised they not be put to any test. The good news was that the Wiltshire Militia was on its way. The bad news was that most of their musket locks were discovered to be rusted away – and there were no bullet moulds to make ammunition in any case. Oh – and London was probably safe for the moment because the Surrey Militia had mobilised at Croydon, and ferocious 'Old Patch', Bishop of Winchester, was on his way because he had property interests in the rebellious area.

Churchill had picked up fifteen hundred half-dependable men of the Dorset Militia en route. His younger brother, John, was heading West with five companies of Trelawney's Regiment, escorting an artillery train drawn off the Portsmouth garrison. If all went well he might just muster four hundred horse and a thousand (discounting the Militia as all sensible men now did) foot against Monmouth's reputed five thousand men.

Relieved, in every sense, of command the Duke of Albermarle could now afford to smile and tell Churchill he had complete faith in him. They had nothing to fear he said: the enemy was miles away, twenty-two of them to be precise – in Taunton. Some saving miracle would come along he was sure.

By the time they spoke, England had two Kings.

Anthony Wharton *LLb.*, Vicar of Godalming, liked to stroll a mile or two after matins, and commune with God and nature – on the faulty assumption they weren't one and the same. Some days he would strike towards Farncombe and Shalford, on others, according to merest whim, he'd proceed in the contrary direction, through Ockford out to Milford and even Witley. On the morning of Ellen's surprise visitation, he happened to plump for the latter route, the genesis of which took him along New Way and past the Westbrook Estate.

It had come as no surprise that neither of the Oglethorpes graced his service with their presence. The Master of the House was away fighting His Majesty's enemies and his wife was a known and entrenched papist. A tolerant man by the undemanding standards of the time, Wharton was prepared to live and let live in that respect, in deliberate contrast to his predecessor, the martial Dr. Speed. That clergyman, renowned in

214

verse for 'praying like a Christian and fighting like a Turk' (against the Dutch) had harried his nonconformist fellow-countrymen with equal zeal – and arrest and imprisonment and snatch-squads of licentious soldiery – sometimes unto death. Parish life was still wounded by the case of Quaker Patching of Binscombe Manor who Speed said he'd see in either Church or Hell – and who perished of harsh treatment in gaol.

No matter what the issue the Reverend Wharton had vowed before the altar to have no more of *that*. It seemed contrary to the spirit of the texts he daily preached. Besides, he doubted the wisdom of force employed to drag Oglethorpes to orthodoxy. Should Speed have tried his tricks with that particular tribe he'd most like have left Westbrook a head shorter, or be blunderbuss-distributed across the lawn.

The Reverend puzzled over the source of these tumultuous thoughts on a morning of such beauty. Godalming was at its greenest and the Oglethorpe home presented a surpassing picture of domestic peace. Lady Oglethorpe sat on the terrace with her babies, eating breakfast. He waved a cheery greeting but got no reply. Most likely he concluded, engrossed in her cup of chocolate and family concerns, she'd not seen him. Though no admirer of the Anglican cloth, she had no quarrel with him as a man.

Still troubled by violent notions and, now he thought of it, the curious *stillness* of the family group, Wharton plodded on his way.

Arthur's illusion had deceived him, as it would all other casual beholders. The Vicar's gentle mind had caught the merest backwash of the savage battle before the House even though he could not see or hear it.

For once Ellen might have welcomed a pastoral visit from the Reverend. Anyone who could wield a musket in the defence of Westbrook would not be turned away. Gardeners, flunkies, coachmen and even nursemaids were all at the windows seeking to stem the implacable tide. Gnarled old Grimes in particular proved to be an unsuspected Hercules in their midst, rallying the defence and dealing death with a steel-tipped dib-

215

ber. Revealing happy knowledge of all his master's covert arms dumps, he ensured that the second wave of attack met a very warm welcome. In-between volleys he bewailed the quantity of blood on his nice trimmed lawn. It was worse than what 'Master's damn-nuisance strays' did on it.

Ellen yelled that she'd read gore was good for grass, even the black oily stuff these creatures spilled, all the while giving thanks for Theophilus's obsessive military hoarding – the same she'd previously deplored. Then another wave of Eel-men broke against the front of the house, pounding the doors, attempting the defended windows and slithering sinuously up the walls. She called for another, primed, pistol from the frantic loading teams of seamstresses and lady's maids in the day-parlour and meanwhile plied a hatpin on the hands and flippers grappling the windowsill for purchase.

The first, surprise, assault had been a close run thing. Two of the demon-soldiers had actually laid cold hands on her and sought to carry her off, before the Elf's repeater crossbow cleared the kitchen of unwanted life and the door could be barred. There'd followed a chaotic up-and-down fight through the house, as the alarm was spread and they sought to secure each entrance. The Elf had saved the day a dozen times over, locating those who'd already got in and putting them to death. Even now they were unsure that every last one was found and dealt with. There were plentiful dark corners and obscure cupboards where a survivor might lurk and bide its time.

Though murderous to all others they seemed to want to seize any Oglethorpes. Ellen found three in the nursery binding up her shrieking infants with noisome ropes. Whilst determined and well advised of Westbrook's geography, the raiders had then showed themselves as hungry, undisciplined things. One, its task forgotten, paused to feed upon the nursemaid they'd slain. The other two sought to elude Ellen's fury and clung on to life long after hope was vain. She'd not required help in clearing that room.

Other invaders assisted them by delaying to attack harmless cats and dogs and were found as they feasted. Thereby, in pro-

216

viding a diversion and in being devoured, Theophilus's pets at last repaid their owner for all the years of hospitality.

Even so, Westbrook barely escaped overrunning, mainly thanks to the Elf's warning and valiant aid. Vital time was gained to organise the defence and prepare a more considered reply to the next attempt. It wasn't long delayed. There was just opportunity to lock the children securely away, save for Lewis, very much his father's son, who demanded to bear arms by his mother's side. The bodies, human and otherwise, had to be left where they lay.

From above there came a rain of roof-tiles and the sound of sundered beams. Dispatching her most immediate opponent, Ellen ordered the crack reserve of sabre-armed laundry girls aloft to the attic to deal with this second front.

They saw Reverend Wharton pass by and wave, and called to him, in no uncertain terms, to come in or fetch help. When he merely walked on at a stately pace they cursed him with equal vigour and the Anglican Communion lost a score of baptised members there and then. They were not to know Arthur's magic hid the fray from outside eyes.

At the extremity of the zone of falsehood, another regiment of almost-men materialised. Its officers hissed orders and dressed the ranks of musketeers and pikemen, heedlessly closing the gaps torn by snipers up in Westbrook's upper stories. Then, when all was ready, yet another wave charged in.

Grimes the gardener shouted that ammunition was low. Ellen ordered Cook to prepare a pot of boiling oil.

'I come to defend the truths in this book, and seal it with my blood if there be occasion for it!'

Monmouth handed the Bible back to the overheated schoolmistress, whose meagre charms now fairly heaved with passion and the sheer romantic . . . whatever of the scene. Her schoolgirl charges likewise trilled with excitement. The Duke pondered the wisdom of granting this Miss Blake a private interview, but was dissuaded by discretion and her angularity. Sadly, he was a guest in a supporter's house, deprived of privacy and under earnest nonconformist eyes at all times. He had an image to maintain – for the while – and the Crown was worth a temporary suspension of mattress-savaging.

In fact, apart from the hamstringing of his social life, things were going rather well. There was even the delicious rumour doing the rounds that King James the usurper was dead. The Duke couldn't quite believe in such luck but, true or not, it brought over a few waverers. Fortune seemed to be swinging his way, Arthur or no Arthur, and he dared to dream of being the architect of his own success. Those few troops the Government had managed to gather were overawed by his own force, merely following them around, snapping at the army's heels but no more. It was a pity his imperious letters to Albermarle and Churchill received only a rude noise in reply but he knew not to take that for their final answer. When dealing with pure businessmen like them there were no absolute yeas or nays, just haggling over terms.

Meanwhile, this unsolicited visitation of the Maids of Taunton was an example of how well he'd been received everywhere he went. As the Duke looked down the main street it seemed each window bore a sprig of Protestant green, and all the plain and simple folk sported similar favours in their hats.

There'd been a militia garrison in Taunton, veterans of the Axminster Gallop, but they'd fled the town at midnight on hearing of the insurgents' approach. Their arrangement was to rally at Bridgwater the next day but no one showed – not even the Officers who'd commanded it.

Colonel Hucker of the Duke's cavalry, a rich merchant of Taunton, probed forward and liberated his own town in the late afternoon of Wednesday the seventeenth of June. He freed some likely supporters from the gaol and made a happy discovery in the arms and powder the Militia had left behind. Apprised of a new regime in force, the townsfolk were told their Protestant Duke would be with them shortly.

When he entered Taunton, the whole population emerged to meet him with hosannas, strewing the streets with flowers. The sole sour faces were on the Town magistrates and aldermen, royalist appointees and half-fearful of a noose. They'd been herded at gunpoint, arrayed in the glory of their civic robes, to hear the great proclamation read with everyone else.

People had opened their houses to the invaders like long-lost family and all kind of supplies were offered *gratis*. The Duke wisely knew not to presume on such generosity of spirit and parked his lower class partisans out of town. An order of the day was given, forbidding pillage on pain of death. It was hardly necessary but made a good impression. As armies went, his was most well-behaved, being sober, pious men on crusade. Even so, a cider frenzy could descend on the best of crusaders when it was doled out free and frequent.

Fortunately there were no incidents. Nine months after the army's stay there was but one solitary illegitimate baby requiring baptism in the Town – and even he was fondly named 'Gustavus' after the great Swedish Protestant hero. Such restraint was unprecedented. Taunton was convinced and willing to be – politically – seduced. Enough recruits flowed in to form another battalion: the 'Blue' regiment.

The next day, Monmouth had been minding his own business, sprawled out in Colonel Hucker's Taunton town-house and sipping brandy, when a kerfuffle outside announced the arrival of another delegation. The high-pitched calling of his name suggested this one to be a bit out of the ordinary and, emerging to investigate, he'd thereby made the acquaintance of Miss Blake's little academy.

The pupils proved to be quite sweet, though indoctrinated to fanaticism by their governess, and he'd granted each a genuinely chaste kiss. Apparently they'd marched through the main street from their place of confinement, Miss Blake to the fore bearing a drawn sword and Bible. Her girls each waved a banner, made, it was intriguingly revealed, from their own silk petticoats and lovingly embroidered with supportive texts.

The Duke was particularly drawn to one large scarlet example on which the initials 'J R' were surmounted by a crown of gold. Like a message from above, the wishes of the ordinary people were thus made clear to him. Never mind the bitter old Cromwellians and republicans in his command. The weft-and-weave members of society required a King, and that '*J R*' didn't refer to James *Stuart* Rex. Therein lay the key to pulling in the nobles so far missing from his camp, together with their deep pockets and trains of obedient servants. Those great and cautious ones would follow a King but not a rebel.

Monmouth decided then and there, as he looked deep into the pre-orgasmic eyes of Miss Blake, that he'd be King before he left town. It was . . . unfortunate that Preacher Ferguson had put in the proclamation that he'd submit his claim to Parliament, but there again, the Duke didn't feel too bound by the frothings of madmen.

Mounting up each maid in front of one of his Lifeguard of young gentlemen, Monmouth led them back in picturesque horseback procession through the streets. Church bells rang in exultation and the hoi-polloi went wild. As they went he composed his coronation ceremony.

'This is just bursting bladders of bad air!' said Nathaniel Wade. 'A mere going round in circles. Enough!' The Rebel Council of War was surprisingly, obediently, hushed.

Monmouth liked this Bristolian lawyer – he could always be relied upon to get stuck in, either in debate or leading the Red Regiment. The Duke smirked and awaited more.

'It's like this,' Wade went on. 'We may not relish this monarchic business but the matter's agreed and there's an end. Our protests are recorded for the judgement of history and Almighty God. So, as I say, enough. The only worthy question at our feet now is what next?'

The Duke took another pull on his churchwarden and nodded agreement. This was the main trouble in conspiring with Protestants: they were infinitely factious and confident of their own text. One day there'd be a sect for each member – maybe more.

The gathered Colonels and senior figures duly considered. Their forte was conspiracy, assassination, fund-raising and low-level soldiering; not grand strategy and swinging an army across the map of England. Trusting in the power of prayer, they'd all rather expected to just land and be swept to London – and the New Jerusalem – on an unstoppable tide of Godly rage. It was not part of the bargain that the aristocracy stand aloof or the Army profess loyalty to Satan.

Worst of all, Preacher Ferguson looked to be winding up to a prayerful, 'seeking-the-mind-of-God' tirade. These tended to be rich in length and low in enlightenment and were much to be avoided. All present were therefore grateful when Wade once again leapt in with both boots.

'The way I see it there's three choices: back, Bristol or BabyLondon.' He counted them off on one penpusher-soft hand. 'We can turn round and destroy Churchill and his little band of men. With that achieved the West is all ours and we'll be forty thousand strong within the month. Contrary-wise, we can head to Bristol or London, and I plump for Bristol. Babylon's too big a chew for us as we are, unless we're lucky and I don't care to trust to that. With Bristol though, that's the second City of the Realm and I know it as I do the Gospel. We'd have a welcome there and recruits like sand grains on the shore. Somerset-side, I grant, it's well protected, but I know a kinder approach. If we can attain the bridge at Keynsham and gain the Gloucestershire-side, there's only militia 'tween us and the prize.'

'And one's seen how firm *they* stand!' laughed Lord Grey. His amusement met frigid silence and froze to death. Only Grey thought he had any room to comment on others' steadfastness. Already his nickname in the army was '*Earl I'm-off*'.

'The Godly folk therein await us,' Wade continued in calm exposition, 'and the shipyards and all south Wales shall be ours. The Duke's men in Cheshire can then move to link up. And that's when the magnates might move, I reckon; seeing a signal victory. There might well be no more fighting, for the enemy will like as not fade away.'

The Council of War stirred and looked at one another with invigorated zeal.

'What say you, my Lord?' asked Wade. 'Or should I say, Sire

. . . This seems to me our bill-of-fare; would you care to make a selection?'

Monmouth ceased to twiddle with his tobacco pouch. In stroking its soft leather side he'd been reminded of mistresses past.

'I,' he said, uninvolved, unconcerned, 'will eat what's put before me. You suggest a place and I'll lead you there – to triumph, of course,' he added, noting his indifference cause faces to fall.

Witnesses around that time report seeing a decline in the Duke they once knew. A Quaker (and thus well qualified to comment on misery) compared him sadly with the golden youth he'd observed in Monmouth's great 1680 'Tour of the West'; writing that he looked *more thoughtful, more dejected and so much the thinner that he felt sorry for him*. It seemed odd to observers that the Duke was cast down when riding a successful wave of rebellion.

The truth was that Monmouth was merely relaxed. Whether they made for Bristol or London or stormed Lands End made no odds to him. A battle there must be, but its siting was of no great import. Likewise, the issues it would settle were not those held dear by these dupes in the Council. Aspiring to be more than plain and simple King of plain and simple England; to be the ruler of an altered, wilder realm, Monmouth knew that for the moment – until he could in due course betray him – he must wait patiently upon Arthur rising from the grave.

'*Right*,' concluded Wade, hiding his concern and pounding the table, 'Bristol it is then.'

Taunton Market Cross might not be Westminster Abbey and Joseph Tily, a captain of the Red Regiment, a poor substitute for the Archbishop of Canterbury, for all his good bass voice – but they'd suffice.

'Hear ye,' he read, 'that upon the decease of our Sovereign Lord Charles the Second, the right of succession to the Crown of England, Scotland, France and Ireland with the Dominions and Territories thereunto belonging, did legally descend and devolve upon the most illustrious and high born Prince James, Duke of Monmouth, son and heir-apparent to the said King Charles the Second. We do therefore recognise, publish and proclaim the said high and mighty Prince, James, Duke of Monmouth, our lawful and rightful Sovereign and King, by the name of James the Second!'

Actually there'd been a problem as to what to call him, both claimants to the Crown unhappily boasting the same Christian name. Though 'King James' he had to be for official purposes, his followers tended to term him King Monmouth, to avoid confusion. The stop-gap measure would do until the rival James could be divided head from body and thus from life. The new Monarch's first decree-in-state offered a reward of £500 to anyone achieving this end.

Hearing the news a day or so later, the other James was less kind in his terminology. He dubbed Monmouth the 'King of Lyme Regis' (in unconscious imitation of the Duke's own bitter self-description) and the name stuck amongst courtiers keen to curry favour.

Back in Taunton – Taunton-Regis as might be – the response was more favourable and Miss Blake the schoolmarm led the wild cheering, leaping in the air and waving her arms, inadvertently (perhaps) revealing a quite acceptable ankle and an inch or two of pink calf besides. King Monmouth looked down from the stone cross and decided to tip her on her back (and front and side and knees) after all, and to hell with what his more grim-faced subjects thought. Once anointed by God to be beyond the reproach of man, a certain amount of freelance 'bed-piracy' was, he knew, almost expected from a vigorous monarch.

Before advising Miss Blake of her treat in store, the new King of four great Nations issued a second decree. Mindful of his army's deficiency in arms, 'James R.' ordered all the constables and tithing-men of the West to 'search for, seize and take' all scythe blades and other deadly agricultural implements in their vicinity, and deliver them to him.

Then, whilst the republican higher command of his forces averted their gaze in disgust, King Monmouth stepped down to

223

pass among his subjects, touching the sick for the 'King's Evil'.

They set out for Bridgwater on the twenty-first. It being a Sunday, certain proprieties had to be observed. Divine service was thus laid on and scripture ransacked for suitable supportive texts.

Similarly, back in Chard, John Churchill and Theophilus Oglethorpe were regaled from Romans 13: 'And they that resist shall receive to themselves damnation'. Churchill was not consoled, for that could be taken either way. Only the eventual victor would decide who were the rebels and who the staunch upholders of right. Presumably therefore, eternal damnation was rolling about like a loose cannon until the issue was resolved – an uncomfortable thought to take away with you. Also, such intimidation seemed an impertinence, religion's rude intrusion upon a gentleman's peace of mind. Back home, as in many other great houses, Churchill's chaplain doubled up as an under-gardener – and knew his place.

Meanwhile, Preacher Ferguson, eaten up with fury at missing the chance to preach in Taunton's fine Churches, more than made up for it on the march. Sinking his teeth into Deuteronomy 20 he told the passing army: 'fear not, and do not tremble, for the Lord your God is he that goeth with you, to fight for you against your enemies . . .'

Though he paid little attention to it, 'King Monmouth' was most pleased with this sermon. Their rate of march was noticeably speeded as people sought to hurry past the ranting cleric.

On arrival, Monmouth was proclaimed King all over again. Mayor Popham and the Bridgwater Corporation put on a proper show and people went even wilder than at Taunton. He wouldn't stay, though they pleaded, but recruited richly even so. Men hastened from their loved ones on impulse, to take up pike or scythe or gun. Nor were these just the likely types to go; men who'd sooner have a fight than breakfast and find fault in paradise. Along with the would-be rolling-stones delicately poised in every place, there also went the more solid, cautious, kind: men with a stake in the realm and responsibilities to think of. Daniel Defoe, 'Robinson Crusoe' still potential within his head, joined up.

The uncommitted were impressed, edging their opinions another notch Duke-wards. Much more of this and he'd have the mighty force of social conformity on his side and almost nothing, neither virtue, right or justice, can stand against that.

When they issued from the Town, enumerators counted seven thousand in arms.

Best of all, the enemy still did not *understand*. They were getting ever closer to their target and the foe could not see it. The tiny Royal army stayed out of their way, fearful of swamping or desertions. Up to now they had made only the merest, pin-prick, token attacks, and even then, got as good as they gave. Doubtless reinforcements were en route but they were only positioned against a dash on London. The Duke of Beaufort, the greatest landowner in the West, meanwhile sat in Bristol, commanding the useless militias of Wales and Gloucestershire, and deluding himself he was safely bypassed. When ordered, by King James himself, to destroy the bridge at Keynsham, the magnate thought it a shame and waste. In all likelihood, when things were settled, the cost of repairs would have to come from his own deep but not bottomless pocket. He therefore settled for the option of technical compliance and had his men knock a hole in the middle of the span. It could be truthfully said the Avon was no longer bridged at Keynsham – but a long-legged man could have stepped over the gap.

Monmouth had numerous spies in Bristol, even at Beaufort's right hand, and they told him all this. Such luck seemed implausible, almost suggesting a better protector watching over him than mere fortune.

On the other hand, as they headed for Glastonbury and his patron's place of rest, the weather changed. Up to now they'd been blessed with heart-warming sunshine and the sort of days that positively incited adventure and recruitment. Now it started to rain – and rain in endless, drenching, discouraging, buckets. 'King Monmouth' wondered about that.

*

He had hoped something might happen at Glastonbury to save them the trouble of bothering Bristol. However, Arthur was as good as his word and continued to slumber. The rain, natural or otherwise, continued. His crusaders might have drawn some cheer from capturing the fountainhead of their religion in Britain but it was too tainted by Popery to really appeal. The Abbey ruins reminded them of the long centuries of monkish-trickery, and legends of St. Joseph's supposed visit grated upon staunch Protestant sensitivities. Ideologists amongst them could only applaud their puritan forbears for chopping down the Glastonbury Thorn. No one climbed the Tor to pay their respects and great fires were lit around the old site of the High Altar, both to spite the site and in vain attempt to dry their clothes.

For himself, Monmouth was more than minded to visit the Tor, to shoot cannon at its hollow sides or set teams to mine within. He was in a mood to sing 'wakey-wakey' to this Judas-ally who allowed him to march through mud, leading an army armed with . . . agricultural implements; even if it was to a glorious, eventual, end.

Sadly, though several such nice ideas occurred to him as they squelched to their quarters, each had to be rejected as giving the game away. The Army considered itself to be serving God – and one particular concept of him to boot. Even more than the Noah-style rain, revealing the contents of the Tor might give them pause for fresh thought. He needed them and their idealism-bred-violence. If he must go to Bristol, he could hardly go alone.

The Duke was – just – human enough to be able to restrain himself and quell his Elfish side wherein desire equalled action. Even so, Mistress Walter's boy got to feel quite petulant about the way the world was serving him. Just how long did it take a supernatural power to wrest a sword off a half-witted Surrey thug? The Duke had *told* Arthur of Oglethorpe's Achilles' heel: why was he so slow to strike at it?

They made recruits at Glastonbury village despite the weather, and a Quaker came in to say the 'Clubmen' were rising; the old Civil War, against-both-sides, mutual protection groups voting to come out in his favour. This was greatly to be wished, for even old Oliver's New Model Army had striven to avoid giving offence to them. 'Take our cattle and we give you battle' had been their motto and they'd resisted enlistment for either side. If *they* should now rise from long sleep, ten or twenty thousand strong as in days of yore, there was hope of other imminent awakenings.

For all the local enthusiasm, the rain, worsening if anything, prevented a fond farewell to the Army. Most people stayed indoors and offered remote-blessings from under tile and thatch. Likewise, the torrent deterred the rebels from noting those few who did turn out to see them go. Slipping forth from secret exits, Arthur's acolytes left the Tor and lined the route, viewing the first army raised in his service since Camlann eleven centuries before.

Men of Snowdonia, furthest Cornwall and the Highland Isles, women of Alba, Elmet and Dalriada, stood in thin, sodden, line, not waving or cheering, but in sullen observation. In fairness, many were not best qualified for joy or speech or seeing. Taking blame for the Elven-Stuart-Oglethorpian incursion of the Tor and marked by the wrath of Arthur, they lacked one eye, an ear or hand or tongue.

There were other wonders abroad that summer. A wise-woman in Kent almost got it right and published her troubled dreams that *Gwyn Ap Nudd*, fairie 'King under the Hill' was rising from his golden chair at Glastonbury, together with his fairie queen, *Annwfn*, and all the 'fairie host', to issue from the Tor and wreak mischief in the world. She died soon after in a freak accident, under the wheels of a coach driven by a Welsh Professor of Literature at Oxford.

St. Keyne was a sixth century princess and renowned turner of snakes into stone whilst in life, and a patron of healing thereafter. She now reappeared to various rustics near her namesake town and beseeched them to tumble Keynsham Bridge down. They listened politely and ever-after reformed their lives – but did not comply. Whilst grateful for the instant curing of their various squints, piles and syphilis, they knew the quarter session judges would not forgive even divinely-inspired vandalism.

The spirits of the Saxon war-dead slain at Badon, rose lamenting from the ground before a clergyman of Bath. He mistakenly took it for a confirmation of his Christian faith and remained resolutely unalarmed. It did not occur to him to contact his brother, a Privy Councillor and a man with much influence in military matters, but also, alas, a scoffer and atheist, with the news.

On 'Faery Hill', near Keynsham, strange patterns appeared in the growing crops: circles and ellipses joined by great avenues through the corn. Though people came to see and farmers recouped their losses by charging admission, cognisance of Mother Earth's handwriting was long gone. They were not warned.

A comet crossed the sky in that season. The diarist, John Evelyn, traced its fiery path, high in the heavens, day by day. It was, he wrote, 'moon-white and very much in the shape of a sword, bending towards London . . .' As the month wore on it became blood-red.

A triple-headed lamb was born, live, in Ludgvan in Cornwall. Its owner debated whether to kill the abomination or put it on display and earn a crust. Settling for the latter, thousands made their way to his village to ponder on the wild whims of Nature.

Only this last event, the product of the granite-based farm's high background radiation, had nothing to do with the great struggle underway.

Three Kings: Arthur, and two James's, and sundry half-seen universal forces, converged on each other in Somerset that summer. The world which awaited a decision and then transformation, could not help but betray symptoms, breaking out in anxious portents.

The sortie was a disaster and Ellen Oglethorpe bitterly repented of her over-confidence. Hitherto she'd found that sufficient determination had been all that was needed for success. The mustering of enough drive and elan always somehow cleared the way to one's wishes. Now she found herself mistaken and others had paid a heavy price for her education. It transpired that Life wasn't light-hearted and punished carelessness.

The Eel-men were not disposed to play by Ellen's rules or find her indomitable spirit disarming. Whereas, by rights, the gallant rush from Westbrook should have taken them aback and soon cut its way to freedom, the enemy's refusal to coop-erate spoilt the tale. The early hour had not glazed their lidless eyes, the sudden fury of the attack did not appal them. They seemed content for their gelatinous bodies to play host to a sabre if it meant delaying, even for a second, the drive to escape. The dying doggedly blocked their path, clinging to the blade that transfixed them. The fallen raised themselves up to clutch and snap at passing feet. In the space of two score paces what started as a charge became like swimming through treacle.

Ellen had chosen the best and fleetest for this task of break-ing the siege and raising the alarm. She reasoned that the remaining garrison could hold out long enough for help to be brought from Godalming. The Elf persuaded her she should stay to ensure that and reluctantly she agreed to it. Providing those selected with the choicest of their stand of arms, and reckoning on the brevity of the lawns they must cross, Ellen felt sure she was acting for the best.

It was no part of her plan that these boys and girls be slowed to a halt amidst a sea of monsters, that they be constrained into a desperate circle, and then, falling one by one, slowly disappear from sight under a frenzied tidal wave of foes.

Ellen watched, impotent, from the drawing-room window and felt like a murderess. If she had not needed to be strong for others she would have howled.

The last stand was made a mere fifty yards from the house, less than a fifth of the distance to freedom. There, amidst the trampled ruin of a flower bed, the last footman and parlourmaid were dragged down and ripped to pieces. The Eel creatures set up a terrible keening of triumph, indifferent to the angry sniper fire now coming from the house.

Ellen Oglethorpe deluded herself the ordeal was over but soon found there was worse to come. Some humans had been taken alive. As the new day dawned Westbrook watched, horrified, and Ellen made penance by witnessing, whilst they were raped and then eaten.

'I *know* the man,' said Theophilus. 'So I know what he's trying to do.'

'Bristol, you say?' said John Churchill, languid and unconcerned. He gestured to the empty chair across the table but Oglethorpe wouldn't sit.

'Bristol or I'll eat m'blade,' he replied, now pacing up and down like a caged tiger.

It struck Churchill as . . . unnatural for someone fresh in from patrol to be so keen to head off on another. He was rather wary of Theophilus when he was in this mood and so just nodded sagely as the rant raged on.

'Oh yes, he's clever all right,' Theophilus continued, 'but I see where these dainty leaps are taking him. Whilst we wear out empty roads round Bath he could cross the Avon at Keynsham. One more swift dash and he'd be 'tween us and the City. The Bridge is meant to be down but Beaufort's just slapped it with his glove. A lady's maid could leap it in modesty. I was there yesterday and reported it but Feversham told me "not to worry". Not worry! It makes you want to pull your teeth out, I tell you!'

He suddenly span out of his chosen pacing route to arrive directly opposite Churchill, slamming his gauntlets on to the table. His superior's cider almost spilled.

'He's outwitting us and will have his prize if he's not stopped. The Duke is Bristol-bound, I'd swear upon scripture. And I know His Majesty thinks likewise.'

'And I agree with you both,' answered Churchill, abandoning his attempts on an unforgivably tough crust to his pigeon-pie supper. He'd had enough of it and all of this; the galley-slave style food, the inns that doled it out, and fruitless riding following an enemy through towns they'd vacated days before. He was disenchanted enough to be candid.

'I'd do just the same if I were King of Lyme Regis, Theophilus. Should Bristol fall then the foundations'll begin to shake – and who can say what interesting bugs and beasties will then come out the thatch. Sadly, however, our opinions count for nought, for our esteemed new commander thinks otherwise.'

Churchill was still sulking about his demotion from command. King James had sweetened the pill by raising him to Brigadier but was implacable about his second thoughts. Not even the sweet abilities of Arabella Churchill could sway him – though the King had a wickedly delicious night or two by dint of pretending to waver. It was not that he doubted the man's military prowess or willingness to fight, but rather awareness of his . . . pragmatism – and the exotic traces that flowed in the family's veins – that led James to act. The more predictable Frenchman, Louis Duras, Earl of Feversham, was sent West to assume control, and James rested easier in his mind for doing it.

Churchill buckled under, as a subject should, but he wasn't happy and now cruised along in mental half-speed. *'My Lord Feversham has sole command here,'* he wrote to a friend, *'so that I know nothing but what it is his pleasure to tell me. I see plainly that the trouble is mine, and that the honour will be another's.'* He also plainly saw what Monmouth was up to, just the same as clever soldier-James did; but if Feversham thought he knew better, it was not his business to correct him. Innocent of the full facts, Churchill thought he could make an accommodation with whatever regime emerged.

'What?'

Oglethorpe was still chuntering on as Churchill daydreamed about this fork in the road of his brilliant career.

'I *said*,' repeated Theophilus, well aware he was being humoured, 'that if we swept south of Bristol in halfway decent strength, we could find the Duke and pin him down and thus convince Feversham of his true intentions.'

Churchill frowned and pursed his thin lips. 'Not so keen on

the "we" bit, Theophilus. The Earl's issued no such instruc-
tions. I dare say it *could* be done – but then you'd have as much
trouble locating our commander. My latest information is that
he's moving to a position astride the London Road at Phillips
Norton. All the reinforcements, every man-jack: the extra
cavalry and dragoons, the Foot Guards and the Coldstreamers
and the Royal Scots and the artillery, are ordered to join him
there.'

'Phillip who? Never heard of him.'

'Place not person, dear boy: charming village; near Bath. I
see you've not given that portion of the map your closest attention, so firm are your convictions. Take my word, if our ex-
friend were to press for the Capital – which he won't – he'd
have to pass that way. Our commander can't be shifted from it.'

'Then someone else must shift him.'

Churchill drew in breath through his teeth. He seemed to be
thinking aloud.

'But who? Couldn't be me: too much of a courageous – politically speaking – thing to do. I suppose that someone less . . .
ambitious, someone rather reckless, might attempt it. They'd
be taking a lot on themselves, it's true. Dissipating our scanty
forces on a wild goose chase could land them in a lot of trouble:
vistas of disfavour and the governorship of Orkney and all that.
But turn the whore around though and there's a better prospect.
If what we think is proven by . . . someone, they'd make poor
Fevers look a bit of a paper chamberpot, mightn't they?'

'And also save the day!' added Theophilus.

'Well, yes,' conceded Churchill, 'that too.'

And so, in due course, Brigadier Churchill arranged to be
elsewhere when, in contravention of his express orders,
Theophilus Oglethorpe stormed off with most of the 'Blues'.

'Damn his eyes! May all his future shits be hedgehogs!'

The rebel Colonels didn't care for that kind of sinful talk
from their supposedly Godly commander. Besides, the rage
seemed disproportionate. It was just another Papist patrol, one
of dozens encountered since they moved out of Lyme. They

were no great danger, merely hanging round to pick off stragglers and justify their wages. A simple *'Boo!'* in their direction was always enough to scatter them. Granted, these annoying gadflies had been shaken off the last few days but their return was hardly a disaster.

'King Monmouth' didn't agree. 'We're rumbled!' he lamented. 'Now they know!' His perspective-glass was lowered and brandished like he wished to shove it up someone.

'What's the problem?' asked Wade, genuinely puzzled and irrepressibly positive as ever. 'Even if they have guessed, what of it? We're over now.'

They were indeed. Captain Tiley of Taunton-Coronation fame had pressed ahead with a troop of horse and seized the bridge at Keynsham. A group of militia cavalry set to guard it did their usual trick and fled at Epsom Races speed at first sight. To Tiley's delight a few stout planks were all that were required to repair the crossing and the work went ahead without tiresome interruption. Word was sent back and the army moved up, ready to cross to the Gloucestershire side and take the prostrate City. Only an absolute opening of the skies prevented an assault then and there but, since they seemed almost unopposed, a timely breather was decreed. The drowned-rat army gratefully took shelter under Keynsham roofs to rest for the victory to come.

Monmouth now cursed himself for being dissuaded. He suspected this freak weather. They should have pressed on regardless.

'You don't understand,' he told Wade. 'I've seen who's commanding them. I know him – and he's got his sword with him!'

The Colonels looked from one to another. Actually, they rather expected soldiers to carry arms, those being the tools of the trade. So what was the big deal?

'We've got one or two swords of our own,' said Colonel Holmes of the Green Regiment, in an attempt to comfort. It didn't succeed. Monmouth continued to glower at the handful of blue-coated cavalry lurking around at the edge of cannon-shot.

'With him there, we'll need them,' answered their King, bluntly. 'And whatever the weather blows, we attack tonight.'

'You must be joking!' Military law didn't exist yet and relations between the ranks were free and easy, reliant on personal force for discipline. In the present situation it was sufficient. Captain John Parker looked at the Lieutenant Colonel and then wished he hadn't. 'No, you're not joking, are you?'

Theophilus's face seemed leaner and thinner and his eyes were afire. Captain Parker hadn't long had the privilege of serving under Mr Oglethorpe and was unfamiliar with his fighting madness. It was like peering on tip-toe into the heart of a volcano.

'As I was saying, Master Parker, sirrah, you will take two hundred and fifty men and charge into Keynsham and do such execution as you are able. I will abide here to deal with whatsoever emerges from the village. Should I perceive your outnumbered venture to be imperilled I will charge in to assist – probably.'

Parker nodded slowly, the ostrich plume atop his hat mimicking the action a second in arrears. 'So it shall be, sir – though as you say, one will be a trifle outnumbered . . .'

'As was Gideon against the Midianites, Parker, and the greater the task the greater the glory. Let us speak straight: do you have a problem?'

'No, sir.'

'Would you like one?'

The Captain thought about it and decided he'd take his chances in Keynsham, two-hundred-odd against seven thousand, rather than the other option. He bowed in the saddle and rode off.

'Up to it?' Theophilus asked his other lieutenant, the rather sinister Irishman, Patrick Sarsfield. He enjoyed battle as much if not more than Oglethorpe, though for less wholesome reasons. Theophilus trusted the man's opinion, if not the man.

'Just being natural,' he opined, looking darkly after the departing Captain. 'Parker'll fight as well as any. This should be good.'

Theophilus agreed. 'I have high hopes of it,' he said, cheerily.

They'd come upon the rebel army in Pensford; not two days' march distant as Feversham imagined, but a mere ten miles off – and five miles from Bristol. Wishing to conceal his true numbers, Oglethorpe put forward mere tens and twenties of men: enough to keep in contact but too few to alarm. Realising he could not deny them Keynsham bridge, he'd sent word to Feversham, sat, as much use as a glass hammer, far away at Bath. Word got to him at midnight and – when he was finally aroused – he and the Royal cavalry set off on a forced night march. The Earl was hardly grateful to have his mistake thus publicised, but neither were there harsh words about Theophilus's truancy.

At least there were now proper troops before the City, albeit tired and wet ones, and the King of Lyme Regis could no longer just stroll in. Even so, it was still a close-called thing: the infantry and guns were all left behind whereas Monmouth had a balanced army of sorts. Theophilus put the odds at fifty-fifty for the concluding struggle and was content.

Then Feversham proceeded to oblige the enemy by methodically screwing up again. A blatant feint by rebel horse deceived the Earl, as Monmouth had hoped but hardly expected. Duly believing the attack would come from the south, Feversham moved his forces round to face the non-existent threat. Once again Bristol lay juicily open to ravishment.

Monmouth's agents in the avowedly Protestant City grew more confident and spoke of a day of reckoning to the occupying militia. Lord Beaufort's coach had dead cats and other, more adhesive, substances slung at it. In the port a great ship, *The Abraham & Mary* was set alight by arsonists, and seeing the glow in the sky far off, the rebels took it for a welcoming beacon.

Feversham meanwhile cleared fields of fire to the south, whilst Churchill obeyed and smirked. Lieutenant Colonel Oglethorpe watched in disbelief and rent more hair from his increasingly threadbare wig. Still he refused, despite all incitements, to despair. Trusting again to mutiny and taking his detached command of the Blues (unrescinded by another oversight of Feversham's), Theophilus had broken camp.

'That'll be Parker, I suppose.'

Sarsfield cocked his head, the better to take in the distant thunder of horse-hoofs and pistol fire. He smiled lovingly.

'So 'tis. Music to me ears . . .'

Oglethorpe couldn't go all the way with him in that. To his mind, children's laughter and a pleasured wife were at least equally agreeable sounds, but it was not an occasion to dispute in minor things. Each to their own and so on. The two men trotted forward into view of the village, the reserve of one hundred arrayed behind them. The rain obligingly died down.

He was well aware they'd been spotted earlier in the day. Theophilus had led a dozen men perilously close for that very purpose. Knowing they were detected might deter the rebels from any rash – and dangerous – moves, thus buying time for Feversham to redeploy. Likewise, concealment of their true strength might delude Monmouth as to his intentions. Small patrols led by rational men, no more convinced of an afterlife than they ought to be, just didn't attack whole armies.

Theophilus approved of what he saw. Assisted by surprise, Parker and companions had got in amongst the narrow lanes of the village and were doing creditable execution. The rebels had been dozy, preparing for the lively night ahead, and the guards unprepared for the onset of a quarter-thousand enemies. It would be a while yet before sufficient rebels bestirred themselves out of shock to make life impossible for the invaders.

Whilst patiently waiting for that stage to arrive, Oglethorpe surveyed the excellent cavalry country around Keynsham. It was flat and open and almost perfect for his purpose. He'd chosen well, both in time and place.

As if on cue, a body of rebel horse drew out of Keynsham, to rally and detach themselves from the confusion. Theophilus calmly pointed them out.

'If you please, Mr Sarsfield . . .'

Sarsfield needed no urging and, as arranged, half the remaining Blues accompanied him. For a brief time there was a drumming upon the turf and the blare of trumpets, and then the two

236

formations of men and beasts collided. Theophilus fastidiously averted his attention. For all it was his chosen profession and he'd gotten used to it, he rather deplored the actual sound of combat; that cacophony of souls evicted from home and metal versus meat. It seemed, on reflection, such a waste of good horseflesh and parental time and love.

Fortunately there was distraction in Parker starting to get into trouble. The more enterprising rebels were now scaling the rooftops and sniping at the horsemen below. Through the medium of his perspective-glass, Oglethorpe even observed one or two Blues hooked from their steeds with the poles used to claw down burning thatch. Once unhorsed into the swirling scrum in the streets they didn't rise again.

Theophilus turned to address those select few entrusted with a mission within a mission.

'Wolrich; you other two, whatever your names are, are you still agreeable?'

The troopers signalled they were.

'Good men. You shall have your reward, in the world or the next.'

Then, though no papist himself, he remembered to cross himself in the manner Ellen strictly instructed he should before entering a fray.

'In we go then.'

They hit Keynsham at the gallop and went through the nearest streets like brandy through a Quaker. Slowly gaining the upper hand with present opponents, Monmouth's men had not expected to be struck by a trinity of attackers. The first rebels met were trodden underhoof without requirement of shot or sword. No more Taunton weaving and West-Country harvests for them.

Oglethorpe led from the front as he was brought up to. The first face he had any space to consider belonged to a straw-headed ploughboy too young to be waving a rusty sword at his elders and betters. Theophilus showed him mercy, merely booting his face, busting his snub nose and crashing him back into the hovel from which he came. Two sturdier types that followed merited a pistol apiece and then he used Excalibur to clear the way. It seemed to be growing fond of him, shifting weight to assist each sweep, and biting deeper than he, unaided, could ever do. Pretty soon people were scaling walls rather than face him. It was like being young and invincible again and, for all the present distractions, Theophilus recognised how corrupting that was. But for his need and fear of alternative owners, he would have flung the blade away.

And then he was through to Parker's force. They had had a steamy time of it, he knew. Theophilus forgave them for the joy with which he was greeted.

'Yes, enough,' he confirmed, shouting to be heard above the shots and screams. 'Away as you will.'

Oglethorpe lingered a little, as was only proper, to see his charges safely home. Several bold rebels sought to detain him and he paid them the honour of his full attention. Excalibur was in independent flow, severing heads from shoulders and parting torsos in two, and Theophilus was repelled, wishing he still had pistols to use instead.

He'd hoped, above all, to meet Monmouth himself and settle the whole issue here, one way or another, but was disappointed in that. By way of compensation, he noted each of his deputed stay-behinds had survived to slip from the saddle and effect plausible capture. Then, as a coda to his composition, he took a pot-shot with his carbine at a Rebel observer in Keynsham Church-Tower. A flukish near-miss caused the man to duck and perhaps parted his hair, provoking a most ungodly flow of abuse. Theophilus was grateful the day should end on a humorous, humane note.

He rode out, leaving Keynsham and the rebel army resembling a well-stirred ants' nest.

'*How* many? asked Monmouth, beside himself with fury.

'Twenty dead of ours, and the same amount as good as,' answered Wade. 'And I'd say five score have deserted. Brand, the Captain of horse, died in the cavalry skirmish and . . .'

'No, no, no,' interrupted the 'King', gripping the ale-house table as though he'd tip it over. 'I should know better than to ask a land-pirate lawyer a straight question! How many did the prisoners report, you mumble-truth?'

'Plus half a dozen papist dead . . . sire,' concluded Wade, very coolly, 'and the three prisoners to who you refer. Under questioning they report that their army of five thousand is "close at hand", to use their exact phrase.'

'They all said that? Each one?'

Wade frowned with a do-you-think-I-was-born-yesterday expression.

'I naturally interviewed each separately, having kept them apart. Their stories tally well, with minor inconsistencies that only serve to convince. Alas, they are to be believed.'

'Have you used torture yet? Gaps in them might put gaps in their stories . . .'

The assembled Colonels' eyes widened – some more than others – but in broad, shocked, agreement.

'You forget yourself, sire,' reproached Colonel Holmes. 'It is the crown of England you aspire to, not the Sultan's turban!'

Monmouth had a sharp reply ready for that, but saw he'd be wasting his time.

'If they've five thousand to hand,' he said, in a tone of ice, 'and regulars all, I suspect we must forget Bristol – and much else that was dear to us.'

'I agree,' said Wade, as though considering a matter of only distant concern. 'Odds of one to one, against regulars behind walls, run contrary to all military science. Note as well that surprise is no longer on our side. The army will take a full day to recover from today's visitation.'

'I told you that Oglethorpe would get amongst us,' snapped Monmouth. 'That is his way – his only poxing, stupid, way!'

'You did tell us,' confirmed Holmes, the old Cromwellian Major, who was damned if he'd be taught war by this puppy. 'On the other hand, what did you do about it?'

Monmouth had no answer to that but impotent rage – which, mercifully, he kept to himself.

'Well then, sire,' interposed Wade who, irritatingly enough, believed every mishap was just an opportunity in disguise. 'We seem agreed that one way is barred. Therefore, where to next?'

Things had come such a pass that 'King Monmouth' could no longer be doing with deception, marching here and there in imitation of a normal rebellion. Frustration let him lay down the burden of pretence and feel a corresponding liberation.

'Back to Glastonbury,' he said. 'There's someone I'd like you to meet.'

There was consternation round the alehouse-cum-council table. They'd expected to hear 'London' or 'Cheshire' or some other bold stroke. Why in God's name should they traipse back on themselves to a half-dead museum of papistry?

Their King's first answer was bad enough, but his second, in response to shouted '*whys?*' caused every chin to grace a chest.

'It's an Elf thing,' he said sweetly, dismissing them. 'You humans wouldn't understand.'

Somehow the army stayed, more or less, together – for where else could they go? The cavalry that had surprised them at Keynsham circled like wolves round a fold, wary of getting too close to the shepherd but ravenous to devour strays and lambs. In the field of treason the only safety lay in numbers and staying together.

James Stuart didn't help in that respect by offering amnesty to all those who laid down arms within eight days. Whispered word of it, like report of the exaggerated Royal Army strength planted by Oglethorpe, did the rebel rounds. Some who were now less than convinced of a Protestant God's protection, and who had families and farms to think of, slipped away. They'd considered the revised odds and decided to take their chances with the Royal 'shoot-first-and-offer-pardon-later' patrols. There was general loss of confidence and verve from wildest Colonel to lowest scythe-man. The former, still reeling in Monmouth's stunning revelation and in a state of shock, steered clear of their 'King'. He in turn allowed them to find solace in activity and giving orders. Thus, though not to be ranked amongst the most notable battles of history, Keynsham proved to be a turning point: literally so in terms of the rebels' line of march. Thereafter, thanks to Theophilus's insubordination, in the eyes of the work-a-day world the insurrectionists had nowhere to go.

'King Monmouth' knew better. It didn't greatly matter to him if his army frayed at the edges as they retraced their rain-plagued steps. So long as he had a force of some kind at journey's end that would suffice. He abandoned thoughts of London or Cheshire or anywhere else that plain men thought important. His one wish now was to dump this squalling baby in Arthur's lap, and thereby force him to act.

That being so there was no great hurry, and they took a circuitous, easier, route back Glastonbury-wards, avoiding the depressing paths they'd already churned to mud. Therein was also the added amusement of putting a blast up Feversham's feathers, once again dissembling ambitions on London. The united Royal Army, a mere half as strong as Oglethorpe had suggested but now a formidable balanced force of horse and foot and guns, scuttled respectfully in their wake. It entertained Monmouth to lead them a dance similar to the one he'd endured.

The welcome on the return route was not as warm as before. Their promised ten thousand 'Clubmen' recruits proved to be a hundred-odd bumpkins armed with pitchforks, hoes and flails. When the rebels summoned Bath to surrender their herald was shot down like a dog.

Henry Fitzroy, Duke of Grafton, was enjoying this. All his life had been spent in the shadow of the graceful, glorious etc. etc. James Walter/Croft/Barlow/Scott, Duke of Monmouth and now King of Lyme Regis. King Charles II had been generous in affection, as in all else, to each of his bastard children, Henry no less than Monmouth, but the mantle of favourite had unmistakenly settled on Lucy Walter's boy.

Henry had tried his hardest and never given cause for grief. Ceaselessly helpful and obedient he'd offered all in his father's wars. When opportunity presented he'd been among the first to

241

take ship and face the Dutch broadsides. Yet, returning to shore, he invariably found precious Monmouth had performed a slightly *braver* deed – or so he said. Charles loved and commended Henry at every stage, but always Monmouth earned the warmest smiles. Unlike some, Henry Fitzroy didn't plot with Charles's enemies or arrange his father's death – and being the side-dish at the feast was his reward for it. Even so, he never complained, though mother, Barbara Villiers, Duchess of Cleveland, constantly incited him to. Instead he kept his peace and accepted second best, doggedly hopeful of justice in God's good time, or even in the world to come. Nevertheless, the waiting rankled and itched his sense of justice.

Now the Good Lord had put his spurs on, and Grafton was duly grateful for a spot of justice on this Earth. Monmouth was widely judged the lowest of the low and it was the pleasure of loyal types to hunt dear Golden Boy through the West Country. Fitzroy had been entrusted with command of the Footguards to this purpose and there were hours on end when he found it hard to keep a straight face. That was doubly true when, as now, he was permitted to lead the chase.

Suddenly the mood changed. He saw movement and the hedgerows to either side sprang to life with musketeers: rebels with more confidence than they'd martial or social right to. It was yet more unfairness. Beaten foes had no business setting traps for their pursuers.

For a second Grafton looked at them and they at him and then the lane dissolved in powder smoke.

It had seemed like a good idea at the time to boot the rebels out of Philips Norton. Their meandering path from Bristol had taken them to Feversham's one-time bastion on the London Road, but they were long since past tackling that great target. Perceiving the rebel army was on its way out and to elsewhere, Earl Feversham decreed a probe in force to assist them along at sprightly pace.

Grafton, granted that honour, dived in with five hundred of his guards, backed up by horse and guns, only to discover that the enemy had learnt a thing or two from Keynsham. This time they weren't taken by surprise. Strong positions were established to cover their retreat and an ambush temptingly set. When the noble Lord saw the hedged lane leading into the heart of Norton, and the rebels apparently streaming out the other side, it seemed only natural to pile on in.

Monmouth heard the firefight and was near enough to turn the Army round. Wade's Red Regiment and Holmes's Greens were ordered on a pincer movement round the trapped Royalists and both did well. Feversham was compelled to puff up in support of the abortive push, desperately committing each unit piecemeal to the struggle as it arrived, in order to stave off defeat.

Grafton, his beloved steed shot from under him, was rescued; out of breath and puzzled and only just. He got out on another man's wounded mount – along with remnants of the Guards – by dint of Feversham throwing in some sacrificial Grenadiers. Meanwhile, the Royalist Foot of the Line were being bustled out of Norton, field-hedge to field-hedge and garden by garden by doughty Wade and Holmes. Lord Grey's horsemen postured and posed threateningly at least, and things looked grim for the Red-coats until the Royal Cavalry arrived in force. After several hours of distinctly difficult moments, Earl Feversham was at last able to draw off his mangled troops.

As the rain came down again, the two sides drew apart and set up for an artillery duel: the Royalists' complete train against Monmouth's four diminutive, if well-served, pop-guns. Fortunately, the technology of the age was still sufficiently civilised such that little was thus achieved and at length the original King James II's Army drew off to lick its wounds. A dose of their own Keynsham-style medicine, particularly dispensed by amateurs, proved hard to swallow, and the regulars now required some time to be alone.

Feversham reproved the Duke of Grafton (his escapade being 'too much of a good thing, though all very well once in a while') and drafted his report to King James, absent-mindedly neglecting to mention three-quarters of the four-score dead they'd left behind. Colonel Holmes meanwhile celebrated his great victory by noting the loss of his son. He wept awhile accordingly and then marched to the kitchen of *The George* in Norton to self-amputate his own musket-ruined right arm.

Despite all this drama, the most significant encounter of the day occurred just before the rebels departed at eleven, leaving vast campfires burning to mask their retreat. Lieutenant Colonel Oglethorpe, through no fault of his own, had appeared late on the scene, being far distant when affairs were at their height. He arrived at the head of his detachment of Blues and was commanded, in terms vigorous enough to get through even to him, that he was not, not, *not* to attack but to cover the Army's inglorious escape. Eighty dragoons were supplied to both reinforce and restrain him. Unlike the Blues, they might actually question his more 'interesting' proposals.

In the event, Theophilus obeyed, though far from content. When evening fell and the guns made long, ineffective, and monotonous, conversation, free at last of pettifogging duty, he rode forward alone. Both proud possessors of perspective-glasses, he and Monmouth spotted each other across the battle-field at the same time.

Two great – if very different – minds thinking alike, they both stood high in the saddle and raised a hand to point, each mouthing to himself '*very soon . . .*'

'Kitchen-staff, fire! Well done. Retire to reload. Chambermaids forward. Pick a target, *wait* for it . . . and fire!'

Eleanor Oglethorpe moved up and down the ragged line, brandishing a sabre and directing the defence. Her hair and face were wild and weirdly streaked with smoke, her gown cut to a cloud of ribbons in half a dozen places. By now the enemy tried to avoid this Celtic goddess of war, but that rarely proved possible. She seemed everywhere, rallying her domestic warriors and laying on herself when occasion demanded, always present when resistance faltered or an eel-soldier attempted some obscure entry.

The last three or four attacks on Westbrook had each

244

promised to be the last. The enemy were infinite, their fallen instantly replaced at the edge of the exclusion zone, whilst her troops were merely men – and women, and boys and girls. Supplies of powder and food were low and there was friction within the house over questions of precedence. Maxted the Butler fell out with Grimes over whether gardeners, however, redoubtable, might issue orders indoors, and they were no longer on speaking terms. Kim the nursery-maid thought it outrageous – loud and often – that she had but a half-pike whilst scullery girls went about with proper muskets.

In the end, Ellen invented martial law, declaring future mutineers and grumblers would be cast forth to feed the eel-men. The garrison rank and file, mulish Godhelmians all, took only partial notice till Ellen was as good as her word and dangled a boot-boy out the window. Thereafter good discipline prevailed.

Thoughts of such penalties reminded Mrs Oglethorpe that even if they should win clear of all this her problems would be far from over. How, she wondered, would she explain such a plethora of dead servants; some of them abundantly chewed-over?

Then the next wave came in, freeing her of concern for anything but the fleeting moment. The Westbrook defenders fired, and those not blessed with guns flung turnips spiked with nails. Gaps appeared in the oncoming lines and then order was lost as they hit the zone Ellen had strewn with tacks and glass. Some monsters howled and hopped in crazy dance but the majority rushed on. They reached the barricade made of their fallen predecessors and wetly surmounted it by sinuous crawling. Bathtubs of boiling water were then tipped up by sturdy footmen to wash away the first line whilst pots of molten oatmeal fell on those behind, as clinging, though less welcome, as an ardent lover. The scalded screamed and fell away – but were soon replaced. The besieged's ingenuity at last exhausted, plain and simple combat was joined.

Whenever all seemed lost the Elven visitor would appear, driving back the enemy with graceful ease. Both he and his blade seemed too slim for all that they aspired to but, combined, proved equal to the task. The serene and untroubled foundation stone of their defence, he rarely spoke, save to point out some new threat. Lewis Oglethorpe chose to remain near him and Ellen was happier in her mind for that.

Noting, on the first or second day, that his crossbow was out of quarrels, she offered him a pistol to use. It was declined. 'That is newcomer distant-killing,' he said graciously enough, 'and not our taste at all.' Though not following such inhibitions, she accepted this one island of independence in her command and left him to ply his saw-edged sword. It transpired there could be no complaint about his use of it.

Somehow this umpteenth assault was thrown back, improbably and perhaps irrepeatably. It wavered and hesitated at its fierce reception – and was lost in that second of self-doubt. The blood-marked housemaids and stableboys redoubled their efforts and contrived to assemble another volley which blasted the clinging few back out the windows. They then rushed forward to belabour the ensuing confusion with various sharp objects.

One parlourmaid leant too far forward, the better to wield her knitting needle. A slimy jaw stretched up to fasten several hundred pin-teeth round her swan-white neck – and snapped. The girl slid back and fountained red around the room.

'Again!' ordered Ellen, averting her eyes. Young Deborah had been like a friend to her. 'Musketeers step forward.'

'No, madam,' countermanded Gardener Grimes. 'We're powerful low on shot. And powder barrel – her's almost empty. We must husband both.'

'I was going to say that!' complained Maxted the Butler.

'You are equally correct,' said the Elf softly, somehow surmounting the tumult. Ellen's emotional rebuke to the menial classes was forestalled. She knew her wish for one further punishing volley was mere indulgence. The eel-enemy were flapping away.

'Talk about heroes!' exulted a stable-boy, finishing off a half-dead intruder and having the adventurous time of his life that he'd never thought to enjoy. 'We've done it again!'

'And for the last time,' whispered the Elf to Ellen. 'A private word if you please, newcomer-mistress.'

They convened in her sewing-room and shared a bottle of old brandy. Though he drank for sociability's sake it did not seem to affect him. The Landlady imbibed and felt better for it, all the while keeping one eye on the window. Rather than lay down her pistol she knocked off the bottle's head. It was the first time for many hours that they'd had any opportunity to speak.

'Do you know how my husband is?' Ellen asked. She was ashamed to have not enquired before, for all the excusing distractions. Now she knew that soldiers' neglect was not always born of cruelty.

The Elf seemed almost to scent the air, looking round and about as though this room were all the world.

'He lives,' he answered. 'That much I can tell. His spark is still shining.'

Ellen breathed again. 'And the rebellion he fights?'

The Elf relaxed, moulding himself into the French divan. 'I cannot say. Our joint enemy is shielding it from sight. We are excluded from any influence over it. All I perceive is a cloud of invisibility over the western portions of this nation – though the corridor of same joining it to London has gone. I take that last item to be good news.'

'You can do no more?' Ellen was disappointed, assuming everything supernatural to be as boundless in power as the realm they inhabited.

Her guest's smile was wintry. 'Very little,' he said. 'My race grows old and impotent. The enemy is profligate with reserves, whereas we must be more cautious, hoping to win through in the long term. If it consoles then know that we strike bargains with the Stormlings so that rebellious zeal shall be dampened with wind and rain. 'Tis a feeble thrust I know, but the best affordable. Your unbaptised babies who ride the upper air are angry spirits who demand a fearful price for cooperation.

247

Likewise, we are not so blessed with Elf-infants that they may be freely bartered . . .'

Suddenly Ellen didn't wish to pursue that topic and the Elf shed whatever humane patina he might have acquired in her eyes.

'So why is that you wish to speak?' she said bluntly – and drank deep.

He knew her attitude had changed, but was indifferent to these usurpers' opinions.

'We are near the end,' he said, simply. 'You should be aware.'

'Us? You? The World?' Ellen snapped. 'Be more specific, sirrah!'

He obligingly thought upon it. 'Well me, certainly. I shall not leave here; I cannot see myself in any of the times to come.'

Despite herself, Ellen was touched by his dignity and resignation. When all was said and done, this was her family's fight and no other's.

'I'm sorry . . .' she told him.

'Are you?' he replied, brightening slightly – but only with curiosity. 'Why?'

Ellen brushed the question aside. 'Go on,' she said, frowning.

'It is hard for us to view the fates of . . . *men*,' he continued, not relishing use of the term. 'You may or may not survive – but you will not prevail here. I sense fresh and more formidable enemies soon to arrive.'

'Who?' Ellen demanded.

'Humans, Madam. The enemy's most fanatic devotees are come, men of your own and kindred races, infiltrated up in ones or two's from throughout the Celtic lands. They will not leave without some or other conclusion.'

'That is what I do not *see*!' wailed Ellen, in anger. 'What have we done to who to arouse such bloody ambitions? Why are we so relentlessly pursued?'

The Elf refused to share her outrage.

'There is not time,' he said, 'and this is not the time, to ponder the mind of the eternal Null with you. You have prised sufficient knowledge of them from us for present needs. Your

248

Theophilus perhaps knows more and may live to tell.'

'*Wait* till I see him!' Ellen fumed, lapsing into fluent Tipperary. 'Still keeping back dark secrets, is it? I'll sort he . . .'

Her companion fastidiously overlooked the outburst. His own race's breeding pairs were not so afflicted by lasting bonds.

'We are both well aware,' he went on, 'that your husband has something the enemy requires – and most ravenously so. Our predicament here makes it plain he will not part with it. Thus, they hope to persuade him through holding you – a clever playing upon this disgusting . . . *affection* you have for one another.'

Ellen didn't rise to the bait, if such it was.

'But if these reinforcements arrive,' she speculated aloud, 'and they are normal men, then the Town will notice. Godalming will raise the alarm and come to our assistance. The militia . . .'

'You are in a zone of thaumaturgic apathy, the product of Arthur's magic. He must judge it important for the spell is too strong for us to pierce. I alone came in before it fell. Have you not thought it strange the lack of visitors these last few days?'

'Offhand,' Ellen tartly replied, 'I'd say there'd been no shortage of callers . . .'

'No: I refer to the normal course of things: to tradesmen, hucksters and people on their social round. The case is that each one approaching here remembers other errands or forgets their purpose, seeing nothing untoward. You observed your priest-man walk on by . . .'

'He's no priest. His Church calls him a *Rector*.'

'The title is immaterial. Either profess the quaint creed of rendering assistance to fellow men. He saw nothing and walked by on the other side. As will all others.'

'So we're quite alone to face this?'

'Yes – though this is hardly the occasion for philosophy.'

'No, dunce: I meant in our present plight.'

'That as well.'

'So what should I do?'

'The matter's easy. Deprive the enemy of his prize. Kill yourself and all your children.'

249

'No!'

'I'll assist.'

'No!' The brandy bottle's jagged neck was pointed at him – though not in invitation.

'But why not?'

'*Because*, Elf.' She stared at him through slitted eyes. He seemed willing to defer.

'Of course I sympathise, Lady Eleanor: you do not have eternal peace to look forward to as we have. You must consider post-grave consequences . . .'

'No, it's not that. Just forget the notion. Expel it from your icy mind!'

He stood lithely up and bowed.

'Very well. I can do no more.' His tone was of mere acceptance, not resentment. 'On entering this house, never to leave, I said I came as your saviour. You would not have it then and so it proves now. Therefore, you must be your own salvation.'

He had been of such assistance that abandonment sparked fear.

'Have you no final word?' she implored him as he left the room. 'No last advice?'

The Elf turned and considered.

'Only,' he said, as charming and pleasant as could be, 'that in whatever you do, be swift. They come!'

The regiments of eel-men, Arthur's dark crop raised from Somerset's marshes, proved to be expendables: sorcerous creations or dark might-have-beens of Nature, cast in to exhaust resistance. Their replacements were even more fanatic. The great mob of men and women came on like a tidal wave, as contemptuous of Westbrook's last store of shot as the sea itself would be. They fell in rows and scampered on, only howling all the wilder.

These were Arthur's people, adorned with the asymmetric cross; his very own, descendants of his closest slaves from when he last trod the Earth. Some lived in attendance on his grave, whilst others trod the wider world in conspiracy, hugging their secret knowledge to themselves and passing it to each new generation. Now, at last, they could unite and strive openly together. They feared Arthur and they loved him, and hearing none but his tale for a thousand years of telling, had no ear for any other.

They suffered grievously in getting to the house and worse in entering it. Like rabid men they ignored their wounds and loved ones being torn from beside them. Then, when each Westbrook gun was empty and every blade was in a foe, they swarmed everywhere like an epidemic and gave forth the note of triumph.

Eleanor Oglethorpe gathered her four children to her, and with their surviving nursemaids, retreated room by room, scything the pursuing Celts with sabres. She saw other small groups look similarly to their own defence, such as Grimes and his remaining staff heading for the garden. The garrison was splitting into component parts, cooks to the kitchen, grooms to the stables; desirous, perhaps, for the comfort of the place they knew best in life before they left both forever. They had lost.

The Elf had no such niche to console him. His abode was out beyond in some unguessable locale, not in the confined homes of men. One spot here was as good as any other. Just before she gained the first floor landing Ellen saw him choose a place to die.

His back was to the morning-room mirror. They could only come at him from one direction at that point. He drew his sword back and forth time and time again, but, though a sheltering body-pile grew, they were simply too many. One at last got through, and whilst the Elven blade was in another's breast, a knife sawed into his own.

Looking through the shattered window the Elf beheld the world one last time – and then was gone. Ellen could not withhold a banshee wail.

His blood was golden, and so frigid that it steamed.

*

After Phillips Norton the rebels were given respectful berth. The two armies moved in stately dance towards and about

Glastonbury, Monmouth taking the male, lead, part. Sometimes one set brushed by the Town, sometimes the other, but still Arthur would not stir. The Duke could not know he was otherwise pre-occupied at Westbrook.

To amuse themselves meanwhile, the rebels vandalised Wells Cathedral (Old Patch's see till last year) as they passed through. Lead from the roof went to make bullets and their horses spent the night (and much else) within its sacred bounds. A beer barrel was plonked on the High Altar and only Lord Grey – who retained some pious sentiments – standing before it sword in hand, prevented worse indignities to the Holy Table.

Monmouth didn't care, having cast all pretence aside. His Colonels now rarely spoke to him, knowing only that he waited for some deliverance invisible to them.

Then suddenly the position changed. Monmouth felt it in the air. Some presence, hitherto withdrawn, looked upon them once again. The very atmosphere was recharged. The 'King' could not guess its nature but he knew some problem of his patron's was now solved.

That very afternoon a stranger visited the rebels' camp with an interesting tale to tell. He said his name was Benjamin Godfrey and that he had long laboured on the land nearby. Now, there were some that would have questioned this; for he seemed rather dark of hair and hue for a son of Somerset, and altogether more like a Cornish man. Strangely though, Monmouth was willing to be incurious – in that respect at least. By contrast, the rest of Godfrey's yarn provoked a hundred probing questions.

'King Monmouth' heard all about the Royal camp at Zog and its tempting lack of preparedness. He took the trouble to ascend the tower of St. Mary's, Bridgwater and, with his trusty perspective-glass, checked all that was alleged. He noted for himself the Royalists' careless dispositions, protected only by a muddy ditch. They were a mere four miles from each other, but once again Feversham was unaware of that interesting, alarming, fact.

There was a path, Godfrey told him, through the murk and mire of Sedgemoor, a route he – and few others – knew in each and every particular, over the drainage dykes or 'Rhines', right to the heart of Zog. He much misdoubted the way would be guarded for 'furriners' were not like to know that it was there. By even happier providence, the Royal guns were parked well away from camp, ill-placed to counter any attack along the trail proposed. Not only that, but he'd seen the soldiers making very merry on local cider. They'd be thick-headed and sluggish by the morrow. His employer, Godfrey said, (which the Colonels took to mean a farmer) had placed him at the King's disposal. Might he have the privilege of guiding them on the suggested stroll?

The Army Council had never heard a 'shift-dirt' talk that way before and accordingly had doubts. Monmouth didn't share them. He wasn't aware that in west-country speak, so carefully reproduced by Arthur's minion, the interposing 'Rhines' deceptively came out as 'Rheens'. It hardly occurred to him to waste time or breath asking Godfrey to write his proposals down since he didn't look the literate type. Thus, misled by his ear and excitement, the connection wasn't made, the warning prophecy went unrecalled and Monmouth was led astray.

The Duke pondered for all of half a dozen seconds before giving orders for a night attack.

Time stood still for the second occasion that day. This pause came around five a.m. when battle had been underway for hours. The outcome was still anyone's guess.

Just who'd raised the first, crucial, alarm ever after remained a mystery. All accounts agreed on a single warning shot. It was that which woke the slumbering outposted sentries and sent them headlong back to camp, but its firer proved strangely shy. Later tales spoke of a traitor in Monmouth's ranks and even named some likely names – who were all safely dead. However, no such Judas came forth to claim the credit and infamy. Consensus of opinion suggested a lowly detached trooper of the

'Blues' who'd gone to his heavenly reward in battle before he could demand his earthly one. Based on inadequate knowledge, it seemed the most reasonable explanation. No one at all posited, say, an Elf/human halfbreed able – shrinkingly – to wield a gun in furtherance of his own agenda.

Whatever the case, that late warning prevented the simple overrunning of the camp. Dragged from drugged sleep by musketry and trumpets, the Royal Foot acquired some degree of readiness and formation before the rebels arrived. They in turn, in their onward haste now surprise was lost, missed the vital 'Upper Plungeon' crossing which would have taken them dryshod into Zog. The foremost amongst them, the Red and the Yellow regiments, then balked at entering the 'Bussex Rhine'. But for that they would have got to push-of-pike (and scythe) and maybe swept the Royal Scots away, before making breakfast of Piercy Kirke's Lambs. Unfortunately, seen in half-light, the inky depths of the Rhine could not be gauged and one might plunge confidently in only to meet watery death. Instead they settled down to fire across the ditch, making a good second best of it. Each successive reinforcement of rebels joined in.

The pleasant or putrid surprise of the moment, depending on which way you faced, was Monmouth's tiny artillery train. Though deprived of a quarter of their strength by the squeaking wheel of one piece, Anton Buyse's inherited skills made the remaining three speak like the array of the Grand Turk.

The Scots and the Lambs had to endure their attentions, more irritating and swifter slaying than the pox, for what seemed like eternity – and scores of them entered same thereby. Their own ordnance, which might have helped to dampen those gales of steel, was far away at Westonzoyland, scratching around for horses to carry them somewhere of use. In the end, Old Patch utilised his own coach-foursome – and oaths such as even hardened soldiers hadn't heard before – to get things moving. They arrived very late and more fearful of the Bishop at their back than any foe ahead.

Lord Grey's rebel cavalry disappointed in the expected manner and then departed the scene. At dawn Oglethorpe and the Blues arrived back from the suspension of time outside Bridgwater, to Feversham's frown and Kirke's curses and an all too brief restitution against Colonel Holmes's Green Regiment of rebels. Theophilus was deep amongst them and had just seen his deputy, Sarsfield, go down, when the seconds ceased to elapse once more. Excalibur had been inches from cleaving yet another head but, it no longer seeming sportsmanlike to strike, Oglethorpe chivalrously dragged it from its kill.

King Arthur came as before, gliding across from Glastonbury, limbs neither touching the ground or matching his headlong pace. If anything he looked . . . larger, more filled-out and for-midable. Then Theophilus saw something else that occupied all of the attention he had to give. The spectre-King was accompanied this time, by an entourage in chains.

He left these in the middle distance, though Oglethorpe already suspected the worst. The King came to stand by Bussex Rhine and, to the sound of creaking iron and skin, surveyed the scene he had made.

'Oglethorpe, come forward.'

Theophilus was already attempting that, it being no simple matter to disengage a horse from close mêlée and trot it in a direction much against its tastes. Eventually he relented on the foaming beast and dismounted, approaching the King on foot. Freed, the steed careered away; a curious bolt of movement to behold in the otherwise still battlefield.

'I said,' rasped Arthur, 'that we would meet again today, Theophilus Oglethorpe.'

The soldier, assuming an ambassadorial role for his race, tried to brazen it out.

'If such is God's will I am content,' he said, coming close. The King loomed high over him. 'What other point is there to all this?'

Theophilus waved his arm to sweep and indicate Sedgemoor and everything that had led to it. Arthur may have followed the gesture – it was hard to be sure. The King's empty eyes, buried deep in a great metal helm, burned bright but unreadable. Oglethorpe desperately wished to deflect their attention for, even sheathed, Excalibur had begun to buzz with recognition. That hadn't happened before. As he suspected, the King had thrived and progressed, becoming more like his former self.

'There *is* a point,' Arthur informed him. 'Although one may think that contrary to the precepts of the Null. We have one purpose and one alone: and when it is achieved there are no more "purposes" anymore for anyone. We strive in order to do away with striving.'

'I don't under . . .'

'No, you don't,' interrupted Arthur, with terrible finality. 'Do not trouble yourself to comprehend – or do anything. Your doing is done. Theophilus Oglethorpe will not see the flowering of our days!'

The Lieutenant Colonel took a step back and checked his balance, hopeful of at least one last blow.

'I thought you would have me serve you in some transformed capacity,' he said, prevaricating. 'That was your threat or promise at King Charles's death.'

'It was,' answered Arthur. 'I saw you soulless, my pliant tool and fool, satrap of some corner of our dimensions. There was even a place reserved; a towering scarlet castle, beleaguered bastion against a race of sentient fungi. That was yours for the price of mere abasement. Think on it, Theophilus; you could have spent your days in ceaseless battle and your nights with brazen, callipygian, maids. Think on and then repine. It shall not be. You have since displeased me even more. It is now my pleasure and intention to annihilate you; to send you back, discorporate, into the swirling soup from which new matter is born. I do not wish to see more like you.'

'But you shall,' Theophilus was resolute. 'Some human types are eternal.'

Arthur's reply was short and sharp and full of confidence. 'I shall arrange otherwise. Meanwhile, give me the sword.'

'Only in your guts, scarecrow-King.'

'I have none, as you see. I require the power within the blade to grow them afresh. With it I dare to wake my Knights. When they ride forth, Monmouth's men will gain courage to cross this little gap: together they will sweep all before them. The help he needs will keep my little "king" chastened and suggestible, and so it will begin. Its end will be a sweeping away of everything you know. Give me the sword.'

'It must be *willingly* given . . .'

'And so it shall be. Behold.'

The little group in chains were suddenly much closer. Oglethorpe had already perceived the truth in his heart of hearts, but – forgivably – denied it.

'Father!' moaned Lewis.

'Daddy . . .' said the younger ones capable of speech.

'Theo,' beseeched Ellen, his wife, her bare arms raised towards him. She'd plainly suffered much. 'Don't let him have us. You can't know what he has done to . . .'

'He can guess,' interjected Arthur, 'which is far worse. Westbrook is afire and all your family seized. Why expound further? You see how far you have demeaned me, Oglethorpe? I, proponent of a . . . calmer way, must descend to fleshy threats. Will you have me lower myself further and specify what I might do?'

'No. Don't.'

'So come forward. Give me my desire and then be slain.'

He found himself well able to do it, free of any inner contesting voice. Love and honour alloyed together forged metal stronger than the desire for life.

Theophilus stepped up and offered the sword. He avoided his family's eye.

Arthur hissed in almost erotic joy. Oglethorpe recoiled from that gale of corpse-breath and hesitated. The King noted it and was enraged. He stretched forth one hand – and over-reached himself.

'Save us, Theo,' said Ellen Oglethorpe. 'Do anything. Die for us.'

Theophilus flinched. His Ellen would not say that. She would not be so finally broken, whatever her ordeal. He turned to look and in that instant knew. This Ellen's nervous gaze flicked guiltily at Arthur, her master – and loveless at her

257

'children'. When caught, her eye was not backed by the unique soul of Eleanor Oglethorpe . . .

'It is!' protested Arthur – but he knew he spoke in vain. Panic rode alongside his soothing words.

'It is not,' answered Theophilus, deceptively, deadly, calm. 'But you may still have the sword.'

In that moment he knew why he was chosen – by Heaven or the Elves or both – to be the wielder of this weapon. His life-long fault briefly became a virtue.

Oglethorpe's fury was like a nova, or the beginning of the Universe. Pre-existing facts vanished in its white, searing glare. Any opposing will evaporated. The blade in his hand whimpered its submission.

And so he gave Excalibur to Arthur – in a huge, traversing blow. The razor edge bit through and briefly sang its returning home as it parted head from shoulder. A lamenting note then arose, when it comprehended the betrayal.

'And down you go and fare ye well!' said Oglethorpe.

Still in its helm, the head bounced down, as bidden, to the ground. In an involuntary act of revulsion, Theophilus then booted the severed part into the Bussex Rhine. It was soon lost to sight beneath the black, brackish water.

If it is possible for a mere torso to betray emotion, Arthur's body evinced . . . disappointment. He could no longer speak but what remained let its feelings be known. The body remained standing, as still as all the other figures in this frozen field. A groan, from everywhere and nowhere, ruffled the air.

Oglethorpe had put all into the strike, not knowing he possessed such strength. Whilst willing to perform miracles most days his body now demanded rest. He lent upon Excalibur.

His 'family' now resembled what they really were: rough shaped dolls of wood and straw; *elf-stocks* empty of the half-life breathed into them. He had almost been deceived. Only knowing Ellen as he did saved him, and them – and everything. Theophilus giggled in nervous reaction. If he had been wrong . . . If it *had* been them . . .

But he hadn't, and it wasn't. They were not here, and Arthur had failed in some way in order for him to try that desperate deception. He did not have them.

Thought of that King made Oglethorpe look up. At first he thought Arthur was gone but then he saw him some way off. The headless remainder was on its hands and knees, painfully dragging itself, agonised yard by yard, back to Glastonbury and safety.

Theophilus steeled himself to give chase to finish the job, but halted as words formed within his head.

'This is no end,' said Arthur's voice, weakened but still crystal clear. 'This is but adjournment.'

The distant creeping body vanished and battle recommenced.

Ellen now saw that the Elf had been right. It would have been better to die calmly and by their own hands than to fall to these wild beasts. Already they had torn one nursemaid from the retreating formation and ripped her limb from limb. These were not the last sights she wished her babies to take with them to Paradise. What seemed intolerable in cold blood, now looked desirable when the hotter variety was covering the floor.

She beheld the great stairwell bay-window, wreathed in sunshine, a few yards off. No decision was necessary. Two stories up and with hard paving stone below, it should suffice. She would have crossed herself but the demands of sabre-play made that impractical. Perhaps a firm desire to do so might be acceptable.

'Only a little pain,' she told her children, 'just a little – and then a new and better place . . .'

The surviving nursemaids saw what was intended and agreed. Lewis did not need guidance but would come of his own accord.

Swords were dropped, the children gathered up, and they turned and ran. They overcame the short resistance of glass and frame and then leapt into unknowing.

And into Gardener Grimes's manure cart, as it turned out.

He and his boys had fought clear and thus being no obstacle to the main aim, were ignored. They might then have scampered into Godalming, just glad to be alive, but nobler feelings steered their proletarian feet. Other than when angry, Master Oglethorpe was a kind employer, and the Mistress was thoughtfully discreet when doling out charity. A web of loyalty had been weaved and though it had been sorely stretched it did not tear. The gardeners – and all the other servants – remained.

Grimes's rustic mind was corkscrew-wily. He observed the running fight move inexorably up the stairs and saw one likely end to it. Though often the subject of heated complaint, especially in summer, he kept his compost transporter close to the house. *'There weren't no other way,'* he always said, *'to make Mother Nature get a move on.'* Now he was vindicated. It was soon fetched and positioned and any opposing Celts dibbered out the way.

The leapers thus had a soft – if fragrant – landing and before they could sit up the wagon was being trundled down the drive. The enemy could not prevent it for they had committed their all to the attack. Nor one bard or druid stood between Westbrook's garrison and escape.

A great lamentation arose from the House.

'The Bussex *what*?'

Monmouth took horrid fright at Lord Grey's crystal-clear, court-English rendition of that particular fly-in-their-ointment; the mere ditch which thwarted the rebels' promising charge.

His aides had looked askance at him for that, unable to understand such passion over mere pronunciation. It was not a straw to break an ant's back, let alone a King's.

Then came worse, though equally invisible, bad news. Monmouth sensed that Arthur was gone – and shortly after so was he. With the battle still at its height, he rode off, with Grey and a few other trusted, worthless, friends, leaving his army to its fate.

Between them, the better-late-than-never artillery and the Horse broke the rebels' gallant regiments of foot. Battered more than flesh and blood can take they finally ran.

The Royal infantry splashed across Bussex Rhine, a much less intimidating obstacle by day than when poorly seen at night, directing pike and shot at unprotected backs. When they were then outrun, the Cavalry took over and commenced a long and bloody chase. Whilst the rebels frantically scrambled down, across and up the deep and boggy Langmoor Rhine, the pursuing horsemen paused and leisurely selected targets for their pistols, able to fire and reload at least twice. In the fields of ripening corn beyond the harvest was turned to red.

Perhaps four hundred of Monmouth's men died fighting upon Sedgemoor but a thousand fell thereafter. The fury of the Royalists was such, contemplating their own several hundred lost, that they buried some rebel wounded along with the slain. A chained group of crude manikins (that much puzzled the casualty enumerators) went in with them.

True to form, Wade fought his way out, rallying a hundred or so of his Red Regiment to make an orderly retreat. The pursuers left such prickly targets alone in favour of easier sport. He made it to Bridgwater and then the coast, commandeering a ship to escape. Forced back to shore by a Royal warship, he was finally taken, though not without a fire-fight which left him hovering at the door of death. He survived and turned King's Evidence, though careful to incriminate only those he knew had died. '*All your friends seem to be dead men, Mr Wade*,' King James laconically remarked when he read Wade's racy account.

Such spirits are a shame to waste and next year he accompanied James back on a tour of the field of battle. He died, full of honours and Town Clerk of Bristol, more than thirty years later in 1718.

Holmes was less lucky and got shot again after giving Theophilus's regiment a hard time. The only man in Monmouth's army to make it over the Bussex Rhine, he was found, dazed and delirious, wandering the Royal camp and when Churchill asked him '*who art thou?*' he could only reply, '*I am in no condition to tell . . .*'

In due course he was repaired sufficiently to meet the true King James and '*regretted rien*'. Having lost son, arm and all, he was then perhaps glad to forego mercy and leave the world, hung, drawn and quartered on Lyme Regis beach, at the very spot he'd landed, full of hope, three months before.

Anton Buyse the gunner made his peace with the victors, as professionals do, though riding far enough to avoid their initial, justified, wrath. When he re-met his father and other artillery-men ancestors, years later, they confirmed they were indeed proud of him.

The Reverend Toogood made it back to Axminster to pray and repent, and finally went to Heaven – only to find it not entirely to his tastes.

Piercy Kirke rampaged through the Western Counties, gain-ing an infamy that survives to this day. His is not a happy name to drop whilst on holiday in Devon, Dorset or Somerset, and still able of its own to spoil the usual welcome.

He got to be very friendly with various young ladies, on the promise of sparing their fathers or brothers – and then drew back the curtain the next morning to reveal their hanging corpse. Innocence was trampled underfoot, every experience sampled in full and a new army drumroll composed to match the dance of hanging men's feet. In short, he thoroughly enjoyed himself and brought a taste of Tangiers to England, before James got to hear and put his lead back on.

Brigadier John Churchill went on to much greater things – as did all his Elf-tinged progeny.

Lord Grey was taken just before Monmouth but in similar fashion: skulking in a ditch in deep countryside. They were both in pitiful condition and the Duke's pockets were found to contain the raw peas that were all he'd had to eat since Sedgemoor. Monmouth wept when he was found. Grey betrayed his location and much else. In return he had his pardon.

No such indulgence could be granted the primary conspira-tor. He was moved under guard via Winchester (Old Patch's hospitality), Farnham and Guildford, to London and the Tower. His spirit broken, Monmouth begged for life, in abject terms and letters embarrassing to read, but James could not grant it. The Stuart King, alone among his counsellors, knew the real nature of the Duke and the true project he'd attempted. Fear of its repetition obligated stern certainty in prevention. James kindly permitted him an interview to explain the whys and wherefores of what must be, but things did not turn out well. His hands bound by a silken cord, Monmouth hurled himself at the Royal feet, tearfully soaking James' velvet slippers. It was all very distressing.

Parliament's bill of attainder meant there was no need for a trial. Fortified by brandy and much badgered by canting Bishops to repent, he went to Tower Hill on Wednesday the fifteenth of July 1685, reasonably composed. That lasted until he approached the axeman, to tip him as per custom and beseech him to strike true.

Then words and all composure fled as he looked into the executioner's hood and observed . . . a pair of golden eyes.

The job was botched and the Duke took many, grievous, blows to die.

The legends started almost directly. They were widespread both in London and the West, just weeks after it required a butcher's knife to finally part Monmouth from life and his shoulders.

At Lyme Regis there were arrests made because of ale-house claims that the Duke was not dead, 'an old man with a beard' having '*plainly*' taking his place on the scaffold. Throughout Dorset it was said '*the real King hath not been taken and would come againe*'. Within six months it was proclaimed from Bolton Market Cross that '*the real King of England is alive*'. Within a year two men were charged and whipped from Newgate to Tyburn for separately impersonating the dead Duke.

Best of all was the story, widely believed, that a brotherhood of five had been prepared for such a day, men of like appearance to the Duke, provided with identical costume and prepared to swop their lives for his. With such a wealth of substitutes credulity was unstrained to think one of these sacrificial lambs went to the slaughter at Tower Hill '. . . *the Duke of Monmouth is not really dead*' wrote one believer, '*but only withdrawn until the*

263

*harvest is over, and then his friends shall see him again in a much
better condition than they ever did yet . . .'*

So now there was another sleeping King, biding his time
before coming back to save his people.

The day after Sedgemoor, as the Army fanned out to occupy
the West and to have fun and retribution, Feversham marched
with three battalions of the Guards and the undisgraced
Wiltshire Militia to Glastonbury. There was no strict military
need to it but he felt obscurely . . . drawn to do so. The
Frenchman sat long outside the *White Hart*, staring at the Tor,
and wondering why he felt so angry.

Before he left they hanged six rebels from the sign-board of
the inn. When the great Earl had departed, the militia stripped
the corpses and left them to dangle naked. There was profit to
be made, even in dead-men's clothes.

Away in Taunton, Miss Mary Blake the schoolmistress heard
the news and cried. As yet unsuspected in her womb,
Monmouth's golden-eyed embryonic son, felt his mother's sorrow within the flow of nutrients. She would die of smallpox in
due course, imprisoned in Dorchester Gaol; but not before
admitting the Duke's little legacy to the world.

And across the sea in the Low Countries, King Arthur was
whispering to William of Orange. It was a shadowy, injured,
more conciliatory Arthur – but Arthur nevertheless.

The Bussex Rhine was a freshwater drainage ditch and had
served its humble purpose to the satisfaction of untold generations. Then, a century or so after the Battle which improbably
made it famous, the agricultural improvers of the age thought
they could do better. The Bussex and its sister, Longmoor,
Rhines were filled in, extended or diverted to create the great
King's Sedgemoor Drain.

In so doing a lot of soil was shifted here and there and the
children of the engineers and navvies played 'princes and
rebels' up and down the mini-mountains created. One particular youth, a draughtsman's son, discovered a weathered skull

peeping from a heap and was much taken with the macabre find. He was learned enough to guess it came from the battle that had happened there – though the rusty iron helm still attached suggested a much earlier era.

He kept it – secretly at first, and then more openly as he grew to manly independence. Research in books taught him that many of the rebels perforce used antique arms and gear, and thus the helmet paradox was solved. The fleshless head was now stored in a sturdy box, the focus and totem of his lifelong interest in Monmouth's rebellion. He wrote a monograph on same and was blessed with favourable reviews. The man's one abiding regret was that his career prevented him from settling in the West: in Bridgwater or Glastonbury, for example. He did not know why he should wish that, for his line were all London born-and-bred – he just felt drawn to it.

He died and the head passed on down the line and is treasured by the family still. The younger members are well known for never missing a single Glastonbury Festival. They now aspire to moving there – lock, stock, skull and barrel.

Theophilus was excused from the post-Sedgemoor butchery and the harrowing of the West Country that was to come. Earl Feversham, who could on occasion be wise, knew the Lieutenant Colonel would be lax in such work. Moreover, since some officers wished to *talk* with Oglethorpe about his tardy arrival on the field, it was desirable to forestall a round of duels and the decimation of his staff.

Thus, directly the battle was no longer in doubt, Theophilus was accorded the honour of taking the good tidings to King James. His own wish was to hasten to Westbrook and ensure the safety of his family but Arthur's desperate resort to deception effectively proclaimed that anyway. Duty took narrow precedence. Still stained with Sedgemoor mud Oglethorpe hammered up the roads to London.

The exhausted soldier finally came upon James in the early hours and at a delicate moment. His Majesty chanced to be in the Queen's bedchamber but announced, through the door, that he would receive this particular visitor – *'if they gave him but a moment'*. Theophilus dozed, his weary head resting on the door and oblivious to the muffled noises beyond, until its opening obliged him to awake. He had never seen a naked king before and hazily wondered why it should seem strange that they were just as other men.

Compacted by fatigue the happy tale was soon told. James sat on the bed and took it all in, his long Stuart face registering no emotion. The young Queen Mary Beatrice, her fair italianate form more decently covered by sheets, in contrast applauded each development and shook cascading black locks in glee. When betrothed to James as his second wife at the age of fourteen, she'd proclaimed the alternative desire to take the veil. Now twelve years later true love had made a surprise arrival and good news for James was likewise joy for her.

When all was said the King slowly nodded and betrayed his hidden lightness of heart by sounding just like his late brother.

'What I want now,' he said, 'is m'clothes and a sword.'

A hovering courtier supplied the first and Oglethorpe the second. Excalibur remained marked with the black blood of Arthur. Theophilus had never before been so unsoldierly as to fail to clean his blade. Fortunately James didn't notice.

'Right then, Master Oglethorpe, now I've got hose and shirt on, you may fall to your knees – and don't go to sleep on me.'

Theophilus obeyed and was lightly brushed with steel on each shoulder. Excalibur buzzed with the desire to bite deeper and avenge its misuse but could not. Where the dried blood touched him his tunic was scorched.

'Arise a Knight, thou good and faithful servant.'

Sir Theophilus Oglethorpe trod unsteadily to his feet, while Mary Beatrice placed two slim fingers to her sensuous mouth and whistled wild acclamation.

And thereafter, as far as the House of Oglethorpe was concerned, things just went on getting better and better.

*

At Westbrook he received a welcome from Ellen that culminated in a broken bed and footprints on the walls. Another

Oglethorpe set off along the road to birth that very night. The convivial memory of that return would remain with the couple always.

Theophilus's initial alarm at the state of the place was soon allayed by finding all essentially well. He was duly grateful, both to Providence and his fellow man and those who'd served his family got to bathe in the torrent of favour that now flowed upon him. When the seat in Parliament arrived, the Colonelship of the King's Holland Regiment was granted, and the forfeited Scottish estates, the property in St James' Park, twelve-hundred acres in Huntingdonshire and the Sir Christopher Wren designed lodge in Windsor Forest – and all the rest – came his way, many others benefited also. Loyalty and virtue were for once rewarded. Theophilus and Ellen made sure of that.

All and everything was suspiciously fine and they were in danger of growing used to it. Though it was hardly to be credited, misfortune seemed permanently banished beyond the boundaries of Westbrook. However, a sensible degree of perching-on-the-edge-of-your-seat style caution remained.

Then, later on, at the christening of Theophilus junior, his father was suddenly struck by the words of the twenty-third Psalm, as recited by the Reverend Wharton.

'. . . *my cup runneth over.*
Surely goodness and mercy shall follow me all the days of my life:
and I will dwell in the house of the LORD for ever.'

Oglethorpe hadn't ever thought to make a personal appearance in Holy Scripture; but there again recent events had familiarised him with all kinds of miracles. Nothing was beyond the realms of possibility.

'Did you hear that last bit?' he whispered to Ellen. She had.

He puzzled for a moment and then surrendered to the happy notion, smiling at his wife.

'Do you know what, Ellen? I think he means *us*.'

From James Boswell's 'LIFE OF JOHNSON' 1791

May 1738. '. . . met with General James Oglethorpe, whose "strong benevolence of soul" was unabated during the course of a very long life: though it is painful to think that he had but too much reason to become cold and callous, and discontented with the world, from the neglect which he experienced of his public and private worth, by those in whose power it was to gratify so gallant a veteran with marks of distinction. This extraordinary person was as remarkable for his learning and taste, as for his other eminent qualities: and no man as more prompt, active and generous, in encouraging merit.'

Sunday, 23 March 1783. '. . . I was glad when General James Oglethorpe's arrival was announced, and we left the ladies. Dr. Johnson attended him in the parlour, and was as courteous as ever. The General said he was busy reading the writers of the Middle Age. Johnson said they were very curious. **OGLETHORPE:** "The House of Commons has usurped the power of the nation's money, and used it tyrannically. Government is now carried on by corrupt influence, instead of the inherent right in the King." **JOHNSON:** "Sir, the want of inherent right in the King occasions all this disturbance. What we did at the 1688 Revolution was necessary: but it broke our constitution." **OGLETHORPE:** "My father, Theophilus, did not think it necessary."

OGLETHORPE, James Edward, 1696–1785. English general, the ninth and final child of staunchly Jacobite parents. He nevertheless succeeded to the Family estate and largely restored its stricken fortunes following the fall of their patron, James II, in the 'Glorious Revolution' (which was neither of those things) of 1688. One elder brother, Lewis, died of a wound taken in an attack on the Hague, whilst serving under Marlborough in 1704. His other brother, Theophilus jnr. was obliged by his inherited Jacobite fanaticism to live abroad. James served under Prince Eugene against the Turks and in 1733 established the colony of Georgia in N. America (heavily mortgaging his house Westbrook to do so), as a refuge for paupers and debtors. He defended it in several campaigns against the Spaniards. His alleged lack of commitment as a general during the Jacobite rising of 1745 was the subject of a court martial but he was acquitted. He was also notable as a Philanthropist, Member of Parliament, prison reformer, viniculturalist (establishing at his home the largest vineyard in England), importer of the edible snail (still to be found in Westbrook's vicinity) and friend of such luminaries as Johnson, Boswell, Burke, Goldsmith, Garrick and Reynolds. Members of the American-Indian "Yamacraw" tribe accompanied Oglethorpe from Georgia to Godalming and were presented at Whitehall, Eton and at Court. The poet Pope favourably immortalised him in his "Imitation of Horace", ep. ii:

> "Impelled by strong benevolence of soul
> To flee like Oglethorpe from Pole to Pole."

I reckon I would have liked the bloke . . .'

Prof. Magali Williams. 'Some Decent Poms'. University of Northern Queensland Press. Cairns. Australia. 1992.

FRIENDS OF OGLETHORPE

GODALMING – GEORGIA LINK

The Oglethorpe Connection.

The 'Friends of Oglethorpe' is a local voluntary organisation formed to foster friendship with the State of Georgia in general and the cities of Savannah and Augusta in particular. Friends reflect the modern day link with one of Godalming's most famous sons, General James Edward Oglethorpe, the local member of Parliament who at the bidding of King George II, took the sailing ship 'Anne' and 100 souls to found the State of Georgia, in the Deep South, 260 years ago in 1733. The friends initiate and organise visits to Georgia and welcome and host visitors from Georgia who come to Godalming to seek the roots of their founder. The Oglethorpe family house was

Westbrook House, now the Meath Home near Godalming Station, which can be visited by arrangement. More information is contained in Godalming Parish Church and in the Oglethorpe Room in the Town Museum where enquiries about membership of the Friends may be made.

  Membership:
  Is open to all with annual subscriptions of £5 per person (£8 per couple). Corporate membership is available at . .

  [Leaflet distributed at 'Godalming Comes Alive' celebrations, 16/10/93]

THE YEAR OF OUR LORD 1702

'Hello,' said Theophilus. 'How are you? Long time no see.'

'We have not met before,' replied the Elf, though sociably taking his place alongside Oglethorpe in the garden chair.

'No? Well, perhaps so. You all seem very . . . interchangeable to us. And besides, memory fades. My acquaintances of your race can hardly be said to have kept in touch . . .'

'No,' agreed the Elf, most amiably and apparently admiring the view of Godalming. 'We saw no point in it.'

'Blunt and honest as ever,' Theophilus smiled wistfully into his cravat. 'And what has now occurred to alter your perception?'

His visitor turned in the seat to regard him.

'Nothing yet – but it is imminent. Your aura fades, your image wavers upon the breeze.'

Theophilus took the news as he always hoped he would. It was no great battle: he wasn't that put out.

'So, I'm on my way, am I?'

The Elf nodded once.

'The Force that gave you birth now calls you home. You cannot hear it yet . . .'

'Oh, I don't know,' answered Oglethorpe, jocularly, 'you should see me struggling out of bed in the morning. Drink? It's decent sherry. I drink a fair bit of it these days.'

Content that his point was made, the Elf once again leant back.

'Well there you are,' he said, downing the offered glass without pleasure or effect, 'your body heeds the call your mind will not admit. By your kind's standard you have had a tumultuous life. So, what did you make of it all?'

For the first time, Theophilus could not strain every bit of bitterness from his voice.

'Depends what you refer to. If it's our fraternisation then I'd say there was little point.'

The Elf didn't dispute it but was merely curious. 'How so?'

The tired old soldier spread wide his hands. At long last the great dammed up backlog of disappointments broke free and flowed out as words.

'Well look,' he said, only too willing to be contradicted. 'What did we achieve? Monmouth got the chop for sure, but James himself only lasted three years in place. The half dozen lordly ones who own this country would rather conspire in treason than have a papist, people's King. Their nominee, Good King Billy the sodomite soon had James out, and my life's been wasted since in trying to undo that. I've been harried up and down the land, arrested, fined to penury and spent years in exile – and Ellen likewise – all to no avail. They even accused us of substituting a baby Oglethorpe for James's new son, of sneaking him in in a warming pan to hide a royal stillbirth. A maid of ours betrayed us – why should she be the odd one out? – and published the lie in a pamphlet. So now we're also unnatural parents. Whiggish wits called the rightful heir "*Prince Oglethorpe of Godalming*". No, I admit it: we were defeated and I've made despairing truce with the regime. I tired of Westbrook being searched and seeing my name on wayside posters. Loyalty staggers when it meets with such divine disfavour. "King" William and all the others were allowed their way and that's the truth. My only comfort is at least I saw him out.'

He suddenly seemed abashed to have made such an impassioned speech – and yet glad to have confessed the venomed wound.

'Though only just it transpires,' he added, smiling ruefully.

'First James, then William, now you,' said the Elf, as gently as he could. 'How curious that all the players should depart in such swift succession.'

'James of melancholy in France, and glad to go. And dear

272

Billy, well, you'd need a heart of ice not to laugh: most reluctantly and thrown from his horse due to a molehill.'

'One hears the party of your persuasion now commence their dinners with a toast to the *"little gentleman in black velvet"*.'

'God bless him. I've never persecuted master mole myself but now he ranges unmolested in many estates thanks to that day's work. By the bye, since you mention the word succession, do we ever get a rightful King or Queen again?'

'Rightful?' asked the Elf, plainly unfamiliar with the term. 'In your terms, you mean? A newcomer of the Stuart blood in legitimate succession? Would you count James's daughter, Anne?'

'That traitress?'

'Then no.'

Theophilus sighed but then rallied.

'And so it ends, as do I,' he concluded, hardly pleased to find his private fears confirmed. 'And what good did any of it do?'

The question was rhetorical but got an answer anyway.

'It seems of small moment to you perhaps,' the Elf replied, 'but concede that mankind has a rather . . . basic perspective. To you, for example, Keynsham was a trifling skirmish, but in other planes it was mirrored in great slaughters of the Null. Swirling cavalry battles with millions of combatants, under skies you cannot conceive, hung upon your charge into that village. Null lancers on lizard steeds fell under your sword although you did not see them. Glorious cities died in flames with each shot you fired. Believe, Theophilus: you do not exist only here. Accept that a pinprick on Earth can be a mortal wound elsewhere.'

Oglethorpe shrugged but did not speak, interested but unmoved.

'And the vision of Nostradamus was fulfilled,' prompted the visitor.

'Who? Oh, him. A great help that was.'

'Prophecies must be opaque lest in speaking clear they abort the very events they predict. You'll admit Monmouth did leave life in London and through the actions of his Uncle.'

'But hardly *"murdered"*,' Theophilus protested.

'Doubtless a fault in translation. Remember the seer was an eavesdropper and a furtive one at that.'

'And the *"Heavenly Temple?"* The *"false peace"*?'

'One lies dormant in the Glastonbury landscape, awaiting our return. The other you have just bewailed. King James would not have disputed the falseness of the peace he so briefly acquired.'

'Hmmmm.' A wealth of scepticism rode alongside that affirmation.

'And above all,' the Elf added softly, 'you did deal with Arthur.'

Oglethorpe considered and then admitted that. 'But only for the moment, I suspect.'

The guest agreed but would not have his host entirely free of consolation.

'That would always have been so,' he told him. 'We swim against the mighty tide of the age, and you chose to swim with us. By its nature it could never be an easy trip. For the present humanity seems to want the Null. Our joint efforts have ensured they shall only have it in dilute form. It will be bad – but not eternal. Arthur was critically weakened. King William and all the others who now bargain with him can interpose their own lowly agendas. Do you really think Arthur cares for the survival of Holland? Or the welfare of homosexuals? No, he has had to *compromise*. Those he contracts with are not mere puppets as Monmouth would have been. Nor do they have knowledge of us. Because of you the Null's ambitions will come in more slowly and in milder form.'

Theophilus considered that as he sipped at his sherry.

'Well, now you put it like that . . . Incidentally, is Ellen joining me?'

They both looked across the grounds to where Mrs Oglethorpe worked, merciless pruner of the great banks of roses. Their planting arose from the need, long ago, to conceal a burial pit. Beneath them lay a jumbled mass of eel-men and Celts, surefire tenured-professorship for some future archaeologist – not to mention amazing fertiliser. Those house servants

274

who'd succumbed to 'the plague' at the same time were more decently interred elsewhere.

One rose of especial splendour rose perennially from what Grimes confirmed was the Elf-soldier's resting place. The old gardener just as regularly won prizes with the uncanny blooms. It thrived with or without libations from his manure cart; though no cutting from it ever took.

'Of course she will. All mortals do. But not yet. She has a long road yet to tread: her flame still burns bright.'

It certainly did. Most of Theophilus's remaining energy was spent in defusing her more gallows-threatening Jacobite conspiracies. But he would miss her, for all that their parting might be short.

'And the children?'

'They will mostly prosper, storm fortresses and maidenheads, found nations and reform the prisons and show every sign of your good upbringing. I see them as profuse as stars in the sky and shining just as glorious. They will be called many things but never petty. By inbred instinct, all unknowing, your progeny will fight the Null.'

'I am answered,' said Oglethorpe, 'and obliged.'

'Curiously enough,' said the Elf, 'we have one question in turn for you. Where is Excalibur?'

Theophilus chuckled to himself.

'Safe – and seemingly frozen to the shape of a standard issue English cavalry sword. I did not care to carry it any more, knowing the spirit that dwells within, and so gave it to Godalming Corporation. Don't look so worried. Their night-watchman required an instrument of intimidation: it saved them the expense of the more customary stave. Those fret-pennies will never lash out to replace it and he is too feeble to lift the blade. Also, Godalming's early hours present no opportunity to indulge its tastes. If it must be *freely* given for another to wield it then I think my choice was good. Our enemy's chiefest resource is hidden in the safest of places – out in plain view.'

'Ah, yes, I can see it now,' said the Elf, his long head tilted up, looking into realms not vouchsafed to mere mortals. 'They do keep it, you are right. A long while from now I note it in their *"museum"*, a place where they store useless objects from the past. It is brought forth on high and holy days to go in procession before their mayor.'

'All's well that ends well,' said Theophilus, half-flippantly.

'Indeed,' agreed the Elf, in all seriousness. 'And that brings me to my main business here . . .'

'Which? Wells or ends?'

'The latter. Here at your end of things I come to tell you of our blessing. We have decided that we liked your company.'

Theophilus poured himself another glass.

'If deciding that took you so long, I'm not sure I should be flattered. Still, I'll take it in the spirit given, for I know you're not a sentimental race.'

'No, we are not. Our motive is, as always, selfish. We merely wish to enjoy you more.'

Oglethorpe looked around the garden. It was almost dusk, an auspicious time for autumnal thoughts.

'Then you needs must be quick,' he said, regarding Ellen's still-supple, bending back, recalling what, in days past, the sight might have led to. 'It seems I am a dwindling asset . . .'

'There is time,' the Elf reassured him, and then stopped time in a most Arthurian way. 'Observe.'

The garden and Godalming and – for all he knew, the World – were held within a second. Beams of evening sunshine were poised, suspended in glorious flight. Before them, amidst these golden insubstantial pillars, had appeared a door.

Theophilus peered within. The whole wide Universe seemed inside – only better. Close to he saw a replica Godalming – more saracenic and gothic than he was used to but improved and how it ought to be. Further in was London, similarly transformed; crystal walled and festooned with skulls. Dark forest lapped against the City, watered by purple minarets which reached up to pierce the clouds. Beyond, the scene extended without limit, reproducing every place he had ever graced or wished to see. Therein lay hope – even confidence – of finding . . . everything.

276

'Behold our home,' said the Elf, 'our personal variant of Earth. It has never known the Null. Because of your great service you have a dispensation. You may join us there.'

A waft of spice came from the view. Theophilus inhaled – and his mind blossomed with a kaleidoscope of pictures. By some unknown mechanism he was *told*.

There were wars within that world: but either victories or glorious last stands, not inconclusive tramps through mud with butchery to follow. He sensed sharp-faced Elf girls who hated the will-she/won't-she game as much as he when young. He honestly admitted to himself he would like just one more long night of warm-hearted fun, when love was new and jadedness no problem. He longed immoderately for wine in good company when thirsty, for the thrill of holding one's new-born child and then the growth of their innocent, total-trusting, childish affections. He wanted to be free of his own, Null-tainted, world's touch, to spit on all the compromises, to no longer be so . . . shabby.

'Is this offer . . . approved of?' Theophilus spoke hesitantly. It seemed amiss to prise the gift horse's mouth open but they were talking serious business here.

'At the very highest level,' the Elf replied. 'By that Judge against whom there is no appeal. The Deity feels your long slavery to duty has earned you a holiday.'

'I *could* do with it,' conceded Oglethorpe – and in eventually owning up to frailty, shrugged off a heavy yoke.

'There you are then. In fact, the more we consider, new-comer, the more likely it seems your parents were guided in naming you. Theophilus: "*the beloved of God*" – as per the Grecian form of monkey-speak. Observe how two – and only two – of your holy books are dedicated to an individual, and both to a previous holder of your name.'

'"Luke" and "Acts",' said Theophilus, accepting the fact but not the implications. 'I know.'

'Knowing or not, you were marked out as the target for suchlike rare honours. There are signs therein for those who would see. Be glad. Surrender to the sweet caress of fortune and just . . . agree.'

Oglethorpe couldn't straightaway oblige. A whole life history of restraint weighed down the opposing scale.

'How long could I stay?'

'For a while,' said the Elf. 'Perhaps for a long while before we evict you. Meanwhile you shall act as you wish without consequence. For that sweet span you may forget all about "sin".'

'And then?'

'You will return to the judgement that all your species must face, and answer for your earthly deeds against a set of standards that we are exempted from. Ellen will find you dead in that seat, peacefully passed away whilst in sight of her. She will mourn, as your kind tend to do, but . . .' once more he consulted the upper air, 'yes, I thought as much: you will meet again: this time never to part.'

Theophilus was more than content. It was all he'd ever asked of life – the promise of justice, for good or ill. There were those who'd sneered at it and him, jeering that 'justice' was extinct. They no longer looked so sleek and clever compared to simpletons such as he. Loyalty wasn't only cause for gales of laughter after all.

He need hesitate no more. Accepting his reward, Theophilus Oglethorpe stepped forward and through the door, to prepare for paradise in Elfland.

Epilogue

' . . . On his quitting this place; he sold the Manor of Westbrook to Sir Theophilus Oglethorpe, Knt. son of Sutton Oglethorpe Esq. of Oglethorpe in the Parish of Bramham in the West-Riding of Yorkshire; who, for his loyalty to King Charles I. was fined by the Parliament in the sum of 20,000l. for which his Estates were sequestered, and afterwards forfeited and given to General Fairfax . . . Sir Theophilus his son was bred to arms, and fought under the Duke of Monmouth in the affair at Bothwell Bridge, where a tumultuary insurrection of the Scots was suppressed, 22 June, 1679. He was afterwards Lieutenant Colonel in the Duke of York's Troop of Horse Guards, and, being first Equerry to King James II, and a Major General in his army, commanded a party of Horse at Sedgemore fight, where the Duke of Monmouth was defeated, 6 July 1685.

. . . having represented the Borough of Haslemere in the Parliaments of 10 and 12 William III. Å 1698 and 1700–1, departed this life in the 50th year of his age, on the 10th of April Å 1702; leaving Eleanor his Wife (daughter of Richard Wall Esq. of Rathkien in the County of Tipperary) surviving, who died 19 June 1732m. He was buried in the Parish Church of St. James, Westminster, where the following Inscription was put up to his memory:

"Hic jacet THEOPHILUS OGLETHORPE, Eques auratus, ab atavo Vicecomite Eborum, Normanno victore, ducens originem. Cujus armis, ad pontem BOTHWELLIENSEM, succubuit SCOTUS: Nec non SEDGMORIENSI Palude fusi Rebelles. Qui, per varios casus et rerum discrimina, magnanimam erga Principem

279

et Patriam fidem, sed nec temere, sustinuit. Obiit Londini, Anno 1701, œtat. 50."'

[*'Here lies Theophilus Oglethorpe, glittering cavalier . . . At Bothwell Bridge the Scots were defeated by his troops and he also stood firm at the Battle of Sedgemoor Marsh. He maintained, but not blindly, high-minded loyalty towards monarch and country throughout diverse events and various circumstances. He died in London, in the year 1701, aged 50.'*]

From the 'Victoria County History of Surrey'

Theophilus was laid to rest on the 14th April 1702, on the north side of the altar in St. James's, past worrying about conspiracy-distracted Eleanor getting his date and place of death wrong.

His memorial, re-sited, survives and may still be seen, looking down upon the antics in St. James's above the south gallery door. Pilgrims and respect-payers shall have their reward, but for Theophilus himself they look in vain.

On the night of the fourteenth of October 1940 new enemies of the nation destroyed his grave, exhuming him with high explosive. Therefore, Theophilus Oglethorpe has no known grave.

EARTHLIGHT

THE SUM OF ALL MEN

Prince Gaborn Val Orden is visiting Sylvarresta, whose
Crown Princess, Iome, he is expected to marry.
Speaking incognito to the people, he finds the matter is
not as cut and dried as expected. However, that pales
into insignificance when it becomes clear that Raj Ahten,
overlord of the Southern Lands, is planning to invade the
Northern Realms and add them to his power base.

Val, Iome and Raj Ahten are only three of the host of
characters which inhabit this wonderful novel. As the
war goes on, so the teenage lovers must come to maturity
too quickly. And the magical system by which people
give their overlords "endowments" comes to be used for
horrific ends...

PRICE £9.99

ISBN 0 684 84028 6

EARTHLIGHT

Quicker Than The Eye

by Ray Bradbury

Ray Bradbury has not published a story collection
for a decade. Now, one of SF and Fantasy's Grand
Masters shows that he never went away. His vision
is still both dark and romantic. In these tales of the
fantastic, every one of Bradbury's long-time fans
(and many new converts) must prepare to be thrilled,
terrified and enchanted...

PRICE £5.99

ISBN 0 671 01784 5

EARTHLIGHT

ESCARDY GAP

by Peter Crowther & James Lovegrove

A former bestselling author sits at his typewriter everyday, unable to produce a sentence. Until one night he hears a sound which he can't place but which prompts him to try and describe it. He realises it is a train pulling into Escardy Gap, a small, midwestern town in the US, which is a recreation of the writer's hometown. The townspeople expect many things from the company which debarks. But not death. Awful death. Horrific death.

Only two people understand the true nature of the "show" that is visiting their community. Only two people can save Escardy Gap from total destruction by the forces of evil.

PRICE £5.99

ISBN 0 671 01605 9

EARTHLIGHT

A SELECTED LIST OF SCIENCE FICTION AND FANTASY TITLES AVAILABLE FROM EARTHLIGHT

THE PRICES SHOWN BELOW WERE CORRECT AT THE TIME OF GOING TO PRESS. HOWEVER EARTHLIGHT RESERVE THE RIGHT TO SHOW NEW RETAIL PRICES ON COVERS WHICH MAY DIFFER FROM THOSE PREVIOUSLY ADVERTISED IN THE TEXT OR ELSEWHERE.

All Earthlight titles are available by post from:

Book Service By Post, P.O. Box 29, Douglas, Isle of Man IM99 1BQ

Credit cards accepted. Please telephone 01624 675137,
fax 01624 670923, Internet http://www.bookpost.co.uk or
e-mail: bookshop@enterprise.net for details.

Free postage and packing in the UK. Overseas customers allow
£1 per book (paperbacks) and £3 per book (hardbacks).